Firestar knew that her touch should have comforted him, but he couldn't get the wailing of terrified cats out of his head, or forget the reflection he had seen in the puddle. He stared down at the river, at the ruffled water spilling around half-covered rocks . . . no, they weren't rocks, he realized, his pelt bristling with fear. They were *cats,* desperately swimming cats, churning the water with their paws, their drenched bodies dragged by the swirling current.

He blinked, and the vision was gone. All he could see was the river sliding past on its endless journey, with the shivering starlight trapped in its depths.

Great StarClan! he thought. *What's happening to me?*

WARRIORS

Book One: Into the Wild

Book Two: Fire and Ice

Book Three: Forest of Secrets

Book Four: Rising Storm

Book Five: A Dangerous Path

Book Six: The Darkest Hour

WARRIORS: THE NEW PROPHECY

Book One: Midnight

Book Two: Moonrise

Book Three: Dawn

Book Four: Starlight

Book Five: Twilight

Book Six: Sunset

WARRIORS: POWER OF THREE

Book One: The Sight

Book Two: Dark River

Book Three: Outcast

WARRIORS MANGA

The Lost Warrior

Warrior's Refuge

Warrior's Return

The Rise of Scourge

WARRIORS FIELD GUIDE: Secrets of the Clans

WARRIORS: Cats of the Clans

ERIN
HUNTER

HarperTrophy®
An Imprint of HarperCollins*Publishers*

 For information address HarperCollins Children's Books, a division of HarperCollins Publishers, 1350 Avenue of the Americas, New York, NY 10019.
www.harpercollinschildrens.com

Library of Congress Cataloging-in-Publication Data
Hunter, Erin.
Firestar's quest/ by Erin Hunter. — 1st ed.
p. cm. — (Warriors)
Summary: Firestar, leader of the ThunderClan, sets off on a harrowing journey to find a long-lost Clan of cats that had been forced to leave the forest many moons ago.
ISBN 978-0-06-113167-7
[1. Cats—Fiction. 2. Fantasy.] I. Title.
PZ7.H916625Firs 2007 2007006989
[Fic]—dc22 CIP
AC

Typography by Rob Hult
❖
First Harper Trophy edition, 2008

Special thanks to
Cherith Baldry

FIRESTAR'S QUEST ~ ALLEGIANCES

THUNDERCLAN

LEADER — **FIRESTAR**—ginger tom with a flame-colored pelt
APPRENTICE, BRAMBLEPAW

DEPUTY — **GRAYSTRIPE**—long-haired gray tom

MEDICINE CAT — **CINDERPELT**—dark gray she-cat

WARRIORS (toms, and she-cats without kits)

MOUSEFUR—small dusky brown she-cat

DUSTPELT—dark brown tabby tom

LONGTAIL—pale tabby tom with dark black stripes

SANDSTORM—pale ginger she-cat
APPRENTICE, SORRELPAW

WILLOWPELT—very pale gray she-cat with unusual blue eyes

CLOUDTAIL—long-haired white tom
APPRENTICE, RAINPAW

BRACKENFUR—golden brown tabby tom

THORNCLAW—golden brown tabby tom
APPRENTICE, SOOTPAW

ASHFUR—pale gray (with darker flecks) tom, dark blue eyes

APPRENTICES (more than six moons old, in training to become warriors)

BRAMBLEPAW—dark brown tabby tom with amber eyes

SORRELPAW—tortoiseshell-and-white she-cat with amber eyes

RAINPAW—dark gray tom with blue eyes

SOOTPAW—lighter gray tom with amber eyes

QUEENS (she-cats expecting or nursing kits)

FERNCLOUD—pale gray with darker flecks, green eyes

BRIGHTHEART—white she-cat with ginger patches

ELDERS (former warriors and queens, now retired)

GOLDENFLOWER—pale ginger she-cat

FROSTFUR—beautiful white she-cat with blue eyes

DAPPLETAIL—once-pretty tortoiseshell she-cat

SPECKLETAIL—pale tabby she-cat

ONE-EYE—pale gray she-cat, the oldest cat in ThunderClan, virtually blind and deaf

SHADOWCLAN

LEADER **BLACKSTAR**—large white tom with huge jet-black paws

DEPUTY **RUSSETFUR**—dark ginger she-cat

MEDICINE CAT **LITTLECLOUD**—very small tabby tom

WARRIORS **OAKFUR**—small brown tom
APPRENTICE, TAWNYPAW

ELDERS **RUNNINGNOSE**—small gray-and-white tom, formerly the medicine cat

WINDCLAN

LEADER	**TALLSTAR**—elderly black-and-white tom with a very long tail
DEPUTY	**MUDCLAW**—mottled dark brown tom
MEDICINE CAT	**BARKFACE**—short-tailed brown tom
WARRIORS	**WEBFOOT**—dark gray tabby tom
	TORNEAR—tabby tom
	ONEWHISKER—brown tabby tom
	RUNNINGBROOK—light gray she-cat
QUEENS	**ASHFOOT**—gray queen
	MORNINGFLOWER—tortoiseshell queen
	WHITETAIL—small white she-cat

RIVERCLAN

LEADER	**LEOPARDSTAR**—unusually spotted golden tabby she-cat
DEPUTY	**MISTYFOOT**—gray she-cat with blue eyes
MEDICINE CAT	**MUDFUR**—long-haired light brown tom
WARRIORS	**BLACKCLAW**—smoky black tom
	HEAVYSTEP—thickset tabby tom
	STORMFUR—dark gray tom with amber eyes
	FEATHERTAIL—light gray she-cat with blue eyes
QUEENS	**MOSSPELT**—tortoiseshell she-cat

MODERN SKYCLAN

SKYWATCHER—very old dark gray tom with pale blue eyes

LEAFDAPPLE—brown-and-cream tabby she-cat with amber eyes

SHARPCLAW—dark ginger tom

PATCHFOOT—black-and-white tom

SHORTWHISKER—dark brown tabby tom

RAINFUR—light gray tom with dark gray flecks

CLOVERTAIL—light brown she-cat with white belly and legs

PETALNOSE—pale gray she-cat

ECHOSONG—silver tabby she-cat with green eyes

SPARROWPAW—dark brown tabby tom

CHERRYPAW—tortoiseshell she-cat

ROCKKIT—black tom

SAGEKIT—pale gray tom

MINTKIT—gray tabby she-cat

BOUNCEKIT—ginger tom

TINYKIT—small white she-cat

ANCIENT SKYCLAN

LEADER — **CLOUDSTAR**—pale gray tom with white patches and very pale blue eyes

DEPUTY — **BUZZARDTAIL**—ginger tom with green eyes

MEDICINE CAT — **FAWNSTEP**—light brown tabby she-cat

BIRDFLIGHT—light brown tabby she-cat with long, fluffy fur and amber eyes

FERNPELT—dark brown tabby she-cat

MOUSEFANG—sandy-colored she-cat

NIGHTFUR—black tom

OAKPAW—gray tabby apprentice

ANCIENT THUNDERCLAN

LEADER **REDSTAR**—dark ginger tom

DEPUTY **SEEDPELT**—gray she-cat with darker flecks

MEDICINE CAT **KESTRELWING**—dark brown tabby tom

NETTLECLAW—gray tabby tom with dark gray stripes

ANCIENT WINDCLAN

LEADER **SWIFTSTAR**—dark gray tom

DEPUTY **MILKFUR**—creamy white tom

MEDICINE CAT **LARKWING**—silver-and-black tabby she-cat

HAREFLIGHT—light brown she-cat

ANCIENT RIVERCLAN

LEADER **BIRCHSTAR**—light brown tabby she-cat

DEPUTY **SLOEFUR**—black she-cat

MEDICINE CAT **ICEWHISKER**—silver-gray tom

FOXCLAW—russet-colored tom

ANCIENT SHADOWCLAN

LEADER **DAWNSTAR**—creamy brown she-cat

DEPUTY **SNAKETAIL**—brown tabby tom

MEDICINE CAT **MOLEPELT**—small black tom

HOLLOWBELLY—black-and-white tom

CATS OUTSIDE CLANS

BARLEY—black-and-white tom that lives on a farm close to the forest

RAVENPAW—sleek black cat that lives on the farm with Barley, formerly of ThunderClan

SMUDGE—plump, friendly black-and-white kittypet that lives in a house at the edge of the forest

HATTIE—pretty brown tabby kittypet who lives in Firestar's former home

SKYROCK
LEADER'S DEN
SKY'S DEN

TWOLEGPLACE
THUNDERPATH
WARRIORS' DEN
DERS' DEN
NURSERY
APPRENTICES' DEN
MEDICINE CAT'S DEN
FALLEN TREE
RIVER
KPILE
TO THE FOREST →
THE GORGE

St. Andrew's Road
Blofield
Warehouse
(Disused)
Deepsands
Gorge

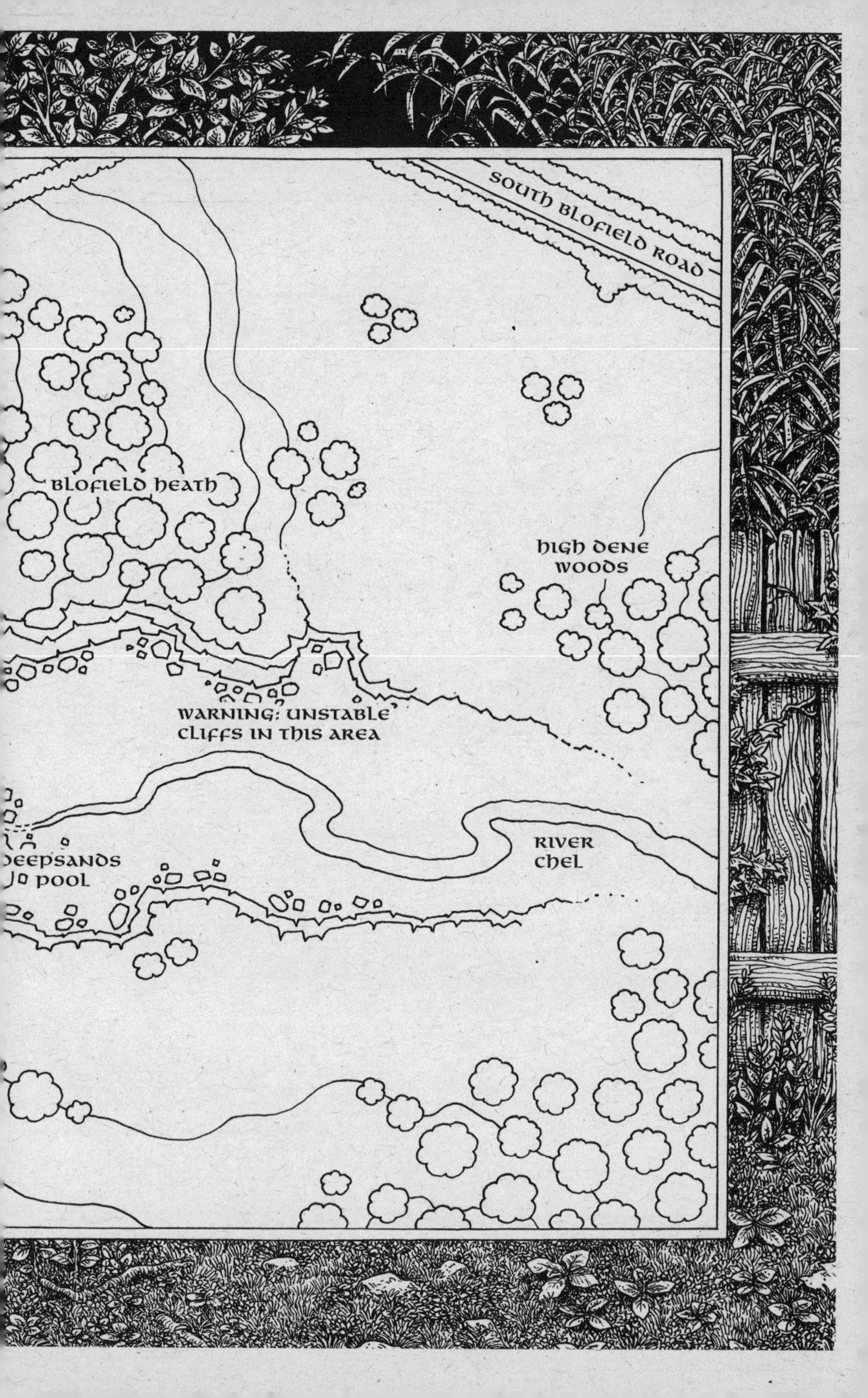
SOUTH BLOFIELD ROAD
BLOFIELD HEATH
HIGH DENE WOODS
WARNING: UNSTABLE CLIFFS IN THIS AREA
RIVER CHEL
DEEPSANDS
POOL

PROLOGUE

The full moon floated in the sky, shedding its cold light over the forest. A faint breeze murmured through the leaves of four massive oak trees; dappled light and shadow moved over the pelts of many cats as they slipped into the hollow below.

A muscular, bracken-colored tomcat emerged from the bushes that lined the sides of the hollow. He bounded across the clearing and leaped to the top of the great rock that stood in the center.

Three other cats were waiting there. One of them, a she-cat with a brown tabby pelt, dipped her head in greeting. "Welcome, Redstar," she meowed. "How's the prey running in ThunderClan?"

"We've plenty, thank you, Birchstar," the ThunderClan leader replied. "Is all well in RiverClan?"

Before Birchstar could reply, one of the other leaders interrupted, scraping his claws on the harsh surface of the rock. His gray-black pelt was a shadow in the moonlight. "It's time this Gathering started," he rasped. "We're wasting time."

"We can't start yet, Swiftstar," the fourth cat mewed. Her

creamy brown pelt held the frosty shimmer of starlight. "We're not all here."

Swiftstar let out an impatient snort. "WindClan have better things to do than sit about waiting for cats who can't be bothered to come at the proper time."

"Look!" Redstar pointed with his tail toward the top of the hollow. The shape of a cat was outlined against the pale moonlight. He stood motionless for a heartbeat, then waved his tail and vanished into the bushes. More cats followed him, pouring over the rim of the hollow, the branches rustling as they streamed down the slope.

"There!" Dawnstar mewed. "SkyClan are here at last."

"About time, too," Swiftstar muttered. "Cloudstar!" he called as the first cat emerged into the clearing. "What kept you?"

The SkyClan leader was small for a tomcat, with a lithe body and a neat, well-shaped head. His fur was pale gray, with white patches like clouds. He didn't reply to Swiftstar's question, but thrust his way through the cats until he reached the rock and sprang up to join the other leaders.

Behind him, more and more cats were emerging from the bushes. A group of young apprentices ventured out, bunched together, their eyes wide with a mixture of fear and excitement. They were followed by the Clan's elders, some of them limping, one leaning heavily on the shoulder of a warrior. Two she-cats each carried a tiny kit in her jaws; several older kits stumbled wearily beside them. The remaining warriors circled them protectively.

"Great StarClan!" Swiftstar exclaimed. "Cloudstar, any cat would think you'd brought your whole Clan to the Gathering."

Cloudstar steadily met the WindClan leader's puzzled gaze. "Yes," he mewed, "I have."

"Why in the name of StarClan did you do that?" Birchstar asked.

"Because we can no longer live in our territory," the SkyClan leader told her. "Twolegs have destroyed it."

"What?" Redstar stepped forward. "My patrols have reported more Twolegs in your territory, and noise from monsters, but they can't possibly have destroyed it all."

"They have." Cloudstar stared across the clearing, as if he were seeing something else in place of the moon-washed bushes. "They came with huge monsters that pushed over our trees and churned up the earth. All our prey is dead or frightened off. The monsters are crouched around our camp now, waiting to pounce. SkyClan's home has gone." Turning to the other leaders, he went on. "I have brought my Clan here to ask your help. You must give us some of your territories."

Yowls of protest rose from the cats below the rock. At the edge of the clearing the SkyClan cats huddled together with the strongest warriors on the outside, as if they were braced for an attack.

Swiftstar was the first to reply. "You can't just walk in here and ask for our territory. We can barely feed our own Clans as it is."

Redstar shifted his paws uneasily. "The prey is running

well now in greenleaf, but what's going to happen when leaf-fall comes? ThunderClan won't be able to spare any then."

"Nor will ShadowClan," Dawnstar meowed, rising from her place on the edge of the rock and facing Cloudstar with a challenge in her green eyes. "My Clan is bigger than any other. We need every pawstep of ground to feed our own cats."

Cloudstar's gaze flicked to the only leader who hadn't spoken. "Birchstar? What do you think?"

"I'd like to help," the RiverClan leader mewed. "I really would. But the river is very low and it's harder than ever to catch enough fish. Besides, SkyClan cats don't know *how* to fish."

"Exactly," Swiftstar added. "And only WindClan cats are fast enough to catch rabbits and birds on the moors. There's certainly nowhere in our territory where you could make a camp. You'd soon get tired of sleeping under gorse bushes."

"Then what is my Clan supposed to do?" Cloudstar mewed quietly.

Silence spread over the clearing as if every cat were holding its breath. Redstar broke it with a single word.

"Leave."

"That's right." There was a hint of a snarl in Swiftstar's meow. "Leave the forest and find yourselves another place, far enough away that you can't steal our prey."

A young black-and-silver she-cat rose to her paws in the clearing below. "Swiftstar," she called, "as your medicine cat, I can tell you that StarClan won't be pleased if the rest of us drive out SkyClan. There have always been five Clans in the forest."

Swiftstar looked down at his medicine cat. "You say you know the will of StarClan, Larkwing, but can you tell me why the moon is still shining? If StarClan didn't agree that SkyClan should leave the forest, they would send clouds to cover the sky."

Larkwing shook her head, unable to answer her leader's question.

Cloudstar's eyes stretched wide with disbelief. "Five Clans have lived in this forest for longer than any cat can remember. Doesn't that mean anything to you?"

"Things change," Redstar replied. "Is it possible that the will of StarClan has changed also? StarClan gave each Clan the skills they need to survive in their own territory. RiverClan cats swim well. ThunderClan are good at stalking prey in the undergrowth. SkyClan cats can leap into trees because there's not much cover in their territory. Doesn't this mean that each Clan couldn't live in another Clan's territory?"

A thin tomcat with rumpled black fur rose from where he sat at the base of the Great Rock. "You keep saying that StarClan wants five Clans in the forest, but are you sure that's true? There are four oaks here at Fourtrees. That could be a sign that there should be only four Clans."

"SkyClan don't belong here," hissed a silver tabby beside him. "Let's drive them out now."

The SkyClan warriors bristled as one, unsheathing long, curved claws.

"Stop!" Cloudstar called. "Warriors of SkyClan, we are not cowards, but this is a battle we cannot win. We have seen tonight what the warrior code is worth. From now on we will be alone, and we will depend on no cat but ourselves."

He leaped down from the Great Rock and shouldered a path through his warriors until he came face-to-face with a beautiful light brown tabby. Two tiny kits were mewling pitifully at her paws.

"Cloudstar." The she-cat's voice was a murmur of distress. "Our kits are too small to make a long journey. I'll stay here with them, if any Clan will have us."

Kestrelwing, the ThunderClan medicine cat, pushed his way between two SkyClan warriors, ignoring their snarls, and bent his head to sniff the kits. "You will all be welcome in ThunderClan."

"Are you sure?" Cloudstar challenged him. "After what your leader said to us today?"

"I believe my leader was wrong," Kestrelwing meowed. "But he won't condemn helpless kits to die. They will have a future in ThunderClan, and so will you, Birdflight."

The light brown cat dipped her head. "Thank you." She turned to Cloudstar, sorrow brimming in her amber eyes. "Then this is good-bye."

"Birdflight, no." The SkyClan leader looked horrified. "How can I leave you?"

"You must." Birdflight's voice quavered. "Our Clan needs you, but our kits need me just now."

Cloudstar bowed his head. "I'll wait for you," he whispered. "I'll wait for you forever." He pressed his muzzle against Birdflight's side. "Stay with Kestrelwing. He'll find warriors to help carry the kits back to ThunderClan's camp." To the ThunderClan medicine cat, he added, "Take care of them."

Kestrelwing nodded. "Of course."

With a last anguished look at his mate, Cloudstar signaled with his tail to the rest of his Clan. "Follow me."

He led the way toward the slope, but before he could plunge into the bushes Redstar called from the top of the Great Rock, "May StarClan go with you!"

Cloudstar turned and fixed a cold gaze on the cat he had once called friend. "StarClan may go where they please," he hissed. "They have *betrayed* SkyClan. From this day on, I will have nothing more to do with our warrior ancestors." He ignored the gasps of shock around him, some from his own Clan. "StarClan allowed the Twolegs to destroy our home. They look down on us now, and let the moon go on shining while you drive us out. They said there would always be five Clans in the forest, but they *lied*. SkyClan will never look to the stars again."

With a last flick of his tail he vanished into the bushes, and the rest of his Clan followed.

Chapter 1

Firestar slid around the edge of a hazel thicket and paused to taste the air. The moon was nearly full, and he could see that he was close to where the stream followed the border with ShadowClan. He could hear its faint gurgling, and picked up traces of the ShadowClan scent markers.

The flame-colored tomcat allowed himself a soft purr of satisfaction. He had been leader of ThunderClan for three seasons, and he felt as if he knew every tree, every bramble bush, every tiny path left by mice and voles throughout his territory. Since the fearsome battle when the forest Clans had joined together to drive out BloodClan and their murderous leader, Scourge, there had been peace, and the long days of newleaf and greenleaf had brought plentiful prey.

But Firestar knew that somewhere in the tranquil night an attacker was lurking. He made himself concentrate, all his senses alert. He caught the scent of mouse and rabbit, the green scent of grass and leaves, and very faintly the reek of the distant Thunderpath. But there was something else. Something he couldn't identify.

He raised his head, drawing the breeze over his scent

glands. At the same instant, a clump of bracken waved wildly, and a dark shape erupted from the middle of the curling fronds. Startled, Firestar spun to face it, but before he could raise his paws to defend himself the shape landed heavily on his shoulders, knocking him to the ground.

Summoning all his strength, Firestar rolled onto his back and brought up his hind paws to thrust his attacker away. Above him he could make out broad, muscular shoulders, a massive head with dark tabby markings, the glint of amber eyes. . . .

Firestar gritted his teeth and battered even harder with his hind paws. A forepaw lashed out toward him and he flinched, waiting for the strike.

Suddenly the weight that pinned him down vanished as the tabby cat sprang away with a yowl of triumph. "You didn't know I was there, did you?" he meowed. "Go on, Firestar, admit it. You had no idea."

Firestar staggered to his paws, shaking grass seeds and scraps of moss from his pelt. "Bramblepaw, you great lump! You've squashed me as flat as a leaf."

"I know." Bramblepaw's eyes gleamed. "If you'd really been a ShadowClan invader, you would be crow-food by now."

"So I would." Firestar touched his apprentice on the shoulder with the tip of his tail. "You did very well, especially disguising your scent like that."

"I rolled in a clump of damp ferns as soon as I left camp," Bramblepaw explained. He suddenly looked anxious. "Was my assessment okay, Firestar?"

Firestar hesitated, struggling to push away the memory of Bramblepaw's bloodthirsty father, Tigerstar. When he looked at the young apprentice, it was too easy to recall the same broad shoulders, dark tabby fur, and amber eyes that belonged to the cat who had been ready to murder and betray his own Clanmates to make himself leader.

"Firestar?" Bramblepaw prompted.

Firestar shook off the clinging cobwebs of the past. "Yes, Bramblepaw, of course. No cat could have done better."

"Thanks, Firestar!" Bramblepaw's amber eyes shone and his tail went straight up in the air. As they turned toward the ThunderClan camp, he glanced back at the ShadowClan border. "Do you think Tawnypaw will be near the end of her apprentice training, too?"

Bramblepaw's sister, Tawnypaw, had been born in ThunderClan, but she had never felt at home there. She was too sensitive to the mistrust of cats who couldn't forget that she was Tigerstar's daughter. When her father had become leader of ShadowClan, she had left ThunderClan to be with him. Firestar always felt that he had failed her, and he knew how much Bramblepaw missed her.

"I don't know how they do these things in ShadowClan," he meowed carefully, "but Tawnypaw started her training at the same time as you, so she should be ready for her warrior ceremony by now."

"I hope so," Bramblepaw mewed. "I know she'll be a great warrior."

"You both will," Firestar told him.

On their way back to camp, Firestar felt as if every shadowy hollow, every clump of fern or bramble thicket, could be hiding the gleam of amber eyes. Whatever Tigerstar's crimes, he had been proud of his son and daughter, and his death had been particularly dreadful, with all nine lives ripped away at once by Scourge's sharpened claws. Was the massive tabby watching them now? Not from StarClan, for Firestar had never seen him in his dreams; the ThunderClan medicine cat, Cinderpelt, had never reported meeting him when she shared tongues with StarClan, either. Could there be another place for coldhearted cats who had been ready to use the warrior code for their own dark ambitions? If there was such a shadowed path, Firestar hoped he would never have to walk it—nor his lively apprentice. Bramblepaw was bouncing through the grass beside him, excited as a kit; surely he had shaken off the legacy of his father?

As they slipped down the ravine toward the camp, Bramblepaw halted, his gaze serious. "Was my assessment *really* okay? Am I good enough—"

"To be a warrior?" Firestar guessed. "Yes, you are. We'll hold your ceremony tomorrow."

Bramblepaw dipped his head respectfully. "Thank you, Firestar," he mewed. "I won't let you down." His eyes blazed; he gave a sudden bound into the air and pelted down the rest of the ravine to wait by the entrance to the gorse tunnel. Firestar watched him, amused. He could still remember when he had felt as if he had too much energy to contain in his four paws, when he felt as if he could run through the forest forever.

"You'd better get some sleep," he warned as he joined his apprentice. "You'll have to sit vigil tomorrow night."

"If you're sure, Firestar . . ." Bramblepaw hesitated, working his claws in the sandy ground. "I could find you some fresh-kill first."

"No, go on," his leader told him. "You're so excited right now you wouldn't notice if a fox ate you."

Bramblepaw waved his tail and bundled through the gorse tunnel into the camp.

Firestar lingered outside the camp for a while, settling down on a flat rock with his tail curled around his paws. He could hear nothing but the faint rustle of leaves in the breeze, and the tiny scufflings of prey in the undergrowth.

The battle with BloodClan had cast its shadow over all the Clans; for more than a season after, every cat in the forest jumped at a cracking twig, and chased out strangers as if their lives depended on it. They were even scared of going too close to Twolegplace, in case any surviving members of BloodClan happened to be lurking there. But now, five moons later, ThunderClan was thriving. Tomorrow there would be a new warrior, and the apprentices Rainpaw, Sootpaw, and Sorrelpaw were all doing well after three moons of training. In time, they would be good warriors too—they were bound to be, considering who their father was. Every day they reminded Firestar of his first deputy, Whitestorm, who had died battling the vicious BloodClan deputy, Bone. He still grieved for the old white warrior.

His mind wrapped in memories of his old friend, it was a

moment before Firestar realized he could hear a faint sound: the footfalls of a cat stepping lightly through the undergrowth. He sprang to his paws, looking around, but he saw nothing.

He hardly had time to sit down before the noise came again. This time Firestar whipped his head around in time to glimpse the pale shape of a cat standing a little farther up the ravine.

Am I dreaming? Has Whitestorm left StarClan to come and visit me?

But this cat was smaller than Whitestorm and its fur was gray, patched with white. It stared straight at him, its eyes dark and earnest, as if it were trying to tell him something. Firestar had never seen it before. Could it be a rogue? Or worse—could BloodClan have recovered from their defeat and come back to invade the forest?

He sprang to his paws and raced up the ravine toward the strange cat. But as soon as he began to move, it vanished, and when he searched among the rocks he couldn't find it. There weren't even any pawmarks, but when he tasted the air there was a faint trace of an unfamiliar scent, almost swamped by the ThunderClan scents that came from the camp.

Slowly Firestar retraced his pawsteps and sat on the rock again. All his senses were alert now as he gazed into the shadows. But he saw nothing more of the strange gray cat.

CHAPTER 2

While he still waited to see if the cat would return, clouds massed above Firestar's head, blotting out the stars. Huge raindrops pattered on the rocks of the ravine, quickly growing to a steady downpour. Firestar squeezed through the gorse tunnel into the camp and raced across the clearing to his den at the foot of the Highrock.

Beyond the curtain of lichen, the den was dry. An apprentice had changed his bedding, piling fresh moss and bracken into a soft heap. Firestar shook the rain from his pelt and curled up, wrapping his tail over his nose. Rain drumming on the earth outside his den soon lulled him into sleep.

The noise of the rain faded and Firestar opened his eyes, feeling cold to the bone. His cozy nest had vanished, along with the familiar scents of ThunderClan. He was surrounded by dense, clinging mist. It swirled around him, breaking up now and then to show stretches of desolate moorland. He could feel tough, springy grass beneath his paws. At first he thought he must be on WindClan territory; then he realized that he had never seen this place before.

"Spottedleaf?" he called into the mist. "Are you here? Does

StarClan have a message for me?"

But there was no sign of the beautiful tortoiseshell who had once been ThunderClan's medicine cat. She often visited Firestar in dreams, but now he couldn't pick up even a trace of her sweet scent.

Instead, he heard the faintest sound, so distant that he couldn't make it out. He strained to listen, and an icy chill froze him from ears to tail as he heard a savage, wordless wailing, the dreadful sound of many terrified cats. He stiffened, ready to flee with them, but though the shrieks grew louder, all he could see were blurred shapes. They seemed to advance toward him through the mist, only to vanish before he could see them properly. The scent of unfamiliar cats drifted in the air.

"Who are you?" he called. "What do you want?"

But there was no reply, and soon the shrill wailing faded into silence.

Firestar jumped as something prodded his side. Blinking awake, he saw warm yellow sunlight angling through the entrance of his den, shining on the pale ginger fur of his mate, Sandstorm.

"Are you okay?" she asked. "You were twitching in your sleep."

Firestar let out a groan as he sat up. His muscles felt as stiff as if he had really been trekking over that barren moorland. "It was just a dream," he muttered. "I'll be fine."

"Look, I brought you some fresh-kill." She pushed the limp body of a vole toward him. "I just got back from a hunting patrol."

"Thanks." The vole must have been freshly caught; its warm scent made his mouth water, and his belly felt hollow with hunger. Bending his head, he devoured the prey in a few rapid bites.

"Better now?" Sandstorm inquired with a glint of mischief in her green eyes. "That'll teach you to let young cats jump all over you."

Firestar flicked her ear with the tip of his tail; word of Bramblepaw's successful assessment had obviously spread through the camp. "Hey, I'm not an elder yet, you know." The damp shadows of his dream were melting away in the bright sunlight. He stepped out of his nest and gave himself a quick grooming. "Do you know if all the patrols are back yet?"

"The last ones just came in." A shadow fell across the entrance of the den, and Firestar looked up to see his deputy, Graystripe, standing just outside. "The hunting patrols caught so much prey, Thornclaw has taken the apprentices out to collect it. Why, did you want them?"

"Not right away, but I need to know what they reported," Firestar replied. He beckoned the gray warrior inside with his tail. Remembering the unfamiliar cat he had seen in the ravine the night before, he asked warily, "Did any of them see any sign of rogues in our territory?"

Graystripe shook his head. "Not a trace. Everything's peaceful out there." His yellow eyes narrowed with concern. "Firestar, is something bothering you?"

Firestar hesitated. His old friend knew him well enough to tell when something was on his mind. But he didn't think this was the time to share his dream or the vision of the cat in the ravine. He had so little to go on; his solitary brooding on Tigerstar and Whitestorm could have made him see things in the shadows.

"No, I'm fine," he replied, pushing the strange gray cat to the back of his mind. "Bramblepaw did an amazing assessment last night. He jumped on me by the ShadowClan border. Come on," he meowed to Graystripe and Sandstorm. "I want to hold his warrior ceremony as soon as the apprentices get back."

He led the way out of his den and leaped onto the Highrock. The rain had stopped; above the trees the sky was blue, with scudding white clouds. Sunlight reflected from puddles, dazzling his eyes, and the barrier of thorns around the camp sparkled with raindrops. Thornclaw was emerging from the gorse tunnel with his apprentice, Sootpaw, behind him, both cats laden with fresh-kill. Moments later Cloudtail appeared with Rainpaw and Sorrelpaw.

Firestar let out a yowl. "Let all cats old enough to catch their own prey gather here beneath the Highrock for a Clan meeting."

Pride surged through him as he watched his Clan collect below the rock. The three youngest apprentices dashed over from the fresh-kill pile to sit near the base of the Highrock. They chattered excitedly, maybe imagining what it would be like when they became warriors too. Speckletail led the other elders from their den beside the burned-out shell of the fallen tree. Cinderpelt the medicine cat appeared from the fern tunnel that led to her den and limped across to sit beside Brackenfur, Willowpelt, and Mousefur.

Firestar spotted Brightheart emerging from the nursery. As an apprentice, she had been injured by a pack of dogs, leaving one side of her face torn away. Now, with her belly swollen with the kits she would bear soon, Firestar thought she had never looked happier. She padded slowly across the clearing to join her mate, Cloudtail, near the fresh-kill pile; the white warrior touched her ear affectionately with his nose.

Behind her came Ferncloud with her two kits, who dashed off with squeals of excitement toward the nearest puddle.

"Shrewkit! Spiderkit! Come back at once," Ferncloud scolded them.

The two kits sat down at the edge of the water, but they kept shooting glances at their mother and dabbing the surface with an outstretched paw. Firestar watched, amused, as their father, Dustpelt, padded over to them, said something sternly to them, then went to sit by Ferncloud. Barely a heartbeat passed before a tiny paw flashed out again.

"Spiderkit!" Dustpelt called, loud enough for Firestar to hear him. "*What* did I just tell you?"

Both kits glanced at their father and then went scampering off, tiny tails stuck high in the air. Soon Shrewkit found a ball of sodden moss lying on the ground. Hooking it up with one paw he tossed it at his brother; Spiderkit ducked, and the moss sailed over his head and struck Speckletail right in the chest. The tabby elder sprang to her paws, batting at soaking chest fur with one paw, and letting out a furious hiss. Though

Speckletail could be cranky. Firestar knew she would never harm a kit, but Spiderkit and Shrewkit weren't sure of that. They flattened themselves to the ground and crept backward to sit beside their mother and father.

Firestar had missed the moment when Bramblepaw emerged from the apprentice's den. Now he was approaching the base of the rock; as Firestar was his mentor, he was escorted to his warrior ceremony by Graystripe, the Clan deputy, instead. His brown tabby pelt was groomed to shining sleekness, and his amber eyes looked solemnly up at his leader.

Firestar leaped down from the Highrock to meet him. Close to him, he could see that Bramblepaw's serious expression hid an almost unbearable excitement. He realized how much this ceremony meant to his apprentice; had Bramblepaw sometimes doubted that he would ever be accepted into ThunderClan as a full warrior?

Firestar summoned up the words that had been spoken to every apprentice in the forest for season upon season. "I, Firestar, leader of ThunderClan, call upon my warrior ancestors to look down on this apprentice. He has trained hard to understand the ways of your noble code, and I commend him to you as a warrior in his turn." Meeting Bramblepaw's gaze, he went on. "Bramblepaw, do you promise to uphold the warrior code and to protect and defend this Clan, even at the cost of your life?"

"I do." No cat could doubt how much Bramblepaw meant it.

"Then by the powers of StarClan," Firestar continued, "I give you your warrior name: Bramblepaw, from this moment you will be known as Brambleclaw. StarClan honors your courage and your loyalty, and we welcome you as a full warrior of ThunderClan."

Brambleclaw's eyes widened as Firestar spoke of his loyalty, and Firestar felt his fur prickle with the weight of meaning behind that word. He had never doubted Brambleclaw's commitment to the warrior code, but he had often struggled to trust the son of Tigerstar. He could see a few of the other cats murmuring to one another, as if they too understood why he had chosen to mention loyalty in Brambleclaw's warrior ceremony.

Taking a pace closer, Firestar rested his muzzle on the top of Brambleclaw's head. He could feel shivers running all through the new warrior's body. Brambleclaw licked Firestar's shoulder in response, then stepped back, his eyes glowing.

"Brambleclaw! Brambleclaw!"

His Clanmates greeted him with his new name. In spite of being Tigerstar's son, he was popular in the Clan, and most cats were pleased that he had become a warrior at last.

Firestar took a couple of paces back, his gaze drifting to the puddle a couple of tail-lengths away where Shrewkit and Spiderkit had been playing. The surface had stilled since they dabbed at it, and now it was a shining silver disk on the ground. It was reflecting an odd-shaped cloud. . . .

Firestar blinked. That was *not* a cloud. It was a cat's face: a pale gray cat, with white patches on its fur and huge water-colored eyes, staring straight at him. A wisp of the same unfamiliar scent that he had detected in the ravine drifted around him.

"Who are you?" Firestar whispered. "What do you want?"

There was a high-pitched shriek of excitement as Shrewkit launched himself into the air and landed in the middle of the puddle, splashing every cat within reach and shattering the reflection into tiny fragments.

Firestar looked up: the sky above the ravine was blue and cloudless. He glanced around, half-embarrassed, hoping that none of his Clanmates had seen him talking to a puddle. But as he watched the cats who were still crowding around Brambleclaw, he couldn't get the gray cat's face out of his mind.

Firestar led the evening patrol as far as Tallpines and Twolegplace, still wary of possible trouble from BloodClan on that side of the territory. Night had fallen by the time he and his Clanmates returned. As he emerged into the camp from the gorse tunnel, he found Brambleclaw sitting alone in the middle of the clearing.

"He must be tired out," Sandstorm murmured sympathetically. "He was out late with you last night, doing his assessment, and he hunted with Ashfur and Graystripe all afternoon."

"He'll be fine," Firestar replied. "All new warriors sit vigil the first night."

"So the rest of us can get a good night's sleep." Cloudtail, the other member of the patrol, stretched and yawned.

Leaving his mate and his kin to head for the fresh-kill pile, Firestar strode out into the clearing toward Brambleclaw. "Everything okay?" he asked.

Brambleclaw nodded; according to tradition a new warrior had to keep his vigil in silence. He was obviously bursting with pride, and taking his new responsibilities very seriously.

"Good," mewed Firestar. "Don't hesitate to fetch me if there's trouble."

Brambleclaw nodded again, and fixed his gaze on the entrance to the thorn tunnel. Firestar left him there and returned to his den. He curled up in his nest, but the moment he closed his eyes he found himself back on the mist-covered moorland, with the wails of cats shivering in his ears. *No!* He could not spend another night listening helplessly to their terror.

Struggling back to wakefulness, Firestar stumbled out into the clearing again. Brambleclaw still sat in solitary vigil, while Sandstorm was heading across the clearing toward the warriors' den. As soon as she spotted Firestar she veered aside to join him.

"Is anything the matter?" she asked. "Can't you sleep?"

"I feel restless, that's all," Firestar replied, reluctant to tell even Sandstorm about the dream. "I'm going for a walk." Suddenly longing for the warmth of her company, he added, "Do you want to come with me?"

He was sure his desperation must have shown in his eyes,

but Sandstorm just nodded. She crossed the camp beside him and followed him out through the gorse tunnel. Without consciously deciding, Firestar turned his paws toward Sunningrocks, the tumble of smooth gray boulders beside the river that divided ThunderClan territory from RiverClan.

They climbed one of the rocks and sat side by side, watching the water whisper past, dappled with starlight.

After a moment, Sandstorm broke the silence. "Are you worried about Brambleclaw? About whether you were right to make him a warrior?"

Her question surprised Firestar. Did his Clanmates think he still distrusted Brambleclaw because of who his father was? The surprise was followed by a sense of guilt that they were so close to being right.

"No," he answered, trying to make his voice firm. "Brambleclaw is *not* the same cat as his father."

To his relief, Sandstorm didn't push him to tell her what was really on his mind. She just leaned her head on his shoulder; her scent wreathed around him as they gazed together at the river of reflected starlight.

Firestar knew that her touch should have comforted him, but he couldn't get the wailing of terrified cats out of his head, or forget the reflection he had seen in the puddle. He stared down at the river, at the ruffled water spilling around half-covered rocks . . . no, they weren't rocks, he realized, his pelt bristling with fear. They were *cats,* desperately swimming cats, churning the water with their paws, their drenched bodies dragged by the swirling current.

He blinked, and the vision was gone. All he could see was the river sliding past on its endless journey, with the shivering starlight trapped in its depths.

Great StarClan! he thought. *What's happening to me?*

CHAPTER 3

Though Firestar didn't dream again that night, he slept badly, and he still felt tired when he emerged from his den the next morning. He blinked in the strong sunlight to see Ashfur padding across the clearing toward Brambleclaw. "Your vigil's over," Firestar heard him meow. "Come on; I'll find you somewhere to sleep."

They disappeared into the warriors' den while Firestar crossed the clearing and slipped down the fern tunnel that led to Cinderpelt's den.

The gray-furred medicine cat was sitting outside the cleft in the rock, turning over some herbs with one paw. Brightheart sat beside her and bent her head forward to give the leaves an interested sniff.

"This is borage," Cinderpelt explained. "You should start eating some now, so when your kits come you'll have plenty of milk."

Brightheart licked the herbs up, making a face as she swallowed them. "They taste as bitter as mouse bile. But I don't mind," she added hastily. "I want to do my best for my kits."

"You'll be fine," Cinderpelt assured her. "Come back every

morning for some more herbs, and call me right away if you think the kits are coming. I don't think it'll be long now."

"Thanks, Cinderpelt." Brightheart dipped her head to the medicine cat and padded across the clearing, passing Firestar at the end of the tunnel.

"Make sure you get plenty of rest," he meowed as she made her way back into the main camp.

Cinderpelt dusted a few scraps of borage from her paws and limped into the clearing to meet Firestar. Once she had been his apprentice, but an accident beside the Thunderpath had injured her leg and made it impossible for her to be a warrior. Firestar knew how hard it had been for her to give up the future she had always dreamed of; he still blamed himself for not taking better care of her.

"Cinderpelt, I have to talk to you," he began.

Before the medicine cat could reply, a wail sounded from behind Firestar. "Cinderpelt! Look at my paw!"

"Great StarClan, what now?" the medicine cat muttered.

Sorrelpaw, the smallest of the apprentices, lurched into the clearing on three legs, holding out her forepaw. "Look, Cinderpelt!"

The medicine cat bent her head to examine the paw. Firestar could see that a thorn was driven deep into the pad.

"Honestly, Sorrelpaw," Cinderpelt mewed, "from the noise you were making I thought a fox must have bitten your paw off. It's only a thorn."

"But it hurts!" the apprentice protested, her amber eyes wide.

Cinderpelt tutted. "Lie down and hold your paw out."

Firestar watched as the medicine cat expertly gripped the shank of the thorn in her teeth and tugged it out. A gush of blood followed it.

"It's bleeding!" Sorrelpaw exclaimed.

"So it is," Cinderpelt agreed calmly. "Give it a good lick."

"Every cat picks up thorns now and again," Firestar told the apprentice as her tongue rasped busily across her pad. "You'll probably pick up a good many more before you're an elder."

"I know." Sorrelpaw sprang to her paws again. "Thanks, Cinderpelt. It's fine now, so I'll go back to the others. We're training in the sandy hollow." Her eyes shone and she flexed her claws. "Sandstorm's going to show me how to fight *foxes*!"

Without waiting for a response she charged off down the fern tunnel.

Cinderpelt's blue eyes gleamed. "Sandstorm's got her paws full with that one," she commented.

"You've got your paws full yourself," meowed Firestar. "Is it always this busy?"

"Busy is good," Cinderpelt replied. "Just as long as there's no blood being spilled. It's great, being able to use my skills to care for my Clan."

Her eyes shone with enthusiasm, and once again Firestar was reminded of the apprentice she had been. What a warrior she would have made! But her accident had diverted all her energy, like a clear, sparkling stream, into the path of a medicine cat.

"Okay, Firestar," she prompted. "You're busy too, so you haven't come here just to gossip. What can I do for you?"

Twitching her ears for Firestar to follow her, she made her way to the cleft in the rock and began to put away the remaining stems of borage. Firestar sat beside her, suddenly reluctant to tell any cat about the strange visions he had seen.

"I've been having these dreams. . . ."

Cinderpelt shot him a swift glance; usually only medicine cats received dreams from StarClan, but she had learned long ago that their warrior ancestors came to Firestar too.

"It wasn't a dream from StarClan," Firestar went on. "At least, I don't think it was." He described the mist-shrouded moorland where the desperate wailing of cats had surrounded him. He couldn't bring himself to tell Cinderpelt about the pale gray cat he had seen in the ravine when he was awake, or the reflection in the puddle and the cats struggling in the river. They could be explained away too easily: odd cloud formations, tricks of the light, or the pattern of starlight in the dark water.

Cinderpelt finished tidying the herbs and came to sit beside him, her eyes thoughtful. "You've had this dream twice?"

"That's right."

"Then I think it's more than a tough bit of fresh-kill stuck in your belly." She blinked several times and added, "That many cats could only belong to a Clan . . . and you're sure it wasn't WindClan?"

"Positive. The moor wasn't anywhere in WindClan territory, I'm sure of it, and I didn't recognize any of the voices.

Besides, there's been no report of trouble in WindClan."

Cinderpelt nodded. "And none in any of the other Clans, either. Do you think you're remembering the battle with BloodClan?"

"No, Cinderpelt, what I heard wasn't battle yowling. It was cats wailing as if something was terribly wrong." Firestar shuddered. "I wanted to help them, but I didn't know what to do."

Cinderpelt brushed her tail across his shoulder. "I could give you some poppyseed," she suggested. "At least that would give you a good night's sleep."

"Thanks, but no. It's not sleep I want. It's an explanation."

Cinderpelt didn't look surprised. "That's something I can't give you, not right now," she meowed. "But I'll let you know if StarClan show me anything. And be sure to come and tell me if you have any more dreams."

Firestar wasn't certain he wanted to do that. Cinderpelt had enough to keep her busy without worrying about him. "I'm probably making a fuss about nothing," he told her. "I'm sure the dreams will go away if I stop thinking about them."

He hadn't managed to convince himself, and as he padded away through the fern tunnel with the medicine cat's pale blue gaze following him, he was sure that he hadn't convinced Cinderpelt, either.

On the second night after his talk with Cinderpelt, Firestar had the dream again. He stood on the pathless moorland, straining to make out the blurred shapes that were all around him, yet never close enough to see clearly.

"What do you want?" he called. "What can I do to help you?"

But there was no reply. Firestar was beginning to feel as if he were doomed to stumble across this mist-shrouded moor forever, calling out to cats who could not or would not hear him.

The sun had risen high above the trees when he woke the next morning. A warm wind ruffled his fur as he stepped out into the clearing. Sootpaw was hurrying across the clearing with a huge ball of fresh moss for the elders' bedding. Ferncloud and Brightheart were sunning themselves at the entrance to the nursery, watching Shrewkit and Spiderkit play-fighting.

Firestar stiffened at the sound of high-pitched caterwauling coming from outside the camp. Somewhere close by, a cat was in terrible distress. Had his dream followed him into the waking world? Or was he still asleep, trapped in the same dream?

He forced his legs to carry him over to the gorse tunnel. But before he reached the entrance to the camp, Cloudtail and Brackenfur appeared, supporting Longtail, whose jaws were stretched wide, letting out loud wails of anguish. Cloudtail's apprentice, Rainpaw, followed them into the camp, his fur bristling with shock.

Longtail's eyes were closed; blood welled from beneath the swollen lids and spattered over his pale tabby fur. "I can't see! I can't see!" he wailed.

"What happened?" Firestar demanded.

"We were out hunting," Brackenfur explained. "Longtail caught a rabbit, and it turned on him and scratched his eyes."

"Don't worry," Cloudtail reassured Longtail. "We'll get you to Cinderpelt right away. She'll fix you up."

Firestar followed them as they guided Longtail across the clearing and through the tunnel of ferns. Cloudtail called for Cinderpelt, who appeared from the cleft in the rock and limped rapidly to Longtail's side. "How did this happen?"

Brackenfur repeated what he had told Firestar, while Cinderpelt rested her tail gently on Longtail's shoulder.

The tabby warrior's wailing had died away into shallow, rasping breaths. He was shivering violently. "I can't see," he whispered. "Cinderpelt, am I going to be blind?"

"I can't tell until I've examined your eyes," Cinderpelt replied. Firestar knew she wouldn't try to comfort Longtail with a lie. "Come over here and sit down in the ferns where I can get a proper look at you."

She led him to a clump of bracken just outside the opening to her den. Longtail slumped onto his side, still panting hard.

"Rainpaw, bring me some moss soaked in water," Cinderpelt directed, "as fast as you can." The apprentice glanced at his mentor, and when Cloudtail nodded he sped off, leaving the ferns of the tunnel waving behind him. "The rest of you can go," the medicine cat added, "and let Longtail have a bit of peace and quiet."

Cloudtail and Brackenfur turned to leave, but Firestar padded over to Cinderpelt, who was calming Longtail with one paw stroking his flank.

"Is there anything I can do?" he asked.

"Just go with the others and let me get on with it," Cinderpelt replied, her tart tones reminding Firestar of her mentor, Yellowfang. As Firestar turned away, she added, "Oh, you might ask Cloudtail to let me have Rainpaw for the rest of the day. An apprentice to fetch and carry would be useful."

"Good idea," Firestar replied. "I'll tell him."

His heart was torn with pity for Longtail. The tabby warrior had challenged Firestar when he first arrived in the forest, and he had been far too close to Tigerstar. But when the murderous deputy's plans became clear, Longtail had realized where his true loyalties lay, and since then he had become one of Firestar's most trusted warriors.

When Firestar reached the clearing he saw Cloudtail and Brackenfur standing with Brightheart, who was anxiously questioning them. Mousefur and Graystripe had come out of the warriors' den to find out what was going on.

Firestar padded over to Cloudtail and passed on Cinderpelt's request about Rainpaw.

"Sure," the white warrior meowed. "It's all good training for Rainpaw, anyway."

"What's going to happen to Longtail?" Brightheart fretted. "Will he really go blind?"

"Cinderpelt doesn't know yet," Firestar replied. "Let's hope the damage isn't as bad as it looks."

"I was lucky," Brightheart murmured, half to herself. "At least I've still got one eye."

Glancing around at their troubled faces, Firestar tried to give them something else to think about. "What about the hunting patrol?" he asked Cloudtail and Brackenfur. "You'd better carry on, and I'll come with you. Whatever happens, the Clan still needs to be fed."

"I'll lead another," Graystripe offered. "Mousefur, are you up for it?"

The wiry brown warrior nodded, lashing her tail. "I'll fetch Dustpelt," she meowed.

As she loped off toward the warriors' den, Firestar cast a final glance back at the fern tunnel. Everything was quiet now in Cinderpelt's clearing. "Oh, StarClan," he whispered, "don't let Longtail lose his sight."

That night Firestar was too restless to settle in his den. He was afraid the dream would return. He had come to dread the unknown moorland and the cries of distress from cats he had no power to help.

As he paced the clearing, he heard a murmuring sound coming from Cinderpelt's den, and brushed through the fern tunnel to find out what it was. Longtail lay in the ferns outside the split rock. His eyes were closed, but he looked too tense to be asleep. Sticky tears seeped from beneath his eyelids.

Cinderpelt sat beside him, stroking his forehead lightly with the tip of her tail, murmuring to him words of comfort that a mother might use to soothe an injured kit. She glanced up as Firestar appeared.

"Shouldn't you be resting?" he asked.

Her blue eyes glinted in the moonlight. "I could ask you the same thing."

Firestar shrugged and went to sit beside her. "I couldn't sleep. How's Longtail?"

"I'm not sure." Cinderpelt dabbed up a pawful of chewed-up herbs from a leaf beside her and patted them gently onto Longtail's eyes. Firestar recognized the sharp scent of marigold. "The bleeding has stopped, thank StarClan," the medicine cat went on, "but his eyes are still very swollen."

"Firestar." Longtail raised his head, though he kept his eyes shut tight. "What will happen to me if I go blind? If I can't be a warrior anymore?"

"Don't worry about that," Firestar mewed firmly. "Whatever happens, there'll always be a place for you in ThunderClan."

Longtail let out a long sigh and lowered his head again. Firestar thought he had relaxed a little, and hoped he would be able to sleep.

"Listen, Firestar." Cinderpelt dabbed some more of the marigold poultice onto Longtail's eyes as she spoke. "As your medicine cat, I'm telling you to get some rest." More quietly, she added, "Your dream isn't going to go away; you know that as well as I do. You need to find out what it means, and the only way to do that is to dream it over and over until you figure it out."

Firestar hesitated; he wasn't sure he agreed. Dreaming hadn't told him much so far. "All right," he mewed reluctantly.

"But if StarClan are trying to tell me something, I wish they would make it clearer."

Obeying Cinderpelt, he padded back to his den. But this time he slept without dreaming at all.

Early the next morning he went back to the medicine cat's den, taking her a squirrel from the fresh-kill pile. He found Cinderpelt still sitting beside Longtail, who was curled up asleep.

"Have you been here all night?" Firestar asked, dropping the squirrel at Cinderpelt's side.

"Where else would I be? Longtail needs me. Don't worry; I'm not tired." She contradicted herself by stretching her jaws in an enormous yawn.

"Last night you told me to get some sleep," Firestar pointed out. "Now, as your Clan leader, I'm telling *you*. It won't do Longtail any good if our medicine cat gets ill."

"But I'm worried about him." Cinderpelt lowered her voice, even though Longtail was asleep. "I think his eyes are infected. The rabbit's claws must have been dirty."

Firestar peered at Longtail's closed eyes. He couldn't see much difference from the night before: they were still red and swollen, with sticky fluid and marigold pulp crusted around them.

"That's bad news," he mewed. "All the same, I think you should eat that fresh-kill and then get some rest. I'll send Rainpaw to you again," he added persuasively. "He can keep an eye on things and call you if Longtail wakes up."

Cinderpelt rose to her paws and arched her back in a long

stretch. "Okay," she agreed. "But will you tell Rainpaw to fetch some more marigold first? There's plenty near the top of the ravine."

"Provided I see you eating that squirrel."

Cinderpelt crouched down beside the squirrel, only to look up at Firestar again before she started to eat. "I'm so scared that I won't be able to save Longtail's sight," she confessed.

Firestar gently touched his nose to her ear. "Every cat in the Clan knows you're doing your best. Longtail knows it most of all."

"What if my best isn't good enough?"

"It will be. ThunderClan couldn't have a better medicine cat."

Cinderpelt sighed and shook her head before beginning to gulp down the squirrel. Firestar knew that he was wasting his breath trying to reassure her. If Longtail did go blind, Cinderpelt would blame herself, just as she had done when Graystripe's mate, Silverstream, died bearing their kits.

Resting his tail briefly on the medicine cat's shoulder, he went to look for Rainpaw.

Firestar led the way up the slope toward Fourtrees. Rain had fallen earlier that day, and drops clung to his pelt as he brushed through the long grass. But now the clouds had vanished and the full moon floated in a clear sky, surrounded by the glitter of Silverpelt.

The warriors Firestar had chosen to attend the Gathering

followed hard on his paws. Brambleclaw was bounding along at his shoulder, his eyes gleaming as if he could hardly stop himself from taking the lead and racing up the slope.

"Calm down," Graystripe meowed to him. "It's not like this is your first Gathering."

"No, but I was always an apprentice before," Brambleclaw pointed out. "Graystripe, do you think Firestar will tell all the Clans that I've been made a warrior?"

Firestar glanced over his shoulder. "Yes, of course I will."

"But they might not believe it unless you stop behaving like an apprentice," Graystripe warned, flicking Brambleclaw's ear with his tail.

Firestar could already hear the sound of many cats ahead, and he picked out the scents of WindClan, RiverClan, and ShadowClan on the warm breeze. He quickened his pace. His dreams were still haunted by unfamiliar voices raised in misery, and it would be good to spend time among cats he knew well. He wanted to deal with problems he had met before, instead of struggling to find out what the strange cats wanted from him.

But as he climbed the last slope to the edge of the hollow, he came to an abrupt stop. For a couple of heartbeats he was convinced that cats were rushing toward him, many cats, a whole Clanful. He blinked, and saw nothing but shadows. But the scent he had tasted in his dreams flowed around him, stronger now. Behind his eyes he had an impression of flattened ears and ruffled fur, as if the cats were fleeing from a Gathering that had broken up in disorder.

A moment later the sensation vanished, and Firestar was aware of Dustpelt bumping into him from behind.

"For StarClan's sake," the brown tabby warrior grumbled, "do you have to stop dead like that? Any cat would think you'd forgotten the way."

"Sorry," Firestar mewed.

His paws still tingling, he took the last few paces that brought him to the top of the hollow. In front of him the four great oaks rustled their branches, sending shifting patterns of light and shadow over the cats in the clearing. He paused for a few heartbeats longer than usual, searching for any other traces of the strange cats. But there was nothing to tell him who they were, and no trace of the pale warrior whose reflection he had seen in the puddle. Forcing himself to concentrate on the Gathering, he raised his tail to signal to his Clan and plunged into the bushes.

When Firestar reached the clearing, Brambleclaw raced past him and stopped in front of a tortoiseshell she-cat sitting a few tail-lengths away. "Tawnypaw!" he panted. "Guess what?"

His sister stared back at him. "Tawnypaw? Who's she? I'm Tawny*pelt* now, if you don't mind."

Brambleclaw's tail curled up in delight. "You are? That's great! So am I—I mean, I'm a warrior too. My name's Brambleclaw."

Tawnypelt purred and twined her tail with her brother's. "Congratulations!"

Just beyond them, Graystripe was greeting his son and

daughter, Stormfur and Feathertail, whose new warrior names had been announced by Leopardstar, the RiverClan leader, at the previous Gathering. Stormfur was a muscular gray tomcat, very like his father, while Feathertail had the beautiful light gray pelt of her mother, Silverstream.

Sandstorm headed straight for Mistyfoot, the RiverClan deputy, who was sitting near the Great Rock. The two she-cats had become friends when Mistyfoot had been driven out of her own Clan by Tigerstar, and had spent some time in ThunderClan.

Seeing that the rest of his warriors were also greeting friends from other Clans, Firestar headed for the Great Rock, where Leopardstar, Blackstar, and Tallstar were waiting.

Tallstar stepped forward as Firestar sprang up to join them. "Greetings, Firestar. Now that we're all here, the Gathering can start."

Firestar dipped his head to the other three leaders while Blackstar let out a yowl, signaling for the cats in the clearing below to be quiet. "I will begin by speaking for ShadowClan," he announced, narrowing his eyes at the other leaders as if they might challenge his right to make his report first.

None of the other leaders tried to argue with him, though Tallstar shot a glance at Firestar, and Leopardstar irritably twitched the tip of her tail.

"The prey is running well in ShadowClan," Blackstar began. "And we have made a new warrior, Tawnypelt."

A chorus of yowls broke out as the cats of all four Clans

congratulated Tawnypelt and called out her name. Firestar glanced down to see the young tortoiseshell warrior sitting beside her brother, her eyes shining proudly. But he couldn't help noticing that a few of her own Clanmates—the deputy, Russetfur, for one—kept silent, giving Tawnypelt suspicious stares. Firestar bit back a sigh. Some ShadowClan cats clearly mistrusted her because she had been born in ThunderClan.

"We have seen more Twolegs in our territory," Blackstar went on. "They stride around yowling at one another, and sometimes they let their monsters leave the Thunderpath and crash through the woods."

"Leave the Thunderpath?" Mistyfoot called out from below. "Why? Are they chasing your cats, Blackstar?"

"No," the ShadowClan leader replied. "I don't think they even know we're there. They'll be no trouble so long as we stay away from them."

"They must frighten the prey, though," Tallstar muttered to Firestar. "I wouldn't want any more of them on *my* territory; that's for sure."

"ShadowClan cats are better than most of us at hiding," Firestar pointed out under his breath.

Blackstar stepped back, nudging Tallstar. "Go on, it's your turn," he meowed.

The WindClan leader dipped his head before advancing to the edge of the rock. "All is well in WindClan," he reported. "Ashfoot has a new litter of three kits. Onewhisker and Mudclaw chased off a fox who seemed to think it would be happier living on the moors than in the woods."

"We soon changed its mind!" Mudclaw, the WindClan deputy, yowled from where he sat at the base of the Great Rock.

"You'd better keep a lookout for it," Tallstar continued to Leopardstar. "It crossed into your territory near the river."

"Thank you for that, Tallstar," the RiverClan leader replied dryly. "Another fox is just what we need. I'll warn the patrols."

Firestar reminded himself to do the same. RiverClan territory was narrow there, and if the fox had kept going it could easily have crossed into ThunderClan.

Meanwhile, Leopardstar had stepped forward. "As usual in greenleaf, there are more Twolegs around," she meowed. "They bring boats onto the river, and their kits play in the water and frighten the fish. This season the river is low, so there aren't quite as many Twolegs as usual. However, we have no problem feeding ourselves."

Firestar wondered if that was completely true. If the water was low in the river then surely there wouldn't be so many fish either. But it wasn't his place to argue, and he knew that Leopardstar, like all the leaders, wouldn't want her Clan to seem weak from lack of food.

"ThunderClan has a new warrior too," he announced when Leopardstar stepped back. "Bramblepaw had his warrior ceremony, and is now Brambleclaw."

Another chorus of congratulations broke out, while Brambleclaw sat beside his sister and acknowledged them with an embarrassed dip of his head. While he waited for the noise to die down, Firestar decided not to mention Longtail's accident. Before the next Gathering, Cinderpelt would probably have healed the tabby warrior's eyes, and the whole incident would be forgotten.

"Our prey is plentiful and the Twolegs aren't bothering us," he finished.

It wasn't often that a Gathering ended so quickly, with no serious disturbances to report from outside, and no reason for quarrels among the Clans. As Blackstar brought it to a close, Firestar looked down into the hollow. It was harder and harder to remember how it had looked after the battle with BloodClan, when the grass was stained red and the bodies of forest cats and the invaders from Twolegplace lay scattered across the clearing. He had lost his first life then, seeing a pale outline of himself take its place among the warriors of StarClan.

The starry cats had given him the courage to fight on when they told him there had always been *four* Clans living in the forest, and there always would be.

Life would go on like this forever; Firestar found the thought comforting. The daily routine of patrols, the toil of finding prey and training apprentices—even disturbing events like Longtail's injury and his own unexplained dreams—seemed small and insignificant when placed beside the unending pattern of Clan life. Firestar was part of a long, long line of cats all driven by loyalty to their Clanmates and the warrior code. Even when he had lost his last life, the Great Oaks would still be here, one for each Clan, until his name had been long forgotten.

CHAPTER 4

The Gathering was over. Firestar bunched his muscles to leap down into the clearing. As he looked for a space to land, he froze, gripping the surface of the rock with his claws. The hollow suddenly seemed more crowded than usual. Sleek, starlit shapes were weaving among the forest cats, close enough for their pelts to brush. The forest cats passed them without a glance, calling out to their Clanmates as they prepared to leave. The other three leaders leaped down into the midst of the strangers like water voles leaping into a pool. Leopardstar almost landed on top of a shimmering white warrior, and bounded away without even a twitch of her whiskers.

Firestar shivered. *None of the others can see them!*

His gaze was drawn to one cat among the starry shapes: the gray-and-white cat he had seen twice before. He was staring directly at Firestar, his jaws open in a silent plea, but before Firestar could respond, Mudclaw of WindClan passed in front of him and the gray-and-white cat vanished.

Firestar knew these were the same cats he had seen leaping in the river, the same cats that had appeared to him indistinctly through the mist in his dreams. *Who are they?*

And what are they doing here?

"Hey, Firestar!" Graystripe called from the foot of the Great Rock. "Are you going to stay up there all night?"

Firestar gave himself a shake. He couldn't go on like this. These cats had stalked him through his dreams, and now they were haunting him in the waking world as well. He had to find out why, and if Cinderpelt couldn't help him, there might be other cats who could.

He leaped down to where Graystripe was waiting for him with Sandstorm, Brambleclaw, and the rest of the ThunderClan warriors. "Graystripe, I want you and Sandstorm to lead the Clan back to camp."

"Why, where are you going?"

Firestar took a deep breath. "I need to go to the Moonstone. I have to share tongues with StarClan."

Graystripe looked surprised, but Sandstorm's green gaze met Firestar's with a look of understanding.

"I knew something's been troubling you," she mewed quietly, brushing her pelt against his. "Maybe you'll feel better after you've spoken to our warrior ancestors."

"I hope so," Firestar responded.

"Shall I come with you?" Graystripe offered. "The rest of the Clan don't need me to take them home, and you never know what might be lurking on the moors. What if that fox has come back?"

"No, thanks, Graystripe," Firestar meowed. "I'll go with WindClan as far as their camp, and after that I'll be fine."

"Okay." Graystripe gathered the rest of the ThunderClan

warriors together with a sweep of his tail. "When you pass Barley's farm, say hi to Ravenpaw for me."

"I'll do that." Firestar turned to Sandstorm and touched his nose to hers. "Good-bye. I'll be back soon."

"Good luck." Sandstorm blinked at him. "I hope you find some answers. It feels like you're a long way away just now."

Giving her ear a final lick, Firestar plunged into the bushes up to the top of the slope on the WindClan side of the hollow. Tallstar was already leading his cats onto the moor: small, dark shapes outlined against a wash of moonlight. Firestar raced after them until he overtook the cat who brought up the rear.

"Hi, Onewhisker," he panted. "Is it okay if I travel with you? I need to go to Highstones."

"Sure. No trouble, I hope?"

"Nothing to worry about," Firestar replied, hoping that was true.

He said good-bye to the WindClan cats on the slope above the hollow where they camped. Dawn was breaking as he set out for Highstones, the pointed mass of rock dark against the pale sky. A chill wind ruffled the short, springy grass, pressing Firestar's fur against his sides. Up here the sky seemed huge, without any trees for cover. The scents were unfamiliar, too: a mixture of gorse, heather, and rabbits, with a sharp tang of peaty earth.

A small, reed-fringed stream crossed Firestar's path. He leaped it easily, startling a rabbit that jumped up under his paws and fled down the slope, its white tail bobbing.

Firestar's paws itched to chase it, but he wouldn't take prey on another Clan's territory; besides, a Clan leader who traveled to Highstones to meet with StarClan at the Moonstone wasn't allowed to eat on the journey.

The sun had risen by the time the barren moorland gave way to lush meadows bounded by hedges and Twoleg fences. A Twoleg nest came into sight, and Firestar heard the distant barking of a dog. He looked around warily, tasting the air, but the dog scent was stale, and he reminded himself that by now the farm dogs, who were left to run loose at night, would be tied up again.

He skirted the Twoleg nest, slinking along in the shadow of a hedge. Another scent drifted toward him, stronger and fresher than the scent of dog: rats! Firestar paused, remembering how on his first journey to Highstones Bluestar had lost a life in a battle with rats very near this place. Pinpointing the source of the scent, he realized that he was downwind of it; with any luck he could pass without letting the rats know he was here.

Not far away from the Twoleg nest was a barn built of rough stone. Firestar headed for it and halted outside the door. A strong scent of cats flowed out of a gap at the bottom. Firestar felt a purr growing in his chest. "Hi," he mewed. "Can I come in?"

"Firestar!" A delighted meow came from inside the barn, and a black cat's head poked out of the gap. "What are you doing here?"

Firestar slid through the door and stood among the dusty

scraps of straw on the floor of the barn. He was greeted enthusiastically by Ravenpaw, who had been a ThunderClan apprentice when Firestar first came to the forest. Ravenpaw had known too much about Tigerstar's crimes, and Firestar had brought him to the barn before the bloodthirsty deputy murdered him to keep him quiet. Ravenpaw had been scrawny and nervous back then; now he was sleek and full-fed, his black pelt shining in the sunlight that angled through a hole in the barn roof.

"It's good to see you again," Firestar meowed. The last time he and Ravenpaw had met was at the battle with BloodClan, when the black cat and his friend Barley had joined in the fight with the forest cats.

"Welcome." Ravenpaw touched noses with his former Clanmate. "Is all well in ThunderClan?"

"Fine," Firestar replied. "But I—"

He broke off as another voice called out a greeting. Barley, the black-and-white cat who shared the barn with Ravenpaw, appeared at the top of a pile of straw bales and dropped neatly down at Firestar's side. He was a short, compact cat, well muscled, even though his belly was a bit too plump from all the mice that lived in the barn.

"Do you want to hunt?" he offered. "There's plenty of prey. Take as much as you like."

"I'm sorry, I can't," Firestar answered regretfully. Water flooded his jaws at the smell of mice; he could hear the tiny squeakings among the straw. "I'm on my way to the Moonstone, so I'm not allowed to eat."

"That's tough," meowed Ravenpaw. "But you can rest here, can't you? There's no point in going to Highstones yet. You'll arrive long before sunset."

"Thanks. I'm so tired I could sleep on my paws."

Ravenpaw led the way to the opposite side of the barn, where he and Barley had made nests in a loose heap of hay. Barley left them to talk together, giving Firestar a friendly nod before sliding out of the barn.

Firestar turned around two or three times, making himself a comfortable spot before curling up with the sweet-smelling stems tickling his nose.

"So, what brings you to the Moonstone?" Ravenpaw asked, and added hastily, "You don't have to tell me."

Firestar hesitated. So far the only cat he'd confided in was Cinderpelt, and he hadn't told her everything. He suddenly realized what a relief it would be to share his worries with a cat who didn't look upon him as a leader, but as a friend.

"I've had strange dreams," he began, describing for Ravenpaw the stretch of unfamiliar moorland and the shrill wailing of cats lost in the mist. "And that's not all. I've started to see things when I'm awake, too. There's one cat—a pale gray warrior—that I've seen three times now. Not just him . . . a whole Clan of cats, shining like starlight. I saw them last night at the Gathering, but no other cat knew they were there. Sometimes I think I'm going mad."

Ravenpaw's green eyes were filled with concern. "Are you sure they're not from StarClan?"

For a heartbeat Firestar felt how strange it was to talk

about StarClan with a cat who didn't belong to a Clan anymore.

"Don't think I've forgotten my warrior ancestors," Ravenpaw put in, as though he guessed what his friend was thinking. "I may not go to Gatherings anymore, but there's a part of me that will always be a Clan cat."

Firestar blinked, understanding. "I'm sure the cats I've seen aren't any of the warrior ancestors I know. I don't recognize any of them, or their scent. I don't know who or *what* they are, or why I keep seeing them. That's what worries me."

Ravenpaw flicked the white tip of his tail. "StarClan will probably be able to explain when you share tongues tonight. Why don't you sleep now, so you'll be ready?"

"I think I will," Firestar murmured. "Wake me at sunhigh, please."

With a drowsy purr, he settled himself more comfortably in his nest of hay. Sunlight slanted through the dust-filled air, the motes dancing like tiny stars. His eyes closed, and he drifted into a warm, hay-scented sleep.

Only a few heartbeats seemed to have passed before Firestar felt a paw prodding him in the side. He blinked his eyes open to see Ravenpaw standing over him.

"It's sunhigh," the black cat meowed.

Firestar rose and arched his back in a luxurious stretch. He couldn't remember the last time he had slept so soundly. In the ThunderClan camp, even if he didn't dream of the moorland, his sleep had been disturbed ever since he first saw the pale gray cat. He wondered if he had rested so well because he was away from the forest. Was it only there that the strange cats could reach him?

He said a quick good-bye to Barley and Ravenpaw. The prey scent in the barn was more enticing than ever, reminding him of his empty belly. He wished he had taken the time to hunt and eat before he left Fourtrees, but it was too late now. He left the barn and temptation behind him, and set out for Highstones.

By the time he reached the ridge, crossing the Thunderpath and scrambling up the rocky slopes, the sun was going down. The dark hole of Mothermouth gaped in the hillside. Firestar found a flat-topped stone and sat looking out across the Twoleg fields and nests, until darkness fell and the moon shed its silver light over the jagged rocks.

He had walked down the lightless tunnel that led to the Moonstone many times, but fear still gripped his belly as he stepped into the hungry shadows. Only his whiskers brushing the walls on each side and his paws on the rough, downward slope told him which way to go. Once he had left the opening behind him, the air was stale, with a tang of dust and stone. Firestar shivered to think of the weight of rock above his head, pressing down on the fragile tunnel.

At last came the moment when the air grew fresher again, bringing the scents of the moor to his nose. The tunnel opened out into a large cave, and he caught a glimpse of the stars glittering far above, shedding their faint light through a hole in the roof. He could just make out the dark shape of the

Moonstone in front of him, stretching three tail-lengths high from the floor of the cave. Wrapping his tail around his paws, he sat down to wait.

The change came with a blinding flash, as if every star in Silverpelt had poured down into the cave at once. The moon shifted in the sky until it shone down through the hole in the roof; in its light the Moonstone glittered like dew, shedding a pale, sparkling light on the cavern walls and the high, arched roof.

Firestar lay in front of the Moonstone and stretched out until he could touch it with his nose. Cold spread through him from muzzle to tail tip, and he remembered the last time he had come here, to receive his nine lives and his name. It seemed such a long time ago. He closed his eyes and let the darkness take him.

For countless heartbeats he felt nothing but wind and the scent of night rushing through his fur. Fear swelled up inside him; he gritted his teeth, refusing to lift his nose from the cold, cold stone.

Then his ears picked up a faint sound that gradually grew louder: the rustling of leaves in the breeze. His eyes flew open. Huge branches stretched above his head, barely visible against a dark sky. There was no moon, but the stars of Silverpelt were burning brightly, close enough to look as if they were tangled among the leaves.

Firestar scrambled up and looked around. He was back at Fourtrees, but this time the clearing was empty.

Then starlight sparkled at the edge of his sight, too low to come from Silverpelt; he spun around to see a blue-furred she-cat padding out of the shadows. Her pelt shone silver, and she left a frosty glitter on the grass where she set her paws.

"Bluestar!" Firestar was overjoyed to see the ThunderClan leader before him. "It's good to see you. Have you come here alone?"

Bluestar padded closer until Firestar could see the gleaming depths of her blue eyes. "I know why you have come," she replied, "and the questions you want to ask would not be welcomed by many of your warrior ancestors."

Firestar stared at her. "Do you mean that StarClan know the cats in my dreams? Are they from StarClan too? Why have I never seen them before? And what do they want from me?"

Bluestar brushed her tail across his mouth to silence him. Her eyes were troubled. Firestar felt as though he stood on the verge of a dark secret, and suddenly he didn't want to know what lay in its depths.

"Firestar." Bluestar's voice was uncertain, hesitant. "Is there any way you would be content to go away without the answer you seek?"

There was a hint of desperation in her eyes; Firestar almost gave way to her, but then he remembered why he had come. If he left without an explanation, the terrified wailing would invade his dreams over and over again, and there would be no escape from visions of the fleeing cats.

"No, Bluestar," he answered steadily. "I have to know the truth."

"Very well." Bluestar sighed. "The cats you have seen are from SkyClan."

"SkyClan?" Firestar echoed. "What is that?"

Bluestar bowed her head. "They are—they were—the fifth Clan."

CHAPTER 5

"But there have always been four Clans in the forest!"

"Not always," Bluestar replied. Her voice and her eyes were cold. "Once there were five. SkyClan's territory lay downriver from ThunderClan, where the Twolegplace is now. When the Twolegs built their nests, many, many seasons ago, SkyClan left the forest. There was no room for them then—and there's no room for them now."

"Where did they go?" Firestar asked.

"I don't know. Far from these skies where StarClan walks."

"And did StarClan never try to find them?" Firestar was shocked that Bluestar sounded so dismissive, as if the spirits of their warrior ancestors didn't care that a whole Clan had gone away.

"Their own warrior ancestors went with them," Bluestar explained. "There was no reason why SkyClan couldn't have found another home somewhere else."

"Then what do they want with me?" Firestar asked, bewildered. "Are they trying to tell me that they want to come back? Why would they do that, if they found another home?"

"I don't know," Bluestar admitted. "But from the first

moment I saw you, all those seasons ago, I knew you were the fire that would save our Clan. I knew you would leave pawsteps behind you that will be remembered as long as the warrior Clans survive. Perhaps SkyClan sees this also. Perhaps they think that only you can help them."

Firestar shivered. "Are you telling me that I have to find SkyClan and bring them back to the forest?"

"I'm not telling you anything of the kind," Bluestar snapped. "Where is there room for another Clan?"

"But the dreams—" Firestar protested.

"Firestar, are there bees in your brain?" Bluestar's tail lashed. "You are ThunderClan's leader, and your Clan needs you. There's nothing in the warrior code that says you have to help a Clan that has been missing for so long, no living cat remembers them."

Firestar narrowed his eyes. Bluestar was right about his responsibility toward ThunderClan, but he couldn't forget the wailing of the cats on the moor. How could he ignore them, if there was anything he could do to help? It wasn't Bluestar's dreams that were filled with the shrieks of terrified, fleeing cats; she didn't see a pleading, haunted face in every pool of water.

And yet the only reason he had found the courage to lead the forest Clans into battle against BloodClan was because he had believed his warrior ancestors when they told him there had always been four Clans in the forest. The fifth Clan was StarClan, forever protecting the four below. Had StarClan *lied?*

Bluestar rested her tail tip on his shoulder and spoke more calmly. "Your warrior ancestors are watching over you now, just as they have always done. Nothing has changed. Your duty is to your own Clan now."

"But SkyClan—"

"Has *gone*. There is no gap where they used to be, no prey or territory waiting for them to return. The forest is perfectly divided between the four Clans who remain."

"Then it's the will of StarClan that I just ignore these cats?" Firestar challenged her. "Don't you care that they are suffering?"

Bluestar blinked. "There are cats who would argue that there should never have been a fifth Clan in the forest at all. Why are there four oaks at Fourtrees, if not to stand for the four Clans?"

Firestar gazed up at the massive oak trees, then back at Bluestar. Fury pure as a lightning flash rushed through his body. "Are you mouse-brained?" he snarled. "Are you telling me SkyClan had to leave because there weren't enough *trees*?"

A look of shock and dismay filled Bluestar's eyes. Not waiting for her reply, Firestar whipped around and raced to the edge of the hollow. Brambles tore at his fur as he plunged through the bushes, but the pain meant nothing. Ever since he came to the forest he had trusted his warrior ancestors. But they had been lying to him all along. He felt as if he had taken a step on ground he thought was solid, only to fall into deep and bitter water.

He fought his way through the last of the bushes, but

instead of reaching the rim of the hollow, he found himself blinking awake in the cavern of the Moonstone. His breath was coming in harsh rasps. His fur felt torn and rumpled. His paws stung, and when he licked them he tasted the salty tang of blood, as if he had been running a long way over stony ground.

Far above, through the hole in the roof, clouds covered the moon and stars. The cave was utterly dark. Firestar rose to his paws and limped across the cave floor, close to panic until he stumbled into the entrance to the tunnel. When he emerged onto the side of the hill a stiff breeze was shredding the clouds like wet cobweb. Firestar caught only fitful glimpses of the moon, but stars were shining overhead once more.

He crawled onto the flat rock where he had waited earlier and collapsed there, gazing upward. He could not see the kindly eyes of his warrior ancestors in the starlight any longer. The desperate cries of the lost and tortured SkyClan echoed through his mind. *How am I meant to help them?*

All those cats must be dead by now. They had fled so long ago that no cat remembered them. But where were their descendants, the living SkyClan?

Firestar lay on the rock until the sky grew milk-pale with dawn. Then he made his way, pawstep by painful pawstep, down the hill and into the fields, leaving the jagged peak of Highstones behind him. A feeling of betrayal still swirled through him like a flooding river. He had always respected StarClan, trusting them to want what was best for all the

Clans. Now he had discovered that they could make mistakes, just like any living cat. If he couldn't trust them, would he ever come here to share tongues with his warrior ancestors again?

His belly felt hollow with hunger. Passing Ravenpaw's barn, he fought the temptation to go in to see his friends, to feast on their prey and rest in the soft heap of hay. But Ravenpaw was bound to ask him what StarClan had said about the strange cats, and he could not think what he would answer. Ravenpaw still clung to his faith in StarClan, even though he had left the forest; could Firestar shatter that faith by revealing how their warrior ancestors had lied to all the cats in the forest, over and over again?

Once he had left the Twoleg farm behind, Firestar stopped to hunt, swiping an unsuspecting mouse as it nibbled seeds in the shelter of a hedge. It scarcely took the edge off his hunger, but he was too exhausted to go looking for more. He curled up under a hawthornbush and fell headlong into sleep.

When he woke it was almost sunhigh. Feeling better, Firestar set off again, skirting the edge of a field where the corn grew tall, beginning to turn golden in the sun. He spotted another mouse as it slipped between the stiff stems, pounced on it, and killed it with a swift bite to the neck. Gulping down the last few mouthfuls he headed for the moors.

The sun was going down when he limped at last into the ThunderClan camp. Red light bathed the clearing, barred with the shadows of trees. Firestar let out a long, despairing sigh. It was good to be home, but could he really go on as Clan leader, knowing what he knew now?

As he hesitated at the mouth of the gorse tunnel, Graystripe came charging across from the warriors' den. Sandstorm glanced up from where she crouched beside the fresh-kill pile and padded more slowly to join him.

"Firestar, you're back!" Graystripe exclaimed. "It's great to see you." Halting in front of his friend, he added more doubtfully, "Is everything okay?"

"I'm fine, thanks," Firestar replied, every word an effort. "I'm tired; that's all."

Sandstorm brushed her tail sympathetically along his flank. Her green eyes searched his face, and he knew she realized that it was not only weariness that troubled him. But she didn't question him, just mewed, "Then it's time you got some rest."

"Listen, Firestar," Graystripe went on, "the afternoon patrol just got back. They think that fox Tallstar was talking about has crossed over into ThunderClan territory. At least, they picked up strong, fresh fox scent on the border, not far from the Twoleg bridge."

Firestar squeezed his eyes shut, trying to concentrate on what this would mean for his Clan. "Did they follow the scent?"

"They tried, but they lost it in a boggy bit of ground near the stream." Graystripe was looking expectantly at Firestar, waiting for his leader to tell him what to do. His expression changed to alarm as the silence lengthened.

Firestar felt as if he were trying to struggle through brambles inside his head. He could understand the problem about the fox, but it felt as if it belonged to another cat, a long time ago, and had nothing to do with him.

"Firestar?" Sandstorm murmured, moving closer so that he could feel the warmth of her pelt.

The excited squeals of kits brought Firestar back to the present. In the center of the clearing Shrewkit and Spiderkit were pouncing on a bundle of moss.

"Take that, Scourge!" Spiderkit squealed. "Get out of our forest!"

"And take your Clan with you!" Shrewkit landed in the middle of the moss, paws flying, scattering the scraps in a wide circle around him.

"Hey!" Rainpaw came bounding up from the direction of the elders' den. "I just collected all that!" he protested. "How am I supposed to fix the elders' bedding if you keep messing it up?"

The two kits exchanged a glance, then scampered off side by side, back to the nursery, their tails waving in the air. Rainpaw watched them go, neck fur bristling, then began to collect up the scattered scraps of moss.

Watching the kits at play reminded Firestar that Clan life was not just about StarClan, or even the warrior code. His duty as leader was to provide for his Clanmates *now*, and make sure they lived long and happy lives in the forest. Feeling a trickle of energy begin to flow into his tired limbs, he turned back to Graystripe.

"Right—the fox. Double the patrols on that part of the border. And tell the hunting patrols to keep a lookout. We don't want it to settle here."

"Sure." Relief flooded into Graystripe's eyes as Firestar took control again. "I'll make sure all tomorrow's patrols know about it." He headed toward the warriors' den.

Sandstorm stayed with Firestar. "You can tell me, you know," she meowed quietly.

"I know. I promise I will, but not yet."

His mate nodded. "Why don't you go to your den and rest? I'll bring you some fresh-kill."

"Thanks, but I'd better visit Cinderpelt first. I want to check on Longtail."

While Sandstorm went back to the fresh-kill pile, Firestar padded across the darkening camp and brushed through the fern tunnel to Cinderpelt's den.

The medicine cat was bent over Longtail, examining his eyes. As Firestar called out a greeting, the tabby warrior sat up and turned to him. Firestar stopped dead, his pelt prickling with horror. Though Longtail's eyes were open now, they were clouded and still weeping stickily.

"Can you see?" Firestar forced himself to ask, choking back an exclamation of pity. That was the last thing Longtail would want.

"A bit," Longtail replied. "But everything's blurred."

"His eyes are still infected," Cinderpelt explained. She looked exhausted; her gray fur was rumpled and her blue eyes were dull with defeat. "I've tried every herb and berry I can think of, and nothing will clear it up."

Longtail clawed at the bracken where he sat, his head lowered. "I'm just going to be a burden to the Clan," he growled.

"No!" Firestar exclaimed. "I won't let you say that. Look at Brightheart—she's learned to fight with only one eye."

"At least she *has* one good eye," Longtail hissed. "You might as well leave me in the forest for the foxes."

"That will never happen, not while I'm leader of this Clan," Firestar hissed back. Fury shook him, not against Longtail, but against himself for not having enough power to protect his warrior from the consequences of his injury. Trying to sound calmer, he added, "Besides, you haven't lost your sight yet. Cinderpelt will do her best to find an herb that works."

"I'll keep trying," Cinderpelt vowed. Beckoning Firestar with her tail, she led him over to the fern tunnel. "You'd better leave Longtail alone for now," she advised quietly. "He's badly shocked, and he needs a while to get used to the idea that his eyes might not get better."

Firestar nodded. "Okay." Raising his voice, he added, "Don't worry about a thing, Longtail. You'll always have a place in ThunderClan. I'll come and see you again soon."

Returning through the tunnel to the twilit clearing, Firestar still felt choked by pity—and fury, too, that this should happen to one of his warriors. He remembered the life that Brindleface had given him when he became Clan leader—a life for protection, the care of a mother for her kits. He had expected that life to be warm and gentle, but instead it had entered him with the shock of fire and ice together. He had felt the raw, ravenous urge to fight and kill, to spill rivers of blood to protect young, helpless cats. Now, thinking of Longtail as he struggled to cope with losing his sight, Firestar understood more clearly what that instinct meant. As Clan leader, he would rip out all his claws to protect any one of his Clanmates.

His den under the Highrock was cool and quiet. Sandstorm had left a rabbit for him, and Firestar settled down to eat. Now that he was alone, he felt as limp as a drooping leaf. Yet he was beginning to see a way forward, a way to care for his Clan even though his trust in StarClan had been shattered.

He was curling up comfortably when a shadow fell across the den entrance. He looked up to see Cinderpelt, her head and shoulders thrusting back the screen of lichen. "Longtail's asleep now," she explained. "So I thought I'd take the chance to come and ask what happened at the Moonstone. Did you find the answers you were seeking?"

"Yes, but they weren't the answers that I wanted to hear." He felt it was still too soon to tell what had happened, even to his medicine cat.

To his relief, Cinderpelt didn't press him. Coming into his den, she bent her head to give his ear a comforting lick. "Have faith," she urged him. "StarClan are watching over us, and everything will be all right."

A claw of anger pierced Firestar. He longed to tell her that StarClan had lied to them, that their ancestors had allowed a

Clan to leave the forest in spite of everything in the warrior code.

But he could not bring himself to poison Cinderpelt's faith, to spill bile onto everything she believed. Somehow he knew that this was his problem, and his alone. Without the help of StarClan, without any remnant of faith in his warrior ancestors, he must find a way of dealing with it.

CHAPTER 6

Wind swept across the moorland, shredding the mist, and Firestar saw the fleeing cats clearly for the first time. They were following a river; the familiar tang of water in the air told him this was the forest river he knew, though here, beyond WindClan territory, it flowed more swiftly through the hills.

"Wait!" Firestar called to them. "Cats of SkyClan, wait for me! I've come to help you."

He raced across the springy turf, but the SkyClan cats sped away from him as if they had not heard his cries.

Suddenly a kit tumbled into the river, its mother letting out a yowl of dismay as the current swept it away. Then a young apprentice, straying away from the main group, was picked off by a fox. Firestar heard its squeals of terror cut off abruptly as the fox bounded away, outpacing a couple of warriors who tried to chase it. An elder lagged farther and farther behind; she kept limping after her Clan, though her paws left smears of blood on the grass. Another staggered to a halt, then fell on one side and didn't get up again.

At the head of the journeying Clan Firestar spotted the gray-and-white cat. Thin, hungry-looking warriors clustered around him. Even though Firestar still couldn't catch up to them, their voices came clearly to him.

"Where are we going?" one of them meowed. "We can't live here . . . there's no prey, and nowhere to camp."

"I don't *know* where we're going," the gray-and-white cat replied. "We just have to keep on until we find somewhere."

"But how long?" one of the other warriors asked. No cat replied.

Firestar saw a small, light brown tabby she-cat shouldering her way through the warriors until she reached the gray-and-white cat. "Let me speak to StarClan," she begged. "They might know of a place for us."

The cat rounded on her. "No, Fawnstep!" he spat. "Our warrior ancestors have failed us. As far as we're concerned, StarClan no longer exist."

He must be the Clan leader! There was authority in his voice, and the small tabby—SkyClan's medicine cat, Firestar guessed—bowed her head, and didn't try to argue.

Firestar called out to the SkyClan cats again and made one last effort to catch up to them, but he was falling farther and farther behind. Mist swirled around him again, cutting him off from the fleeing Clan. At last his paws wouldn't carry him any longer. He sank down, and opened his eyes to find himself in his own den.

Gradually he became aware of another cat sitting in the shadows. "Sandstorm?" he murmured, longing for the warmth and comfort of his mate's presence.

The cat turned toward him, and the light from the den

entrance fell onto a soft tortoiseshell pelt.

"Spottedleaf!"

The former ThunderClan medicine cat rose and came toward him, gently touching her nose to his. Firestar drank in her familiar sweet scent. He couldn't think of her as one of the warrior ancestors who had betrayed him; no matter what the rest of StarClan might do, he would always trust Spottedleaf.

Gazing at the shape of her head and her slender, graceful body, he found himself thinking of the gray-and-white cat, the SkyClan leader he had seen in his dreams.

"Have you come to tell me about SkyClan?" he asked.

"Yes," Spottedleaf replied gravely. "When I lived in ThunderClan, I never knew there had once been five Clans living in the forest. I learned their story after I joined StarClan."

"I don't understand." Firestar scratched restlessly at a piece of moss. "How could StarClan allow a whole Clan to leave the forest?"

Spottedleaf crouched beside him. He could feel the vibrations of her soothing purr. "I know it is hard for you," she mewed. "But StarClan do not control everything in the forest. We could not banish the dog pack that threatened you, or drive out Scourge and BloodClan."

Firestar sighed; he knew that was true. But it didn't explain why StarClan had lied, and pretended that SkyClan had never existed. "Have you met any of the SkyClan cats?"

Spottedleaf shook her head. "We do not walk the same skies."

"I spoke to Bluestar," Firestar meowed. "She told me my duty is to ThunderClan. She said there is nothing I can do for SkyClan. But if that's true, why do I keep seeing them?"

"If the SkyClan leader has appeared to you in dreams," Spottedleaf replied, touching his shoulder with her tail, "then he must believe you *can* help him."

"But how?" Firestar persisted. "What can I do? It all happened so long ago."

"The answer will be shown to you," Spottedleaf promised. "Rest now."

She pressed closer to his side, and Firestar drifted more deeply into sleep, comforted by her warm scent. This time no dreams disturbed him.

Bright sunlight shone into his den when Firestar woke. Spottedleaf was gone, though he caught a trace of her scent among his bedding. He rose and stretched, feeling new energy coursing through him.

Skirting the Highrock, he found Graystripe in the main clearing with several cats standing around him as he arranged hunting patrols. "Cloudtail, you can go with Thornclaw," he was telling the white warrior. "Who do you want for a third? Willowpelt?"

"I'll go," Firestar interrupted, bounding up to them. "I feel as if I haven't had a good hunt for moons."

"Thanks." Graystripe nodded to him. "In that case, Willowpelt, you can come with Brackenfur and me. We'll head toward Fourtrees and see if we can spot that fox."

Once outside the camp, Firestar let Thornclaw take the lead. The tabby warrior took them down a trail that led to Twolegplace. Everything was quiet; even the prey seemed to be hiding. Firestar paused, gazing through the trees at the fence that edged the Twoleg nests, and wondered where SkyClan's territory had been. The border must have been near here, if they had been driven out when the Twolegs built their nests. When they built *his* old Twoleg nest, Firestar realized with a jolt. His paws prickled at the thought that he might have once lived in part of SkyClan's old territory!

Cloudtail and Thornclaw had vanished among the trees to search for prey. Firestar dragged his thoughts away from SkyClan. He had a Clan to feed. He opened his jaws; a strong scent of mouse flowed over his scent glands, and he spotted the creature scrabbling at the edge of a bramble thicket. Dropping into the hunter's crouch, he prowled forward, setting each paw down as lightly as a falling leaf.

But before he came within pouncing distance, a white blur appeared at the corner of his eye. He whipped his head around, furious with Cloudtail for creeping up on him. *Go and catch your own prey!* But the white blur had vanished, and a wisp of now-familiar scent told him that it hadn't been Cloudtail after all. The SkyClan leader had crossed his path once more.

Firestar stood still, his tail flicking back and forth. "Are you there?" he called softly. "What do you want? Come and talk to me!"

There was no reply.

By now the mouse had vanished. Firestar opened his

mouth and breathed in, trying to track down more prey. His ears strained to pick up the least sound of tiny paws; instead, all he could hear was a furious yowling and scuffling that broke out somewhere ahead, near the Twoleg fence. Was something—maybe a Twoleg dog—attacking his warriors?

He raced through the trees until he came to the edge of the wood. Ashfur and Brambleclaw were scuffling with an unfamiliar black-and-white cat. Brambleclaw had climbed onto the cat's back, clawing at its neck fur, while Ashfur bit down hard on the end of its tail.

The black-and-white cat was writhing on the ground, his flailing paws barely touching his attackers. "Get off me!" he yowled. "I need to see Rusty—I mean Firestar!"

Firestar suddenly recognized the disheveled bundle of black-and-white fur. It was Smudge, the kittypet who had been his friend before Firestar left his Twolegs to live in the forest.

"Stop!" He ran over to the wrestling cats, lowering his head to butt Brambleclaw hard in his flank. Brambleclaw slid off Smudge's back, glaring up with a furious hiss that broke off when he realized who had interrupted the fight.

"Leave him alone," Firestar ordered.

"But he's an intruder," Brambleclaw protested, scrambling to his paws and shaking dust from his pelt.

"A *kittypet* intruder," added Ashfur, reluctantly letting go of Smudge's tail.

"No, he's not," Firestar corrected them. "He's a friend. What are you two doing here, anyway?"

"We're the border patrol," Brambleclaw told him. "With Dustpelt and Mousefur. Look, here they come."

Following the direction of his pointing tail, Firestar spotted the two older warriors bounding rapidly through the trees.

"In StarClan's name, what's going on?" Dustpelt demanded. "I thought a fox must have gotten you from all that noise."

"No, just a kittypet," Firestar mewed, faintly amused at Brambleclaw's and Ashfur's outraged expressions. "Okay, carry on with your patrol," he added.

"But what about the kittypet?" Ashfur asked.

"I think I can handle him," Firestar mewed. "You're doing fine, but just remember that not everything you haven't seen before is a threat."

Brambleclaw and Ashfur fell in behind Dustpelt and Mousefur as they continued their patrol; Brambleclaw cast a threatening glance back at Smudge and hissed, "Stay off our territory in the future!"

Smudge heaved himself to his paws, glaring at his attackers. His fur was covered in dust and stuck out in all directions, but he didn't seem to be hurt.

"You're lucky I was here to save your pelt," Firestar remarked as the patrol vanished among the trees.

His old friend let out a furious snort. "I'll never understand you, Firestar. You actually *want* to live with these violent ruffians?"

Firestar hid his amusement. There was no point trying to

explain that these violent ruffians were warriors who had risked their lives at his side time and time again.

"It's good to see you again, Smudge," he meowed. "Why did you come so far into the forest? You know it's dangerous for you."

Smudge looked away, scuffling the ground with his forepaws.

"Well?" Firestar prompted, when Smudge had been silent for several heartbeats.

The kittypet blinked. "I . . . I think," he began haltingly, "that is, I'm afraid I might have to come and live in the forest with you."

"Great StarClan! What's happened? It's not BloodClan, is it?" Firestar asked fearfully.

Smudge looked up for a moment. "Who?"

"Never mind. Your Twolegs, then—they haven't thrown you out, have they?"

"No! My housefolk have always been very good to me." Smudge cast a longing look over his shoulder toward the red stone nest where he lived. "It's just . . . well, I've been having these weird dreams, and I remember you told me that *you* had dreams before you went to join the forest cats." Horror gleamed in his eyes, and Firestar, for all his sympathy, found himself hiding a purr of amusement that his old friend couldn't imagine anything worse than having to live in a Clan. "I thought my dreams must mean I'd have to leave my housefolk."

Firestar swept his tail around to touch his old friend on

the shoulder. "I wouldn't worry. Dreams have many meanings, and sometimes a dream is just a dream. I'm sure you won't have to eat bones just yet."

Smudge didn't look reassured. "But these dreams are terrible!" he mewed. "I keep seeing lots of cats—they're running away, but I never get to see what's chasing them. They're wailing and shrieking as if they're scared or in pain. And sometimes I see a gray-and-white cat on his own. He keeps opening and closing his mouth as if he's trying to tell me something, but I can't hear what he's saying."

Every hair on Firestar's pelt bristled. Smudge was having the same dreams as him! But why? Surely SkyClan didn't think that a *kittypet* could help them?

"What do you think?" Smudge asked nervously. "*Do* I have to come and live in the forest?"

Firestar knew he had to decide how much to tell his friend. Though his faith in StarClan had been badly shaken, he still felt some loyalty toward them. At least, he didn't think he could tell Smudge how StarClan had allowed SkyClan to be driven from the forest, and then lied about it afterward. Besides, if he tried to explain, how much would Smudge understand? He had no idea about the warrior code, or what it was like to live in a Clan.

"Don't worry about it," he meowed at last. "There's no reason for you to leave your Twolegs."

"Are you sure?"

"Positive. I know a bit about these dreams already, and I'm trying to sort everything out."

Smudge looked puzzled but relieved as well. "I guess I'll let you handle it, then."

Firestar was glad he didn't think to ask how a forest cat—even a Clan leader—could know about another cat's dreams. "I'll come back with you to your Twoleg nest," he mewed. "Just in case any of those violent ruffians are still hanging about."

Smudge looked down at his messy fur and gave it a few swift licks. Then he and Firestar padded side by side through the trees. As the Twoleg fence came into sight, Firestar spotted a vole pattering through the long grass. He made a swift pounce, and straightened up with the limp body hanging from his jaws; he tried to push down a stirring of pride that he had been able to show off his hunting skills in front of Smudge.

His friend's eyes were wide, but not with admiration. "Don't you ever get tired of having to catch your own food?"

Firestar dropped his fresh-kill and scraped leaves over it so that he could collect it later. "No, never. That's what warriors do."

Smudge shrugged, and went on toward his nest. Catching up with him, Firestar spotted another cat, a pretty brown tabby, jumping down from the fence around the Twoleg nest where he had once lived. He remembered seeing her before when he had been showing the territory to his new apprentice, Bramblepaw.

"Hi," she meowed. Her amber eyes examined Firestar

without a trace of fear. "Who's this, Smudge? I've never seen him before."

Smudge twitched one ear. "His name's Firestar. He lives in the forest."

"I'm called Hattie," the tabby introduced herself. "I've never met a forest cat before. How do you know Smudge?"

"I've known him since I was a kit," Firestar explained. "I used to live here, in this Twoleg nest."

"Really? But this is my home now!" The tabby's eyes stretched wide. "Why did you leave?"

"It's a long story." Firestar didn't expect any kittypet, even this lively tabby, to understand what had called him out of his safe life with Twolegs to the danger and excitement of the forest.

"I've got time to listen," Hattie meowed.

Firestar was aware of Smudge close beside him, quivering with tension. "Sorry," he meowed. "Maybe another time."

Hattie looked disappointed. "Don't you want to see where you used to live?" she mewed persuasively. "My Twolegs dug up a bush that was so old its roots stretched nearly the whole way across the garden, and planted some new trees that are great for scratching."

Firestar opened his jaws to refuse, but the words didn't come. He stood silent, gazing at the fence. An old bush . . . how old? Suppose it had been here before the Twoleg nests were built? Did that mean it had been here when *SkyClan* lived in the forest? Were there any other remnants of SkyClan's former territory that might have survived?

CHAPTER 7

"Firestar, why are you standing there with your mouth open?" Smudge asked crossly.

"Sorry." For a moment Firestar had been caught up in the lost world of SkyClan, gaping as if he expected prey to jump into his jaws. "Okay," he added to Hattie. "I'll have a quick look from the fence." Flicking his tail to draw Smudge a couple of pawsteps away, he murmured, "I won't be long. This might help with your dreams."

Smudge looked doubtful, and shot an anxious glance at Hattie.

"Don't worry; I won't tell her anything," Firestar promised.

He sprang up to sit on the fence and looked down into the garden. He remembered the bush now: it had been brittle and straggly, and some of its branches had been leafless. In the place where it had been a new young tree was growing with soft, tempting bark; from his place on the fence Firestar could see Hattie's claw marks scoring the trunk.

Hattie leaped up beside him and pointed with her tail. "That's where the bush used to be, and there's the scratching tree. And there's another new one, next to Smudge's fence, that's even better."

Firestar heard scrabbling farther along the fence, and Smudge hauled himself up to sit beside Hattie. "Well, what do you see?" he demanded in a low voice.

"Nothing yet," Firestar admitted. He studied the Twoleg nests, trying to imagine what this part of the forest would have been like before the trees were cut down.

His eyes narrowed as he glanced up and down the row of nests. Smudge's nest lay in a slight dip, lower than the others. If Firestar had been leading a Clan back then, and had to choose a place for a camp, he would have wanted it in a sheltered hollow, perhaps with bramble bushes for extra protection, like the WindClan camp. He drew in a swift breath, feeling every hair on his pelt stand on end. Could Smudge's nest have been built right on top of the old SkyClan camp? That might explain why he had been dreaming so vividly about the fleeing cats.

"Smudge," he began, interrupting a discussion between his friend and Hattie about catmint, "is it okay if I stay with you tonight?"

Smudge blinked in surprise. "Of course. But will it be okay with . . . with the other cats in your Clan?"

His concern moved Firestar. Smudge might be a kittypet, but he was a true friend. "They'll be fine, I promise. I just think this will help me figure out, you know, what we were talking about earlier."

"Oh, I see." Smudge looked alarmed as he added, "But I'm

not sure how easy it'll be getting you inside the nest."

"I don't need to come inside," Firestar told him. *StarClan forbid!* "I'll be fine in the garden, thanks."

The black-and-white cat nodded. "Okay. Well, come on over."

"I've got to find my Clanmates first and let them know I won't be back tonight."

Firestar jumped down from the fence, back into the forest. Behind him, he heard Hattie meowing inquisitively, "Why does Firestar want to stay in your garden? Why doesn't he want to stay in mine?"

Firestar raced through the trees until he reached the place where he had last seen his Clanmates. Before he could begin tracking them by scent, Thornclaw appeared from behind a clump of brambles, carrying two mice by their tails.

He dropped his prey in front of Firestar. "I thought you must have gone back to camp."

"No, something's come up." Firestar was reluctant to explain any further. "I won't be back until tomorrow. There's nothing wrong," he added, seeing that Thornclaw was starting to look worried. "Just tell Graystripe that he's in charge until then."

"Okay. Cloudtail and I are just about ready to take our prey back."

Firestar said good-bye and retraced his pawsteps through the trees to the Twoleg nests. There was no sign of Smudge, but Hattie was sitting where he had left her.

"You still haven't told me how you joined your Clan," she

mewed as Firestar leaped up onto Smudge's fence. She sounded put out. "Don't you want to visit your old home properly?"

Firestar didn't want to upset her, and he *was* curious to see the place where he had spent the first moons of his life. Balancing carefully, he walked along the fence to Hattie's side. "All right, I'll come for a little while."

Hattie let out a little trill of pleasure and leaped down into her garden. Firestar followed; his nose twitched at the unfamiliar scents. The flowers seemed to glare at him in the sunlight, and the close-cut grass pricked his pads. Everything seemed familiar and yet strange, as if he were gazing through some other cat's eyes at something he had never experienced himself.

"Come and have a scratch," Hattie invited, racing over to the tree and standing on her hind paws to score her claws down the length of the trunk. "It's really good." Whirling, she pointed with her tail. "And that's the bush where birds come hopping after snails. Did they do that when you were here?"

"Yes," Firestar replied, chasing the vague memory. "Have you ever tried to catch one?"

Hattie wrinkled her nose with distaste. "Why would I want to do that? There would be blood and feathers everywhere—ugh!"

Firestar bit back an annoyed response. A kittypet couldn't understand that a bird—even the scrawniest, toughest thrush—might be the only thing that kept a Clan cat from starvation.

"I used to stalk the birds," he remarked, padding over to the bush and ducking underneath its branches. "I never caught one, though. They were too quick for me. I learned how to catch prey when I went into the forest."

"I can't understand why you left your housefolk," Hattie mewed, padding over to sit beside him. "They—"

She broke off at the sound of footsteps approaching. Firestar sprang up and whipped around to see his former Twolegs walking down the path that led around the side of the nest. They had a kit with them—a female, staggering along on short, stubby legs, and clinging with one paw to her mother.

Before the Twolegs could spot him, Firestar darted out of the bush; one outlying branch raked through his fur. He flung himself up the wooden strips of the fence, over the top, and down into the shade of the forest. As soon as his paws touched the ground, he dived into the shelter of a clump of ferns and crouched there, his ears straining for the sound of the Twolegs coming after him. Had he moved fast enough, or had they seen him? He couldn't even be sure they'd recognize him after so many seasons, but it wasn't worth the risk.

Gradually his breath slowed. Everything was quiet in the Twoleg gardens. He couldn't hear any sounds of Twolegs searching for him, only the rustle of the trees and the tiny sounds of scuffling prey. But he stayed hidden until the sun began to set, bathing the forest in scarlet light.

Venturing out of the shadow of the fern fronds, he scented the vole he had killed earlier, dug it up, and devoured it in hungry gulps. Then in the twilight he crept cautiously back to the Twoleg nests and scaled the fence to land unseen in Smudge's garden.

He padded forward, looking for a place to sleep near the center of the dip, where he imagined the SkyClan camp would have been. A faint sound made him jump, but it was only Smudge, dropping down from the low branch of a tree.

"There you are!" the kittypet gasped. "I thought you'd gone back to the forest. Hattie told me what happened with your old Twolegs."

Firestar didn't want to talk about that. "I just kept out of sight until they'd gone," he explained.

Smudge gave his chest fur a few rapid licks, as if he was trying to hide how anxious he had been. "Are you sure you'll be able to sleep out here?" he went on. "It'll be cold now that the sun's gone."

"Smudge, I sleep out every night," Firestar reminded him. "I'm used to it. I don't think I could sleep inside a Twoleg nest if I tried."

Smudge blinked. "Oh, okay. I just thought—"

He broke off as the door of the nest swung open and yellow light poured out into the dusky garden. A female Twoleg stood there, yowling, with a bowl in her hand.

"I've got to go," Smudge meowed, while Firestar crouched down behind a clump of feathery grasses. "My supper's ready. Are you sure—"

Firestar suppressed a sigh. "I'll be fine, honestly."

"Good night, then." Smudge ran across the grass with his

tail in the air and rubbed against the Twoleg. She bent down to stroke him, then closed the door.

Firestar padded down into the dip until he reached a bush covered with sweet-smelling white flowers that glimmered pale in the dim light. Sliding underneath the low-growing branches, he scraped out a rough nest, and sneezed as a couple of petals drifted down onto his nose.

As he curled up, he thought how strange it felt to be back in Twolegplace after so long. The faint sounds coming from the nest were oddly familiar, and so was the orange light spreading over the sky. The harsh glow hid the stars, so that Firestar felt even farther away from his warrior ancestors. Gazing up through the branches, he formed a silent prayer, but it was not to StarClan.

Warrior of SkyClan, wherever you are, visit me in my dreams.

Damp cold woke him, soaking into his pelt. Above his head, the orange sky was softened by mist. Shivering, he crawled out from under the bush to stretch his stiff legs, and froze midway through a stretch.

The gray-and-white cat was sitting a few tail-lengths away. Mist wreathed around him, and he watched Firestar with eyes the color of a pale winter sky.

"I have been waiting for you," he meowed.

CHAPTER 8

"Wh-who are you?" Firestar stammered. "What's your name?"

The strange cat looked at him blankly. "It's been so long since any cat spoke my name, I don't need it anymore." His eyes spoke to Firestar of deep sadness; his voice ached with it, so that Firestar could hardly bear to listen.

"Do you come from SkyClan?" he asked, though he was almost sure what the answer would be.

The pale-furred cat twitched his whiskers in surprise. "You know of SkyClan, then?"

"A little," Firestar mewed. "I spoke with a warrior of StarClan. She told me that there were once five Clans in the forest, but SkyClan left when—"

"Left?" The SkyClan warrior's voice was full of contempt. "We didn't *leave*. The other Clans drove us out of the forest because they said there was no room for us anymore."

Firestar stared at him. When he had spoken to Bluestar, she had let him believe that SkyClan had gone away of their own accord when the Twoleg monsters had invaded their territory. She never told him that the other Clans had driven them away. Surely the warrior code wouldn't allow it? Yet he couldn't suppress a nagging thought: would *he* want to give up any of ThunderClan's territory if another Clan had asked for it?

"Couldn't StarClan do anything to help you?" he asked.

"StarClan!" The SkyClan cat spat out the word, lashing his tail. "StarClan betrayed us. They allowed the other Clans to chase us out like rogues. When we left the forest, I vowed that I would never look to the stars again."

"A Clan without warrior ancestors?" Firestar was bewildered.

"Our medicine cat still walked with them in dreams," the SkyClan cat told him. "And many of our warriors kept to the old ways. I never tried to stop them. They had lost their home; how could I take the warrior code away from them as well?"

The strange cat spoke as though he had been the leader of his Clan. But before Firestar could ask him if this was true, the pale-furred warrior straightened up and looked around. "Once we roamed over all this territory, patrolled our borders, and caught as much prey as we wanted. But then the Twolegs came." The throbbing note of sadness returned to his voice, raising every hair on Firestar's pelt. "This was once our camp," he went on, indicating Smudge's garden with a sweep of his tail. "Where we are standing used to be the warriors' den. The Twoleg nest stands where our nursery was. Our apprentices' den was beneath ferns along the line of the fence, and under those bushes over there was where our elders slept." He sighed. "It was all so long ago. . . ."

"Where is the SkyClan camp now?"

The gray-and-white cat stared at his paws. "SkyClan have no camp," he mewed quietly. "My Clan has broken apart and scattered."

Firestar was puzzled. "Then there's no SkyClan anymore?"

The SkyClan warrior's neck fur bristled and he drew back his lips in the beginning of a snarl. "I did not say that. I said that our home has gone and my Clanmates have scattered. Some became rogues, and some went to live with Twolegs as kittypets. But SkyClan still lives, although the cats have forgotten their heritage and the warrior code."

Bewildered, Firestar wondered how the other cat could insist SkyClan survived without any territory, if it had broken up and no cat knew the warrior code. What made a Clan if their home and heritage were gone?

"So why have you come to me?" he asked.

"Because you're the only cat who can help us," the warrior replied. He padded forward until he stood within a tail-length of Firestar, and his faint, fugitive scent wreathed around the ThunderClan leader. "You must rebuild SkyClan before it is lost forever."

Firestar stared at him. How could he rebuild a scattered Clan, when he had no idea how to find its cats, and he had a Clan of his own to lead? "But I—"

The SkyClan warrior ignored him. "You must follow the river to its source," he commanded. "We fled upstream, and that is where you will find the remnants of the Clan, and a place where they can live."

Firestar's mind whirled. "But . . . but why me?"

The gray cat fixed his gaze on Firestar, his eyes glowing with sorrow. "I have waited long for you to come, a strong cat, a leader, and one who bears no taint of our betrayal in his blood. You are not descended from the cats that drove us out, and yet you are a true Clan warrior. It is your destiny to restore SkyClan."

Mist swirled around him and his pelt seemed to fade into it, leaving Firestar gazing at the patch of grass where he had stood. Only his scent lingered.

Firestar sat down and wrapped his tail over his paws. He still had not moved when the first traces of dawn appeared in the sky.

The faint wailing of a cat roused him. He sprang to his paws, fur bristling. Was the camp being attacked? Then he remembered where he was; besides, the wailing sounded more impatient than terrified.

Suddenly the door of the Twoleg nest opened and Smudge shot out.

"Honestly!" he panted, hurtling over the grass. "Sometimes I think my Twolegs are *stupid*! I asked and asked to come out, but would they get up and open the door?"

"Well, you're here now," Firestar meowed, glad that he didn't have to depend on Twolegs for his freedom.

"Well? Did you dream about my cats?" Smudge demanded.

Firestar nodded. "I spoke to the gray-and-white cat, and I know what I have to do now."

"What *you* have to do? But what about me? Why did I get the dreams as well?"

Firestar raised his tail to silence Smudge's anxious questions. "The cats you saw left the forest a long time ago," he explained. "Now they're asking for help. You dreamed about them because this is where they used to live."

"Here?" Smudge gazed around his garden as if he expected the long-lost cats to emerge from the bushes right then. "So you're going to help them?"

"Yes, if I can."

When Firestar saw the relief in Smudge's eyes, he wondered if that was exactly true. He would have to leave his Clanmates and go on a long journey without knowing where it led. He would have to find a scattered Clan that had long since been abandoned by StarClan. Why should it be his destiny to save them, whether or not ThunderClan's ancestors carried the guilt of driving them out? His duty lay with ThunderClan, and with the warrior code he had known ever since he came into the forest.

"I'd better go," he mewed to Smudge. "I'll tell the patrols to keep a lookout for you—and not to jump on you."

"Thanks," Smudge replied. "I'm really grateful, Firestar. You're a good friend, but I'm glad I don't have to come and live with you in the forest!"

"I'm glad too." Firestar gave Smudge a friendly flick on the ear with the tip of his tail. "I know you wouldn't like it."

"Good-bye, then. I'll see you around sometime." Smudge began retreating toward the door of the nest, glancing over his shoulder to add, "Let's hope they can be a bit quicker letting me *in*."

Determined to be gone before Smudge's Twolegs found him in their garden, Firestar bounded across the grass and leaped to the top of the fence.

"Good-bye, Firestar!" It was Hattie's voice; Firestar spotted her in the next garden, balanced on a low branch of the scratching tree. He waved his tail to her in farewell. "Come and see us again!" she called as he sprang down from the fence and plunged back into the shadow of the trees.

Once he was out of sight of the Twoleg nests he slowed his pace. For once the forest seemed strange to him. He felt oddly detached from it, as if it weren't real anymore. Instead, he kept thinking of the moorland, and the wails of fleeing cats. Was he really meant to be following in their pawsteps?

After the damp night, the sun had risen into a clear blue sky. Every bush was draped with glittering cobwebs, and dew sparkled on every blade of grass, soaking Firestar's fur as he brushed through. He halted, his paws tingling when he picked up the scent of approaching cats, only to relax as Thornclaw pushed through a clump of ferns, closely followed by Sootpaw, Sootpaw's mother, Willowpelt, and Ashfur.

Firestar gave his pelt an annoyed shake. Of course, this was the dawn patrol! Was his mind so full of SkyClan that he couldn't recognize the scent of his own Clanmates?

"Hi, Firestar." Thornclaw padded up to him. "Everything okay?"

"Yes—everything's fine." Firestar wasn't about to explain

why he had spent the night away from camp.

Thornclaw exchanged a swift glance with Willowpelt, then turned back to his Clan leader. "Graystripe suggested I should take Sootpaw out with me today," he meowed, resting the tip of his tail on the apprentice's shoulder. "Longtail can't mentor him when his eyes are so bad."

"Good idea." A pang of guilt stabbed Firestar like a claw; he should have thought about Sootpaw's training as soon as his mentor, Longtail, had his accident. His dreams of SkyClan were distracting him from his duty to his Clan. "In fact," he went on, "I think you should take over as Sootpaw's mentor until Longtail is fit again." *If he ever is.* Firestar didn't dare say it out loud. He was reluctant to admit, even to himself, that Cinderpelt wouldn't be able to save Longtail from blindness.

Thornclaw's eyes gleamed. He was a young warrior, and so far he hadn't had an apprentice. "Thanks, Firestar!" he meowed.

"I'll announce it later today," Firestar promised. "Providing Longtail agrees."

"I'm sure he will," Sootpaw put in. "I've been taking him fresh-kill and fixing his bedding, and I can still do that."

"Good." Firestar gave him an approving nod. Needing to plunge himself back into the life of his Clan, he added, "I'll join you on patrol, and Sootpaw, you can show me your tracking skills."

The apprentice's eyes shone with excitement at the thought of training with his Clan leader. As Thornclaw led the way along the border toward the Thunderpath, Sootpaw kept his nose to the ground, pausing to scent the air every few pawsteps.

"What can you smell?" Firestar meowed.

"The Thunderpath," Sootpaw replied promptly. "And vole. And a Twoleg with a dog has been along here. No—two dogs."

"How long ago?" Willowpelt asked.

"Not today," Sootpaw mewed. "The scent is stale. Maybe yesterday."

"That's what I think, too," Firestar meowed, while Willowpelt let out a purr of satisfaction. "Okay, carry on. Sootpaw, tell me if you scent anything else."

They were so close to the Thunderpath that Firestar could hear the growling of the monsters as they rushed up and down. Soon they emerged from the undergrowth at the edge of the smooth black surface.

Sootpaw wrinkled his nose. "It's really yucky," he complained. "It hides all the other scents."

"Right," meowed Thornclaw. "That means you have to be extra careful."

With the rest of the patrol following, he picked his way along the edge of the Thunderpath, keeping well away from the huge black paws of the monsters. Firestar felt his fur buffeted by the wind as they passed by.

He helped Thornclaw, Ashfur, and Willowpelt renew the border scent markings, and watched Sootpaw as the apprentice went on practicing his scenting skills. Suddenly the young black cat veered away from the border.

"Hey, where do you think you're going?" Thornclaw called.

Sootpaw glanced back, eyes alight with a mixture of excitement and apprehension. "I've found a really weird scent," he explained.

"Well, you can't follow it now," Thornclaw told him. "This isn't a hunting patrol."

"What sort of weird?" Firestar asked. The reek of the Thunderpath was still blocking out most other scents.

"Strong," Sootpaw replied. "I've never smelled it before."

Firestar exchanged a glance with Thornclaw. "Okay, let's follow it."

This time Sootpaw led the way deeper into the undergrowth, and as they left the Thunderpath behind, Firestar began to pick up the new scent. He halted, his fur prickling. "Badger!"

"Oh, no!" Willowpelt protested.

Thornclaw snorted. "Just what we need." Ashfur remained silent, but his blue eyes widened.

"Are badgers bad?" Sootpaw asked.

"Pretty bad," Ashfur replied.

"We certainly don't want one on our territory," Willowpelt agreed.

Firestar remembered one leaf-bare, when snow was on the ground and prey was scarce. Cloudtail had been a kit then, and a hungry badger had attacked him in the ravine. Only swift action from Firestar and Brackenfur had saved him. Badgers didn't normally prey on cats, but if they were hungry or scared they made formidable, deadly opponents.

"The scent's fresh," he meowed. "We'll have to follow it to find out where the badger is and whether it's going to make a den here. Well done, Sootpaw. That was a useful bit of tracking."

The apprentice's eyes glowed.

"Firestar's right," Thornclaw added. "Now, keep behind me, and let's go."

He took the lead, with Sootpaw and Willowpelt hard on his paws. Ashfur followed them, while Firestar brought up the rear, padding along with the strong scent of the badger in his nose. He felt his muscles tensing beneath his fur; he half expected a chunky black-and-white body to come trampling out of the undergrowth.

The trees began to thin out; the badger trail was leading toward Snakerocks. Firestar felt exposed and vulnerable, convinced that small, malevolent eyes were watching him from every thornbush or bramble thicket. This was a bad place for ThunderClan cats. When the dogs were loose in the forest they had made their den at Snakerocks; Swiftpaw had died in their jaws, and Brightheart had received her terrible injuries. Firestar imagined he could still scent the reek of spilled blood.

The tumbled rocks came into view, rising from the center of a clearing where the gritty soil was covered with small creeping plants and seeding grasses.

"Stay here," Thornclaw instructed Sootpaw, gesturing with his tail toward a sheltered spot at the base of some brambles.

"Don't move, but give a good loud yowl if you see anything dangerous."

Sootpaw hesitated, as if he wanted to go on tracking the badger, then went to crouch in the shelter of the brambles with his forepaws tucked under his chest. His gray fur melted into the shadows.

Thornclaw, Willowpelt, and Firestar began to search among the rocks. Firestar paused at the mouth of the den where the dogs had lived, shivers rippling through him from ears to tail tip. He was prepared for the reek of dog to come flowing out of the dark hole, but there was nothing more than a trace of stale fox. Even the fresh badger scent had faded. At first he thought it was because the rocks and thin soil wouldn't hold the odor for long. But when he explored further, brushing under the low-growing branches of a tree at the edge of the clearing, he realized that the badger hadn't come this far into the territory. The scent trail had vanished before he reached the rocks.

"Willowpelt? Thornclaw?" he called. "I've lost the trail over here."

He broke off as a fresh whiff of scent reached him. Firestar spun around to see a huge shape, black and yellowish white, rearing up from behind the bramble thicket, its massive paws ready to slam down on the cowering apprentice.

Chapter 9

"Sootpaw! Move!" Firestar yowled.

He sprang forward but he didn't see how he could reach Sootpaw before the badger swatted him with its blunt, powerful paws.

Then he spotted Willowpelt diving from the top of a rock to streak across the ground and shove Sootpaw out of the way with outstretched forepaws. The badger landed heavily on her back; her shriek was cut off with a sickening crunch as the huge creature snapped her neck. It scooped up her limp body with one paw and tossed it into the clearing.

Sootpaw let out a thin, wailing cry. Firestar flung himself at the badger, snarling as he raked his claws down its side. The huge striped head turned, snapping at him with gleaming white teeth. Ashfur dashed in from the other side, leaping up to bury his claws in the badger's neck and fasten his teeth in its ear. It shook him off easily; Ashfur hit the ground and lay still, winded.

Thornclaw crouched in front of the badger, spitting and clawing at its eyes as it loomed over him. Firestar scored its flank again, feeling a fierce satisfaction as blood welled up in the tracks of his claws. The badger let out a bellow of pain. It swung its head from side to side, then turned and lumbered off into the undergrowth. Thornclaw and Ashfur charged after it with earsplitting caterwauls.

"Come back!" Firestar yowled. "Let it go!"

Panting, he closed his eyes briefly, listening as the sound of the badger's paws faded into the distance. Then he braced himself and padded over to where Sootpaw was crouched beside the body of his mother. He looked up as Firestar approached, his eyes pleading.

"She's not dead, is she? She can't be dead."

"I'm sorry." Firestar bent his head and touched Sootpaw's forehead with his nose. Only five moons had passed since the young cat's father, Whitestorm, had died in the battle with BloodClan. *How could StarClan let this happen?* "She died bravely, like a warrior."

"She died saving me!" Sootpaw's voice was shrill with anguish.

"Don't blame yourself." Firestar gave his shoulder a comforting lick. "Willowpelt knew what she was doing."

"But she . . ." Sootpaw fell silent, trembling with shock, and pushed his nose into his mother's fur.

Firestar looked up to see Thornclaw and Ashfur returning; Ashfur was limping heavily.

"It's gone toward the Thunderpath," Thornclaw reported. "I hope a monster gets it." He padded over to Sootpaw and sat beside him, looping his tail over the young cat's shoulders. Sootpaw didn't look up.

"Are you okay?" Firestar asked Ashfur.

The younger warrior flexed his shoulder muscles. "I think so. I landed hard; that's all."

"Better let Cinderpelt take a look anyway, when we get back to camp."

Ashfur nodded. Together he and Firestar lifted Willowpelt's limp body and began to carry her back to the ravine. Her drooping tail scored a faint line in the dust. Thornclaw followed, leading the stunned Sootpaw.

Wrapped in grief, Firestar didn't notice the sound or scent of approaching cats until Cloudtail emerged from a clump of bracken almost under his paws.

"Firestar, you're back!" the white warrior exclaimed. "Are you—" He broke off, his blue eyes flaring with alarm. "That's Willowpelt. What happened?"

Dustpelt and Brackenfur joined Cloudtail to listen, horrified, as Firestar set down the dead warrior and described how she had given her life to save Sootpaw.

"Let me get my claws on that badger," Cloudtail hissed when Firestar had finished. "I'll make it wish it had never been kitted."

"Shouldn't we follow it?" Dustpelt suggested. "We should make sure it really has gone."

Firestar nodded. "It headed for the Thunderpath," he meowed. "Cloudtail, take your patrol and see if you can pick up its scent. Follow it and find out what it does, if you can, but *don't* attack it. Is that clear?"

Cloudtail lashed his tail. "If you say so."

"If it settles in our territory, we'll make a plan to get rid of it," Firestar promised. "But I won't risk losing more cats unless I have to."

Muttering under his breath, Cloudtail led his patrol back along the trail toward Snakerocks. *Great StarClan, let them all come back,* Firestar prayed as they vanished into the undergrowth.

Firestar's legs felt heavy with exhaustion as he and Ashfur struggled to maneuver Willowpelt's body through the gorse tunnel. Pain for his Clanmates stabbed deep into his heart. He was their leader; he was supposed to protect them, not let cats die when he was with them.

When he reached the clearing, Graystripe and Sandstorm were sitting together by the fresh-kill pile. They exchanged a questioning glance when they spotted him; Firestar guessed they were wondering why he had spent the night away from camp. SkyClan's troubles crashed over him again, heavier than the weight of Willowpelt's body, but he had to push them away. There was no time to think of the lost Clan now.

Both cats sprang up and raced over to him.

"Firestar, what happened?" Graystripe asked.

"I'll tell you soon," Firestar promised hoarsely. "I have to take Willowpelt to Cinderpelt first, so she can prepare for the vigil."

"I'll let her know." Sandstorm spun around and sped off to the medicine cat's den.

By the time Firestar and Ashfur had crossed the camp, Cinderpelt had emerged from the fern tunnel.

"Lay her body there," she directed, pointing with her tail to a shady spot under the ferns. "She'll be out of the sun until dusk falls."

The two cats did as she suggested; Sootpaw settled down beside his mother's body as if his legs couldn't hold him up another moment. His eyes stared into the distance, glazed with horror, as if he couldn't stop reliving that terrible moment.

"Sootpaw needs something for shock," Firestar murmured to Cinderpelt. "And Ashfur might have damaged his shoulder."

The medicine cat nodded. "I'll fetch him some poppy-seeds. Ashfur, come with me."

As the gray warrior followed Cinderpelt to her den, another shriek sounded from the opposite side of the camp. Firestar's head whipped around, and he saw Rainpaw and Sorrelpaw racing across from the apprentice's den. Sorrelpaw flung herself down beside her mother's body, pressing herself against her cold flank, while Rainpaw halted in front of Firestar.

"What happened?" he demanded.

"A badger killed her," Firestar replied. "I'm sorry, Rainpaw. No cat could have stopped it."

The apprentice glared at him for a moment more, his fur bristling. Then his head and tail drooped and he turned away without a word, to settle down beside his brother and sister.

"They'll all need Cinderpelt to look after them," Sandstorm murmured.

Firestar was too sick at heart to reply. Brushing his mate's fur with his tail, he trudged across the camp and scrambled up onto the Highrock to call the Clan for a meeting. Already cats were creeping out of their dens, shocked and bewildered as they learned about Willowpelt's death.

"Cats of ThunderClan," Firestar began when they were all assembled. "Willowpelt is dead. She died bravely, and her spirit will be honored in StarClan."

"How did it happen?" Speckletail called out.

Firestar felt as if an extra weight of sorrow descended on him every time he had to tell the story. "The badger ran off toward the Thunderpath," he finished. "I sent Cloudtail's patrol to track it."

Brightheart, sitting outside the nursery, flinched when he mentioned her mate, while Ferncloud drew her kits closer to her with a sweep of her tail. Spiderkit and Shrewkit pressed themselves into her fur, gazing up at Firestar with huge scared eyes.

"What about my kits?" Ferncloud demanded. "What if the badger comes here?"

"Unlikely," Firestar replied, flexing his claws on the hard rock. "It was a young one, and I think it's learned that cats aren't easy prey. We'll know more when Cloudtail comes back. I promise you," he added, "we'll do everything we can to make sure it doesn't settle in our territory."

Ferncloud didn't look convinced, but there wasn't any more he could say to reassure her.

"Tonight we will sit vigil for Willowpelt," he announced, and sprang down from the Highrock to show that the meeting was over.

"They're badly shaken," Graystripe commented, padding over with Sandstorm to join Firestar outside the entrance to his den.

"Those three apprentices especially," Sandstorm added, compassion in her green gaze. "This is a bad time for them to lose their mother."

Firestar nodded sadly. "It's the first cat we've lost since the battle with BloodClan. I think it's hard for all of us to understand that even if we're at peace with the other Clans, the forest isn't completely safe."

For some reason, alarm lit in Graystripe's and Sandstorm's eyes as he spoke, and they exchanged a swift glance. Firestar didn't understand, but after the stress of his meeting with the SkyClan warrior, and the horrible shock of meeting the badger, he didn't have the energy to question his friends.

"We'll talk later," he mumbled, and padded slowly across the camp to the fresh-kill pile.

When night had fallen, the elders brought Willowpelt's body into the center of the camp for her vigil. Firestar joined them there; he looked up to see the stars of Silverpelt blazing, as if they waited to welcome Willowpelt's spirit.

"She was much loved," Dappletail rasped, smoothing the gray warrior's fur with one forepaw. "And far too young to die. She had much more to give her Clan."

"I know," Firestar agreed, feeling hollow with grief. He had been with Willowpelt when the badger attacked Sootpaw, but he had been unable to save her. *Call yourself a leader?* he asked himself savagely.

He watched as Cinderpelt guided the three apprentices to their mother's side; the medicine cat murmured comforting words as the young cats crouched down and pushed their noses into the still gray fur. More of the Clan gathered around, some staying for a little while before going silently to their dens, while others settled beside Willowpelt's body to keep watch during the night.

How can I leave now? I can't abandon my Clan to go off into the unknown, searching for a Clan that doesn't exist anymore. Maybe I can't protect them from badgers that kill or rabbits that blind them, but my place is still here, serving my Clan. That's what it means to be a leader.

Firestar looked up at Silverpelt, wondering if the starry warriors approved of his decision. But the glittering specks of light seemed very far away, and they gave no answer.

He kept watch beside his dead warrior's body until the first rays of dawn reached through the trees. A faint breeze ruffled Willowpelt's fur. Speckletail rose to her paws. "It's time," she meowed.

She and the other elders lifted Willowpelt's body and carried it slowly out of the camp for burial. The rest of the Clan emerged from their dens and watched them go in respectful silence. When Willowpelt's gray fur was lost to sight in the gorse tunnel, Cinderpelt swept her tail around to gather the three apprentices close to her.

"No training for them today," she told Firestar. "They need to rest."

Firestar nodded. "You know best, Cinderpelt."

His limbs stiff from crouching all night, he stumbled to his paws and headed for his den. As soon as he sank into the soft moss of his bedding, darkness swept over him like a crow's wing.

The sparkling scent of swift-flowing water flooded around him, and Firestar found himself walking beside a river. Sunlight danced on the surface; the silver shapes of fish flickered in the shallows. He paused and looked around. The trees and bushes on the riverbank were unfamiliar, and he knew that he was dreaming.

There was a sudden turbulence in the water, and a cat's head broke the surface, a plump silver fish gripped tightly in its jaws. As it swam to the bank and padded out of the water, Firestar recognized Silverstream, the RiverClan cat who had fallen in love with Graystripe and died bearing his kits. The drops of water clinging to her fur shone as brightly as stars.

Dropping the fish in front of him, she meowed, "Greetings, Firestar. This fish is for you." When he hesitated, she pushed it closer to him. "Go on, eat."

"But it isn't a ThunderClan fish," Firestar protested. "I don't want to steal prey."

Silverstream let out a little *mrrow* of amusement. "You're not stealing; it's a gift. It's not a RiverClan fish either. You looked hungry, so I thought I would catch you some food."

"Thank you." Firestar didn't hesitate any longer. Sinking his teeth into the fish, he thought he had never tasted anything so delicious. With every mouthful he felt strength pouring back into his tired body.

While he was still eating, Silverstream padded closer to him and mewed softly into his ear, "Remember the life I gave you when you became leader of your Clan? I told you it was for loyalty to what you know to be right. Firestar, that isn't always the same as following the warrior code." When he turned to her in surprise, she added in a whisper, "I always knew it was right for me and Graystripe to be together, even though we came from different Clans. There are some things that are too big to be contained in the warrior code."

She touched her nose to his flank, then padded back to the river and launched herself into the water.

"Good-bye, Silverstream," Firestar called.

He thought he heard her last word of farewell shivering in the air as the dazzle of light on the water swallowed her up. Where she had vanished, the image of fleeing SkyClan cats appeared, leaping and flickering through the waves. Then Firestar was blinking awake in his own den, with the taste of fish in his mouth and his belly comfortably full.

Silverstream obviously believed he should go on the journey to find SkyClan. The warrior code did not account for everything that happened beneath the stars, and now he had to make amends for what the other four Clans had done so long ago. Since a StarClan cat had come to tell him this, was it the will of his warrior ancestors that the lost Clan should be restored? Perhaps even StarClan felt guilty for what they had allowed to happen.

"I must go," Firestar murmured aloud. Even though he felt his heart torn in two when he thought of leaving his Clan, he knew that Graystripe was as loyal to ThunderClan as he was, and would care for them until he returned.

He got to his paws, shaking scraps of moss from his pelt. When he brushed past the screen of lichen and into the clearing, he saw that it was almost sunhigh. The long sleep, and the fish Silverstream had given him, had brought back his strength, and he knew there were many things he must do before he could leave.

First he padded through the fern tunnel to Cinderpelt's den. Willowpelt's three kits were curled up asleep in the ferns, huddled together for comfort. Longtail was lying outside the split in the rock and raised his head as Firestar emerged into the clearing. "Hi, Firestar."

Hope tingled in Firestar's pads. "Can you see me?"

Longtail blinked, and Firestar saw that his eyes were still inflamed. "Yes . . . no. I'm not sure," he replied. "You're just a blur. I think I recognized you by your scent."

"Your eyes are no better, then?"

Longtail sighed. "No. I think they're getting worse."

"But I'm not giving up yet." Cinderpelt emerged from her den, speaking around the leaf wrap she carried in her jaws. Setting it down beside Longtail, she added, "This is a poultice of marigold with juniper berry juice. We'll see if it helps."

"Okay." Longtail didn't sound hopeful, but he kept his head still while Cinderpelt dabbed the poultice on his infected eyes.

"Did you want something, Firestar?" she asked when she had finished, cleaning her paws on the grass.

"A word with Longtail," Firestar replied. "It's about Sootpaw," he began awkwardly, wondering how Longtail would react to losing his apprentice.

"I know, he's not being mentored," Longtail mewed promptly. "It's been worrying me."

Firestar was relieved that he didn't have to explain what was on his mind. "As soon as he's fit to train again, I think I should find another cat to take over. Just until your eyes are better."

Longtail's ears twitched. "You don't have to lie to me, Firestar. I know perfectly well I'm going blind. I'll never train another apprentice."

Firestar exchanged a glance with Cinderpelt. The fact that the medicine cat didn't protest showed him that Longtail was probably right.

"We'll worry about that when it happens," he meowed. "Right now, we need to find Sootpaw another mentor. Do you think Thornclaw would be a good choice?"

"Yes, he's very keen. It's time he had an apprentice." Longtail suppressed a sigh. "Sootpaw will do fine with him."

"That's settled, then. Thanks, Longtail." He hesitated, knowing he had to tell Cinderpelt about his decision to leave, but not knowing how to begin.

Her eyes narrowed. "I can tell you've something on your mind, Firestar," she meowed. "Spit it out."

"I need to talk with you," he began. "Will you come for a walk with me in the forest?"

Cinderpelt looked startled. "What, now?" She flicked her

tail toward the sleeping apprentices. "I've got my paws full with those three."

"No, after sunhigh," Firestar replied. "I need to talk to Graystripe and Sandstorm, too. We'll go once the afternoon patrols have been sorted out."

Cinderpelt's blue eyes still looked puzzled, as if she was wondering what Firestar had to tell her that couldn't be said in her own den. "Okay, I'll take Sootpaw, Sorrelpaw, and Rainpaw to the nursery. Ferncloud and Brightheart can look after them. It'll do them no harm to be treated like kits for a day or two, so soon after losing their mother."

"Great," Firestar mewed. "I'll meet you by the fresh-kill pile."

But as he brushed back through the fern tunnel, a cold stone seemed to weigh in his belly as he wondered how his friends would react to his decision.

Firestar led the way out of the gorse tunnel with Graystripe, Sandstorm, and Cinderpelt following close behind; his claws flexed nervously as the time came closer when he would have to tell them about SkyClan.

"Cloudtail reported to me just before sunhigh," Graystripe meowed as they climbed up through the ravine. "He and his patrol tracked the badger as far as the stream, and then they lost the scent in a patch of boggy ground."

"It sounds as if it was making for ShadowClan territory," Firestar commented.

Graystripe let out a faint growl of satisfaction. "ShadowClan are welcome to it."

"But if any of our cats spot one of their border patrols, we should pass on a warning," Firestar pointed out.

His deputy flicked an ear. "That's just like you, Firestar. You want to help every Clan, not just your own. Okay, I'll tell the next patrols when they go out."

"And what's all this about wanting to go into the forest to talk to us?" Sandstorm's whiskers twitched irritably. "Why couldn't you tell us in the camp?"

Firestar let his gaze travel over her sleek ginger pelt and luminous green eyes. He knew he had a lot to explain, but he couldn't work out why she was so upset now, before he had said a word.

"I wanted to talk somewhere we wouldn't be interrupted," he meowed. "You'll understand soon."

He padded on, not saying any more until the four cats came to a glade hidden deep among the trees. The ground was covered with sweet-smelling grass and soft mounds of moss. Firestar found a place to sit among the knotted roots of an oak tree, and his friends settled around him in the sun-dappled shade. The only sounds were the rustle of wind in the branches and the high piping of birds.

Firestar looked at the three cats who meant more to him than any others in the Clan. "I've been having a lot of dreams recently," he meowed, feeling as if he were about to plunge over the edge of a bottomless gorge. "For a long time they confused me, but I think I know their meaning now. And I've had to make a very hard decision. . . ."

"But what about us?" Sandstorm blurted out, her claws

tearing at the moss. "How can you go off and leave us?"

Firestar stared at her. How could she possibly have guessed that he meant to leave ThunderClan? "You'll be fine, honestly—"

"No, we won't!" Sandstorm spat back at him. "We need you. ThunderClan needs you as their leader! How can you even think of abandoning us like this?"

Firestar glanced from his mate to Cinderpelt and Graystripe. The medicine cat's eyes were blank with shock, but Graystripe's gaze was full of sorrow and compassion.

"I don't understand," Firestar mewed. "How did you know? And what makes you think I'll never come back?"

"Because you spent the night with your old Twolegs," Graystripe rasped. He turned his head away as if he couldn't bear to go on looking at his old friend. "Do you really care for them more than you care for us?"

"What?" Firestar's eyes stretched wide with dismay. "You think I'd abandon my Clan to go and be a kittypet?"

"Isn't that what you've brought us here to tell us?" Sandstorm challenged him.

"No! It's not that at all. This is my *home*. StarClan are my warrior ancestors just as much as yours. I couldn't live anywhere else but the forest."

"So perhaps you'll tell us what you *are* going to do," Cinderpelt meowed tartly.

"It's true that I have to leave—but only for a while." Firestar took a deep breath and told his friends how he had been visited by an unknown cat, and dreamed of a wailing, fleeing Clan. He explained how he had met Bluestar when he visited the Moonstone, and what she had told him about SkyClan.

"You mean there were once *five* Clans in the forest?" Sandstorm gasped.

"Yes. A long time ago, before Twolegplace was built."

"But Twolegplace has *always* been there!" Graystripe protested.

"Not according to Bluestar," Firestar told him. Not wanting to shake his friends' faith, he skirted around how StarClan had lied, and hurried on to the next part of his story. "That's why I spent the night in Twolegplace. I wasn't with my old Twolegs. I slept in Smudge's garden—Graystripe, do you remember my friend Smudge?"

Graystripe nodded. "That fat black-and-white kittypet."

"I thought his garden was a likely place for SkyClan to have made their camp, and I was right. The SkyClan leader spoke to me in a dream. He told me it was my destiny to go and find the scattered cats of SkyClan and bring them together again."

Graystripe snorted. "And if he had told you it was your destiny to fly to the moon, would you have believed him?"

Firestar reached out with his tail and touched his deputy gently on the shoulder. "I know it seems impossible. But I've decided that's what I must do. I must go on a journey to find SkyClan and repair the damage done by the other Clans."

Graystripe stared at him, his eyes stunned with shock. Sandstorm's gaze was fixed on him too, anger and grief flickering in her eyes like minnows in a deep green pool. Only Cinderpelt remained calm.

"I can tell how much this means to you," she mewed. "And if it is really your destiny, then you must go wherever your paws lead you. But be careful—StarClan may not be able to watch over you. Our warrior ancestors do not walk in all skies."

"I don't know how you can even *think* of doing this!" Sandstorm sprang to her paws before Firestar could reply to the medicine cat. "What about ThunderClan? What about your friends?" She paused, then added shakily, "What about *me*?"

Firestar felt her pain as if it were his own, like a sharp stone that would pierce his pads on every pawstep of the journey. Glancing from Graystripe to Cinderpelt, he rose and beckoned Sandstorm with his tail.

"Come."

He padded a few tail-lengths from the others to a sun-warmed spot near the center of the clearing. Sandstorm followed reluctantly.

"I know you never really wanted me for your mate," she mewed as soon as they were out of earshot of the other cats. "You've always been in love with Spottedleaf."

Firestar thanked StarClan that he had not mentioned his dream encounter with the former ThunderClan medicine cat. "I loved Spottedleaf," he admitted. "But even if she had lived, what could I have done? She was a medicine cat. She would never have chosen a mate."

"So I was second-best?" Sandstorm spoke bitterly, not looking at him.

"Sandstorm . . ." Firestar pressed against her side, curling his tail around her as she tried to move away. "You're not second-best to any cat."

"But you can still go off and leave me."

"No." Firestar had spent a long time thinking about this. Meeting Sandstorm's gaze steadily, he went on. "I never meant to abandon you. Graystripe and Cinderpelt must stay here to look after the Clan, but I don't want to make the journey alone. Sandstorm, there's no other cat I'd rather have with me than you. Will you come with me?"

As he spoke, the grief and anger faded from Sandstorm's eyes. Her green gaze shone, and the sun warmed her ginger pelt to the brilliance of flame. "You really want me to come?"

"I really do." Firestar pressed his muzzle to her shoulder. "I don't think I can do it without you, Sandstorm. Please."

"Of course I will! I—" Sandstorm broke off. "No, I *can't*, Firestar. What about Sorrelpaw? I'm her mentor."

Firestar hesitated. Sandstorm had desperately wanted an apprentice, and he knew how seriously she took the little tortoiseshell's training. "It won't do Sorrelpaw any harm to have another mentor for a while," he meowed. "It won't be the first time an apprentice has had to change—Sootpaw will have a new mentor now, because of Longtail's bad eyes."

Sandstorm nodded slowly. "The experience could be good for her," she murmured.

"Then that's settled." Firestar didn't ask himself what

would happen if he hadn't returned before the apprentices were ready to be made warriors. He had no idea *when* he would come back—or if he and Sandstorm would come back at all.

With Sandstorm close by his side, he padded back across the grass to the roots of the tree where Graystripe and Cinderpelt waited.

"Sandstorm is coming with me," he announced.

Neither Graystripe nor Cinderpelt looked surprised.

"That's good," Graystripe meowed. His shock had faded; he had a resolute look in his eyes, and Firestar realized all over again what a good friend he was, and what a worthy deputy of ThunderClan. "Cinderpelt and I will take care of the Clan for you," he promised. His whiskers twitched. "I always knew you had a destiny that stretched beyond our territory. Perhaps it's time for fire to save another Clan."

"We swear by StarClan, we will keep ThunderClan safe for you," Cinderpelt meowed.

"Thank you," Firestar replied, feeling very humble. The leaves rustled above his head and he looked up, half expecting to see the pale-furred SkyClan leader looking down at him from a branch. He saw nothing, but in the whispering breeze he seemed to hear his words repeated.

Thank you . . .

CHAPTER 10

Firestar padded through Cinderpelt's fern tunnel, swiping his tongue around his jaws to clear the bitter taste of the traveling herbs. Behind him, he could hear Sandstorm talking to the medicine cat.

"Let me make sure I've got this straight. Cobweb to stop bleeding, marigold for infection, yarrow to get rid of poison . . ."

"That's right," Cinderpelt replied. "And if you get bellyache, watermint or juniper berries are good."

Sandstorm began repeating the remedies under her breath. In the two days since Firestar had asked her to come with him, she had spent most of her time learning what she could from Cinderpelt. "It'll be dangerous, going off without a medicine cat," she had explained to Firestar. "At least I can learn what the most useful herbs are."

Firestar emerged from the ferns and bounded across to the Highrock. His cats parted in silence to let him through; their gazes followed him as he sprang up onto the Highrock.

"They don't want you to go," Sandstorm murmured, joining him a few moments later.

"I know." Firestar suppressed a sigh. Apart from leading

his warriors into battle against BloodClan, this was the hardest thing he had ever had to do as Clan leader.

He looked down to meet the puzzled eyes of his Clan. It broke his heart that they seemed hurt by his reluctance to tell them about his journey; yet how could he tell them where he was going, when he didn't know himself? He had to let them think it was StarClan sending him away, not a Clan they'd never heard of, with no place left in the forest.

Graystripe stood at the base of the rock with the Clan warriors around him. Firestar spotted Sootpaw with Thornclaw, and Sorrelpaw with her new mentor, Dustpelt. Rainpaw and Cloudtail sat next to them; Firestar was glad to see the three apprentices beginning to get over the shock of their mother's death, enough to return to training. Brambleclaw was sitting with Ashfur and Mousefur. Speckletail was glaring up at Firestar as if he were an apprentice who had scratched her while searching for ticks. Dappletail and One-eye sat close together, whispering and casting swift glances up at the cats on the rock. Cinderpelt guided Longtail out of her clearing and brought him to sit nearby. Outside the nursery Ferncloud sat with Brightheart; instead of playing, Ferncloud's two kits crouched close to their mother, as if even they understood how troubled the Clan was.

"Cats of ThunderClan," Firestar began. "It's time for us to leave—"

"And what for, that's what I want to know," Mousefur interrupted, the tip of her tail twitching. "StarClan are supposed to look after the *forest*. Not send a Clan leader gallivanting off who knows where."

"What can be more important than caring for your Clan?" Thornclaw added.

Firestar couldn't answer. His warriors were right. But they hadn't heard the cats wailing in the mist; they hadn't seen how desperate the SkyClan leader was to find his lost Clan.

"And what about my kits?" Ferncloud fretted. Her claws worked on the dusty ground. "There's a badger somewhere in the territory. Have you thought about that?"

"Yes, of course I have," Firestar replied, finding his voice. "But ThunderClan has a deputy. I trust him to look after the Clan just as well as I do. And you have Cinderpelt to take care of any injuries and interpret the signs of StarClan. No Clan could have a better medicine cat."

Cinderpelt bowed her head; Graystripe's eyes glowed, while a murmur of agreement rose from the rest of the Clan.

"Firestar wouldn't leave us unless he had to." It was Brightheart, stepping forward from where she had been sitting next to Ferncloud. "If StarClan has told him he must go, then we must trust our warrior ancestors to take care of him and bring him safely back. They have never let us down before—why would they take our leader from us now if it wasn't the right thing to do?"

Firestar's pelt crawled as the other cats agreed; they were obviously comforted by the thought that there were good, wise cats watching over them, always making the right decisions and fighting for truth and honor. But if their faith meant they would let him go . . .

"They don't like you going," Sandstorm murmured, "but they will accept it if it is the will of StarClan."

Firestar hoped she was right; selfishly, he didn't want to leave with the protests of his Clanmates ringing in his ears. He straightened up, even though every bone in his body was screaming at him to change his mind, to stay in the forest where he belonged. "Good-bye, all of you."

There was an ominous silence, and Firestar felt his pelt singed by many scorching stares. He knew what was in his Clanmates' minds as clearly as if they had spoken out loud. *Where are you going? Why are you leaving us? Has StarClan promised to bring you back?* He longed to reassure them, but telling them he was being sent away by a warrior ancestor they'd never even heard of would only cause them more pain and confusion.

At last Sootpaw stepped forward. "Good-bye, Firestar!" he called.

Slowly the other cats joined in.

"Good-bye!"

"Travel safely!"

"Come back soon!"

Firestar leaped down from the Highrock and wove his way through his Clanmates with Sandstorm at his shoulder.

Cinderpelt was waiting for him beside the entrance to the gorse tunnel. "Good-bye," she mewed, swiping her tongue over his ear. "May StarClan light your path."

"And yours," Firestar replied. A sudden bolt of sorrow choked him and he couldn't say any more.

Dustpelt came up to Sandstorm, with Sorrelpaw bouncing along behind him. "I'll take care of your apprentice," he promised, fixing the lively tortoiseshell with a severe look. "You've obviously been far too lenient with her." Though his words were harsh, there was a glimmer of amusement in his eyes.

Sorrelpaw waved her tail, not at all crushed by her new mentor's words. "I think Sandstorm is a *great* mentor!"

Taking a last look at his Clan, and the clearing that had been his home for so many seasons, Firestar pushed through the tunnel and out into the ravine. Sandstorm and Graystripe followed him.

The sun had just cleared the tops of the trees, shining from a blue sky with a few puffs of white cloud. A gentle breeze stirred the branches, carrying the scents of prey and green, growing things. Firestar stood still for a moment, feeling it ruffle his fur. He knew that whatever he found on his journey, there could be nowhere as beautiful as this. SkyClan must have been devastated to leave. Two days of rest and good food had restored his energy, and now that he was actually beginning his journey his paws tingled with excitement. Though his heart was torn about leaving, he wanted to see what lay beyond the forest, and to find the cats who had once been SkyClan.

At the top of the ravine he halted and turned to face his deputy—his best friend, and the cat without whom he would never have been able to lead his Clan. "Will you come to the edge of the forest with us, Graystripe?"

The gray warrior shook his head. "This is your journey,

yours and Sandstorm's. I'll say good-bye here. Good luck, both of you."

Sandstorm and Firestar leaned forward to touch noses with their old friend. "I couldn't leave if I didn't have you to look after things while I'm gone," Firestar murmured.

"Every cat knows I can't fill your pawprints," Graystripe replied. "But I'll do my best."

"You'll have to take Firestar's place at Gatherings," Sandstorm reminded him.

Graystripe nodded. "We mustn't let ThunderClan seem weak. I'll tell them you've been called away by StarClan, but you'll be back soon."

"I hope you're right," Firestar meowed softly. "But if I don't come back—"

"Don't say that!" Graystripe's tail lashed. "You *will* return; I know it in my heart. I'll wait for you however long it takes. Whenever you come back, I will be here, just the same."

"Which way first?" Sandstorm asked.

They had left Graystripe behind and were heading through the forest toward Sunningrocks.

"The SkyClan warrior told me that his Clan fled upstream," Firestar replied. "I guess that means we should follow the river."

"How far?"

Firestar felt his neck fur begin to bristle, and he made himself relax until it lay flat. He didn't have a clue where to find the scattered Clan, or a place where they might live. He was even less sure what he would have to do to bring the Clan together again. He had hoped for more guidance, but his dreams since the night he spent in Smudge's garden had been dark and empty. Did that mean that the SkyClan ancestor wasn't watching him any longer? He felt as if he were stepping into a dark, dark night without moon or stars to guide him.

"I don't know," he admitted. "I suppose StarClan will show us, or maybe it'll be obvious."

Sandstorm's green eyes glinted, and Firestar braced himself for a scathing comment, but his mate only twitched her whiskers and went on in silence.

From Sunningrocks, Firestar led the way along the RiverClan border until the Twoleg bridge over the river came in sight. Here he paused, tasting the air. The RiverClan scent markers were strong, but there was no fresh scent to suggest that a patrol might be nearby.

"Okay, come on," he muttered.

He and Sandstorm slipped cautiously down the slope as far as the bridge, dodging between rocks and clumps of gorse to stay out of sight. From there they headed upstream, along the top of the gorge. Firestar half expected to see the leaping forms of SkyClan cats around him, reassuring him that this was the way he should go, but there was no sign of them.

Looking down at the foaming white water, he remembered how Bluestar had hurled herself over, taking with her the leader of the dog pack. Firestar had plunged in to save her; he shivered at the memory of the roar of water in his ears, the weight of his soaking fur, the exhaustion in his legs as he tried to swim with Bluestar's body gripped in his teeth.

Then he thought of the last time he had seen her, with starshine in her pelt and frosty starlight around her paws. She hadn't wanted to tell him about SkyClan, and she had done her best to discourage him from going on this journey. Determination flared in Firestar like a flame in dry grass. This was *his* quest, not StarClan's, and if he had to, he would carry it out without any help from his warrior ancestors.

He felt exposed along the bare edge of the gorge, but he and Sandstorm reached the border between RiverClan and WindClan without being spotted by a patrol. A stiff breeze was blowing from the moorland, flattening the tough grass and making Firestar feel it might blow him off his paws and into the tumbling river below. It brought the strong, fresh scent of WindClan cats with it.

"There could be a patrol about," Sandstorm mewed.

Firestar tasted the air again; with the wind so strong, it was hard to be sure how far away the cats were.

"We'd better keep going," he murmured. "Keep a lookout behind."

"I would if I had eyes in my tail," Sandstorm retorted.

They headed across the border, but they had hardly set paw in WindClan's territory when a rabbit streaked across the crest of the moor with a WindClan warrior hard on its paws.

"Get down!" Firestar crouched instinctively, but there was no cover in sight. They stayed unseen only because the hunter was so intent on his prey.

Then he noticed a spot on the edge of the gorge where the ground had crumbled away. "Quick—that way!" he hissed.

Pushing Sandstorm ahead of him, he crept down the cliff face for a tail-length or so, and into the shelter of an overhanging rock. He was pulling his tail into hiding when he heard the rabbit's shriek abruptly cut off, and another cat call out, "Good catch!"

"That was close!" Sandstorm breathed.

Firestar peered out of his hiding place to see two cats standing on the edge of the cliff, their heads outlined against the sky. He couldn't make out their features, but he recognized his friend Onewhisker's voice.

"You know, I swear I can smell ThunderClan scent, but I can't see any cat."

"They'd better not set paw here." The second voice, an aggressive growl, belonged to Mudclaw, the WindClan deputy. "If I catch them, they'll wish they'd never been kitted."

"Maybe some cat is going to Highstones," Onewhisker suggested.

Mudclaw's reply was an ill-tempered snort. "This isn't the way to Highstones, mouse-brain."

Firestar pulled his nose back into cover and pressed himself even closer to Sandstorm.

"You know," she murmured, "you could just *tell* them where we're going."

Firestar shook his head. He didn't want the other Clans to

know that he had left the forest; they would find out at the next Gathering, and that was soon enough for him.

Gradually the WindClan scent faded and Firestar dared to emerge from their hiding place. Scrambling back up the crumbling stones, he had time to glance down into the gorge and imagine what it would be like to lose his footing and go plummeting down into the turbulent river. Every hair on his pelt was on end by the time he regained the safety of the cliff top.

"Have they gone?" Sandstorm asked from just behind him.

"I think so. Let's keep going quickly in case they come back."

Picking up the pace, he bounded along the edge of the gorge with Sandstorm beside him. When he next paused to check for patrols, the ginger she-cat meowed, "You don't have to be so secretive about this, you know. You didn't even tell the whole story to your own Clan."

"The SkyClan cats came to me alone," Firestar told her. "There's no need to tell every cat about them. It's not as if I'm going to bring SkyClan back to the forest."

"Then what's all this about?" Sandstorm demanded, her neck fur beginning to fluff up. "If you don't plan on bringing SkyClan back, what *are* you going to do?"

"I'm not sure," Firestar replied. "But I know that SkyClan need help that only I can give."

"And what if that help means sharing ThunderClan territory with them?"

"It won't. The SkyClan cat said there would be a place for them to live."

Sandstorm didn't look reassured. "What if he's wrong?"

Meeting the challenge in his mate's green eyes, Firestar realized he couldn't answer.

The gorge came to an end, and the cliffs sloped down to rejoin the river as shallow, sandy banks once more. Firestar breathed a sigh of relief when they crossed the border scent markings and left WindClan territory behind. Soon after, the moor gave way to farmland, small fields divided by Twoleg paths and hedges; Firestar led the way down a narrow track between a hedge and a field of wheat.

"Smell those mice!" Sandstorm exclaimed. "I'm starving!"

She plunged in among the crackling stems, and, with a quick look around for dogs or Twolegs, Firestar followed. He caught one mouse with a swift blow of his paw as it ran along a furrow, and a second only heartbeats later. Carrying his prey to the edge of the field he found Sandstorm already there, crouching down to eat.

Firestar joined her, water flooding his jaws at the warm scent of food. Neither of them would take prey from another Clan's territory, so they hadn't eaten since they left ThunderClan that morning. When the last bite was gone, Firestar swiped his tongue around his jaws and arched his back in a long stretch. "Let's rest for a bit," he suggested. "If we wait until sunset, there won't be so many Twolegs about."

Sandstorm yawned, murmured agreement, and curled up in a patch of sunlight. Settling down beside her, enjoying the warmth of the sun on his fur and the comfortable fullness of his belly, Firestar tried to imagine how SkyClan had felt when they came this way. They must have been terrified, driven out of their home with no clear idea of where they were going. And so many cats—a whole Clan!—would be terribly vulnerable to dogs or foxes. He looked around, searching the shadowy places under the hedge for a familiar pale pelt, and strained his ears to catch the sound of the lost Clan's wailing. But all he could hear was the rustle of wind in the wheat and birdsong high in the sky. He blinked drowsily, rasped his tongue a few times over Sandstorm's ear, and slept.

Loud voices broke into his dreams. Not the yowls of the fleeing cats of SkyClan, but real, and closer, and getting even louder. Firestar scrambled to his paws to see Sandstorm standing rigid beside him, her pelt bristling as she stared up the line of the hedge. Coming toward them were two young Twolegs and a brown-and-white dog. The dog ran a little way ahead of its Twolegs, then bounced back to them, letting out a flurry of high-pitched yaps.

"Into the hedge!" Firestar ordered.

Thorns tearing at his pelt, he flattened his belly to the ground and crept into the middle of the hedge. Then he began to claw his way up the trunk of a hawthorn bush, forcing the spiny branches to let him through.

Sandstorm was scrabbling her way up another bush, but the branches crisscrossed so thickly that she came to a stop, unable to go any farther. Her green gaze, full of terror and frustration, met Firestar's.

The dog was whining alongside the hedge. Firestar caught

a glimpse of it trying to thrust its way through a gap, its tongue lolling and its white teeth gleaming.

"It's found our scent," Sandstorm whispered.

Firestar searched for a way to reach her and drag her higher, but they were separated by too many prickly branches. The dog's forepaws tore at the earth as it tried to force its way through the gap to reach the cats. Its jaws were no more than a tail-length away from Sandstorm's hind paws.

Then Firestar heard a Twoleg yowling. A Twoleg paw appeared in the gap, grabbed the dog's collar, and dragged it out again. The dog let out a bark of protest. Firestar waited, hardly daring to breathe, as the sounds died away and the scents of dog and Twolegs gradually faded.

"I think they've gone," he murmured. "Stay there while I check."

Leaving tufts of his flame-colored fur on the thorns, he crept to the edge of the bushes and looked out warily. The wheatfield was empty, the rays of the setting sun pouring over it like honey.

"It's okay," Firestar meowed, glancing back to where Sandstorm still clung to her branch.

He padded a little farther out, taking deep breaths as he tried to control his trembling. It was Sandstorm's danger, not his own, that had turned his blood to ice. Would it have been easier to have made this journey on his own, with no other cat to worry about? But when Sandstorm joined him, shaken but unhurt, he kept the disloyal thought to himself.

* * *

They padded through the night, under the light of the half-moon. This was the best time to travel without being seen, and they kept going until both cats were too weary to take another pawstep. They found a place to sleep in a hollow among the roots of a beech tree.

For the next two days they continued to follow the river through fields of wheat that stretched as far as they could see on either side. On the third day they left the fields and slid through a gap in the hedge onto a stretch of rough grass that sloped gently down to the river. Rushes thickly fringed the bank. Hot gusts of wind rattled them together; as Firestar drew closer he picked up the scents of voles and waterbirds, and heard small creatures rustling among the stems. The sun was going down, turning the river to flame.

Before they had gone far along the bank, Firestar heard the roaring of monsters in the distance. Tasting the air, he picked up a familiar harsh tang. "There's a Thunderpath up ahead."

"Then we'll have to cross it." Sandstorm's tail twitched. "There might not be so many monsters out now."

Soon Firestar made out a line of trees, black against the scarlet sky. The setting sun glinted on the bright, unnatural colors of swift-pawed monsters. Rounding a bend in the river, he caught sight of a Twoleg bridge made of stone, with monsters hurtling across it.

"The Thunderpath goes over the river. We'll be safe underneath." Sandstorm sounded pleased.

But Firestar felt uneasy as they approached the bridge. It

cast a dark shadow over the path, and as the daylight died the monsters shot brilliant beams of light from their eyes, sweeping across the riverbank. He froze as one beam picked them out, and heard a gasp from Sandstorm, but the monster snarled and rushed on.

Firestar let out a sigh of relief. "It didn't spot us."

"I don't like this," Sandstorm meowed. "Let's get out of here."

Firestar let her take the lead as they ran under the bridge. The stones were damp, and water dripped from the arch into the river. From the depths of the shadows Firestar saw the light beams of another monster, approaching fast along the Thunderpath above their heads. Suddenly its roar was all around them, echoing and reechoing from stone and water. Firestar froze, imagining the creature's huge jaws parted to swallow them.

Sandstorm let out a panic-stricken yowl. "Run!"

Terror crashed through Firestar; his legs propelled him forward until he was racing along the riverbank. He fled along the edge of the reed beds until the bridge was left far behind and he couldn't hear the monsters above the rasping of his own breath.

Only exhaustion slowed him down. He stood panting on the bank, his paws stinging and every hair on his pelt bristling. Sandstorm crouched beside him, looking back the way they had come, her tail lashing.

"Are you okay?" she asked when she had caught her breath.

Firestar tried to make his pelt lie flat. "I thought we were crow-food for sure. And I feel I've lost every scrap of skin from my pads. I don't know if we'll be able to go much farther tonight."

Sandstorm's eyes gleamed in the gathering darkness, and she parted her jaws to taste the air. "Wait there," she instructed, and vanished through the reeds toward the water's edge.

"What—" Firestar broke off as he realized she had gone. Collapsing onto one side, he licked his stinging pads until his mate reappeared, carrying a bunch of broad leaves in her jaws.

"Dock," she announced, dropping the leaves beside Firestar. "Rub it on your pads. Cinderpelt said there's nothing better for soreness."

"Thanks." Firestar blinked gratefully at her and rubbed his pads against the surface of the leaf. The cool juices soothed the discomfort, and he stretched his jaws in a yawn; it would be good to sleep, but there was still light in the sky, and he knew they should go on for as long as they could.

The river chattered swiftly through the rushes, narrower than where it flowed through the forest. Looking back the way they had come, Firestar saw a single warrior of StarClan shining in the sky. Just below it, hills stood up like jagged teeth, and Firestar realized that he was gazing back at Highstones; that last glimpse of the world he had known made him feel lonelier and more lost than ever.

He shook his head and stood up. "The dock leaves worked fine," he meowed. "Come on. We'd better try to get a bit farther."

Sandstorm gave her pads a last rub on the leaves and got up to follow him. Instead of being comforted by her presence, Firestar wondered if she really understood what was driving him to make this journey, and if she was wishing that she had stayed at home in ThunderClan.

The breeze dropped; although the sun had gone, the night was hot and sticky. Clouds gathered in the sky, spreading until they covered the moon and stars.

"I can't see my paws in front of me," Firestar muttered. "At this rate, we'll end up in the river."

"We'd better stop for the night," mewed Sandstorm. Firestar could just make out her pale ginger shape in the gloom, her head raised as she tasted the air. "There's a strong scent of vole," she went on. "Suppose I hunt, while you find us a place to sleep."

"Fine." Firestar knew his mate was the best hunter in ThunderClan. "Don't go too far, though."

"I won't." Sandstorm slipped away into the darkness.

More by scent than sight, Firestar located a clump of reeds and circled in the middle of them, trampling them down until he had created a makeshift nest. He sighed as he remembered the comfort of his den under the Highrock.

Before he had finished, Sandstorm reappeared with two voles hanging from her jaws. She dropped them and pushed one over to Firestar. "We won't starve, at least," she meowed. "There's plenty of prey, and they act like they've never seen a cat before."

So SkyClan doesn't hunt around here, Firestar thought as he gulped down his vole. *There's still a long way to go.*

He curled up, wrapping his tail over his nose, and tried to sleep in the stifling darkness. Though Sandstorm lay close enough for her pelt to touch his, he felt as if she were farther away than the hidden stars.

CHAPTER 11

Raucous quacking sounded in Firestar's ear. He jumped up, staring around wildly until he spotted a duck in the water beside the reed bed. As he watched, it took off, speeding low over the river with whirring wings. At the same moment, Firestar felt the ground begin to shake with the heavy tramp of Twoleg feet.

Sandstorm looked up. "What—"

Firestar slapped the end of his tail over her mouth. "Ssshh! Twolegs."

Peering out of the reeds, he saw three male Twolegs walking up the riverbank toward him. All of them carried the long, thin sticks that Twolegs held over the water to catch fish. To his relief there was no sign of a dog.

Firestar stayed very still while the Twolegs passed his hiding place and disappeared downstream. Then he beckoned Sandstorm with his tail. "Let's get out of here."

With his mate just behind him he ran lightly along the bank in the shadow of the reeds until the Twoleg scent faded. Then he paused to catch his breath, anxiously scanning the sky. Thick cloud still covered it; yellowish gray and seeming low enough to touch the tops of the trees. The air was hotter than the night before, and utterly still.

"There's a storm coming," Sandstorm meowed. "It'll break before nightfall."

Firestar nodded. "Then we'd better get moving, as fast as we can."

They set off again, side by side, at a steady, loping pace. In spite of what he said about needing to hurry, when he thought about what might be happening back in the forest Firestar's courage seemed to be draining out through his paws, and it was hard not to turn around and go racing home to his Clan. What if the badger had come back? How would the other Clans react when they discovered he had gone? Only a few moons ago, they had all been united against BloodClan. But how long would that alliance survive? Leopardstar would steal back the Sunningrocks if she thought she could get away with it, while Blackstar would take any opportunity to extend ShadowClan's territory. Firestar suddenly felt scared and exposed; he had left the forest and the warrior code far behind him, and he wasn't sure any longer that he knew why.

He wanted to share his fears with Sandstorm, but every time he glanced at her, padding alongside, her green gaze fixed intently on the path ahead, the words died in his throat. He didn't dare ask her if she thought he had made the wrong decision, in case she said yes.

As they continued along the riverbank, the air seemed to grow hotter and more oppressive. Firestar panted with thirst, which the river water quenched for only a few heartbeats. Sandstorm surprised a vole slipping from a hole in the bank into the water, tossed it into the air, and killed it as it hit the ground again.

"Great catch!" Firestar exclaimed.

Sandstorm's eyes shone with pride as she dragged the fresh-kill over to him so that they could share it. For a few moments Firestar was warmed by a sense of their old companionship, but he still didn't feel he could share his worries with his mate. What if she insisted on going back to the forest?

They had hardly moved off again after eating when Firestar picked up a strong scent of dog from ahead, and heard the sound of Twoleg voices. Sandstorm had heard them too. Flicking her tail to beckon him, she raced away from the river to a clump of elder bushes growing a few fox-lengths farther up the bank. Firestar followed, clawing his way up the trunk and crouching beside Sandstorm on the lowest branch.

Through the leaves he could see a couple of Twolegs walking past, with two dogs bouncing around them. One of them suddenly took off for the trees, barking loudly.

"It's scented us," Firestar mewed.

He felt Sandstorm tense; her lips drew back in the beginnings of a snarl and her claws scraped on the branch.

Then one of the Twolegs yowled loudly. The dog skidded to a halt, then turned and trotted back, glancing once or twice over its shoulder as it went.

"Good riddance," Sandstorm muttered.

Waiting until the Twolegs and their dogs were well away, Firestar looked out from his perch to get a better view of what lay upriver. "Twoleg nests," he meowed.

Sandstorm gave a disgusted sniff. "I suppose our luck couldn't last. Wherever there are Twolegs, there's trouble."

Firestar could see only the tops of the Twoleg nests from the elder bush, but when he and Sandstorm continued upstream the first one soon came into full view, very close to the edge of the river.

"Look at it!" Sandstorm halted, swishing her tail in disgust. "It's *swarming* with Twolegs."

Firestar stopped beside her, puzzled. Most Twoleg nests held only a Twoleg and his mate, and maybe their kits. But there were far more than that outside this nest, too many to count. Most of the adults were sitting around, eating Twoleg food, while their kits ran shrieking down to the river to throw stones in the water. Some of the Twolegs yowled at them, but the kits didn't take any notice.

"Don't they ever apprentice their young?" Sandstorm asked with a sigh.

"If we stay on the riverbank we'll have to go right through the middle of them," Firestar meowed. "We'd be spotted for sure. We'll have to go around."

A white wooden fence enclosed the nest and the Twolegs, leading down to the river. Skirting it, Firestar led the way up the bank and around the back of the nest. Close to the nest wall, where he would have expected to find a garden, was a wide space covered with the same hard black stuff as a

Thunderpath. Several monsters were crouching there.

"Are they asleep?" Sandstorm whispered.

As if in answer to her question, one of the monsters broke into a throaty roar and began to creep slowly away from the others and through a gap in the fence onto a small Thunderpath. Then it leaped forward and dashed away, passing two other monsters on their way in.

Firestar felt his pelt bristle. Crossing a Thunderpath was bad enough, but here he felt as if the crouching monsters were watching him, ready to spring as soon as he ventured onto the hard surface.

Setting down his paws as lightly as if he were stalking a mouse, his belly fur brushing the grass, he crept up to the edge of the Thunderpath. There were shrubs for cover on the other side, but he didn't dare dart across yet. He could hear the growling of another monster, and a few heartbeats later it sped down the Thunderpath, slowed at the gap in the fence, then went to sleep beside the others near the nest. A couple of Twolegs emerged from its belly.

"Run when I say 'now,'" he murmured to Sandstorm.

"Get on with it, then," she replied edgily.

Firestar's gaze flicked from the nest to the Thunderpath and back again. Everything was still. "Okay, now!"

He sprang forward with Sandstorm beside him. At the same moment, the snarl of a waking monster broke out near the nest. Firestar flung himself forward and hurtled into the bushes, where he squeezed his eyes shut tight and tried to stop shaking.

"It spotted us!" Sandstorm gasped, thrusting her way into cover beside him. "But it can't follow us in here."

Firestar hoped she was right. When he opened his eyes and peered through the leaves he could make out the monster's gleaming color as it prowled onto the Thunderpath and paused. Was it trying to scent them? Surely it would be hard for a monster to scent anything except its own harsh reek. All the same, Firestar's breathing didn't slow until the monster gave up and went on, its roar dying away into the distance.

"Okay, let's go," he mewed. He would have liked to rest for a bit longer, but he hated this weird nest crammed with Twolegs, and their monsters that seemed to have learned how to hunt.

Sandstorm muttered agreement; both cats pushed their way through the shrubs until they reached the river. Firestar's pelt didn't lie flat until they had rounded a bend and left the Twoleg nest far behind.

By the time the next Twoleg nest came into sight, Firestar guessed that sunhigh was long past, though there was no sun to be seen. The clouds had darkened and a sharp wind had picked up, bringing the scent of rain. White-flecked ripples appeared on the river; in the distance Firestar heard the rumble of thunder. The storm would break soon.

Sandstorm stopped to taste the air. "Mice!" she exclaimed. "The scent's coming from that nest."

"Are you sure?" Firestar asked.

He broke off at Sandstorm's scathing look. Without bothering to reply, she stalked toward the nest.

"Hey, wait!" Firestar broke into a run to catch up with her. "You don't know what's in there."

"I know what *isn't*. There's no Twoleg scent, no dogs." Sandstorm sighed. "Do you want fresh-kill, Firestar, or don't you?"

Firestar had to admit that his belly was yowling with hunger. All day so far they had done nothing but avoid Twolegs. There had been no chance to hunt. "Okay, but . . ."

Ignoring him, Sandstorm prowled closer to the nest. Following her, Firestar realized that she was right about the scent: lots of mice, but no trace of Twolegs or dogs. The nest looked abandoned. The door sagged open, and the square holes in the walls were dark and empty. There had been a wooden fence around the garden once, but most of it was broken down and rotting, while the garden itself was overgrown.

Sandstorm crept up to the door and paused to taste the air again before she slipped inside. Firestar followed, the powerful aroma of mouse flooding over him as he entered.

Inside the light was gray and cold, filtering through dusty air. A thick layer of dust and debris covered the floor. On either side, doors to separate dens stood open, while straight ahead an uneven slope led to a higher level. Sandstorm began to climb upward.

"Be careful," Firestar warned her.

Her tail twitched. "Stay here and keep watch."

Firestar waited at the bottom of the slope until Sandstorm had vanished. Then, ears pricked for the sound of danger, he padded through the empty dens. Every tiny movement woke an echo; Firestar found himself remembering what it had been like when he lived with his Twolegs, before he had ever set paw in the forest. Their nest had been warm and cozy, the floors covered with thick padding that muffled every sound. The holes in the walls were filled with shiny stuff like ice, and pelts hung there to be drawn across at night. The Twolegs had slept in a den on the higher level, while he stayed in the . . . What was the name of the den where they ate food? Yes—the *kitchen*.

The unfamiliar word popped into his mind as he stood in the empty nest. The trickle of memory was becoming a flood; Firestar thought of Hattie and Smudge, living happily with their housefolk. Would he have been as happy if he had stayed, if he had never known the excitement of stalking prey in the rustling shadow of leaves, never curled up in the warriors' den beside his Clanmates, never fought for his Clan or shouldered the burden of being their leader?

No. Even in the Twoleg nest, he had walked the forest in his dreams. When he joined ThunderClan he knew that he had found the place where he belonged. But if ThunderClan meant so much to him, why had he left to help a Clan who had been driven from the forest so long ago that no Clan remembered them? Was it enough that he felt he was doing the right thing?

He started at the sound of a pawstep behind him and spun around to see Sandstorm padding into the kitchen with the limp body of a mouse in her jaws.

"You look as if you've got a lot on your mind," she meowed, dropping the fresh-kill. "What's the problem?"

Firestar shook his head. "Nothing important."

Sandstorm held his gaze for a heartbeat as if she didn't believe him, but she said nothing more.

Crouching side by side, they shared the mouse. Outside the wind had grown stronger, buffeting the nest and hurling sharp rain at the walls and through the holes to spatter in the dust on the floor.

"Maybe we should stay here overnight," Sandstorm suggested.

Firestar knew she was right. They could catch more prey and sleep full-fed until the storm was over. But the walls of the Twoleg nest seemed to be closing in on him. He couldn't bear to be inside any longer, struggling with old memories. He wasn't a kittypet anymore, and this wasn't where he belonged!

"No," he mewed. "It's not dark yet. We can't waste the rest of the day."

Sandstorm opened her jaws to argue, but something in Firestar's face must have stopped her, because she followed him without protest as he led the way out of the nest.

The wind battered Firestar as soon as he emerged. Rain slapped him in the face and soaked his fur within heartbeats. He knew it would be more sensible to go back, but pride wouldn't let him change his mind. Lowering his head, he fought his way into the wind and down to the riverbank.

The river had changed since he and Sandstorm had left it

to enter the nest. The water level had risen much higher, churning with muddy brown waves that slopped against the top of the bank. Wind lashed the reeds, blowing them nearly flat; the stems whipped the cats' fur with stinging blows as they battled through the gloom. The waning moon showed fitfully among the clouds, its faint light useless to guide their pawsteps.

Firestar heard an angry hiss from Sandstorm, and knew she thought they should find shelter, but he also knew that she was too stubborn to ask twice. He was desperate to keep going, whatever the weather, to find SkyClan and reassure himself that he had been right to leave the forest.

Soon the river rose higher still, washing through the reeds and around the cats' paws. On the side away from the river they were hemmed in by bushes, the thorny branches growing too thickly for them to force a way through. Lightning stabbed down from the sky, followed almost at once by a crack of thunder right overhead, as loud as if the sky were splitting into fragments. The cold light turned the driving rain to silver and shone blackly on Firestar's and Sandstorm's drenched pelts, plastered against their bodies.

At the next flash Firestar looked up and thought he caught a glimpse of the SkyClan cat's face in the rolling purple clouds. Before he could be sure, the face changed to Bluestar's. Firestar thought she was gazing down at him with a pleading expression, as if she was terrified for her former Clanmates and wanted them to turn back. Firestar wanted to yowl a question to her, but at that moment lightning split the sky again and the face vanished.

We can't turn back, Firestar told himself. *Not now that we've come so far.*

He splashed on, head down and tail drooping under the driving rain. Suddenly a surge of water washed over the path. Firestar was swept off his paws. He opened his jaws to yowl a warning to Sandstorm and gulped in icy water as his head went under.

Paws working frantically, he struggled upward. At first when his head broke the surface he couldn't see anything but tossing waves. Then he caught a glimpse of the bushes on the bank and swam toward them. The cold made his legs feel stiff, and his sodden fur dragged at him. The surge began to recede, carrying him away from the bushes again. Firestar swam even more desperately, terrified of being swept out into the churning river.

Then his paws touched the ground. He dug in his claws and managed to cling on as the wave gurgled past him, leaving him in water that washed against his belly fur. Shaking with cold and terror, he looked back. "Sandstorm!" he yowled.

There was no reply, and at first Firestar couldn't see his mate. Then he spotted her, clinging with teeth and claws to a jutting root a few tail-lengths downstream. As Firestar waded back to her she scrambled to her paws and spat out river water.

"Are you okay?" Firestar panted.

"What does it look like?" Sandstorm hissed, lashing her

tail. "We could have been washed away. Why can't you listen to me for once, instead of being so stubborn?"

Guilt washed over Firestar like another wave. Sandstorm was right; if they had stayed in the shelter of the abandoned nest they would have been warm and safe now.

"I'm sorry—"

"'Sorry' catches no prey!" Sandstorm snapped back at him. "Admit it, Firestar; you don't really want me here at all."

"That's not true!" Firestar protested.

"I don't believe you!" Sandstorm glared at him, then added more softly, "I know you love me, Firestar, but is that enough? Don't you wish Spottedleaf were with you right now?"

The question took Firestar by surprise. What would it be like to have the StarClan medicine cat by his side? Would she be able to convince him that he was doing the right thing?

As he hesitated, the anger faded from Sandstorm's gaze, replaced by a look of horror. "Don't say a word, Firestar," she mewed. "I know what your answer would be."

"No, I didn't mean—"

Not listening to him, Sandstorm spun around and dashed off, back the way they had come, her paws splashing along the flooded path.

"Sandstorm, wait!" Firestar yowled. He forced himself to bound through the water until he caught up with the fleeing she-cat. "You've got to listen to me."

Sandstorm rounded on him. "I don't want to listen!" she hissed. "I'm going home. I know you don't want me. You've never wanted me as much as you want Spottedleaf."

"It's different; that's all!" Firestar protested. "You can't ask me to choose between you. You're *both* important, and I—"

Lightning crackled across the sky again, clawing at a beech tree on top of the bank. Thunder rolled out, and a deep groaning sound answered from the tree. The top began to tilt, slowly at first, then faster and faster, as the tree fell across the river, the highest branches crashing down on the opposite bank. Firestar and Sandstorm leaped back as sharp, whipping twigs lashed the path where they had been standing.

The two cats crouched on the flooded path until the noise died away. As the fallen tree rustled into silence, Firestar rose cautiously to his paws. "Wait for me here," he mewed. "I'll check out the other bank. It doesn't look so wet over there."

For a moment Sandstorm stared at him in silence. Her gaze was cold, as if she wasn't in the mood to obey his order. Firestar wondered what he would do if she insisted on leaving. Then she nodded abruptly. "Okay."

The falling tree seemed to have ended their quarrel—for now. Firestar breathed silent thanks to StarClan as he clambered onto the tree trunk, trying to sink his claws into the smooth gray bark.

The first few paces were easy, but as the trunk grew narrower it began to bounce under Firestar's weight. Once he reached the branches he had to climb over them. He dug in his claws even harder, terrified that he would slip into the churning current. He flinched as water splashed up between the branches, and felt the surging black river swirl around his hind legs. He clawed his way to safety, half-blinded by bunches of leaves. Twigs scraped his face and snagged in his fur. For a heartbeat he froze as the trunk shifted under his paws; the whole tree was threatening to roll over and pitch him into the water. Bunching his muscles, he sprang forward, pushing his way through the slender upper branches, and landed safely on the far side.

The bank was higher here, with water sucking a couple of mouse-lengths below the top. Trees spread their branches over it, giving some shelter from the driving rain. Firestar drew a few panting breaths, then turned back toward Sandstorm, still waiting on the opposite bank.

"It's okay!" he called. "You can—"

A rumbling sound interrupted him. At first he thought it was thunder, but it grew louder and louder. Sandstorm was staring upstream, her eyes stretched wide with horror. Firestar whipped around. A huge wave was bearing down on them, brown and topped with foam, bearing sticks and debris along with it, roaring louder than any monster.

Firestar let out a screech of shock. Dashing to the nearest tree, he leaped up and sank his claws into the trunk. Then the wave was upon him. It surged past, swirling over the tree trunk less than a tail-length below him. Spray spattered his fur. Firestar clung there until the wave had passed. When he climbed down he stared in horror at the river. The fallen tree had been swept away.

How will Sandstorm cross now?

As he looked across to the opposite bank a cold claw sank into his heart. Sandstorm was gone.

CHAPTER 12

"No!" Firestar yowled. "Sandstorm! Sandstorm, where are you?"

There was no reply. Firestar ran up and down the bank, yowling his mate's name over and over. He couldn't see any sign of her, no trace of ginger fur among the debris thrown up on the far bank.

He raced downriver, scrambling over rocks slick with water. Desperately he scanned the banks and the surging water, convinced that every scrap of tossing debris might be his beloved mate.

He had to stop at last, sides heaving, his paws scraped and bleeding. Standing on a boulder, he stared down at the black, gurgling water a tail-length below. If Sandstorm was dead, he would never, ever forgive himself.

You stupid excuse for a cat!

Bluestar's face in the cloud had clearly been a warning, but he had ignored it. He had been so wrapped up in his quest for SkyClan that he had forgotten what he owed to Sandstorm. Whatever had happened to her, if she was drowned or lying injured somewhere, it was his fault. He let out a whimper of grief. How could he have let Sandstorm believe that he would rather have been with Spottedleaf? It was *Sandstorm* he loved, and he would do anything to live the time over again and send her across the tree trunk first.

Rain still fell, but more gently now, hissing into the river, and the thunder had rolled away into the distance. The gloom of day was fading to twilight. Firestar wanted to go on, but he knew he couldn't search properly in the dark. He could easily miss Sandstorm if she was lying unconscious. Every pawstep painful, he crept underneath the jutting boulder and curled up. Exhaustion surged over him like the black water of the river, dragging him into a cold, dreamless sleep.

Pale light reflected from the surface of the water and woke Firestar. He crawled into the open, shivering in the wind. Clouds raced above his head, tearing away to show blue sky behind them, and the sun was already climbing toward sunhigh. The storm was over. His pelt was almost dry, the fur sticking together in clumps.

For a heartbeat Firestar drew in the clear air, gathering himself for the next stage of his journey. Then memory struck him like the blow from a badger's paw. Sandstorm was gone.

All that mattered was to find his mate. He couldn't go on without her; he had to retrace his pawsteps downstream.

Firestar stood on the edge of the river and looked across at the other bank, measuring the distance. His instincts told him to plunge in and swim, but he held back. The river was still full, and too fast-flowing for even a RiverClan cat to cross safely. With a sigh, he began to pad along the bank.

Soon more boulders reared up in front of him, too steep for Firestar to climb. He was forced away from the edge of the river. Climbing a steep bank, he picked his way through long grass at the edge of a field. The stems were weighted down by raindrops, soaking his pelt afresh as he brushed through them. With every pawstep he peered down at the river through the thin line of trees, scanning for any sign of a familiar ginger pelt.

The clouds began to clear away and the sun shone more strongly, soaking into Firestar's drenched fur. The scent of prey drifted to him from the field, but he ignored it. As he limped onward he spotted another tree fallen slantwise across the river, but several tail-lengths separated its upper branches from the far bank, and Firestar didn't dare risk using it to cross. He picked up his pace when he spotted a narrow wooden Twoleg bridge, only to halt in frustration as he realized that the middle section was broken away, leaving a gap too wide to leap.

The sun was already going down when he came to another bridge. His paws itched to cross, but Twolegs blocked his path: two adults and a kit. A dog padded beside them. Firestar's neck fur bristled and he crouched down in the grass; then he noticed that the dog was old and plump, and tethered to the Twoleg kit by some sort of tendril. That meant it was much less of a risk, as long as he ran fast enough.

Taking a deep breath, Firestar streaked down the bank and across the bridge, darting between the legs of the Twolegs.

He heard a bark of surprise from the dog. One of the Twolegs called out, but Firestar didn't look back. He skidded off the far end of the bridge and plunged into the shelter of the bushes, his heart thudding.

When he dared to peer out, he saw the Twolegs staring after him, the old dog straining on its tendril, but after a moment they carried on, turning downstream on the far bank. Firestar let out a sigh of relief. Once they were out of sight he emerged and set out down the path.

The ground beneath his paws was covered in sticky mud, with debris scattered over it. The enormous wave must have washed right up to the bushes; Sandstorm couldn't possibly have escaped it.

Firestar looked and looked for her, dreading the sight of lifeless ginger fur caught up in a branch or rammed against a boulder. The sun had already disappeared when he came to the abandoned Twoleg nest. In the twilight he padded up the path, hope flickering in his heart. Sandstorm had wanted to shelter here; if she had survived the wave she might have spent the night inside. But when he reached the door Firestar could pick up only a faint, stale trace of her scent, along with his own.

Unable to give up without a search, he slipped inside the nest. The dust rose under his paws, stinging his nose. "Sandstorm?" he called.

There was no reply. Staggering with exhaustion, Firestar dragged himself up the uneven slope and explored the dens above, but there too, the only scent of Sandstorm was stale.

Grief and fear overwhelmed him; he curled up on the bare wooden floor and closed his eyes, but sleep was hard to come by. When unconsciousness overwhelmed him at last, his sleep was disturbed by broken memories of his life with his Twolegs, as if he had never left them to become a warrior, or known the joy of leading his Clan.

He woke shivering in the gray light of dawn. As he padded down the slope again, his heart lurched when he heard movement coming from the Twoleg kitchen. Without pausing to scent, he rushed through the opening. "Sandstorm?"

He was halted in his tracks by a fierce snarling. A fox raised its red-streaked muzzle from a meal of pigeon, its white teeth bared among the blood and feathers.

Firestar backed slowly away until he reached the outer door. Then he turned and fled, racing down the path with his belly fur brushing the ground and his tail streaming behind him. He was braced to feel the hot breath of the fox on his neck and its teeth meeting in his scruff, but he reached the riverbank safely. Panting, he looked back. The fox hadn't pursued him.

Firestar trotted along the bank until he reached the other Twoleg nest where the monster had almost caught them. Rounding a bend in the river, he halted in surprise. Where the Twolegs and their kits had been was a vast stretch of water, flat and silver-gray, spilling out from the river and pooling around the nest. A few Twoleg things bobbed forlornly in the middle of it. Close to the nest two or three Twolegs were standing, staring out at the water and wailing.

Keeping an eye on the Twolegs in case any of them spotted him, Firestar skirted the edge of the water, hoping to cross the Thunderpath behind the nest, as he and Sandstorm had done before. But the flood stretched much farther than he had thought. The Thunderpath itself was underwater. Firestar had to pick his way through marshy woodland, slipping into muddy hollows and snagging his fur on brambles.

At last he reached the little Thunderpath again. Out of habit he crouched beside it, glancing cautiously up and down, but there were no monsters today. Everything was silent except for steady dripping from the trees.

Firestar pushed his way through the undergrowth on the other side of the Thunderpath, hoping to follow the edge of the flood back to the river. But as he emerged from the woods again he heard loud yapping. A Twoleg and a little fox-colored dog were rounding the corner of the nest.

Whipping around, Firestar fled, but he was too late. The dog rushed at him with a flurry of high-pitched yaps. Firestar heard the Twoleg yowl, but the dog kept on coming. Firestar could hear it blundering through the trees behind him. He forced his legs to move even faster. A wall reared up in front of him; without thinking, Firestar took a flying leap, clawed his way up the stones, and paused to look down at his pursuer.

The dog panted up to the wall and sat at the foot, howling. Firestar bared his teeth in a furious hiss, then jumped down into the garden on the other side. As he slid into the shelter of a bush he heard the dog's Twoleg come crashing up, snarling irritably. The dog's yapping faded into the distance as it was dragged away.

Firestar crouched in the shelter of the dripping bush and caught his breath. Where could the water have taken Sandstorm? If the river had flooded this far, she could have been swept away from the bank altogether. *If she managed to struggle free,* he thought, *she might have come this way to escape the flood.*

It would be worth searching a few gardens, Firestar decided, to see if he could pick up any trace of her. At least there was no more rain, and the pale sun drew up steam from the sodden grass.

Firestar peered out from behind his bush and examined the garden. It looked empty. There were no sounds coming from the Twoleg nest. But when he tasted the air he couldn't scent Sandstorm. She wasn't here; he would have to go on.

Streaking across the grass, he plunged through the bushes at the far side and leaped up onto the opposite wall. Beyond it was a narrow passage; after checking for scent, Firestar jumped down. The wall on the other side was too high to climb, so he trotted along the passage, senses straining for any trace of Sandstorm.

The passage emerged into a tangle of Twoleg nests joined by a small Thunderpath. Everything was quiet, and there were no monsters in sight, not even sleeping ones. All the same, Firestar's pelt prickled. Being in a Twolegplace didn't feel right, and he was already beginning to doubt that he would find Sandstorm so far from the river.

I'll just take a quick look.

But all the nests and gardens looked alike, and the rain had washed away any scents that might have guided him. Jumping up onto a wall that he thought overlooked the passage back to the woods, Firestar found himself staring down into yet another garden.

"Fox dung!" he spat. "Now I'm lost. What else can go wrong?"

He tried to retrace his steps, but somewhere he must have taken a wrong turn. More unfamiliar gardens stretched in front of him, separated by the winding alleys that seemed to turn back on themselves. Several times he crossed his own scent trail, but it didn't lead him anywhere. By the time night was falling, he still hadn't found his way back to the river.

He felt too tired to go on searching; warily he dropped down from a fence into one of the gardens and crawled underneath a bush with strong-smelling blue flowers. With luck they would hide his scent from any passing kittypets.

This time his dreams were filled with the voice of his mate, wailing for him in the distance, but however far and fast he ran, he couldn't catch up with her. When he woke he still felt exhausted, and so miserable that it took an immense effort for him to drag himself out from underneath the bush.

Across the garden a movement caught his eye, and he spotted a plump white cat emerging from the door of the nest. It yawned and stretched, then lay down in a patch of sunlight on some flat stones and began to wash its long, snowy fur.

He looks like Cloudtail, Firestar thought, leaping down and approaching cautiously in case the kittypet displayed any of his kin's fighting skills.

The cat looked up in surprise and fixed a brilliant blue gaze on Firestar as the ThunderClan leader paused at the edge of the stones and dipped his head politely. Firestar suppressed a spurt of contempt that this kittypet couldn't be bothered to defend his own territory. He didn't look as if he had ever raised a claw in anger in his life.

"Greetings," he meowed.

The white cat blinked at him. "Hi. Who are you?"

"My name's Firestar. Have you seen a ginger cat recently?"

The kittypet blinked again. "I've seen you."

Firestar gritted his teeth. "Yes, but I'm not looking for me," he pointed out. He wanted to sink his claws into the kittypet and shake some sense into him, but he managed to stop himself.

"Well . . ." the white cat went on, "I think I saw a ginger cat . . . oh, about five days ago. Or was that a tortoiseshell?"

Firestar took a deep breath and let it out. "Okay. Never mind. Can you just tell me how to get back to the river?"

The kittypet twitched his whiskers. "What river?"

Firestar dug his claws into the ground. "Thanks for your help," he hissed.

Turning his back on the kittypet, he raced across the garden and climbed the wall. Yet another narrow passage lay beyond. With nothing else to do, Firestar padded along it until it emerged into a wide space covered with black Thunderpath stuff. A Thunderpath led out of it from the other side, and all around it were small, square nests with featureless walls and gaping entrances. Some of them were empty, but one of them had swallowed a monster whole.

Every hair on Firestar's pelt rose. What if one of the nests swallowed him, too? His paws were itching to run back the way he had come, but he thought that if he could get out on the other side, along the Thunderpath, he might be able to find his way back to the river.

Cautiously, pawstep by pawstep, he ventured out onto the hard black surface. He was almost halfway across when he froze at the roar of a monster, growing rapidly louder. The huge creature swept through the opening, sunlight glinting off its shiny pelt, and bore down on Firestar.

Fear slammed into Firestar's throat. He dodged to one side. The monster followed him. *It's hunting me!* Its throaty snarl seemed to be all around him. Letting out a terrified caterwaul, Firestar clawed his way up the wall of one of the nests, across the roof, and crashed down on the other side, too panic-stricken to look where he was going.

His paws sank deep into a pile of Twoleg rubbish. Its reek billowed out around him. Choking, Firestar scrabbled furiously to drag himself out of the mess. Shaking pieces of the stinking stuff from his fur, he collapsed on his side, his head spinning. There was a vile taste in his mouth, and he felt as if every muscle in his body were aching.

Despair crashed over him. He had failed Sandstorm and SkyClan. He had failed his own Clan by abandoning them. Every decision he had made had been wrong, and he was too exhausted to do any more.

His belly was caterwauling with hunger, but Firestar was too miserable even to try scenting prey. A few tail-lengths away he could see a pile of Twoleg stuff covered by a stiff, shiny pelt. His muscles shrieking in protest, he crawled over to it and slunk into the shelter of the pelt. With a tiny sigh he closed his eyes and let darkness take him.

His dreams were dark and chaotic. Over and over again he saw the enormous wave bearing down on him, and heard Sandstorm yowling to him for help he couldn't give. Then the Twoleg dog chased him, gripped his scruff in its teeth, and shook him until he thought it would rip his pelt off.

CHAPTER 13

"I've never seen him before in my life. What's he doing here?"

"He's not moving. Is he dead?"

"No . . . here, you, wake up!"

The voices pulsed loud and soft in Firestar's ears. He blinked painfully and saw a blur of black and brown blocking the gap where he had crept into shelter. A paw was fastened in his neck fur, giving him a vigorous shake.

"Wha . . . ? Get off." Firestar batted feebly at his assailant.

"Keep your claws to yourself," a voice growled.

Firestar blinked again. Crouched in front of him were two cats: one was a black she-cat, the other a scrawny brown tom with a torn ear.

"You can't stay there," the black she-cat meowed. "Twolegs come in and out of here all the time. Move your paws."

"I'll move when I'm ready." Firestar tried to sound defiant, but his mouth was so parched with thirst that he could hardly speak, and his head spun from hunger.

"You'll move when we tell you," the scrawny tom snarled. "Flea-brain!" He gave Firestar a sharp poke in the ribs with one paw.

Firestar was too weak to argue. He dragged himself out from beneath the shiny pelt and staggered to his paws.

"About time." The she-cat sniffed. "Follow us."

She set off down a winding path that led between the mounds of Twoleg rubbish. Firestar briefly thought of making a break for freedom, but he had no idea where to go. Besides, he could barely totter along, and while the she-cat led the way, the brown tom padded along beside Firestar and kept his yellow eyes fixed on him.

Where are they taking me? Firestar wondered.

He thought of Scourge and BloodClan, and wondered if there was another Clan of vicious Twolegplace cats here. If they knew he was from the forest, they might see him as an enemy. Were these cats taking him to be killed?

The black she-cat led him through a gap in the wall. Firestar emerged into a patch of bare ground where a few stunted trees struggled to survive in the thin soil. He couldn't see any other cats, but there was powerful cat scent all around him. His fear of finding another BloodClan grew stronger and stronger until it rose in his throat and almost choked him.

"That way." The brown tom gave him another push, almost carrying Firestar off his paws.

He stumbled forward, slid down a dip in the ground, and came to a halt as his forepaws splashed into the edge of a puddle.

"Keep your paws out of it," the tomcat growled. "I don't want to drink it if you've been paddling about in it."

Firestar backed away hastily.

"Go on, then, drink," the she-cat snapped. "It's perfectly safe, you know. We're not trying to poison you!"

Firestar gave her a doubtful glance. These cats had brought him to the water he needed so desperately. Did that mean they wouldn't kill him after all?

He crouched by the edge of the pool and lapped at the water. He knew it was stale, tainted by Twoleg scents, but right then it tasted more delicious than the clearest stream in the forest.

When he sat up, twitching drops of water off his whiskers, he saw the black she-cat standing beside him with a sparrow in her jaws.

"Here," she mewed, dropping the fresh-kill at his paws.

Firestar stared at it. These cats were *feeding* him?

"Honestly," the she-cat muttered, rolling her eyes as she pushed the sparrow closer to him. "Eat. Haven't you ever seen prey before?"

"Er . . . thanks." Firestar fell on the sparrow, gulping it down in huge bites.

"I can see you haven't eaten for a long time," the brown tom remarked. "Have you come far?"

Firestar swallowed a mouthful of sparrow before he replied. "Far enough," he meowed. He dipped his head and added, "My name is Firestar."

"I'm Stick, and she's Cora," the brown tom told him.

Firestar felt a shiver of hope stir his pelt. Maybe he wasn't the only wanderer they had rescued. "I'm looking for another ginger cat. Have you seen her?" he asked.

The two rogues exchanged a glance. Firestar felt sick with disappointment as Cora shook her head, shrugging.

"One of the others might have," Stick added.

"Others? What others?" Firestar demolished the last scrap of prey and heaved himself to his paws. Energy was beginning to trickle back into him now that he had eaten and drunk. "Are you part of a Clan?"

Cora looked puzzled. "What do you mean, a Clan?"

"Other cats come here," Stick explained. "Cats like us."

"Where are they now?" Firestar demanded.

"Dunno," meowed Stick. He gestured with his tail. "Around."

"Can you take me to them?"

"No need," replied Cora. "They'll turn up here sooner or later. They always do."

Firestar glanced around. There were still no other cats in sight, but the strong scent he had picked up at first told him that this must be a meeting place for many cats. The memory of BloodClan made him nervous. Stick and Cora had treated him well up to now, but what about the others? Firestar's instincts were telling him to run, but he was so desperate to find Sandstorm that he knew he had to stay and ask more questions.

"Could you introduce me to the other cats?" he asked.

Cora twitched her tail. "You'll be fine without us."

"We don't usually hang around with them," Stick added.

"Please!" Firestar dug his claws hard into the ground. "I

need to be sure that the other cats will talk to me. I've got to find my friend!"

The cats hesitated, glancing at each other again.

"Who is this cat you're looking for?" Cora asked. "Why is it so important to find her?"

"Because it's my fault she's lost!" Firestar burst out. "We were traveling along the river, and she got washed away in the storm. I've looked everywhere for her, but I can't find her. I can't go on without her, and I can't go back home and leave her here." His claws scraped the dusty ground. "I can't give up looking for her!"

"Keep your fur on," Cora meowed. Her voice was still sharp but her eyes were sympathetic. "We'll stay."

"Thank you." Firestar held her gaze, hoping she would understand how much this meant to him.

Stick and Cora padded over to a shady spot under one of the scrubby trees, shared tongues briefly, then curled up for a nap. Firestar stretched, wishing that he could sleep too, but he didn't want to miss the arrival of the other cats. He couldn't trust Stick and Cora to wake him because he wasn't sure that they realized how important it was for him to find Sandstorm.

He found a sun-warmed patch of earth and settled down for a really thorough grooming. The hairs of his flame-colored pelt were clumped together, with bits of debris from the river matted among them. Even worse, he was covered with smears of disgusting Twoleg stuff from the rubbish heap. If his Clanmates could see him now they would hardly recognize him! Rasping his tongue over his shoulder, he pulled a face at the vile taste, but he kept on until his fur was smooth and glossy again.

Firestar found it harder and harder to keep awake. The sun was going down, casting the long shadows of trees and Twoleg walls across the open space. Suddenly he spotted movement from the corner of his eye; a cat was slinking out from behind one of the trees.

Firestar stiffened, glancing toward Stick and Cora. The black she-cat rose to her paws, arched her back in a long stretch, then padded over to him. "Here they come," she mewed.

More cats followed the first, emerging from between the trees or through the gap where the rogues and Firestar had entered. Others leaped down from the walls. Firestar watched them greet one another with friendly reserve, just as different Clan cats did at Fourtrees.

Cora waved her tail. "Come on; I'll introduce you."

Stick joined them as they headed for the nearest group of cats, three of them, who were sitting by the puddle where Firestar had drunk.

" . . . and so I said to the rat," a black tom was meowing, "'Come one step farther and I'll rip your pelt off.'"

A brown tabby looked up from the puddle. "What happened then?"

"Its mate jumped him from behind," the third cat, a beautiful white queen, replied with a *mrrow* of amusement.

The black tom bared his teeth in a snarl. "So what? I

ripped the pelts off *both* of them."

"That's Coal," Cora murmured in Firestar's ear. "He's the biggest boaster around."

"But his claws are sharp," Stick added.

The white she-cat yawned. "Who wants to eat rat, anyway? *I* had some Twoleg milk."

"And hedgehogs fly," Coal snapped.

"I *did*!" The white she-cat's eyes stretched wide with indignation. "The bottle was standing on the step, so I tipped it over and all the milk flowed out." She swiped her tongue around her jaws. "It was delicious."

"The white cat is Snowy," Stick told Firestar. "She spends a lot of time around Twolegs. She might have seen your friend there."

Firestar shook his head. "I doubt it. Sandstorm wouldn't go near Twolegs if she could help it."

"Snowy, I saw you near that nest." The brown tabby got up from the puddle, and Firestar saw that half his tail was missing. "You might not have noticed that they have a new dog there. It chased me off when I was stalking a mouse in their garden. I'd stay well away if I were you."

Snowy stretched and extended her claws. "I've seen the dog—stupid hairy lump. I can deal with it."

Coal snorted. "I'd like to see you try."

The brown tabby padded over to sit between Coal and Snowy. "Hi, there. I saw a strange cat today," he began.

Firestar's ears pricked.

"A couple of Twoleg kits had grabbed her," the tabby tom

went on, flexing his claws. "*I* soon showed them what's what."

Snowy turned toward him with an angry glare. "Shorty! You didn't claw young Twolegs, did you?"

"What if I did?" Shorty snapped back. "They deserved it, mauling a cat. But no," he went on, "I didn't hurt them. I had my claws sheathed. I just distracted them so the ginger cat could escape."

"Ginger!" Firestar exclaimed.

Stick's eyes gleamed. "That could be your friend."

"Why didn't you bring her to meet us?" Snowy asked Shorty.

"No time." The tabby tom's amber eyes shone with admiration. "She jumped over the fence as if she'd sprouted wings. I don't think I've ever seen a cat move so fast."

Firestar touched Stick on the shoulder with his tail. "I've *got* to talk to that cat."

"Okay," Stick replied. "Follow me."

He strolled forward, tail waving, until he came up to the group of three cats. "Hi," he meowed. "There's a cat here who wants to meet you."

All three cats fixed their gaze on Firestar. He dipped his head respectfully. "Greetings. How's the prey running?"

Coal and Snowy exchanged a glance, as if they thought he'd said something odd. Firestar hoped he hadn't sounded too weird.

"You're new around here," Coal mewed. "Where are you from?"

Firestar didn't want to tell these cats about the forest.

What if they decided to invade his home, like BloodClan? "Downstream," he replied, hoping that was vague enough.

"His name's Firestar," Cora added, padding up to his side. "Firestar, meet Snowy, Coal, and Shorty."

"Have you come to stay?" Snowy's brilliant blue gaze was friendly.

"No, I'm just passing through," Firestar told her. "I was with another cat, but we got separated in the storm." Eagerly he turned to Shorty. "I heard what you said about the ginger cat. I think it might have been my friend."

Shorty's whiskers twitched; he got up and came to sniff Firestar. "Could be," he meowed. "She had the same sort of scent as you: trees and leaves and river water."

Firestar took a breath, his heart thudding painfully. "Can you show me where you met her?"

Shorty waved the stump of his tail. "Sure."

"But not tonight." Cora thrust her way between Firestar and Shorty. "Look at you," she added, interrupting Firestar as he tried to protest. "A puff of wind would blow you over. You need a good night's rest and some more prey before you're fit to go anywhere."

Firestar dug his claws into the ground in frustration. *I'm a warrior!* he thought resentfully. *I don't need to rest.* "But Sandstorm might leave," he meowed. He didn't voice his other fear, that Shorty might wander off and Firestar would never see him again.

"Your friend won't go anywhere by night in a strange place," Cora snapped. "Not unless she's flea-brained. Shorty, if you take him with you now, I'll claw off the rest of your tail."

Shorty shrugged good-humoredly. "I can't argue with that," he mewed to Firestar. "Don't worry; I'll take you to the place tomorrow."

Firestar could do nothing but agree. He found a dip in the ground to sleep in, and though he was convinced that worry would keep him awake, he slept almost as soon as he curled up. This time no dreams disturbed him.

He woke the next morning to find himself lying in warm sunlight. Though he hadn't wanted to delay, he had to admit that he felt much better. Springing to his paws he glanced around, but the only cat he could see was Stick, padding over to him with a mouse dangling from his jaws.

"Here you are," he meowed, dropping his prey in front of Firestar. "Eat."

"Where's Shorty?"

Stick flicked his ears. "Dunno."

"But he promised to take me to find Sandstorm!"

"Then he will. Keep your fur on; he'll be back sooner or later."

Firestar wasn't sure. Muttering thanks for the fresh-kill, he crouched down to eat, his senses alert for the first sign of the tabby tom's return. But he was still so weak that exhaustion crept up on him and he slept again.

He woke with a start to see the trees casting long black shadows across the stretch of open ground. Red light washed between them; the sun was sinking again!

Firestar scrambled up, his heart thudding in panic. He spotted Shorty, sitting under the nearest tree, his amber eyes fixed unblinkingly on him.

"Why didn't you wake me?" Firestar demanded.

"What for?" Shorty twitched his whiskers. "Don't worry; we've got plenty of time."

Firestar bit back what he would have liked to say. If he offended this cat, he might never find Sandstorm at all.

"Come back here if your friend's not there," Cora told him, padding up from behind. "We'll ask around and see if we can find out anything else."

"I'll do that," mewed Firestar. "Thanks."

"Okay," meowed Shorty. "Let's go."

The brown tabby leaped over the wall and into another of the confusing passages. Trotting down to the end and around a corner, he squeezed through a gap in a wooden fence. Firestar followed and found himself behind bushes in another Twoleg garden. Night had fallen; yellow light poured from a single square hole in the wall of the Twoleg nest.

"This was the place," Shorty murmured. "The young Two-legs live here. They caught your friend by that grass over there."

He flicked his tail toward a clump of long grass in the middle of the garden. The stems rose for three or four tail-lengths, with plumy tops that glimmered yellow in the strange light. Keeping a cautious eye on the nest, Firestar crept into the open until he reached the clump.

He closed his eyes to concentrate better, and drew in air

over his scent glands. The powerful scent of Twoleg flowers almost swamped everything else, but Firestar could distinguish the scent of Twolegs, several different kinds of prey, and . . . yes! Very faint, and growing stale, but still recognizable.

"Sandstorm!" he breathed. "She was here. She's alive!" *Thank StarClan!* he thought.

Shorty bounded up to him. "Any luck?"

"Yes—yes, it's her. Which way did she go?"

Shorty pointed the stump of his tail toward the opposite fence. "Over there, into the next garden."

Firestar raced across the grass to the fence; to his surprise Shorty kept pace with him. "You don't have to come with me," Firestar meowed.

Shorty flicked his ears. "That's okay. I'll tag along, if you don't mind. Snowy's bound to ask me if we found your friend."

"Thanks," mewed Firestar. Though he didn't say so to Shorty, he was surprised that the rogues were being so helpful. He had been too quick to assume they would be his enemies.

The two cats scrambled over the next fence. Firestar thought he caught another trace of Sandstorm's scent among the clumps of flowers, but the Twoleg scents were very strong here, and there was a powerful aroma of dog. His neck fur lifted when he heard it barking from the nest.

"I've lost her trail," he told Shorty, padding up and down in frustration.

"Let's follow the fence," the tabby tom suggested. "We

might pick up the spot where she left."

"Good idea." Firestar slipped along the bottom of the fence, concealed from the Twoleg nest by thick shrubs, but there were no other signs that Sandstorm had been there, not even the imprint of a paw in the soil. He wished he had Cloudtail with him; the white tom was the best tracker in ThunderClan.

StarClan help me! he prayed, gazing up at the glittering warriors of Silverpelt and wondering if they could see him when he was so far away from the forest.

As he lifted his head, a tuft of fur snagged on the top of the fence caught his eye, and he made out the pale ginger of Sandstorm's pelt.

He pointed with his tail. "That's where she crossed the fence. Come on, Shorty!"

But the tabby rogue was looking uneasy, his claws working in the thick leaf mold under the bushes. "There's a kittypet over there," he meowed. "She's a good fighter, and . . . well, a bit short-tempered."

Firestar couldn't believe that any kittypet could fight well enough to give him trouble. "I can handle it," he promised.

He leaped for the fence, clawed his way to the top, and gave the tuft of fur a quick sniff. Sandstorm's scent flooded over him. The garden below him was overgrown with shrubs and a wild tangle of Twoleg flowers. Trees spread their branches over it, casting deep shadows. Firestar's paws tingled. This garden was almost like the forest; it was just the sort of place where his mate might hide.

"Sandstorm!" he called softly. "Sandstorm, are you there?"

There was no reply. Firestar dropped down into the garden and prowled through the undergrowth, his nose filled with the scents of leaves and flowers and other cats. He had lost Sandstorm's scent again, but he was sure she had to be close by. "Sandstorm!" he called again.

Just behind him a snarl broke the silence. Firestar whirled to see a tortoiseshell kittypet standing a tail-length away. Her back was arched and her teeth bared; her fur bristled, and her quivering tail was fluffed up to twice its size.

"What are you doing in my garden?" she spat.

Firestar gulped; obviously not all kittypets were lazy about defending their territory. "Look, keep your fur on," he began. "I'm only—"

He broke off as the tortoiseshell leaped on him, hissing with rage, and bowled him off his paws.

"Shorty!" he yowled.

He battered at the tortoiseshell with his hind paws, but he still didn't have his full strength, and he couldn't throw her off. His side stung as she raked her claws down it.

"Trespasser!" she hissed in his ear.

Firestar struggled to bring his head around and sink his teeth into her neck. Then from somewhere close by he heard the furious yowl of another cat. Suddenly the tortoiseshell's weight vanished. Firestar lay limp on the ground for a couple of heartbeats, thankful that Shorty had come to his rescue.

Then he looked up and scrambled to his paws with a gasp of amazement. The newcomer wasn't Shorty at all; it was

Sandstorm! The ginger she-cat had flung the tortoiseshell to the ground; she jabbed her hind paws into the kittypet's belly and fastened her teeth into her ear. The kittypet fought furiously for a moment longer, then tore herself away and fled toward the Twoleg nest.

"Sandstorm!" Firestar panted. He stood gazing at his mate; her sides were heaving, and blood welled from scratches on her shoulder.

"Think yourself lucky I turned up in time to save your pelt!" Sandstorm hissed.

"I didn't ask you to!" Firestar flashed back. "I could have taken care of myself."

Sandstorm's lip curled disbelievingly. "Oh, sure."

Firestar stared at her. This wasn't how he had imagined his reunion with Sandstorm would be. "Listen—"

"Is everything okay?" Shorty interrupted; Firestar looked up to see his head popping up over the fence. "Hey! You found her!"

"No, *I* found *him,*" Sandstorm growled. She sounded as if she wished she hadn't. "I'm surprised you even bothered to look for me," she went on to Firestar, her green eyes glittering with hostility. "After all, what's one Clanmate compared with all the nameless cats who are depending on you who knows where? Why didn't you go on looking for them, instead?"

Firestar was too worn-out to quarrel with her any more. Padding over to her, drinking in her warm, familiar scent, he murmured, "I would have searched for you forever. I would never have gone on without you."

Sandstorm gazed at him for a long moment. "I meant it when I said I wanted to come on this journey," she mewed. "But I want to *share* your mission. I want to understand why you need to help this Clan, and play an equal part in finding them."

"But StarClan sent the dream only to me—" Firestar began.

"That's not true," Sandstorm pointed out. "What about Smudge? This Clan must be desperate for help if they would try talking to a kittypet. Surely two cats are better than one?"

Firestar rested his muzzle against hers. He remembered how he had felt when he thought he had lost her forever. Now he knew that he could never complete his journey without Sandstorm by his side.

"Excuse me for interrupting," Shorty meowed from his perch on the fence, "but are you two going to stay down there all night?"

For a heartbeat Firestar met Sandstorm's green gaze. So much passed between them that could never be put into words. Then he tore himself away.

"Sorry," he mewed, leaping to the top of the fence to balance beside Shorty. "Can you show us the way out of here?"

"We need to get back to the river," Sandstorm added as she joined them.

"No problem. Follow me."

Shorty led them back across the gardens. They crossed a small Thunderpath, quiet but lit by the glare of orange

Twoleg lights, and padded down yet another passage between two Twoleg nests.

"Not far now," Shorty announced cheerfully.

At the end of the gardens the passage came out into a rough grassy space. Firestar lifted his muzzle as the scent of the river washed over him. He could hear the soft rush of water in the distance.

"Thank you," he meowed to Shorty. "Thank you for everything. I'd never have found Sandstorm without your help."

Sandstorm dipped her head. "Thanks for scaring off those Twoleg kits, too."

The brown tabby gave his chest fur a few licks to hide his embarrassment. "Good luck." His eyes narrowed. "I reckon you're up to something where you might need all the luck you can get."

"You're right; we do," Sandstorm agreed.

"I hope we might see you again someday," Shorty meowed.

"I hope so too," Firestar replied.

Shorty waved the stump of his tail in farewell. He stood watching at the mouth of the passage while Firestar and Sandstorm padded side by side across the tussocky grass and down to the river.

CHAPTER 14

Throughout the night, Firestar and Sandstorm traveled slowly upstream beneath a claw scratch of moon. They left behind the familiar stretch of river with the Twolegplace standing forlornly in a sea of mud, and the path that led to the deserted Twolegplace. The river shrank and flowed more swiftly, chattering over stones; a thick hedge bordered it, leaving only a narrow path for the cats to pass.

Firestar didn't feel the need to talk; it was enough to have Sandstorm back with him, padding alongside him.

At last the first traces of dawn appeared on the horizon. The sky grew milky pale, and one by one the warriors of StarClan winked out.

"Do you think we should eat now?" Firestar suggested. He didn't want Sandstorm to think he was making all the decisions. "Then we could rest for a bit."

"What?" Sandstorm's green eyes flew wide with shock. "Rest? Eat? Are you completely mouse-brained? We should keep going."

Firestar stared at her. "Well, if that's what you want . . ."

Amusement glimmered in Sandstorm's eyes, and she let

out a tiny snort of laughter. "No, you daft furball, I'm only joking. Eating's a great idea, and as for resting, I'm practically asleep on my paws!"

Flicking her ear with his tail tip, Firestar halted and stretched his jaws wide to taste the air. There was a strong scent of vole. Sandstorm angled her ears forward. "There," she murmured.

Firestar caught sight of the creature pulling itself out of the water a couple of tail lengths farther up the bank. "If we're not careful, it'll go straight back into the river."

"Stay there," Sandstorm breathed.

Slinking up the side of the hedge, she passed the vole and started creeping back toward it. When she was close to it, she leaped to the edge of the river, the water splashing up around her paws. Startled, the vole dashed up the bank, straight into Firestar's paws. He killed it with a swift bite to the neck.

"That was brilliant!" he exclaimed as Sandstorm joined him, shaking her wet paws.

"Don't expect me to make a habit of it," she replied, flicking a droplet of water crossly from her nose. "I'm not a RiverClan cat."

As they shared the vole, the daylight grew stronger and the sun came up. The sky was blue, with only a few faint traces of cloud, high and misty. Firestar felt the warmth of the sun soaking into his fur.

"Let's find a comfortable place to sleep," he suggested when he had finished the last mouthful of vole.

Sandstorm's only reply was a yawn.

Not much farther along the path, they discovered a soft patch of moss among the hedge roots. Sunlight shone through the branches, dappling their pelts as they curled up together. Feeling Sandstorm's tongue rasping along his neck, Firestar relaxed for what felt like the first time in days. He bent his head to his mate's, sharing tongues until sleep drifted over them both.

Firestar stood on the riverbank. It looked like the place where he had fallen asleep, but the hedge wasn't so tall and bushy, and there was no sign of Sandstorm. Panic clawed at him for a moment. Then he realized that he was standing at the edge of a large group of cats. Some of them were sitting at the water's edge, while others lay stretched out as if they were exhausted.

Sound gradually faded up around him, the fretful mewling of kits and wails of distress from older cats.

"How much farther?" a tabby kit was asking his mother.

"My paws are sore!" a little tortoiseshell added.

Their mother, a beautiful gray-furred queen, bent to give them both a comforting lick. "Not far now," she promised them. "And then we'll find a nice new home."

"I don't *want* a new home," the tortoiseshell kit protested. "I want to go back to our camp."

Her mother gave her ears a gentle lick. "Our camp is gone," she mewed. "Twolegs have taken it. But we'll find a better one; you'll see."

The anxiety in her green eyes told Firestar that she wasn't

sure she was telling her kits the truth. He followed her gaze over the cats sprawled on the bank until he spotted the gray-and-white cat he had seen so many times, who had spoken to him in Smudge's garden. He stood commandingly on the brink of the river, his head turned upstream.

"Is this the right way?" he meowed quietly.

A small tabby she-cat, sitting on the bank beside him, replied, "You're our leader, so you have to decide. I've had no signs from StarClan since we left the forest."

"StarClan don't care about us, Fawnstep," growled the gray-and-white cat. "If they did, they would never have let the other Clans drive us out of the forest." He bowed his head. "All we can do is keep going until we find a place to live."

Movement in the corner of his eye distracted Firestar. He froze as a long-furred tabby kit darted straight at him. He waited for it to spot him and raise the alarm, but it bundled past him, so close that their pelts almost brushed, and never noticed him.

Suddenly realizing that none of the cats could see him, Firestar began to pad among them. He was horrified by how thin they were, their ribs visible through dull, ungroomed pelts.

A black-and-white elder was lying on his side, his breath coming in short gasps. "I can't go any farther," he rasped. "You'll have to go on without me."

"Rubbish," a ginger warrior growled. "No cat is staying behind."

The elder closed his eyes. "We should never have left the forest."

A brown tabby she-cat came to stand beside the ginger tom. "We'll find a good place to stay; I promise."

"Better than the one we left," the ginger warrior agreed, lashing his tail. "Without the other Clans to bother us. No more border raids, no more prey stealing. And especially no more Twolegs. We'll have it all to ourselves."

The black-and-white elder let out a faint hiss. "Buzzardtail, there have always been *five* Clans in the forest."

"Not anymore," the ginger tom muttered.

"We'll find you some fresh-kill," the tabby meowed, "and you'll soon feel better." Glancing at the tom, she added, "Let's hunt."

The two cats left their Clanmates and began to prowl up the hedge. A squirrel sat chittering in a tree that spread its branches over the riverbank; the tabby she-cat gave an enormous leap and grabbed it in strong jaws, falling back to the ground with her prey between her paws.

Firestar stared in amazement. What a catch! He had never seen a cat jump so high. At first he was surprised that the ginger tom didn't congratulate her. Then he noticed that both cats had strong, muscular back legs; jumping must have been SkyClan's special skill, just as RiverClan cats could swim well and WindClan cats could run fast after rabbits.

The hunters took their fresh-kill back to the rest of their Clan. A couple of other warriors had killed voles, but it still wasn't enough. He saw the fresh-kill being shared among the elders and mothers with kits first, just as he would expect from cats who followed the warrior code.

When the Clan had devoured the prey in a few ravenous bites, the gray-and-white leader padded into their midst. "It's time to go on," he meowed.

The whole Clan rose to their paws. The gray-and-white cat took the lead, heading upriver. The ginger tom and the tabby supported the black-and-white elder. As they limped past Firestar, he realized he could see river and grass through each pelt. The SkyClan cats seemed to walk one by one into a bank of pale mist, and Firestar found himself blinking awake in the sunlight under the hedge.

"I *must* help them," he murmured aloud. "Whatever happens, SkyClan must be found."

For the next three sunrises Firestar and Sandstorm journeyed on. The river grew steadily narrower, foaming around sharp gray rocks. Everywhere Firestar could see traces of the huge wave that had swept Sandstorm away: scattered branches, debris caught in the hedge, drying puddles left on the path. In the shallows under the bank, moorhens called miserably for lost chicks.

"Do you think it's much farther?" Sandstorm meowed. "If the river gets much narrower, it'll vanish altogether."

"You're right. We should start looking for signs of SkyClan," Firestar replied.

"What sort of signs? Border scent markings?"

Firestar shook his head. "I doubt it. That would mean

there's still a Clan protecting its territory. The SkyClan cat I spoke to said the Clan had been scattered."

"But there must be *some* SkyClan cats left," Sandstorm pointed out. "Otherwise what are we doing here?"

"Maybe there'll be just a few cats, trying to live by the warrior code," Firestar suggested.

Sandstorm nodded, then sighed. "I wonder. Or maybe they don't remember who they are anymore."

Looking ahead, Firestar saw the jagged tops of a range of hills. They didn't look as sharp and bleak as Highstones, but they were higher than WindClan's moorland. It might have looked like a refuge to a fleeing Clan who wanted to be far away from other cats and Twolegs.

The path grew sandy, staining their paws orange and stinging their eyes when a breeze picked up. The sun was still strong; Firestar and Sandstorm were glad of the shade from trees that grew along the hedge.

Firestar felt his neck fur begin to bristle as two or three Twoleg nests came into view. Was this the beginning of another Twolegplace to get lost in? The path led right past the front of the nests, and a litter of Twoleg kits were running up and down.

Sandstorm touched his shoulder with her tail tip. "Let's see if we can get around."

She found a gap in the hedge and led the way through into a field of rough grass. The two cats padded across it, skirting the fences of Twoleg gardens, until they came to a narrow Thunderpath.

Firestar paused; the reek of monsters was faint and stale. He glanced at Sandstorm. "Do you think it's safe to cross?"

Sandstorm gave a quick glance up and down, then darted across. Firestar followed hard on her paws. On the other side was more rough grass, and it didn't take long to skirt the remaining Twoleg nests until the river came in sight again.

As they drew closer, Firestar could hear the squeals of more Twoleg kits. He let out a faint hiss of annoyance; he thought they had dodged all the Twolegs by avoiding the nests. Once he reached the path again he could see that here the river widened into a round, shallow pool. Several Twoleg kits were bouncing around in the shallows, shrieking happily and splashing one another with water. On the bank two older Twoleg females sat on pelts.

"Playing in water!" Sandstorm wrinkled her nose with disgust as she came to stand beside Firestar. "I always knew Twolegs were mad. They'll freeze to death without any hair on their pelts."

Before she finished speaking, a louder screech came from the young Twolegs. A couple of them bounded out of the water and dashed toward Firestar and Sandstorm with their paws outstretched, sending drops of water flying.

"Run!" Firestar meowed.

The first Twoleg kit nearly grabbed him as he whisked away. Behind him, he heard a yowl from one of the older Twoleg females. Glancing back, he saw that she had risen to her paws and was calling the young Twolegs, who trailed back toward her. Still, he and Sandstorm kept running until the river curved away and the Twoleg kits were left behind.

At last they halted, sides heaving, where an elder bush cast deep shade over the riverbank.

"I can hear something," Sandstorm whispered.

Firestar pricked his ears. From somewhere ahead came a roaring sound like the waterfall in RiverClan territory. Cautiously he led the way around the next bend.

In front of him, water slid in a smooth curve over the top of a cliff, turning to white foam as it tumbled over jutting rocks and crashed into a pool below. The air was full of mist, splitting the sunlight into tiny dancing rainbows.

Firestar stood still for a moment, enjoying the cool spray as it soaked into his hot fur. Meanwhile Sandstorm padded up to the edge of the pool and ventured out onto an overhanging rock.

"Be careful!" Firestar called out, his heart lurching as he imagined her falling into the churning pool. "The rocks will be slippery."

Sandstorm waved her tail to show she'd heard him; Firestar hoped she wasn't annoyed that he'd tried to warn her. A couple of heartbeats later, the ginger she-cat darted a paw down into the water; silver flashed in the air, and a fish lay wriggling on the rock. Sandstorm planted a paw on it to stop it from flopping back into the pool.

"Hey, I thought you said you weren't a RiverClan cat," Firestar teased as he bounded up to her.

Sandstorm picked the fish up in her jaws and joined him on the bank. "The stupid creature practically came up and begged to be caught," she told him, dropping her prey at his paws.

ThunderClan cats didn't usually eat fish, but Firestar found the unfamiliar taste delicious as he devoured his share. Cleaning his whiskers when he had finished, he looked up at the cliff face beside the waterfall. Moss-covered rocks jutted out of it, with clumps of fern spilling over them.

"It doesn't look too hard to climb," he mewed. "We'd better try, before the sun goes down."

He started to claw his way up the rocks, anxiety throbbing through him as he struggled to keep his balance. The water thundered down less than a tail-length away; if they slipped into it they would be flung into the pool below. Where the rocks were bare they were slick with spray, and the moss pulled away when Firestar tried to put his weight on it. Ferns slapped him in the face, showering him with drops of water.

Dragging himself onto a flat rock, he paused for a moment to rest, his flanks heaving as he fought for breath. Looking back to check on Sandstorm, he spotted her balanced precariously on a boulder at the bottom of a sheer slab of rock.

"Are you stuck?" he called to her. "Hang on; I'll come down and help."

Sandstorm gazed up at him and bared her teeth in a hiss that was drowned by the thunder of the water. "Stay where you are," she called back. "I can manage."

Firestar flicked his tail irritably. Why did Sandstorm always have to prove that she could cope on her own? "Don't be mouse-brained. You can't—"

"I said I can manage!" Sandstorm interrupted. "It's no good putting us both in danger. One of us has to survive to find SkyClan."

Before Firestar could respond, his mate launched herself upward, snagging her claws in a clump of moss above her head. As the moss started to give way, she scrabbled with her hind paws until she reached a deep crack in the rock. From there she managed to spring across to where Firestar stood waiting, his heart pounding with alarm.

"See?" Sandstorm shook herself, scattering drops of water from her pelt. "I told you I'd be fine."

Firestar pressed his muzzle against hers and tried to stop his legs from trembling. Then he began to climb again. His breath came fast and shallow, his pelt bristling with tension by the time he hauled himself up over the cliff edge and collapsed onto level ground. A heartbeat later Sandstorm joined him and flopped down by his side. He felt her warm breath on his ear.

"Sorry," she murmured.

The sun was close to setting; the river reflected the red sky, barred with the long shadows of trees that lay across it. Firestar and Sandstorm padded on upstream; the river grew narrower still, and the banks rose until they were traveling through a sandy gorge, close to the edge of the water. It was smaller than the gorge at the edge of WindClan territory, but the sides were just as steep, and although there was still light in the sky they were soon walking through shadow.

"We'd better find somewhere to spend the night,"

Sandstorm suggested. "If there are any signs of SkyClan here, we could miss them in the dark."

As much as Firestar wanted to keep going, he knew that what she said was sensible. They found a small cave in the side of the gorge, sheltered by a stunted gorse bush, and crawled into it. The sandy floor was more comfortable than Firestar expected, and it was not long before he slept with Sandstorm's sweet scent all around him.

Daylight filtering through the spiky gorse woke him. Alarm stabbed him when he saw that Sandstorm was not there. He pushed his way past the thorny branches and emerged beside the river, blinking in the bright sunlight and shaking seeds from his pelt. To his relief, Sandstorm was trotting toward him.

"I thought I'd hunt," she mewed as she came up to him, an annoyed look in her eyes. "But I haven't found any prey. There's hardly anywhere up here for them to live."

"Don't worry. We'll carry on and hunt on the way. There's bound to be *something.*"

Sandstorm's only response was a sniff. Firestar knew how proud she was of her hunting skills; it was unusual for her not to bring back any prey at all.

In full daylight he could see that their surroundings were very different from the lush territory below the waterfall. The sides of the gorge had turned into sandy cliffs, with a few straggly bushes and clumps of tough grass rooted in cracks. The path beside the river almost vanished on both sides, so the cats had to scramble over boulders in order to keep close to the water. Though they kept on stopping to scent the air, there was only the faintest trace of prey.

"This is no good," Firestar meowed after a while. "No cats could live this close to the water, with no space for a camp. We'd better climb to the top of the gorge."

This time the climb was easier; although the sandy cliff was smooth and slippery, there were cracks and occasional shallow ledges to give them plenty of pawholds. When Firestar scrambled over the edge wind buffeted his pelt, and he bounded a few pawsteps away from the cliff in case he was blown over. He found himself looking out over a wide stretch of sandy earth, with patches of scrubby grass dotted with stunted trees. In the distance he could just make out the walls of a Twolegplace, and the glitter of monsters speeding along a Thunderpath.

"We'll stay away from there," he muttered as Sandstorm climbed up to join him.

His mate was already scenting the air. "Rabbits!"

Firestar didn't feel too hopeful. He was used to stalking prey in thick woodland; he wasn't a WindClan cat, swift enough to run it down in the open. "Let's keep going," he mewed. "There might be a better place to hunt farther on."

As they padded along the edge of the gorge, his paws began to tingle. He could smell cats! Tasting the air carefully, he tried to pick out the SkyClan scent that was familiar from his encounters with the Clan leader. But these scents were completely different.

Sandstorm had drawn a few paces ahead, and had paused

at the foot of a tree to sniff the bark. "Come and look at this," she called, beckoning with her tail.

Bounding up to her, Firestar saw long claw marks scored into the bark. The cat scent was stronger here, too.

"A cat made those marks," Sandstorm mewed, her green eyes gleaming.

Firestar nodded. "One with long, sharp claws, by the look of it. Come on," he meowed, eagerly drawing air over his scent glands again. "Let's see what else we can find."

A few pawsteps farther on, a cloud of flies buzzed into the air when he almost stumbled onto the half-eaten body of a rabbit.

"Ugh!" Backing away, he swiped his tongue over his jaws. "Crow-food."

Sandstorm examined the dead rabbit from a distance. "Some cat killed that. It didn't die naturally, and there's cat scent on it. So there are cats around here who hunt for prey."

Firestar made himself pad forward again and give the carcass a more careful scrutiny. "I'd guess the cat was hunting alone," he meowed. "That would explain why it didn't finish its meal."

"And they must be fast, like WindClan, to catch rabbits."

Firestar retreated, and they set out again along the edge of the gorge. "The scent on that rabbit was different from the scent by the tree. These are rogues, not Clan cats."

"But isn't that what the SkyClan cat said?" Sandstorm asked. "That his Clan had been scattered?"

Firestar didn't reply. Although the signs of cats were encouraging, he had never really considered, until now, what it would be like to put a Clan together from rogues and kittypets. He would have to treat every cat as if he were training an apprentice—no, a kit, because these cats would have no knowledge of the warrior code, or what it meant to live in a Clan. The task was so daunting that for a heartbeat he thought of turning around to go home. Then he gritted his teeth with determination. He wouldn't give up his quest until he had discovered exactly what cats lived here, and whether there was any hope of restoring SkyClan. But right now he felt as if his quest would never end, and he would never see the forest again.

Sunhigh was past when they came to a sandy bank with several rabbit holes leading down into the earth. The scent of rabbits grew stronger. Suddenly one burst out from behind a gorse bush and fled along the edge of the gorge. Firestar raced after it but Sandstorm flashed past him, and he slowed to watch while she chased the prey and brought it down.

"Well done!" he meowed, padding up to meet Sandstorm as she dragged the rabbit back. "Now you're a WindClan cat!"

When he and Sandstorm had shared the fresh-kill, Firestar felt full-fed for the first time in days. If his mate could catch prey here, so could the SkyClan cats.

Sandstorm blinked at him. "You're excited, aren't you?"

Firestar nodded. "Every pawstep we take is bringing us closer."

"I'm glad I'm here with you."

Firestar touched his nose to her ear. "I'm glad you're here, too. I don't think I could do this without you."

They spent that night curled among the roots of a spreading oak tree, one of the few full-sized trees growing on this windswept cliff. With the scents of sap and bark wreathing around him, the rustle of leaves in his ears, Firestar could almost imagine that he was at home in the forest.

Sunlight shining into his face woke him. His eyes flew open in alarm; how had he managed to sleep for so long? Then he realized that the roots where he had settled to sleep had vanished, replaced by the sandy walls and roof of a cave. Sunlight was angling in through the opening, a few tail-lengths away. The air around him was warm. He could hear the murmurs of many sleeping cats, and SkyClan scent surrounded him. Raising his head, he saw the furry shapes of warriors curled up among moss and bracken.

A shadow fell across the cave, and Firestar saw a muscular tomcat outlined against the light. He recognized the ginger tom he had seen in his vision by the river. Fear clawed at him; what would these cats do to him when they found him in their den? But the ginger tom stared straight at him without seeing him, and Firestar realized that once again he was invisible to the SkyClan cats.

"Come on," the ginger warrior meowed. "It's time you were moving."

All around Firestar the warriors began to stir and raise

their heads. One of them—the brown tabby she-cat who had caught the squirrel—got up and arched her back in a long stretch. "Keep your fur on, Buzzardtail. We're coming."

"Okay, Fernpelt, you can lead the dawn patrol," the ginger tom went on. "Pick a couple of others to go with you, and keep your eyes open for that fox we spotted on the other side of the gorge."

Fernpelt flicked her tail. "Don't worry. If we come across it, it'll be crow-food."

The ginger tom stalked across the cave and prodded a sandy colored she-cat with one paw. "Up you get, Mousefang. You're coming hunting with me, and we'll pick up Oakpaw on the way. Nightfur," he added to a black tom on the other side of the cave, "you can lead another hunting patrol."

By now all the cats had risen to their paws and were shaking moss and bracken from their pelts. "This is our home now," meowed Buzzardtail, glancing around approvingly. "You know where to go. . . ."

As he spoke, he and all the rest of the cats began to fade. For a heartbeat Firestar saw the sandy walls of the cave appearing through their pelts; then the cave walls dissolved too, and he was blinking awake in the gray dawn. Buzzardtail's voice still echoed in his ears. *You know where to go. . . .*

Firestar padded out from the shelter of the tree. The sky shone with a milky light, and a gentle breeze teased his fur. All his senses strained to pick up traces of the lost Clan. His paws tingled with their nearness; would this be the day when he found them?

"I'm here," he mewed aloud.

Turning back to where Sandstorm still slept, he spotted a mouse scuffling among the oak roots. He dropped into the hunter's crouch and pounced on it, killing it swiftly with a bite to the throat.

He woke Sandstorm by trailing the end of his tail across her nose. "Time to get up," he announced, as her whiskers twitched and she opened her eyes. "There's fresh-kill waiting for you."

When they continued their journey, they had to skirt thickets of gorse and bramble that grew close to the edge of the cliff. Firestar still picked up occasional traces of cats, but nothing to tell him where the Clan had gone.

Then as the bushes dwindled, Sandstorm padded up to the edge of the cliff again. Firestar, who had scented a mouse among the brambles, heard her let out a gasp. He whirled around to see her staring down into the gorge.

"Firestar, come and see!" she exclaimed. "The river has vanished!"

CHAPTER 15

Abandoning his prey, Firestar rushed to her side and looked down. The sides of the gorge sloped down steeply to a narrow, bone-dry valley strewn with reddish rocks. There wasn't even a trickle of water.

His heart began to pound. "We must have passed the place where SkyClan camped," he mewed to Sandstorm. "The gray-and-white cat told me to follow the river."

Sandstorm's tail lashed. "Mouse dung! We'd better climb down and head back along the gorge."

Firestar took the lead as they climbed carefully down the steep cliff. Loose pebbles skidded beneath their paws; Firestar tried not to think about slipping all the way down in a flailing tangle of legs and tail, ending up broken at the bottom. He tried to step lightly, picking his way from one jutting rock to the next and using his tail for balance.

By now the sun was high in the sky, and the rocky sides of the gorge reflected the heat. The hot ground scorched Firestar's paws. Panting, he felt as if his fur were about to burst into flame. He disturbed a lizard basking on a rock; it whisked down a crack when his shadow fell on it.

"At least we won't starve," he commented, pointing at the creature with his tail.

Sandstorm wrinkled her nose. "Only ShadowClan eat scaly things," she meowed. "I'd have to be really hungry before I tried it."

At last they reached the bottom of the gorge and began padding back the way they had come, weaving among the boulders. Firestar's pelt prickled; nothing grew in this part of the gorge except for a few clumps of wiry grass and stunted bushes; there was no shelter, no undergrowth to conceal the cats from hostile eyes.

"It's a good thing we're not black or white," Sandstorm murmured. "At least our pelts will help to hide us."

Firestar nodded tensely. "Stay alert. We don't know what might be lurking down here."

As the sun slid down the sky, the shadow of the cliff fell across them. Firestar breathed more easily as the air grew cooler. He began to make out the sound of water up ahead. He took a deep breath, detecting the first traces of moisture in the dry air.

Sandstorm's tail went up. "I can hear the river!"

Wishing for the soft ground of the forest instead of these sharp pebbles, Firestar picked up the pace until he and Sandstorm were bounding among the rocks. Rounding a bend, he stopped dead when he saw a pile of reddish boulders blocking the gorge. The lapping of water was louder, but he couldn't see it.

He scrambled up the pile of rocks, claws scraping on the

crumbling stone, and peered cautiously over the top. Directly below him, water flowed smoothly out of a gaping black hole into a round pool before winding away down the gorge and out of sight.

Sandstorm clambered up beside Firestar. "So this is where the river begins."

Firestar glanced around, half expecting to see the pale shapes of SkyClan warriors watching him from the cliffs. There were no cats in sight, but halfway up the side of the gorge he spotted several caves, dark, narrow openings tucked underneath the cliff. Narrow trails zigzagged across the cliff face, leading from one cave to the next.

Firestar remembered his dream of waking among SkyClan warriors in a sandy cave. The deputy's words echoed once more in his mind. *This is our home now. You know where to go.*

"We are here," he told Sandstorm quietly.

"You think SkyClan lived in those caves?" Sandstorm sounded dubious. "Climbing up and down the cliffs every day?"

"I think so."

Sandstorm rose to her paws. "Okay, but I'm not going to look until we've had a drink. My mouth feels as dry as the gorge."

She began to pick her way down the pile of boulders on the other side, following the river until she reached the pool where the river flowed out. Firestar joined her as she crouched down and began to lap. The water was icy cold; it soaked through his scorched fur and Firestar thought that he would never want to stop drinking.

The water flowed swiftly but without making a sound. A blue-green light sparkled under the surface, but further under the heap of boulders everything was dark. The cave gaped like an open mouth, silently waiting. . . .

Firestar shivered and sat up, shaking droplets from his whiskers. Sandstorm was staring at something on the dried mud beside the pool.

"Look at that," she mewed.

In the mud were the clear pawprints of a cat! "It could be a rogue, just passing through," Firestar pointed out, "or even an adventurous kittypet."

Sandstorm sniffed. "*Very* adventurous, for a kittypet. Let's have a look at those caves."

The side of the gorge was even steeper here than where they had climbed down. Firestar struggled to keep his footing among the loose pebbles, convinced he was about to slip. After the first few tail-lengths he left the shadows behind, and the blazing heat struck him like a blow. Dust puffed up under his paws, making him as thirsty as ever.

But when he reached the first of the trails, the going became easier. It looked as if the cliff face had been scraped out to expose a flattened trail that led back and forth in a gentle slope, connecting each of the caves. Firestar headed for the highest entrance, which also looked to be the biggest. He pressed close to the cliff, avoiding the drop on the other side. Sandstorm was just behind him, puffing her breath out in a sigh of relief as she followed him onto the level floor of the cave.

Firestar stared around him. He had been here before. The

cave was several times the size of his den in the ThunderClan camp. Inside it was cool and shadowy, with sheer walls and a sandy floor. It was sheltered from rain or blistering heat, and it would be difficult for enemies to reach.

For a few heartbeats he stood still, imagining how the SkyClan cats would have felt when they reached this refuge. Had they been joyful to find shelter, or wary of danger lurking in the shadows? Had they longed for their camp in the forest? Or were they just too tired to care? For a moment they were all around him again; he could hear their mews and feel their pelts brushing against his own.

"What do you think of those?" Sandstorm asked, pointing with her tail to a few shallow scrapes in the floor at the back of the cave. "Filled with moss and bracken, they'd make pretty good nests."

"Yes, but where would they find moss and bracken around here?" Firestar asked. "I didn't see any growing in the gorge."

"There might be some on the cliffs."

Firestar nodded, tasting the air again. The cave was full of animal scents: he could discern mouse and vole, and even cat, but none of them smelled fresh. He padded forward, nosing around the scrapes Sandstorm had spotted; only the memory of his dream assured him that they really were nests, not just natural dips in the cave floor.

"Let's go and explore some of the other caves." Firestar headed for the entrance, only to stop dead a tail-length inside. His heart had started to thump again. "Look at that," he whispered.

At one side of the entrance was a narrow column of rock, attached on one side to the cave wall. Thickly scored down the lower half were the marks of claws. Hardly daring to breathe, Firestar padded across, raised his forepaws, and placed his own claws in the marks.

"A perfect fit!" Sandstorm breathed.

She was right. Firestar's claws slipped into the marks as if he had made them himself. He shivered to think that his paws were resting where those other cats had been, so long ago.

"Look at those other marks." Sandstorm padded up to the stone trunk and laid one paw against it, close to the bottom.

For the first time Firestar noticed some tiny scratches running sideways across the trunk. "Maybe kits made them."

Sandstorm looked doubtful. "Why would they scratch crosswise, instead of up and down?"

Firestar shrugged. "Why do kits do anything? Anyway, it doesn't matter. This is the place," he meowed, suddenly more confident than ever. "This is where SkyClan made their camp."

Sandstorm's green eyes glinted. "Then where are they now?"

They spent the rest of the day exploring the other caves. Firestar's paws tingled as they kept discovering more of the claw marks, proof that all these caves had once been inhabited by cats.

"Look!" Sandstorm murmured in the next cave they visited, resting her tail tip gently against the wall. "Nothing but tiny marks! This must have been the nursery."

Firestar glanced back at the entrance; a boulder blocked most of it, hiding it from hostile eyes and keeping it cool even in blazing sunlight. "The kits and their mothers would have been safe here."

Sandstorm padded farther into the cave, her pale ginger pelt a blur in the shadows. "There are bigger scrapes in the floor, too," she reported. "Just the right size for a queen and her litter."

Further down the cliff face they found smaller caves that might have been dens for the apprentices, the medicine cat, and the Clan leader. Finally they returned to the first cave.

"I guess this was the warriors' den," Firestar meowed, not wanting to bring up his dream. "There's plenty of space, and it's near the top of the cliff. They'd be able to protect the rest of the Clan if foxes or Twolegs tried to get down."

Sandstorm thoughtfully tasted the air. "There's cat scent here," she announced. "Not fresh, but it's all we've smelled so far. I think at least one cat was here in the last moon or so."

Firestar padded slowly around the cave and spotted something white glimmering in a crevice between a boulder and the wall. He poked one paw into the gap and drew out a heap of tiny white bones. "A mouse or a vole," he commented to Sandstorm, who had come to have a look. "You're right; cats have been here, but it doesn't look as if they live here permanently. If they did, the scent would be fresh."

"I wonder why they come?" Sandstorm didn't sound as if she expected an answer, and Firestar couldn't give her one.

By now the sun had gone down and the gorge was filled

with shadows. They climbed the last few tail-lengths to the cliff top and hunted among the bushes along the edge. When they had eaten, they returned to the warriors' den for the night.

"I'm so exhausted, I could sleep for a moon." Sandstorm sighed, turning around in one of the shallow scrapes and curling up with her tail over her nose.

Her steady breathing soon told Firestar that she was asleep. He sat beside her, gazing around the cave and picturing the way it had been in his dream: warm, breathing bodies in nests of moss and bracken, and one cat, awake as he was, on watch.

He blinked, and the cats vanished. Pale silver light from the half-moon washed into the cave, lapping at his fur. But there was no sound, no flicker of a pale pelt to disturb the shadows.

Did SkyClan scatter too long ago? he wondered. *Is there any hope of finding their descendants? Or have I come too late?*

CHAPTER 16

The sound of rustling and faint voices woke Firestar. Stretching his jaws in a yawn, he thought it must be time to get up and make sure the dawn patrol had left. When he blinked his eyes open he saw the unfamiliar cave with its sandy walls and bare scrapes in the rock, and the memory of where he was flooded back into his mind. For a moment he had thought that he was back in his old den under the Highrock, sleeping in warm moss and bracken with sunlight filtering through the curtain of lichen at the entrance. Instead he was in a deserted cave that had once been part of the SkyClan camp, with Sandstorm stirring at his side.

Sandstorm raised her head. "I thought I heard something."

"So did I." Firestar sprang to his paws. He could still hear movement from the cliff top, and when he tasted the air he picked up a strong, fresh scent of cat.

Raising his tail to warn Sandstorm to stay still and quiet, he padded toward the entrance. Daylight slanted into the cave from a pale sky; the sun hadn't yet risen above the gorge, and the air was cool. He peered out of the cave mouth. Looking up, he was just in time to see a dark tabby tail whisking out of sight into the bushes that grew on the cliff top.

"Is he there?" a cat meowed nervously.

"I think so!"

Stretching his neck out further, Firestar took a breath to call out, but before he could make a sound a pebble flew down from the cliff top, skimming past less than a mouse-length from his nose, and pattered down into the gorge. More sounds of scrabbling came from above, and a half-stifled *mrrow* of laughter.

The first voice called out, "Did you find what you were looking for in the sky, stupid old furball?"

"I'm not surprised you don't have any friends, dog-breath!" the second voice added. "Bet you can't catch us!"

Another stone came bouncing down the cliff, barely missing Firestar, and he heard the sound of two cats scrambling through the bushes with loud, triumphant meows.

Furious, he launched himself upward. But by the time he clawed his way over the cliff and thrust his way through the undergrowth, the two cats were too far away to be worth chasing. He spotted them, a dark tabby and a tortoiseshell, racing toward the distant Twolegplace.

"Mouse dung!" he exclaimed.

Rustling in the bushes behind him announced the arrival of Sandstorm. "What was all that about?"

"I don't know. But if any Clanmate of mine spoke to me like that, they would spend the next moon searching the elders for ticks."

Sandstorm rubbed her muzzle against his. "Well, they

don't know that you're Firestar, leader of ThunderClan," she consoled him. "For all they know, we might be rogues trying to muscle in on their territory."

"I'm not so sure." Firestar gazed across the scrubby grassland to the Twolegplace, where the two cats had now vanished. "They thought there was only one cat there, so they can't have seen us arrive. And their insults meant something; they seemed to know exactly who they were talking to."

"Then there must be another cat around here," Sandstorm mewed. "Maybe the one who left those bones in the cave?"

"Maybe." He turned back into the thicket and began to explore more thoroughly. He managed to pick up several different cat scents among the bushes, as well as mice and birds.

"No foxes or badgers," Sandstorm commented, coming face-to-face with him around the trunk of a holly bush.

"At least that's something," Firestar mewed. "Most of the cat scents are kittypet, including fresh ones from our visitors. I'd like to talk to them. They might know if cats once lived in the caves."

"They might." Sandstorm gave a disgusted sniff. "But will they be willing to tell us?"

Firestar didn't reply. Turning away from Twolegplace, the two cats hunted in the bushes, then climbed down the stony trails into the bottom of the gorge. Reaching the river, Firestar spotted more caves on the opposite side, lower down than the ones they had already explored.

"I wonder if SkyClan used those caves too," he meowed, pointing with his tail.

"They must have been a big Clan, if they did," Sandstorm replied. "There's plenty of space in the caves we've already seen."

"Still, we'd better check them out."

They climbed the pile of rocks where the river flowed out, and crossed to the far side of the gorge. There was no cat scent in the other caves, and no evidence of claw marks or bones to suggest that cats had ever been there.

"I expect it's because these caves don't get much sun," Sandstorm suggested. "It'd be cold and dark for most of the day."

Firestar thought she must be right. He was thankful to leave the last cave and head for the river again.

A sudden yowl from the top of the gorge froze his paws to the ground. Four Twolegs stood outlined against the sky.

"This way—quick!" Sandstorm hissed at him from the shelter of a boulder.

Firestar bounded over to her and crouched by her side, hoping the Twolegs hadn't spotted him. Peering out, he saw that they were all young males. Yowling loudly, they clambered down the side of the gorge as far as the pool. Firestar didn't know whether they were looking for him and Sandstorm; he could feel her heart racing as he pressed against her side.

Then he saw the young Twolegs pulling off some of their pelts. With the loudest yowl of all, one of them leaped from a boulder at the side of the pool and plunged into the water. His three friends jumped in after him, then climbed out of the pool, shaking water from their head fur, and then leaped in again.

"Thank StarClan!" Firestar let out a sigh of relief. "They don't know we're here. They've just come to play in the water, like those others downstream."

Sandstorm shrugged. "I keep telling you, Twolegs are mad."

They stayed out of sight until the young Twolegs were tired of their game. Once they had put their pelts back on and begun the climb back to the cliff top, the two cats ventured out of the shelter of the boulder.

"I wonder if they come down here a lot," Sandstorm mewed. "SkyClan wouldn't have been happy living so close to Twolegs."

"True," Firestar agreed. "But at least they make enough noise. A cat would always know when they're coming."

He leaped across the rocks to the opposite side of the river, thankful to emerge into sunlight again. "I haven't seen any fish here," he remarked as Sandstorm joined him.

"I haven't seen any fish since below the waterfall," she meowed. "Prey here is mice and voles and birds. And maybe a few rabbits."

"And most of that at the top of the cliffs," Firestar mused. "It can't have been an easy life."

"Maybe that's why they're not here now."

Firestar wondered if she was right. He and Sandstorm had managed to feed themselves without much trouble, but would there be enough for a whole Clan?

They were climbing back to the warriors' cave when Sandstorm halted. "There's another trail here," she announced, angling her ears toward a narrow, stony path that led slantwise up the rock. Firestar could just make out faint pawprints in the dust, as if at least one cat had been that way recently. "I didn't notice it before. Do you think we should follow it?"

Firestar nodded. "It can't do any harm."

The trail led farther up the gorge until it ended at a deep cleft in the cliff face. Beyond the cleft was a flat rock that jutted out over the gorge.

Sandstorm glanced back at Firestar, looking puzzled. "It's a dead end. Why did they come this way when there's nothing here?"

Firestar studied the ledge, the rock, and the sheer walls of the rift. A cat who lost its footing here would go plummeting right down to the floor of the gorge.

"I'm not sure," he replied. "Maybe . . ."

He crouched down, then pushed off with powerful hind legs and leaped, to land with all four paws on the flat rock.

"Firestar!" Sandstorm yowled. "Have you lost your mind?"

He didn't reply, but stood upright on the rock, facing into the breeze that ruffled his fur and brought to him the mingled scents of stone and water, undergrowth and prey. If he looked up the gorge he could see the dry valley growing narrower still as it wound upward; just below was the place where water flowed out from the heap of red rocks, and he followed the river with his gaze until it became lost in the misty distance. The rock beneath his paws was smooth and warm; he wanted to sprawl there and bask in the sunlight, as his Clan did at Sunningrocks.

"Come over!" he called to Sandstorm. "It's wonderful!"

Sandstorm paused, her tail flicking. Then she seemed to make her mind up, gathered herself for the leap, and landed neatly beside Firestar. "Do you want us to get our necks broken?" she asked crossly.

"Just look!" Firestar swept his tail around. "A cat on watch here could see danger coming from anywhere."

As Sandstorm scanned the gorge, her annoyed look vanished and the fur on her shoulders lay flat again. "You're right," she admitted. With a sudden change of mood she lay on her side and dabbed one paw playfully toward Firestar. "It's great up here. Why don't we rest for a bit?"

Firestar settled down beside her on the sun-warmed stone, feeling the heat soak into his fur. Drowsily sharing tongues with his mate, he found his mind drifting back to Sunningrocks and the forest. There would be a Gathering soon, and the other Clans would discover that he had left. What would they do then? Firestar felt his paws itching to carry him home, and had to remind himself that SkyClan still needed him. If he ever found them . . .

As the sun sank they hunted again and ate their prey before they returned to the warriors' cave.

"Where are all the cats we scented?" Firestar wondered. "We haven't seen a single one, not since those rude kittypets first thing this morning."

Sandstorm limped inside the cave and rasped her tongue over one paw. "I'm not surprised they don't come here. This isn't a good place for cats. Okay, there's water and shelter, but prey is hard to come by. My paws are rubbed sore from scrambling up and down rocks all day. I can't even find any dock to rub on them. *And* my claws are nearly wrenched out from hauling myself into caves."

Firestar's paws were sore too, with dust and grit stuck between the pads. He longed for the cool touch of lush grass and fern. For a couple of heartbeats he was tempted to climb down and soothe his paws by wading in the shallows at the edge of the river, but he would only have the long climb back afterward.

"SkyClan must have had paws made of stone if they lived here," Sandstorm added as she finished cleaning one paw and started on another.

Firestar was about to agree with her when he remembered his dream of SkyClan beside the river, and how one cat had jumped up powerfully into a tree. That skill would come in useful here, too, to leap from boulders and into caves without scraping their pads and claws on the rough stone.

Suddenly curious, he padded to the cave entrance and examined the rocks outside. There were fresh scratch marks that he and Sandstorm had made, but hardly any old markings that might have been made by SkyClan. They would have jumped up and down the cliff face instead of having to scramble; even the leap to the flat rock would have been easy for them.

"It wouldn't suit us here," he meowed slowly to Sandstorm. "But it suited SkyClan. They knew how to jump. They already had the skills they needed. This was their home—but where are they now?"

Mist lay thick in the gorge and pressed against the cliff face when Firestar woke the next morning. He looked out cautiously, half expecting another stone to be hurled at him by the kittypets. But everything was silent, even the sound of the river deadened by the fog.

He roused Sandstorm, and they climbed to the cliff top to hunt. Prey scent was harder to pick up in the cool, damp air; Firestar prowled through the thickets without success. "Not even a mouse tail!" he muttered.

Frustrated, he emerged from the bushes and stared across the open ground toward Twolegplace, wondering what the chances would be of tracking down a rabbit. Then he heard a fluttering of wings; glancing to one side, he spotted a sparrow pecking at the ground underneath a bush.

As silently as he could he glided forward, one paw after another, gradually closing the distance between himself and his prey. He was readying himself to pounce when there was a commotion in the bushes and another cat burst out, front paws extended toward the sparrow.

The bird let out a loud alarm call and took off; the newcomer sprang up at once in a tremendous leap. His claws just grazed the sparrow's wings as it fluttered to safety in a tree. A couple of feathers spiraled down. The cat, a dark brown rogue, stood panting, gazing up at the bird and lashing his tail.

Stiff-legged with fury, Firestar stalked up to him until the two cats were standing nose-to-nose. "That was my prey," Firestar hissed. His frustration spilled over; he was hungry, he and Sandstorm had traveled all this way to find nothing but empty caves, and now this mangy, crow-food-eating tom had just frightened away his first chance of food that day.

"Rubbish," the rogue retorted. "It was mine."

Firestar let out a snort of disgust. "I would have caught it if you hadn't come crashing through the bushes like that. Has no cat ever taught you to hunt?"

The rogue's neck fur bristled and he peeled back his lips in a snarl. Firestar arched his back, hissing in anger and flashing out a paw with claws extended. For a heartbeat both cats stood frozen, glaring angrily at each other. Firestar braced himself to spring, but then the rogue flattened his ears and took a couple of paces back. Letting out a last snarl, he whipped around and slunk off down the line of bushes.

"Oh, great!" At the sound of Sandstorm's voice Firestar turned to see her poking her head out from behind a bramble bush. "We're supposed to be talking to the local cats, not scaring them off."

Firestar's fur grew hot with embarrassment. He glanced after the rogue, only to see the stocky brown shape bounding away along the edge of the gorge.

"Sorry," he meowed. "I suppose I was a bit hasty. But it should have been obvious that the sparrow was mine." He gave his chest fur a few quick licks to help himself calm down.

"I'm not used to sharing territory with cats who've never heard of the warrior code."

"Well, you'll have to get used to it." Sandstorm emerged from the bush and padded over to him. "You can't expect the cats here to live by the rules we have at home. I don't suppose they even know about StarClan."

Her words chilled Firestar. She was right; they couldn't expect that StarClan had followed them so far. How could he carry out his mission without his warrior ancestors to protect and guide him? He couldn't even be sure that SkyClan's warrior ancestors walked these skies. He glanced up, wondering if the gray-and-white leader was watching him, but nothing broke the white blanket of fog.

Eventually they managed to catch a couple of mice, and headed back toward the cave. As they were weaving their way among the bushes, Firestar heard rustling ahead of them, and picked up a familiar kittypet scent. He flipped the end of his tail across Sandstorm's mouth for silence, and slipped into the shelter of a gorse bush.

Before many heartbeats had gone by, two cats came into view, thrusting their way through the bushes from the direction of the cliff edge. One was a dark tabby tom, the other a smaller tortoiseshell. Firestar was certain that they were the same two cats who had taunted him the day before.

His paws itched to confront them, but he was too far away to surprise them and he didn't want to make a fool of himself. Besides, if he did speak to them they would probably just deny they had done anything wrong. He let them go back toward the Twolegplace.

"What's the matter?" Sandstorm batted irritably at his tail.

"I think they're the cats who threw stones at me yesterday," Firestar explained. "I need to talk to them, but I want to figure out what to say first."

He headed for the cave, hoping to settle down and think, but as they scrambled down the steep, slippery trail to the entrance a foul smell rolled out to meet them.

Sandstorm curled her lip. "What's that disgusting reek?" She pushed past Firestar and leaped up into the cave.

When Firestar joined her he found her standing over the body of a mouse. It had obviously been dead for days; white maggots were wriggling through the remains of its fur. The stink of it filled the whole cave.

"It must be those kittypets!" Firestar snarled. "I suppose it's their idea of a joke, leaving crow-food in a cave where cats are living."

"If I catch them, I'll show them it's no joke," Sandstorm growled.

"Better get it out of here." Firestar sighed.

Dabbing at it with their paws, they managed to push the mouse out of the cave and over the rocks until it fell down the cliff. Back in the cave, Sandstorm scraped sand over the damp, stinking patch where it had lain.

"It'll take forever to get rid of the smell," she complained. "*And* it's all over my paws. I'll have to go down to the river to wash."

Firestar padded to the cave entrance and took in gulps of clean air. He hadn't expected this sort of welcome. The cats who lived here were rude and interfering, and if they lived by any kind of code he couldn't imagine what it was.

"Rogues aren't like this in the forest," he mewed to Sandstorm. "Mostly they keep to themselves, and stay away from the Clans' territories."

"But there *aren't* any Clans here," Sandstorm pointed out. "Back in the forest, most cats know about the warrior code. And if they don't want to live by it, they know how to stay away from us."

Firestar watched the mist at the bottom of the gorge. The warrior code was the basis of life in all the Clans. Kits drank it in with their mother's milk. Out here no cat knew of it—but they had once, as well as any cat in the forest. He wondered if he would ever be able to awaken the memory of the warrior code in this scorched place.

"I'll have to make a start somewhere," he muttered, speaking half to himself. "And I think I know where." Straightening up, he added, "Sandstorm, tomorrow we're going to talk to those kittypets."

CHAPTER 17

"Ow!" Sandstorm halted at the foot of a thornbush, letting out a yowl of pain and shaking one forepaw.

"Shh!" Firestar hissed. "You'll bring every cat in Twolegplace down on us."

Sandstorm blinked at him. "I thought that was the point? I'm sorry," she added, giving her paw a quick swipe with her tongue. "I trod on a thorn; that's all."

Firestar glanced around. "I don't think any cat heard. Okay, carry on. As soon as the kittypets arrive, get down to the cave. Remember, it's best if they don't get a good look at you."

"I know." Annoyance sparked in Sandstorm's eyes. "We went through all this last night."

"Right, then." Firestar took another quick look around, then pushed through the undergrowth until he reached the nearest tree. Clawing his way up the trunk, he settled himself on the lowest branch, hidden from below by thick bunches of leaves.

Beneath the tree, Sandstorm went on hunting. Water flooded Firestar's jaws when he saw her bring down a mouse.

Neither of them had eaten since the night before. His claws worked impatiently on the branch. He couldn't be sure if the kittypets would come, but the plan he had worked out with Sandstorm seemed to be the only chance of talking to some of the cats who lived near the abandoned camp.

He heard a rustling in the bushes a short way off. Peering through the leaves, he caught a glimpse of a tortoiseshell pelt. His gaze flicked to Sandstorm; she was peering into the depths of a bush. Firestar didn't dare call out to her in case he alerted the kittypets.

Then Sandstorm sat up, jaws parted as if she had detected a scent. A heartbeat later she grabbed up the mouse she had caught and vanished through the bushes toward the edge of the gorge.

"Hey, he's here!" It was the tabby kittypet speaking, pushing through the undergrowth until he stood almost directly under Firestar's tree. "I saw the bushes shaking where he went down to the cave."

His tortoiseshell companion slipped past him, following the route Sandstorm had taken.

Don't they ever pick up a scent? Firestar wondered. *Can't they tell it's a different cat?*

Both kittypets vanished again, but he could still hear their voices, raised as if they were calling down to the cave.

"Hey, dog-breath, did you like the present we left for you?"

"I bet it was the best mouse you've eaten this moon. We saved it just for you."

"Did you, now?" Firestar muttered. *Okay, time to go.*

He leaped down from the tree and followed the kittypets through the bushes to the cliff edge. When their backs came into view he halted, taking up a position beside a thick growth of bramble. The kittypets wouldn't want to push through *that* to get away from him.

"Crazy old furball!" the tortoiseshell called out. "Mangy old—"

"Who are you talking to?" Firestar interrupted loudly.

Both kittypets spun around, jaws gaping in identical amazed expressions. Firestar looked them over, raised one paw and licked it reflectively, then allowed his claws to slide out. The kittypets' eyes widened.

"Er . . . we weren't talking to any cat," the tabby tom replied, his forepaws scuffling on the ground.

"You mean you sit on the edge of the cliff calling out to no cat?" Firestar asked. "You must be really weird to do that."

"We're not weird!" the tortoiseshell flashed back.

"Then tell me who you think is down there."

"We don't know. We haven't done anything." The tabby tom took a pace forward. "Let us go!"

The tortoiseshell stepped forward to stand beside her companion, their pelts brushing. Neither of them seemed to have the confidence to push past Firestar, and he was blocking the only route through the thorns. Both young cats jumped and huddled closer as a rustling came from the cliff edge and Sandstorm hauled herself into view.

The kittypets stared at her.

"You're not—" the tortoiseshell blurted out.

"Not who?" Firestar demanded.

Sandstorm padded forward and sat beside the kittypets, who shrank away from her. "Firestar, don't sound so fierce," she meowed, flashing him a warning look. "They haven't done any harm—well, not much."

"We didn't mean to," the tabby tom insisted.

"I'm sure you didn't." Sandstorm's voice was soothing; Firestar wished the kittypets could have heard her when she was telling off a careless apprentice. "Why don't you start by telling us your names?"

"I'm Boris, and she's my sister Cherry," the tabby replied and added nervously, "What are you going to do with us?"

"We won't hurt you," Sandstorm promised, with another hard look at Firestar, who sheathed his claws and wrapped his tail around his paws. "We're just looking for some cats who might have lived here long ago."

Boris looked puzzled. "Which cats?"

"A Clan of cats," Firestar meowed. When the kittypets still looked blank, he added, "They used to live in these caves . . . warrior cats in one, older cats in another, queens and their litters in another, and so on. They had a leader, and they taught their young cats the warrior code. They defended their borders—"

"Oh, them!" the tortoiseshell, Cherry, meowed impatiently. "We've heard stories about them." She paused. "According to some of the cats around here, there used to be a lot of fierce cats who lived in these caves. They even used to eat kittypets!"

"That's a load of mouse dung," Boris protested. "I can fight as well as any cat. They wouldn't eat me!"

"I didn't see you being so keen to fight *this* cat." His sister flicked her tail at Firestar. "Anyway, those cats have gone now, all except crazy old Moony."

"Who's Moony?" Sandstorm asked, and Firestar added, "Is that who you thought was down in the cave?"

The two kittypets exchanged a glance, beginning to look embarrassed again. Boris ducked his head and started to lick his chest fur.

"He's just this mad old cat," Cherry muttered. "He doesn't live here, but he comes here every full moon, and sits on that rock that sticks out over the gorge. He spends ages staring up at the moon—that's why we call him Moony."

"Then he sleeps one night in that cave before he goes away again," Boris added.

Cherry gave a disdainful sniff. "Every cat around here knows that he's mad. If you try to talk to him, he just tells you weird stories about cats in the stars."

Firestar felt every hair on his pelt stand on end. This was the first clue that any trace of Clan life survived, that any cat knew what it meant to be a warrior.

"Cats in the stars?" he asked sharply. "Are you sure?"

"Of course I'm sure," Cherry mewed. "I've listened to him often enough."

"And if he did have anything to do with those other cats," her brother added, "they can't have been very fierce. Moony never fights back, whatever—"

He broke off as his sister gave him a sharp prod with one paw and hissed, "Mouse-brain!"

Firestar would have liked to cuff both young cats around the ears, but when he met Sandstorm's gaze, she shook her head. Regretfully, Firestar admitted she was right. They would get more out of the kittypets if they didn't scare them.

"Moony hasn't done anything wrong, has he?" Firestar asked, deliberately making his voice gentle. "He hasn't hurt you or stolen your food?"

Both kittypets shook their heads, not meeting his gaze.

"Then you should leave him alone."

The two kittypets exchanged a guilty glance. "I told you this wasn't Moony!" Cherry hissed to her brother. "The moon isn't full yet."

"Well, how was I to know?" Boris complained. "No other cats have ever come here."

"Never mind that." Firestar interrupted their argument before it had a chance to get properly started. "What can you tell us about Moony? Where does he live when he isn't here?"

Cherry shrugged. "Dunno."

"He must come from farther up the gorge," Boris offered, waving his dark-striped tail in that direction. "We'd have noticed if he came up the river."

"And that's all you can tell us?" Sandstorm leaned forward and fixed both young cats with a penetrating green gaze.

"That's really all." Boris's yellow eyes widened. "Can we go now?"

"I think they can, don't you, Firestar?"

Firestar paused for a couple of heartbeats, long enough for the two young cats to understand that they weren't getting off too lightly. "I suppose so," he mewed at last. "But no more tormenting defenseless cats, okay?"

"We won't!" Boris promised. He prodded his sister. "Will we?"

"No, not anymore." Cherry flattened her ears. "We just didn't think . . ."

"Next time, try not to be so mouse-brained," Firestar meowed, drawing aside to leave a narrow tunnel through the undergrowth. "Off you go."

Relief flooded the eyes of both young cats. They crept hesitantly past Firestar, as if they weren't completely sure his claws would stay sheathed. Once they were safely past him, they shouldered their way out of the thicket and broke into a run. As Cherry dashed past the tree where Firestar had hidden, she gave a tremendous leap, batting at the lowest branch. Leaves showered down on her brother as he bounded after her.

Firestar and Sandstorm followed the kittypets to the edge of the bushes and watched them racing back to Twolegplace, their tails held high.

"They're not bad, for kittypets," Sandstorm commented. "Cherry's got spirit, at least."

Firestar suspected that the young tortoiseshell reminded Sandstorm of her apprentice, Sorrelpaw. "They've both got spirit," he responded. "It's a pity they can't be apprenticed in a proper Clan."

"Well, they can't," Sandstorm meowed. "Not unless we can

find SkyClan. They left here a long time ago, by the sound of it."

"Except for Moony." Firestar felt excitement prickling through his pelt again. "A cat who gazes at the full moon and talks about cats in the stars . . . He's a Clan cat, Sandstorm; he must be!"

Sandstorm nodded, a glow in her green eyes. "Then that's our next job. We've got to find him."

"To think I complained it was too hot!" Sandstorm exclaimed.

She and Firestar had finished their hunt and eaten, and were heading along the top of the gorge in search of Moony. The dawn mist had turned to a fine, cold drizzle, soaking the cats' fur. The sky was heavy with gray clouds, and Firestar couldn't see clearly more than a few fox-lengths ahead.

"This is no good," he meowed. "It's just the same as when we were looking for the SkyClan camp. If we stay up here, we'll never find the place where Moony is living."

Sandstorm sighed. "I was afraid you were going to say that."

Climbing down was even harder when the rocks were slippery with rain and the bottom of the gorge was still shrouded in mist. Firestar led the way, scrambling over boulders and slithering down loose pebbles until they reached the narrow valley above the rocks where the river poured out. The path was sticky with mud, covering the cats' legs and splashing up into their belly fur. They plodded along uncomfortably, peering through the rain at the sides of the gorge to find any trace of the old cat.

"There's a slit in that rock." Sandstorm pointed with her tail. "Maybe it leads to a cave." She splashed away from the path to investigate and splashed back almost at once. "No good," she reported. "It's not wide enough for my whiskers. A cat could never live in there."

Firestar wondered whether a cat could live in this barren place at all, but as he and Sandstorm trudged along he began to spot stunted bushes here and there, and scent faint traces of prey. Some of the rainwater had collected in puddles among the boulders.

"This place would support one or two cats," he meowed. "But it's a pretty miserable place to live, all the same."

"Especially on your own," Sandstorm agreed. "If Moony is a bit weird, no cat could blame him."

The cats passed more slits in the gorge wall, but they were all too shallow or too narrow for a cat to live in comfortably. Firestar began to wonder how much farther they would have to go, or whether they had already missed Moony's home.

Gradually a breeze sprang up, wafting billows of rain into their faces. Firestar shivered.

"For StarClan's sake, let's look for shelter," Sandstorm mewed. "We'll never find him in this."

Not waiting for Firestar's agreement, she splashed up to another of the narrow caves and slipped inside it. There was just enough room for Firestar to squeeze in beside her, their sodden pelts pressed together. But in spite of his drenched, mud-plastered fur and his sore paws, he felt more hopeful than he had for a long time. At last they had news of a real

Clan cat, and sooner or later they had to find him.

He drowsed uneasily and woke to feel Sandstorm's tail flicking over his ear. She was standing outside the cave, looking down at him. "Come on," she meowed. "The rain's stopped."

Creeping stiffly out of the cave, Firestar looked up and saw that the clouds were parting. A watery sun shone down into the gorge. The breeze ruffled his damp fur, showering him with a few last drops of rain.

"That's better," he meowed. "Let's get moving."

"In a moment," Sandstorm replied. "I want a drink first."

"Haven't you had enough water?" Firestar asked, as he followed her to a pool in a hollow between two twisted thorn trees.

At the edge of the pool Sandstorm froze, staring down at the ground in front of her paws. "Firestar, look!"

He bounded over. There in the newly wet mud at the edge of the pool were the pawprints of a cat! They were crisp and fresh, larger than his prints or Sandstorm's.

"They could be Moony's!" Sandstorm exclaimed. "Or at least, a cat who might know where to find him. And they must have been made recently—since the rain stopped."

Firestar lashed his tail. If they hadn't gone to sleep in the cave, they might have spotted the cat when it came to drink.

"Whoever it is, they might still be close by," he meowed. "You search that side of the gorge, and I'll look on this side."

He padded slowly along the base of the cliff, alert for any more footprints or the scent of a cat. Then Sandstorm let out a yowl and signaled with her tail. "Over here!"

Firestar bounded across to her. Before he reached her he began to pick up a strong, fresh scent. "I'm sure that's the same scent that was in the cave where we've been sleeping," he meowed.

Sandstorm nodded, tasting the air again. "It was stale there, but it's the same cat. It *must* be Moony who made those prints."

Following the scent, Firestar reached a narrow path that wound behind a huge boulder. The cats could barely squeeze between the rock and the cliff face. On the other side of the boulder the path led steeply upward until it reached a gnarled tree clinging to the side of the cliff. Firestar scrabbled his way up to it, showers of pebbles pattering down under his paws. Sandstorm followed a tail-length behind.

Drawing closer to the tree, Firestar saw that its roots arched out of the reddish stone, forming a den of hard, twisted branches. Outside was a scattering of bones and scraps of fur and a bundle of soiled moss. The cat scent was stronger still.

"This is it," he panted, glancing over his shoulder at Sandstorm. "This must be where Moony lives."

As he began to climb farther up, a dark gray shape shot out from beneath the roots. "Get away from here!" he snarled. "Leave me alone! Haven't you tormented me enough?"

CHAPTER 18

"It's all right," Firestar meowed. "We haven't come to harm you. We just want to talk."

Moony glared at him from huge, pale blue eyes. He must have once been a big, powerful cat, but now he was shrunken and scrawny. His gray fur was thin and staring, his muzzle white with age. "Well, I don't want to talk to you," he growled.

Whirling around, he stumbled back into his den. His gray pelt merged into the shadows; all Firestar could see clearly were his pale eyes, gleaming with a mixture of fear and anger. They were exactly the same color as the eyes of the SkyClan leader he had seen in his dreams. He felt so close to SkyClan, it was as if a single pawstep would lead him to that caveful of warriors.

Slowly, with his claws sheathed, he padded up to within a tail-length of the den. Sandstorm came to stand at his shoulder. "Please," she mewed. "There's so much we want to ask you."

Moony's reply was a defiant hiss. "Leave me alone."

"Is that what you really want?" Sandstorm's voice was gentle. "Haven't you been alone long enough? We want to help you."

"Go away," growled the old cat. "I don't need your help. I don't need any other cats. This is my life now."

Firestar knew he could have bullied the old warrior into answering his questions, but Moony had already suffered enough at the paws of the kittypets—and probably any rogues or loners who came across him, too. Besides, he looked quite capable of giving any attacker a nasty scratch. Firestar wanted to earn his respect, not his hostility. Fighting wasn't the answer.

Beckoning with his tail to Sandstorm, he withdrew a few paces down the path. "Come on; let's leave him alone," he murmured.

Sandstorm's tail went up in surprise. "We've only just found him!"

"Yes, but we're not doing any good here. We'll never force him to talk when he's protecting his own den."

"Then what *are* we going to do?" Sandstorm asked.

"The moon will be full in four sunrises," Firestar explained. "We must go back to the cave and wait until he comes to the gorge. He might not be so defensive out in the open, and at the time of the Gathering he might be more willing to talk about his ancestors."

Sandstorm blinked thoughtfully. "You're right. I'm sure he'd never break the Gathering truce."

Firestar dipped his head to the shadows beneath the tree roots before he turned away from Moony's den. "Maybe at the full moon we'll find out what we need to know," he murmured.

* * *

Firestar hauled himself into the cave with a mouthful of feathers, and carried them to where Sandstorm was lining their nests with bracken. "I found these on the cliff top," he told her. "There was a scent of fox; I think it must have caught a bird."

"Fox?" Sandstorm gave him a worried look from her pale green eyes. "I hoped there weren't any foxes around here."

"There are foxes everywhere," Firestar meowed. "Anyway, the feathers should make the nests a bit more comfortable."

"We really need moss." Sandstorm gave the bracken a dissatisfied prod with one paw. "Ferns alone aren't nearly as good. But there doesn't seem to be any moss at all around here."

"Why don't we go down and search beside the river?" Firestar suggested. "I could do with a drink."

Sandstorm looked doubtful. "It's worth a try."

She took the lead as the two cats headed down the trail to the bottom of the gorge. The heavy rain of the day before had passed, and the sky was blue again, with a scattering of puffy white clouds. Beside the river, puddles gleamed in hollows in the rock.

Firestar made for a sandy slope where the river had scooped out a dip in the bank, and jerked back quickly as his paw sank deep into mud. "Mouse dung!" he exclaimed, shaking his paw. "Did SkyClan get their paws filthy every time they wanted a drink?"

Sandstorm let out a faint purr of amusement. "If they

weren't as impatient as you, they could find the best places—like this," she added, waving her tail at a broad, flat rock that sloped gently down into the water. "Even kits could drink safely from here."

"Yes, they could." Firestar padded down the slanting rock and crouched to lap, with Sandstorm at his side.

"We still haven't found any moss." Sandstorm sat up again, twitching droplets from her whiskers. "Let's try farther downstream."

They hadn't explored this stretch of the river before. Before they had gone many pawsteps, they had to pick their way around huge boulders that came between them and the water. Sandstorm swiped her paw across one of them, and examined the faint greenish smear on her fur. "It's like tiny moss!" She sniffed. "But what good is that for lining a nest?"

"SkyClan would have had a hard time living here without moss," Firestar pointed out. "It's not just important for lining nests. You need moss to carry water to kits and elders."

Sandstorm nodded. "And medicine cats use it to wash wounds."

That was one more mystery about the lost Clan, Firestar mused, as he and his mate padded on. Even more than before, he couldn't wait for the night of the full moon, when Moony might be able to give them some answers.

Farther downstream the river curved around a jutting spur of rock. Firestar clawed his way up it, listening to Sandstorm spitting in annoyance as she scrambled after him. "I'm wearing the skin off my pads," she complained.

From the top of the rock Firestar could see the next stretch of water. The gorge had grown wider; there was a flat, pebbly foreshore that gave way to trees and bushes growing between the river and the cliff face.

"This looks like a better place for prey," he meowed. "I couldn't imagine how SkyClan managed to feed themselves just from—"

"Get down!" Sandstorm interrupted, slapping him across the shoulders with her tail.

Firestar flattened himself against the rock. "What is it?" he whispered.

Sandstorm jerked her head toward the undergrowth at the edge of the river. Firestar saw the branches shaking; then a massive tomcat emerged, his fur a darker shade of ginger than Firestar's flame-colored pelt. He carried a piece of fresh-kill in his jaws.

"Sorry," Sandstorm muttered. "I thought it might have been a fox."

"No, just another rogue." Firestar rose to his paws. "Maybe we should go down and talk to him."

But the ginger tom was heading rapidly downstream, slipping along in the gap between the bushes and the cliff. Firestar wasn't sure if he had even spotted them. Soon he was out of sight.

"We'd never catch him," Sandstorm meowed. "And if we did, he'd probably think we were trying to steal his prey. The cats around here aren't exactly desperate to make friends."

She was right, Firestar thought, frustrated, gazing at the

spot where the ginger tom had vanished. He slid down the rock and stalked up to the bushes, tasting the air for prey. The scents were richer here than at the top of the gorge; he could distinguish mouse, vole, and squirrel, but the strongest were all from birds.

He pricked his ears at a rustling sound close by, and turned his head to see a blackbird pecking among the debris at the edge of the bushes. He dropped into the hunter's crouch, but as soon as he began to creep forward the blackbird cocked its head, its tiny bright eye fixed on him. Firestar launched himself at it, paws extended, but the blackbird shot up, calling out in alarm, and winged away over his head.

Firestar hissed, remembering the sparrow he'd lost a few days before when the brown rogue had interrupted him. Catching birds was always harder than catching prey on the ground. But here there wasn't much choice, unless he wanted to go hungry.

A few tail-lengths along the riverbank a thrush was tugging a worm out of a damp patch of earth. Sandstorm was already prowling toward it. Intent on its own prey, the thrush never noticed her; Sandstorm pounced, and her claws met in its neck.

Firestar bounded up to her. "Well done! I lost mine," he added ruefully.

"Never mind, we can share." Sandstorm patted the thrush toward him. "There's plenty of prey here."

"Still no moss, though," Firestar mewed, looking at the bare rocks beside the river.

"Then SkyClan must have managed some other way," Sandstorm pointed out sensibly.

Firestar tried to imagine the empty riverbanks alive with cats, patrolling, hunting, training apprentices, living by the warrior code as cats in the forest had done for uncountable seasons. If Moony really was the last SkyClan warrior, what could any cat do to rebuild the lost Clan?

"Full moon tonight." Firestar emerged from the warriors' cave; the dawn chill reminded him that greenleaf was drawing to an end. There was just enough light to make out the cliff at the opposite side of the river. A stiff breeze flattened his fur against his sides. "We've got to be ready to meet Moony."

Sandstorm, still curled in her nest, answered him with a yawn. "He won't be here until moonhigh. Go back to sleep." Her green eyes were no more than slits; as Firestar watched they closed completely, and she wrapped her tail tip over her nose.

The nest looked tempting, but Firestar felt too restless to lie down again. His paws itched to be doing something. "I'll go and find us some fresh-kill," he meowed.

Sandstorm's ears twitched to show that she had heard.

Luck was with Firestar; when he scrambled up to the cliff top he found himself nose-to-nose with a mouse and killed it before it had the chance to run. Scratching earth over it, he prowled through the bushes, but there was no other prey about.

By the time he emerged on the other side of the thicket the sun was edging above the top of the Twolegplace, flooding the stretch of scrubland with warm light and glittering on monsters racing past the Twoleg nests in the distance. Firestar hadn't ventured far in that direction before. Without consciously deciding, he found that his paws were carrying him toward the Twolegplace. He wasn't trying to hunt anymore, just scouting this unfamiliar territory.

Darting into the shelter of a gorse bush for cover, he was met by a furious hiss and a paw swiped past his nose, the claws missing him by less than a mouse-length. Firestar reared back in astonishment. A tabby she-cat crouched in front of him, her cream-and-brown neck fur bristling and her amber eyes glaring. Her scent told Firestar she was a rogue.

"Keep your paws off me!" she spat.

"I'm sorry." Firestar dipped his head. "I didn't see you there."

The she-cat relaxed slightly, but her look was still unfriendly. "Stupid furball. Just be a bit more careful next time." She turned and began to stalk off, her tail in the air.

"Hang on." Firestar bounded forward and caught up with her. "I want to talk to you. I need to know—"

"I don't want to talk to *you*," the she-cat interrupted, sounding just like Moony. "Go away and leave me alone." To show she meant it, she picked up speed until she was racing across the scrubby ground toward the Twoleg nests.

Firestar stood looking after her, tail lashing in frustration. Why was every cat in this place so hostile? None of them seemed to care about one another. There wasn't a trace of the warrior code left. Apart from the two kittypets, all the cats he had seen were rogues through and through.

A heavy stone seemed to settle in his heart. Ever since he and Sandstorm found the caves, he had clung to the hope of finding a few SkyClan cats living together, troubled and defiant, but still stubbornly surviving and clinging to the warrior code. Now he realized he was wrong. SkyClan had gone, lost seasons before he ever came to this place.

Why did you send me here? he wailed silently, not knowing if he was speaking to StarClan or to the SkyClan cat who had haunted his pawsteps for so long.

There was no reply.

Turning back toward the gorge, Firestar spotted the two kittypets, Boris and Cherry, sitting side by side on a Twoleg fence. He thought they were watching him. He couldn't see any point in going to speak to them; they wouldn't be pleased to see him after the encounter on the cliff top. He just hoped that they had learned their lesson, and would stay away from Moony in the future.

Moony was their last hope of discovering anything about the lost Clan. He and Sandstorm would do their best to persuade him to tell them what he knew that night. Then, once they found out what had happened to SkyClan, they could go home. No cat could do more; SkyClan were lost forever.

Firestar leaped across the cleft and landed on the jutting rock. During the day the last wisps of cloud had disappeared and now Silverpelt blazed down from a clear sky and glittered on the river far below. The moon, still low in the sky, covered everything with a silver sheen and cast Firestar's shadow huge behind him.

"If Moony sees us here, he might not come," Sandstorm meowed, leaping over the gap to stand beside Firestar. "Do you think we should hide?"

"Good idea." Firestar pointed with his tail toward a heap of boulders where the flat rock met the cliff face. "Over there."

He padded across and slid into deep shadow; Sandstorm squeezed in beside him. Through a gap between two of the boulders they could see most of the surface of the jutting rock and the last section of the stony trail that led up from the gorge. Now there was nothing to do but wait.

The moon crawled higher in the sky and the moon shadows grew shorter. Firestar felt his legs protest with cramps; he would have given anything for a good stretch.

At last he heard the soft pad of paws, and the old gray cat rounded a bend in the trail. His movements were stiff and painful, his belly sagged toward the ground, and his tail dragged in the dust. Yet he held his head high, and the moonlight turned his pelt to dazzling silver.

"He'll never manage the leap!" Sandstorm whispered in Firestar's ear.

Moony paused a few tail-lengths from the end of the trail and raised his eyes to the stars. Then he started forward again, somehow managing to pick up speed, and launched himself in a flying leap over the rift. His forepaws struck the rock, and for a few heartbeats he hung over the gap, paws scrabbling to pull himself up.

Firestar felt Sandstorm's muscles tense, as if she were about to dash out and help him. But before she could move the old cat gave a massive heave and hauled himself to safety. He stood still for a moment, panting, then padded forward and sat down in the middle of the rock. Lifting his head, he turned his face to the moon; he looked like a cat made of shadows, outlined against the shining white circle in the sky.

Moony began to speak very softly; Firestar and Sandstorm crept forward so that they could hear what he was saying.

"Spirits of cats who have gone before," Moony mewed, "I am sorry I am the only cat left of what was once a noble Clan. I will try to preserve the way of the warrior until my last breath. But I fear that when I die it will die with me, and the memory of SkyClan will be lost forever."

He looked up, as if he were listening for a reply that never came. At last he heaved a long sigh, letting his head droop, and sat motionless while the moon began to slide down the sky.

Firestar could not interrupt his silent vigil. For how many seasons had Moony lived alone, surrounded by cats who tormented him? How long had he tried to live by the warrior code, and kept alive the memory of SkyClan?

At last the moon began to dip below the Twoleg nests on the horizon. Firestar was about to step forward when the old cat turned his head. His eyes glowed like moons. "I know you're there," he meowed. "I'm not so old that I can't pick up scent."

Firestar's pelt prickled; he felt as awkward as an apprentice caught eavesdropping. He and Sandstorm emerged from behind the boulders and padded forward to stand in front of the old cat. Firestar dipped his head. "Greetings, Moony. We—"

"That is not my name," the old cat interrupted, standing up so that his shadow slid over the rock and vanished into the bottom of the gorge. "My name is Sky."

CHAPTER 19

Firestar's heart thudded so hard it felt as if it would burst out of his chest. He could hardly breathe, and the words he wanted to say tumbled out in a rush. "Were you once a warrior of SkyClan?"

"I was not," the old cat replied. Before Firestar had time to feel disappointed, Sky went on. "My mother's mother was born into the Clan. By the time I was born, SkyClan was no more, but my mother taught me the ways of a Clan warrior."

Firestar exchanged an excited glance with Sandstorm. Her eyes were stretched wide. "We were right!" she mewed to Firestar. "This *was* SkyClan's home."

"Go on, Sky." Firestar took a step toward the old cat. "Tell us more about SkyClan."

To Firestar's dismay, Sky recoiled. "Why do you want to know?" he demanded. "What is it to you?"

"We want to help you," Firestar explained. "We come from the forest where SkyClan once lived."

"We're cats of ThunderClan," Sandstorm added. "My name is Sandstorm, and this is Firestar, the Clan leader."

The old cat's ears flattened, as if his ingrained mistrust

were fighting with the respect that a true warrior would show for a Clan leader. Firestar realized that he must be the first leader Sky had ever met.

"I had a dream." Firestar sat down, his tail wrapped over his paws to make him look as unthreatening as possible. After a moment's hesitation Sky sat down too, and listened while Firestar told him everything that had happened since his very first vision of the gray-and-white cat in the ravine outside the ThunderClan camp. "I'm sure he was the leader of SkyClan when it was driven out of the forest," Firestar finished. "He begged me to come and find his lost Clan."

"And you came all this way because of a dream?" Sky asked.

"I came because I had to."

Sky sprang to his paws again, the thin gray fur on his shoulders bristling. "Do you think it's as easy as that?" he spat. "Do you think the wrongs of the past can be forgiven so easily?"

"What do you mean?" Sandstorm mewed, bewildered.

"It was thanks to the four Clans left in the forest that my ancestors were driven out of their home. When they came here, they thought they would be safe, but later they found it was as terrible as the territory they had left. Your ancestors destroyed my Clan!"

For a few heartbeats Firestar was afraid that the old cat would leap on him with teeth and claws bared. He braced himself, knowing that he could never raise a paw against this noble old warrior.

Then Sky drew in a deep breath and sat down again. "This is a time of truce. I will not seek revenge while the moon is full for the wrongs done to my ancestors."

Firestar was beginning to feel alarmed. What was wrong with the gorge that meant SkyClan hadn't been able to stay there? With some prey at least, freshwater and shelter, and little threat from Twolegs, the cliffside camp seemed to be a perfect refuge for cats.

"What happened?" he prompted. "Why did they all leave?"

Sky turned his head away. A low keening came from his throat, as if he were mourning for all the cats of SkyClan, driven out, lost, or dead.

Sandstorm padded forward and gently touched his shoulder with her tail. "Tell us why you're called Sky," she urged.

The old cat looked up at her. "My mother gave me that name," he rasped, "so that I would never forget my ancestors. And I never have. That's why I come here every full moon."

"That must get very lonely sometimes," Sandstorm murmured.

Sighing, Sky looked up at the glitter of Silverpelt. "I don't know if my warrior ancestors listen to me, but I will keep the way of the warrior alive until my last breath."

"We know you stay in one of the caves on the night of the full moon," Firestar began hesitantly, not wanting to upset the old cat any more. "Sandstorm and I have been sleeping there. I hope you don't mind."

Sky let out a disgusted snort. "Then you've met those two kittypets. That's how you knew the stupid name they gave me."

"Yes, we've seen them," meowed Sandstorm.

"They live in a Twoleg nest and eat pap!" the old cat exclaimed. "And they say *I'm* mad!"

Firestar caught a glance from Sandstorm, as if she were trying to warn him not to mention that he had once been a kittypet. He certainly didn't intend to; Sky's opinion of him was low enough without that.

"We scared them away," he told Sky. "You shouldn't have any more trouble with them."

Sky twitched his ears; for a moment Firestar thought he looked almost disappointed. "Did you notice anything . . . unusual about them?" he asked.

Firestar cast his mind back to the encounter with the kittypets. He couldn't remember anything distinctive, except for their rudeness, and he didn't think Sky meant that. Then he pictured the two of them as they ran back to the Twoleg nest. "Cherry jumped into a tree," he recalled. "Is that what you mean?"

Sky nodded. "I think those two kittypets are descended from SkyClan cats."

Sandstorm's ears pricked with surprise. "Those two mouse-brains?"

"When the Clan was forced out of the gorge," Sky explained, "most of the cats, including my mother's mother, became rogues or loners. But some of them, those who were too old or too young to hunt, went to live with Twolegs." He stared across the scrubland to where the harsh orange lights of the Twolegplace stained the sky. "Strange . . . ," he murmured. "So many of those cats must share my blood, yet none of them knows who I really am." He bowed his head again.

"What happened?" Firestar asked. "Why did SkyClan have to leave the gorge?"

The old cat did not reply; Firestar wasn't even sure if he had heard the question.

"You look tired," Sandstorm mewed. "Would you like me to hunt for you?"

Sky tensed; Firestar was afraid that Sandstorm's offer had offended him. Then he looked up, blinking gratefully. "Thank you. It's been a long night."

Immediately Sandstorm leaped across the rift and disappeared down the trail into the gorge. Firestar followed more slowly with Sky. He was ready to help the old cat cross the gap, but leaping down from the rock was easier than leaping up, and Sky landed with all four paws firmly on the trail. Firestar let him take the lead to the cave.

As he padded behind, Firestar realized that Sky reminded him of Yellowfang. He had the same proud reserve as the former medicine cat; he was clearly uncomfortable and prickly around other cats, yet he shared Yellowfang's strength and her deep commitment to her Clan. Sky had all the qualities of a true warrior: courage, faith, and loyalty to his Clan. Yet everything he was had been based only on tales told to him by his mother. SkyClan from his nose to the tip of his tail, he had never been part of a real Clan.

Sky clambered up to the mouth of the cave and paused, whiskers twitching. Firestar was nervous that he would feel insulted that he and Sandstorm had brought in bedding, when he must have slept on the bare sandy floor. The old cat let out a faint snort, then padded over to one of the hollows and curled up without any comment in a nest of ferns and feathers.

He was barely settled when Sandstorm appeared in the entrance, a mouse dangling from her jaws. She crossed the cave to Sky and laid it down in front of him.

The gray cat reached out one paw and prodded it. "A bit skinny, isn't it?" Before Sandstorm could defend her catch, he dragged the mouse closer and began devouring it in rapid gulps.

Sandstorm glanced at Firestar, her eyes glimmering with laughter, and mouthed, *Yellowfang!*

Sky finished off the last scrap of mouse, swiped his tongue around his jaws, and let out a long sigh. Then he curled up again and was asleep almost at once, his snores echoing around the cave.

Firestar and Sandstorm squashed up together in the remaining lined nest. Sleep refused to come to Firestar. Bracken pricked against his fur, and Sky's snoring echoed off the sandy walls. Sandstorm was restless too, shifting among the bedding.

But that wasn't what kept Firestar awake. His mind buzzed with troubled thoughts. He wondered whether the SkyClan ancestor was watching him, or his former leader Bluestar. Neither of them had sent him any signs since he came to the gorge. Could the SkyClan leader be trapped somewhere else, unable to watch over his former home?

Eventually he slipped into a disturbed sleep. Sunlight streaming into the cave woke him the next morning. Sandstorm was already sitting up beside him, grooming herself, while Sky snored in his nest opposite.

"Are you ready to go and hunt?" Sandstorm asked.

Firestar heaved himself out of the nest with a huge yawn. His legs were stiff but he knew he wouldn't sleep again. He gave himself a brisk shake to dislodge scraps of bracken from his fur. "Lead on," he mewed.

By the time they reached the riverside, he was beginning to feel better. He waded through the shallows for a few paces, enjoying the sensation of cool water on pads that were still sore from scrambling up and down the cliff. Then he and Sandstorm headed downstream, to where the trees and undergrowth sheltered prey.

It was good to hunt side by side like this, Firestar thought, without having to worry about organizing patrols or keeping a watch on the borders. The forest suddenly seemed very far away. *Could I stay here forever?* he wondered. *Could I live without a Clan?*

Then he heard Sandstorm let out a faint sigh. She was gazing down at an eddy in the river, where the current had scoured out a hollow under the bank beneath a hazel bush. It looked almost exactly like the place where ThunderClan crossed the stream on the way to Fourtrees.

Firestar's thoughts went winging back to his own territory. How had ThunderClan fared at the Gathering the night before, and what did the other Clans think when they heard he had left the forest?

The idea that he might choose not to go back seemed as remote as the stars. He was ThunderClan's leader; the forest was where he belonged. Except for Sky, all the SkyClan cats were long gone. There was nothing more that Firestar could do for them. Once he had listened to the rest of Sky's story, and found out why the SkyClan cats had left the caves, it would be time to go home.

He and Sandstorm hunted and carried their fresh-kill back to the cave. But when he reached the entrance, Firestar stopped in surprise. The hollow in the cave floor was empty. Sky had gone.

Chapter 20

Firestar flattened his ears in disappointment. "I thought he would at least stay until we got back," he meowed. "There's so much more I wanted to ask him."

Sandstorm dropped her prey beside Firestar's and padded across to the hollow where Sky had slept. "He's used to being alone," she pointed out. "I suppose he just didn't feel comfortable around other cats."

Firestar twitched his tail tip, irritation raising the fur on his shoulders. "Now we'll have to trek all the way up the gorge again. I don't want to leave without speaking to him. I *have* to know more about SkyClan, especially why they left these caves."

Sandstorm's green eyes glinted at him. Firestar was afraid she would think he was becoming obsessed with SkyClan, particularly when there was no Clan to restore, nothing but memories and sand.

"I'll feel as if I've failed the cat in my dreams if I don't find out what destroyed the Clan in the end," he defended himself. "It wasn't just leaving the forest. They reached this place, and they could have thrived here, especially with their special ability to leap. So what happened next? Why did they go?" He shook his head in frustration. "I *have* to know," he repeated.

"It's okay." Sandstorm pressed her muzzle against his. "I understand. And if—"

A panting, scraping noise from outside the cave interrupted her. Sky clambered into the cave; a huge bundle of moss was clamped in his jaws.

Relief flooded over Firestar. "You're still here!"

"And you found moss!" Sandstorm added.

The old cat dropped his burden and looked at her as if he thought she was mad. "You do use moss for bedding, don't you? I haven't dragged this stuff all the way up from the river for nothing?" He gave his nest of ferns a scathing look. "Maybe you enjoy being pricked all night."

"Yes, we use moss," Firestar meowed, "but we couldn't find any."

Sky snorted. "I'll show you later." He pushed the bundle of moss toward them with one paw. "There, put it in your nests. I don't need any; I won't be staying another night."

"I wish you would." Sandstorm brushed her muzzle against Sky's shoulder; the old cat tensed, but didn't protest. "There's so much you can tell us."

Sky hesitated, then flicked his ears. "I'm not welcome here. Those kittypets . . . I've been driven out, just like my ancestors."

"I'm sorry—" Firestar began.

"Don't feel sorry for me!" Sky's blue eyes flashed. "I've got a perfectly good den of my own. I don't need anything."

His voice ached with a loneliness that contradicted his words.

Sandstorm padded across to the small fresh-kill pile she and Firestar had made, and picked out a plump vole, which she carried over to Sky. "Please eat," she mewed.

The old cat's eyes glinted with surprise, but he crouched down to devour the vole. Sandstorm fetched a starling for herself, while Firestar used Sky's moss to line their nests. It was paler than the moss that grew in the forest, and he was still puzzled about where Sky had found it. There hadn't been time for the old cat to go far.

By the time Firestar settled down to eat, Sky was swallowing the last scraps of fresh-kill. "Thanks." He grunted. "I've eaten worse."

Sandstorm dipped her head. "Please, will you show us where you found the moss?" she asked. "And maybe some of the other places you remember from when you were young?"

Firestar gave Sandstorm an appreciative glance. It was a good idea to nudge the old cat along the path of his memories; he must want to share them, after being so long alone.

Sky rose to his paws and padded over to the cave entrance. His gaze fell on the scratch marks on the stone trunk; Firestar thought he flinched before he turned to look out at the hazy sky. "I'll show you the moss," he meowed, "and the other places my mother used to take me. But we should go now. It's going to be a hot day, so we'll need to be back before sunhigh."

Firestar gulped down the rest of his sparrow and stood up.

"I'm ready," he mewed to Sky. "Lead the way."

The elderly cat took the stony trail that led to the bottom of the gorge, then leaped up to the top of the pile of boulders where the river appeared. His movements were stiff, but Firestar was impressed by how agile he was, in spite of his age. Sky's flanks were heaving with effort by the time he reached the top, but as he turned back to watch Firestar and Sandstorm scrambling up after him, Firestar thought he could detect a hint of amusement in his eyes.

"This was called the Rockpile," he announced once Firestar and Sandstorm were standing beside him, panting. "The SkyClan leader stood up here when he wanted to call a Clan meeting. The rest of the Clan gathered around the pool." He flicked his tail toward the jutting rock high overhead, behind them. "You already know the Skyrock; that's where the Clan gathered at the full moon."

"Why did SkyClan hold Gatherings when there weren't any other Clans?" Firestar asked.

The old cat's eyes clouded. "Because that is the way of the warrior. The Clan would gather there to be closer to the stars." He turned away from the jutting rock. "Up there were the dens," he went on, pointing to the caves with his tail. "The warriors used the one where we've been sleeping. Below that was the elders' den, and—"

"Oh, we thought the lowest den would be where the elders lived," Sandstorm interrupted. "Because—" She broke off, giving her chest fur a few quick licks to cover her embarrassment.

"Because old cats are too stiff to climb?" Sky growled, though Firestar was sure that his eyes were warm. "No—SkyClan cats never lost the power to jump. That lowest den was the medicine cat's, close to the water and where the herbs grow."

He went on to point out the nursery—which was the cave with the tiny claw marks Firestar and Sandstorm had picked out—the apprentices' den, and the Clan leader's, a little way away from the others, next to the trail that led up to the Skyrock.

"Did the river ever flood?" Sandstorm asked.

"Yes, but never as high as the warriors' cave," Sky replied. "The whole Clan used to shelter there in the worst storms, so my mother said."

He gazed up at the caves for a heartbeat longer, as if he were imagining the trails busy with cats. Then he gave himself a brisk shake. "Come on. I'll show you the moss."

He jumped down from the highest boulder and picked his way down the pile on the opposite side of the river. Firestar wondered where he was going. They were uncomfortably near the black water where it appeared from among the rocks; did Sky expect them to swim?

Instead, the old cat veered around the lowest boulder and vanished. Firestar blinked. Where had he gone? Then he spotted a narrow ledge leading into the cave just above the level of the blue-green water.

A voice came from the darkness. "Are you coming or not?"

Firestar swallowed, exchanging a glance with Sandstorm.

His mate shrugged. "We can't not," she mewed.

Carefully setting down his paws in a straight line, Firestar ventured onto the ledge. The rock was slick with water, and his claws skidded when he tried to cling to it. The river lapped less than a tail-length below his paws. "I must be mouse-brained!" he muttered.

To his relief, after a while the ledge grew wider and opened out into a shallow cave. The river slid silently out of the shadows ahead and past them to the cave entrance, now a ragged gap of light behind them.

Sky was standing at the edge of the shadows. Pale dappled light shone on his gray fur. "All the moss you could want," he announced, sweeping his tail around.

Firestar stared in amazement. Behind the old cat, the walls of the cave were covered with thick hanging clumps of moss. But what really astonished Firestar was the eerie glow that came from it.

"Shining moss!" Sandstorm gasped.

"It's perfectly safe," Sky assured her. "You can use it for carrying water as well as for bedding. No cat knows why it glows like that. This was called the Shining Cave," he went on. "No cat lived here, but the SkyClan medicine cats came to share tongues with their ancestors at each quarter moon."

Firestar felt humbled that Sky had brought them to such an important place. He was glad, too, that he and Sandstorm hadn't discovered it on their own. They might have taken the moss without realizing how special the cave was.

"Thank you for showing us," he murmured to Sky. The

softly spoken words seemed to echo around the cave like a whole Clan of voices answering, and Firestar was relieved when the old cat led the way back to the sunlight.

Once they were all on the bank again, opposite the cave dens, Sky led them downstream until they reached the trees. Firestar noticed that Sky's stiffness seemed to be wearing off; he moved like a younger cat, as if exploring his ancestors' territory with visitors had given him another life. His tail held erect, he followed a twisting path through the undergrowth, farther than Firestar and Sandstorm had explored, until he reached a fallen tree that bridged the stream. Most of its branches had rotted away, and its trunk had been scoured to a silvery gray.

Sky leaped onto it and trotted confidently across to the far bank. Firestar and Sandstorm followed more cautiously, Firestar glancing down at the river bubbling underneath and digging his claws in as he crossed.

"This was the edge of SkyClan's territory," Sky announced as they joined him on the bank. "And that's where I was born."

He waved his tail toward a small cave at the bottom of the cliff, its entrance sheltered by a straggling bush. The sandy floor was littered with sharp little stones; Firestar tried to imagine what it would be like with a warm nest of moss and bracken, and a mother cat caring for her kits.

"What was your mother's name?" Sandstorm asked.

"Lowbranch," the old cat replied. "I never knew my father—another rogue, I suppose. I had a littermate called Twig."

"Does he still live here too?"

Sky stiffened, glaring briefly at Sandstorm. Instead of answering, he muttered, "This way," and swung around to pad off upstream.

"Sorry," Sandstorm whispered to Firestar. "I've obviously upset him. I wasn't trying to be nosy."

"I know." Firestar touched her ear with his muzzle. "I suppose Twig must be dead."

Instead of returning to the caves, Sky began to climb the cliff again. This time there were no trails to follow; Firestar and Sandstorm had a hard scramble over tumbled rocks and along narrow ledges before they reached the top, panting and limping on paws scraped by sharp stones.

Sky was waiting for them, his tail tip twitching impatiently. His pale blue gaze raked across them, but he said nothing, only turned to lead the way through the strip of bushes and into the scrubland. Firestar and Sandstorm plunged into the undergrowth after him, and caught up to him a few tail-lengths into the open.

"Are we still in SkyClan territory?" Firestar panted.

Sky angled his ears toward a tree stump that poked up out of a bramble thicket. "That marks the border. My mother said her mother remembered when it was a tree. And that thicket is where I caught my first mouse." His voice grew softer and he paused, as if he were looking back through long seasons to the young cat he had once been. Then a gleam of amusement appeared in his eyes. "Pricklenose was impressed," he added. "I never told her that the bramble thorns slowed the mouse down. It was an easy kill."

"Pricklenose? Who—" Sandstorm broke off, in case this was another painful question. "Didn't Lowbranch teach you to hunt?"

"Pricklenose was my mother's friend. It was the custom for a mother cat to give her kits to another to be trained. Pricklenose trained me and Twig, and my mother took her kits."

Firestar's ears pricked. "Why did they do that?"

Sky shrugged. "I don't know. It was the custom. Maybe they thought that a mother would be too soft on her own kits, or that she would be tempted to hunt for them instead of teaching them to do it for themselves."

Firestar exchanged a glance with Sandstorm. "It's as if the mother cats were mentors," he murmured. "They must have remembered something of the way warriors were trained when the cats still lived in SkyClan."

"Their names are a bit like Clan names, too," Sandstorm responded. "But somehow they don't sound quite right."

"Do the rogue she-cats still train one another's kits?" Firestar asked Sky, turning back to the old cat.

"I've no idea." Sky snorted. "I have nothing to do with the cats around here."

He set off again. Firestar followed, battling frustration that all these echoes of Clan life were nothing more than that—echoes without meaning, if there were no SkyClan cats left.

"This is a waste of time," he whispered to Sandstorm. "It's interesting, but we're not getting anywhere. We might as well go home."

Sandstorm's green gaze was calm. "Wait. All sorts of things could happen yet."

Firestar stared at her. Before he could ask her what she meant, Sky interrupted to show them a dark hole amid the roots of a gorse bush.

"That used to be a fox's den," he meowed. His gaze grew somber. "Two kits were killed there once, my mother said."

Firestar tasted the air, but there was no fox scent there now.

"It's close to Twolegplace," Sandstorm commented, gazing toward the fences of the Twoleg nests.

"The nests used to be farther off, but then the Twolegs built more," Sky told her. His tail lashed. "I can remember that happening when I was a kit. Huge monsters tearing up the ground, frightening off the prey with their noise."

Firestar shivered. He was used to monsters racing along Thunderpaths; he couldn't imagine what it would be like if they crashed their way into a Clan's territory, tearing up trees and destroying the camp. . . .

"Is that why SkyClan left the gorge?" he asked.

Sky narrowed his eyes. "No. Weren't you listening? SkyClan was already scattered when the monsters came."

"Then why—"

Not waiting for Firestar to finish his question, Sky swung around and led them along the Twoleg fences. Firestar's pelt began to bristle at the thought of being so close to Twolegs; he could see that Sandstorm was uneasy too.

"There are a lot of cats here," he remarked; the scents were almost overwhelming.

Sky gave a grunt of contempt. "Kittypets! What good are they? They can't even hunt."

Firestar could distinguish the scents of Cherry and Boris, but there was no sign of the two young cats. He felt sorry; he wanted them to meet Sky and treat him with respect from now on, especially if Sky was right and the kittypets were his distant kin.

"A dog used to live in that nest," Sky meowed, waving his tail at the closest fence. "Every cat was scared of it, its bark was so fierce!" A hint of amusement crept into his voice. "One day Twig dared me to climb up on the fence and look at it. And do you know, the dog was no bigger than me! I snarled at it, and it went yelping back into its nest."

Sandstorm let out a *mrrow* of laughter. "I wish I'd seen that!"

"Now, in *this* nest," Sky went on, leading them farther along the row, "the Twolegs were friendly. They used to leave out food." All the amusement vanished from his eyes and voice; a deep sadness swept over him, like the shadow of a cloud on a sunny day.

"What happened here?" Sandstorm asked softly.

"Twig ate the food and decided it was easier than hunting." Sky's voice rasped in his throat. "He went to live with the Twolegs. I never saw him again."

Sandstorm touched her tail to his shoulder, while Firestar remembered how his kin Cloudtail, back in the forest, had gone back to living the life of a kittypet, only to discover that it wasn't as good as life in the forest. It must have been hard for Sky to watch his kin scattering, just as his ancestors had done.

Eventually they came to the end of the Twoleg fences. Now they walked alongside a shiny mesh like silver cobweb that Firestar had seen before in Twolegplaces.

"We can go back now," Sky announced, stopping abruptly.

Firestar was surprised. The sky was still hazy and the day was not too hot to carry on. "Are we far out of SkyClan territory?" he asked.

"Far enough," Sky growled. His legs were stiff, his ears pricked, and his neck fur bristling. His pale blue eyes darted swift glances from side to side.

Firestar looked around. Beyond the silver mesh was a broad expanse of white stone, cracked and split with weeds. It surrounded a huge Twoleg nest that reminded Firestar of the barn where Barley and Ravenpaw lived. But this barn was much bigger, with a shining silver roof and gaping holes in the sides. It didn't look as if any Twolegs lived here; all that Firestar could smell was Twoleg rubbish, crow-food, and rats. A ShadowClan cat might be happy to hunt there, but Firestar didn't want to set one paw inside the fence.

"Okay, let's go," he meowed.

Sky's relief was obvious, his neck fur lying flat again as he began to lead the way back to the gorge. Firestar didn't want to ask him what had disturbed him so deeply, and the old cat didn't offer to explain.

As they drew closer to the cliff top, Sky slackened his pace. Firestar guessed he was walking the paths of memory, lost among the shadows of his scattered kin and Clan. He slowed down too, letting the old cat draw ahead; Sandstorm kept pace with Firestar.

"He's so lonely and sad. I wish we could help him," she murmured.

"So do I," mewed Firestar, "but what can we do? He spends too much time caught up in his ancestors' past, like a fly in a cobweb, but those days will never come again."

Sandstorm halted, her green eyes sparking. "Why won't they? We've proved that this is a place where cats can live. And there are plenty of cats around—kittypets and loners—to build up the Clan again. Some of them even have SkyClan blood."

Firestar stared at her. "And who's going to tell the kittypets and loners that they have to come here and live in caves? A Clan isn't just cats, Sandstorm. A Clan belongs together and lives by the warrior code."

"Then you're just giving up?" Sandstorm drew her lips back in the beginning of a snarl.

"What else can I do? SkyClan lived here once, but then something terrible happened—something so terrible that Sky won't even talk about it—and they scattered. They're *gone*. I would stay if I thought I could help, but I can't. There's nothing to work with."

His voice shook, but he couldn't see any other way. All that was left of the once-proud Clan was one old cat, clinging to the fading echoes of Clan life. It wasn't enough. SkyClan was lost forever.

* * *

The haze had cleared away and the sun beat down from a deep blue sky. Firestar was thankful for the shade of the warriors' cave when he and Sandstorm joined Sky there. The old warrior was crouched in the entrance, his paws tucked under him, his gaze fixed on the cliffs opposite.

Firestar dipped his head. "Thank you for showing us the territory. We'll rest until it starts to get cooler, and then we'll have to leave."

Sky rose to his paws and looked from Firestar to Sandstorm and back again, his eyes narrowed. Suddenly he seemed to have grown taller and his gaze was sharper. He seemed less like a lonely elder and more like a true Clan warrior.

"Leave?" he echoed. "What do you mean? What I want to know is, will you do it?"

Firestar stared at him, bewildered, while Sandstorm, who clearly understood more, let out a small mew of satisfaction.

"Do what?" Firestar asked. "Our journey is over. We've found the place where SkyClan used to live, but the Clan is gone."

"*That's* not why you were sent here," Sky spat. "You told me that a SkyClan ancestor visited you in your dreams. He must have known his Clan was long gone, forced out of the gorge by something even more terrible than their reason for leaving the forest. Yet still he asked you to come."

Firestar remembered his vision of the SkyClan leader in Smudge's garden. The cat had told him that it was his destiny to restore SkyClan. But then, Firestar had imagined that he would find at least the remnants of a Clan surviving in their new home. Not one old warrior, surrounded by rogues and kittypets who had never heard of the warrior code.

"Oh, no," he meowed. "You can't ask me to—"

"You must right the wrongs your Clan's ancestors did all those seasons ago," Sky insisted. His pale gaze burned into Firestar's eyes like sunlight on water. "You must rebuild SkyClan."

CHAPTER 21

"I know it seems impossible," *Sky* continued, "but I know too that you have the strength to do this. Have faith in yourself, Firestar. We will meet again soon."

With great dignity he dipped his head and padded down the stony trail, away from the warriors' cave.

"Well?" Sandstorm prompted softly. "Are you going to follow him and tell him you can't do it? Or just leave, and let him discover for himself that all his hopes have come to nothing?"

Firestar shook his head helplessly. The idea of rebuilding SkyClan was so huge that he couldn't even think about it. "I'm going hunting," he announced. "I'm sorry, Sandstorm. I just need to be alone for a while."

Sandstorm pressed her muzzle against his; her eyes glowed with her love for him. "I understand."

Not wanting to catch up to Sky, Firestar headed in the opposite direction, downstream toward the trees near the old boundary of SkyClan territory. His mind was whirling. He was leader of *ThunderClan;* that was where he belonged. Yet Sky was asking him to take responsibility for another Clan as well. Surely it couldn't be the will of StarClan for one cat to lead two Clans, especially when their territories were nearly a moon's journey apart?

He remembered how Tigerstar had made himself leader of ShadowClan and RiverClan, and tried to take over the other two Clans as well. His bloodthirsty ambitions would be remembered in the forest for many seasons.

"I won't be another Tigerstar." Firestar spoke aloud, halting by the edge of the river. "My loyalty is to ThunderClan." But was he right? Should he be loyal to the warrior code, rather than to any individual Clan?

Trying to shrug off the questions, he pressed on down the riverbank. Even though the sun was sliding down the sky, the sand was still hot against his pads, and the scrubby bushes by the cliff face cast very little shade. He longed for the cool, damp glades of the forest, the thick canopy of leaves, and the small rustlings of prey in the undergrowth. He had stayed here long enough that his paws were hardening from constant running on sand and stone, and he was learning how to track prey through the scanty cover that was all the gorge had to offer.

But this isn't my home, he thought. *It never will be.*

He clambered over the rock spur, relieved at the sight of the thicker shrubbery beyond. Slithering down the other side, he caught a glimpse of movement and spotted the dark ginger tomcat he had seen before.

"Hey!" he called out. "Wait up!"

The ginger tom cast a glance over his shoulder, but he

didn't stop. Instead, he pushed his way deeper into the undergrowth; Firestar lost sight of him, and didn't know whether to be glad or sorry.

He picked his way across the pebbles, heading for the nearest clump of bushes, his ears pricked and his jaws open to sense the first traces of prey. Then he paused, puzzled. There was a scent here he couldn't identify: prey, but so thickly covered by the tang of crushed leaves that he couldn't be sure what creature it came from. His fur prickled with the sensation that he was being watched.

Trying to shake off the feeling, Firestar slid into the ground cover, brushing through clumps of fern and seeding grasses until he reached the shadow of the bushes. His conviction that he was being watched grew stronger still. Icy claws raked his spine as he pictured a cold, malevolent gaze fixed on him. Something was lurking in the thicket that didn't welcome cats.

"Who's there?" Firestar hissed. He spun around, disturbing a thrush that shot up into the nearest tree. Disgusted, he realized that its loud alarm call would have alerted all the prey in the gorge.

He crept under a low growing thornbush and crouched there. Nothing moved; he could see nothing that might explain the evil force that he felt so strongly. His heart thudded, and he dug his claws into the ground as he braced himself to meet an attack.

Gradually the sensation faded. Firestar's heartbeat slowed, and, feeling slightly foolish, he crawled out from underneath the bush. *You're not a kit*, he scolded himself. *Haven't you enough problems without imagining more?*

He tried to concentrate on the hunt. Soon he scented a mouse, and spotted it scuffling among the debris underneath a holly bush. Flattening himself to the ground, Firestar began to creep up on it. He was about to pounce when a loud rustling in the undergrowth alerted his prey; the mouse vanished deeper into the thicket with a flick of its tail.

Firestar let out a snarl of frustration and sank his claws into the ground. He was aware of eyes on him again, but this time there was none of the hostility he had felt before. Glancing over his shoulder, he caught a glimpse of tortoiseshell fur and heard a voice hiss, "Be *quiet*! He'll hear us."

"Get off me, then," another voice replied. "Stupid furball."

Firestar heaved a sigh, drawing in kittypet scent. *Cherry and Boris! I might have known it.* He began slipping through the undergrowth, meaning to come up on them from behind and give them the fright of their lives. Then he hesitated.

So they wanted to spy on me? Okay, I'll give them something worth watching.

He tasted the air again, and almost at once found another mouse, nibbling on a seed under a beech tree. Dropping into the hunter's crouch, he crept forward, hardly letting his paws touch the ground. The mouse started to run, but this time Firestar was faster, and he brought it down with one blow from his paw.

From somewhere behind him he heard a gasp of admiration; his whiskers twitched with satisfaction as he scraped earth over his fresh-kill. He wanted to show these kittypets what a Clan cat could do with skills trained by a lifetime of following the warrior code.

A couple of tail-lengths away from the edge of the thicket a blackbird was pecking at the ground. Firestar stalked toward it. *StarClan, please don't let this one fly away!* Bunching his muscles, he pushed off with his powerful hind legs and pounced on his prey as it fluttered up from the ground. "Thank you, StarClan!" he exclaimed aloud, before carrying it back to bury it beside the mouse.

He had only just finished when the scent of squirrel flooded over him; the creature was bounding over the grass toward a tree a few fox-lengths away. Firestar shot out of the bushes, racing at an angle to intercept the squirrel at the foot of the tree, where he killed it with a swift bite to the throat.

Turning back to the thicket, he fixed his gaze on a gorse bush whose branches were waving wildly. "I know you're there," he meowed. "Do you want to come out and try for yourselves?"

For a heartbeat there was silence. Then Cherry pushed her way out through the gorse branches with Boris a couple of pawsteps behind her. "I told you he'd hear you!" she snapped over her shoulder at her brother.

"I could hear both of you," Firestar told her. "Rampaging through the thicket like a couple of foxes in a fit. I'm surprised there was any prey left at all. Come on," he added in a friendlier tone. "I'll show you what to do."

Cherry exchanged a glance with her brother, then ran up

to Firestar with her tail in the air. "Can you really teach us to hunt like that?"

Boris followed more slowly. "Why did you bury the mouse and the blackbird?" he asked. "Don't you want to eat them?"

Firestar dropped the squirrel. "Yes," he explained, "but not yet. We bury fresh-kill to hide the scent so other predators don't find it before we're ready to take it back to the camp."

"But what's the point of taking it back?" Cherry persisted. "Why not eat it here and save yourself the trouble?"

Firestar's memory winged back to one of his first lessons as an apprentice: *the Clan must be fed first*. He had only just left his life as a kittypet; he couldn't have been much different from these two young cats. "Clan cats don't hunt only to feed themselves," he explained. "They take their prey back to camp to feed the elders and the nursing queens and any other cats who can't hunt for themselves. That's a very important part of the warrior code."

Cherry and Boris glanced at each other again, round-eyed. Firestar wondered if they'd understood what he had told them.

"Okay, let's start," he meowed. "What can you scent?"

Cherry let out a little *mrrow* of amusement. "You and Boris!"

"Apart from me and Boris." Firestar sighed. "What about prey?"

Both young cats stood still, drawing in air over their scent glands. At least they seemed to be concentrating hard. Firestar picked up his squirrel and took it across to his other fresh-kill, so they wouldn't confuse its scent with the prey they were searching for.

When he returned, Boris bounced up to him with a triumphant gleam in his eyes. "Mouse! I can smell mouse."

"Well-done," mewed Firestar. "But you won't smell it for long if you go thumping about like that. A mouse can feel your pawsteps through the ground long before it hears you or smells you. Remember how I crept up on the mouse I caught?"

"I remember!" Cherry boasted. She dropped into the hunter's crouch and glided forward, only stopping to sneeze when a drooping grass stem tickled her nose. "Mouse dung!" she spat.

"That wasn't bad at all," Firestar told her. The crouch wasn't quite right, and she would have to learn to set her paws down much more lightly if she hoped to catch a mouse, but for a first effort it was promising. "Boris, you try."

The young tabby wasn't as eager to show off as his sister, and his greater weight made it harder for him to step lightly, but he was doing his best.

"Like this." Firestar began to stalk forward, and the two kittypets followed his movements with fierce concentration.

Then he spotted a mouse just beyond a clump of dry bracken, and pointed to it with his tail. With a twitch of his ears he told Cherry to try catching it.

Her eyes glittered with excitement. Breathlessly trying to get her movements right, she crept closer and closer, but with her gaze fixed on the mouse she didn't notice that the arching fronds of bracken were in her way. She blundered into them, and their shadow swept back and forth over the mouse. An instant later it was gone.

Cherry sat up, her tail lashing. "I'll never get it right!" she wailed.

"Yes, you will," Firestar reassured her, while her brother rested his tail across her shoulders. "It was just bad luck about the bracken."

He glanced around, tasting the air again. He wanted at least one of the kittypets to make a catch before their lesson was over. The only prey he could spot was a squirrel on the lowest branch of a nearby tree.

"What about that?" he suggested, wondering if Cherry would make another of her spectacular leaps. "Do you think you can catch it?"

"I can!" Cherry charged off, with Boris a mouse-length behind her. Reaching the tree, she leaped up, forepaws extended, and snagged one claw in the squirrel's tail. It fell to the ground, where Boris pounced on it and killed it by biting its throat. Cherry stood staring in astonishment, as if she couldn't believe they had really caught something.

"Well done!" Firestar exclaimed. "Great catch, both of you! Can you both jump like that?"

"Sure." Boris scraped the ground with his paw. "The other cats say we're showing off, but it's just something we've always been able to do."

"Well, it's a good skill," Firestar meowed. "And if you both have it, it must mean that your ancestors could jump like that too. If they can see you now, I'm sure they're very proud."

Boris was looking puzzled. "Yeah, but they can't see us, can they?"

Firestar wondered if this was the time to tell the young cats about SkyClan, but he felt it was too soon. "Eat the squirrel if you like," he encouraged them, changing the subject. "You haven't got a hungry Clan to feed."

"It smells yummy," Boris mewed. "Do you want some?"

Water was flooding Firestar's jaws at the warm aroma of the fresh-kill. His belly yowled with hunger after the long day with Sky, but he wouldn't take another cat's prey. Besides, he had fresh-kill of his own to share with Sandstorm when he returned to the cave.

"No, thanks," he replied. "You and Cherry share it."

The two young cats glanced at each other uncertainly. "The thing is," Cherry began, "our housefolk get worried if we don't eat their food. And if we're stuffed full of squirrel, well . . ."

"They might give us less next time!" Boris meowed worriedly.

Firestar, who had seen cats starving for lack of prey, couldn't really sympathize. But some cat had to eat the squirrel. Left lying there, it would only attract foxes.

"You know what?" Cherry put in before he could speak. "It smells so good, I don't care! We can always catch another if our housefolk don't feed us enough."

She crouched down beside the squirrel and began to tear into it. A heartbeat later Boris joined her, ravenously gulping down the fresh-kill. Hiding his amusement, Firestar wished them good-bye and went to collect his own prey.

The sun was going down and the caves were in shadow by the time he returned to the SkyClan camp. Sandstorm was sitting at the entrance of the warriors' cave, gazing across the gorge.

"You had good hunting," she commented as Firestar dropped his fresh-kill at her paws.

"Yes, and I came across those two kittypets again." He told her about the hunting lesson, and how Cherry and Boris had caught the squirrel. He said nothing to her about his odd sensation of being watched by hostile eyes before the kittypets arrived; he might have imagined it, and he didn't want to worry her for nothing.

"They've got the makings of good warriors," Sandstorm commented when he had finished. "Did you ask them if they wanted to join SkyClan?"

"No—"

"Why not?" Sandstorm twitched the tip of her tail. "You have to start somewhere."

"I haven't decided whether I want to start at all."

She tipped her head to one side. "So you're going to let Sky down?"

Firestar couldn't answer. He still felt it was too late to rebuild the lost Clan, but guilt swept over him when he thought of the pain Sky would suffer if he refused to try.

"I think we can do it," Sandstorm went on. "But we can't

stay here forever. We have Clanmates of our own who need us, so we ought to start collecting the scattered SkyClan cats as soon as we can."

She knew him so well, putting her paw on the reason for his doubts. How could he reconcile his duty to his own Clan with the task that Sky had set him? Which path must he choose if he was to stay faithful to the warrior code?

"Cherry and Boris are strong-willed cats," he began. "If they're going to live by the warrior code, they need to adapt to it of their own accord. At the moment, they see nothing wrong with their lives. They have to choose the warrior code because they really believe it's the right way to live."

Sandstorm gave him a doubtful look, clearly wondering if he was just making excuses. Firestar wasn't sure himself.

"Have some fresh-kill," he mewed, patting the squirrel toward Sandstorm. "I'll think about what Sky said. Maybe it will be clearer in the morning."

StarClan, show me the way! Show me how I can help this Clan!

CHAPTER 22

"Firestar! Firestar!"

Firestar opened his eyes to see the dark shapes of two cats outlined against the light in the cave entrance. "For StarClan's sake, what's the matter?" he grumbled, scrambling to his paws.

As the two cats bounced into the cave he could make them out more clearly: Cherry and Boris, their ears pricked and their eyes bright.

"We want another hunting lesson!" Cherry announced.

"Please," her brother added, giving her a nudge.

Sandstorm was stirring too, her green eyes no more than slits. She stretched her jaws in a huge yawn. "I thought all kittypets slept until sunhigh," she grunted, crawling out of her nest and giving herself a shake.

"Sometimes we do," meowed Boris. "But it was so exciting yesterday, and—"

"We had such fun!" Cherry interrupted. "You will take us with you today, won't you?"

Their enthusiasm surprised Firestar, but it pleased him too. A sudden pang of homesickness struck him: these two young cats could easily have been ThunderClan apprentices, begging to be taken out on a hunting patrol.

"We can take one each," Sandstorm suggested with another yawn. "We'll split up; too many cats together will scare off all the prey."

"True," Firestar agreed. "Especially here, where there's so little cover. You take Boris, and I'll have Cherry."

The young tortoiseshell gave an excited little bounce. "I bet we catch more prey than you!" she boasted to her brother.

With Boris following her, Sandstorm left the cave and took the trail that led to the thickets at the top of the cliff. Firestar led Cherry in the other direction, down to the river. The sun had risen into a blue sky dotted with white clouds. Sunlight sparkled on the surface of the water, but the day was still cool. A fresh breeze rippled Firestar's fur.

"Are we going back to where we hunted yesterday?" Cherry asked excitedly.

Firestar paused halfway down the trail. They would find plenty of prey downstream, but he couldn't forget the sense of cold malice that he had felt there the day before. Even though he knew they couldn't afford to abandon a good hunting ground, he wasn't in any hurry to meet what lay behind those invisible watching eyes.

"No," he decided. "We'll go upstream instead today."

For a heartbeat Cherry looked as if she might argue, then obviously thought better of it. Firestar picked his way down to the tumbled rocks where the river welled out into the light. As he leaped the last tail-length to the ground, he set one paw on a sharp chip of rock; pain stabbed through his pad like a claw. Letting out a hiss of anger, he paused to give the injured pad a quick lick. It wasn't bleeding, but it was sore enough to make him limp.

Cherry had bounded ahead, but when she realized Firestar wasn't with her, she came running back. "What's the matter?"

Firestar looked at her. "Aren't your pads sore?"

Cherry shook her head, and lifted one paw to show him. Her pads were tougher than his, with hard gray skin good for walking on rocks. Ruefully Firestar showed Cherry his own pads, the soft black skin scarred and rubbed raw from the rough ground.

Cherry blinked in surprise. "I never thought a cat's pads could get like that!"

"Remember, I don't come from around here," Firestar explained. "I'm more used to walking on soft forest ground." He wondered if this was the opportunity he had been waiting for. Should he tell Cherry about her ancestry? She would need to know if she was ever to become a SkyClan warrior.

He took a deep breath. "You remember that I told you how you inherited your ability to jump from your ancestors? Well, you inherited your strong paws from them too. Your ancestors were able to settle here because they had the right kind of bodies and the right skills."

The young tortoiseshell stared at him, her eyes stretched wide. "Do you mean that? You're not just telling a story?"

"No, it's true."

"How do you know so much about my ancestors?"

With a wave of his tail, Firestar led her into a patch of shade cast by a scrubby thorn tree at the foot of the cliff. When they were sitting side by side, their pelts brushing, he told her about the forest where he came from, and how four Clans of cats lived there.

"Once there were five Clans, but the fifth Clan, SkyClan, was sent away a long, long time ago. The cats came here and settled in the caves, but then they broke up and scattered. There's no SkyClan anymore, but some cats—like you and Boris—are descended from the original Clan."

Cherry's whiskers quivered with excitement. "Wow!"

"Look." Firestar pointed with his tail to the caves in the cliff face and the stony trails that connected them. "This was the SkyClan camp. The warriors lived in the cave where Sandstorm and I sleep. That cave there with the boulder at the entrance was the nursery—"

"Yes, I can see there's room for lots of cats," Cherry interrupted. "But why are you telling me all this?"

"Because Sky believes—"

The young tortoiseshell blinked. "Sky? Who's Sky?"

"The cat you call Moony," Firestar meowed. "Yes, the one you were so rude to. His real name is Sky. He is the last warrior of SkyClan—and he's your kin."

Cherry's fur fluffed up and her eyes stretched wider than ever. "Our *kin*? But we're kittypets!"

"You and Sky are all descended from the cats of SkyClan. And that's why I have come here—to find the scattered Clan and rebuild it."

"Starting with me and Boris?" Cherry's voice was a squeak of surprise.

Firestar suppressed a *mrrow* of amusement. "You'll have to make your own minds up about that," he replied. "I'll show you as much of Clan life and the warrior code as I can, and then you must decide."

For once Cherry was silent. Her gaze traveled up the cliff face where the caves were. Firestar wondered if she was trying to imagine what it would be like to live there with a whole Clan of cats.

And he realized that somehow, without consciously making the decision, he had accepted that he must stay.

They returned to the warriors' cave at sunhigh, laden with fresh-kill. The gorge basked in the heat like a huge, sandy-furred animal. Firestar winced as he set down his pads on the hot rock, but Cherry ran ahead without seeming to notice.

Sandstorm and Boris had already returned. They sat beside a small pile of fresh-kill; Boris was gulping down a sparrow.

Cherry pattered across the cave and dropped her prey on the pile. "Guess what, Boris? We're not kittypets at all! We're from SkyClan! They came from the forest where Firestar and Sandstorm live, all the way down the river, and they made their camp here. They—"

"Sandstorm told me too," Boris interrupted. His amber eyes shone with excitement. "She says we can be SkyClan warriors if we want."

"You'd make good warriors," Sandstorm put in, with an approving glance at the young tabby tom. "Boris hunted really well today."

"So did Cherry." Firestar twitched his ears toward the fresh-kill pile. "Go on; help yourself."

Cherry seized a mouse and began to devour it ravenously. Both cats seemed to have forgotten their worries about not being able to manage their Twoleg food as well.

"That tasted great!" Boris finished his sparrow and cleaned his whiskers with one paw. "Can we come again tomorrow?"

"Of course," Sandstorm replied. "You'll have to, if you want to learn about the warrior code."

"We do!" Cherry meowed enthusiastically.

"Just a moment." Firestar padded across the cave and sat down in front of the two young cats. "You do realize that the warrior code isn't just about having fun? It's a way of life. You can't live with your housefolk and pop to the gorge whenever you feel like it. If you want to be warriors, this has to be your home."

"Leave our housefolk?" Boris looked up from his sparrow, his eyes huge and serious. "I don't know . . . they're kind and they feed us, and they'd worry about us if we went away."

"But if we're really SkyClan cats, then this is where we need to live," Cherry argued. She gave her brother a nudge. "Come *on*! Don't you want to stay out as long as we want, even when it's dark? Wouldn't you rather eat mice and squirrels than that stupid kittypet food?"

Firestar exchanged a glance with Sandstorm. Cherry couldn't understand yet what it truly meant to be a warrior. In leaf-bare, with prey scarce and snow on the ground, she might have second thoughts.

"You don't have to make your minds up yet," he went on; he felt he had to warn her, even though he didn't want to dampen her enthusiasm. "Living by the warrior code can be hard."

"But you said we've got the right sort of bodies." Cherry gave her brother another vigorous nudge, so he almost toppled over. "You know you want to do this, don't you?"

"I guess. . . ." Boris was still thoughtful. Then he rose to his paws, a determined look in his eyes. "Well, I'll give it a try."

"Me too!" Cherry sprang up, gulping down the last mouthful of prey. "Come on, Boris. We can practice stalking in our garden."

Both young cats charged out of the cave. A heartbeat later, Cherry whisked back to mew, "Thanks! Bye!" and vanished again.

Sandstorm's green eyes glinted with amusement. "It looks as if we've found our first two apprentices."

Firestar and Sandstorm slept through the heat of the day. When the shadows were gathering, they set off to explore farther up the gorge.

"Sky showed us the downstream borders of the territory," Firestar meowed, "but he never told us how far it stretches in this direction."

"We could ask him."

Firestar glanced across to the other side of the gorge. They were just passing the huge boulder that hid the twisting path to Sky's den among the roots of the thorn tree. There was no sign of the old cat, and Firestar didn't want to go looking for him. He wanted more to report than a couple of possible apprentices before he talked to Sky again.

"Let's see what we can find for ourselves," he mewed.

The gorge grew narrower until a cat could almost have leaped from one side to the other. The sky above their heads was still bright, but little sunlight penetrated between the soaring cliffs on either side. The ground beneath their paws was dry and sandy, and the air was still.

Suddenly Sandstorm checked. "Fox!"

At the same instant the reek flooded over Firestar, and he heard a drawn-out snarling from the shadows ahead. It was followed by the screech of a cat.

"Come on!" Firestar's paws flew over the ground, his sore pads forgotten.

Sandstorm raced beside him. Around the next curve in the gorge, they saw the fox. It stood stiff-legged, its lips drawn back to bare sharp fangs. Firestar guessed it was starving; its ribs stuck out from a thin, ragged pelt.

In front of the fox crouched a pale brown she-cat; her fur bristled defiantly, but her eyes were wide with fear. Behind her was a pile of sandy rocks surrounded by thick thorn-bushes. Firestar spotted a dark opening in the rocks, and heard the mewling of terrified kits.

"She's protecting her kits!" Sandstorm gasped.

Firestar let out a yowl and flung himself on the fox. It turned on him, its jaws snapping for his throat. Sandstorm dashed in and raked her claws down its other side before it spun around and batted her away with one paw. Spitting with rage, Firestar leaped for its shoulder, snagging his claws in its pelt and trying to bury his teeth in its neck.

Even though the fox was starving, it could still fight furiously, or perhaps hunger had maddened it. Lashing its head from side to side, it dropped to the ground, trying to crush Firestar beneath it. His muzzle was buried in its fur; its hot scent was all around him as he struggled to breathe. He felt the sharp pain of claws in his belly. With a massive heave he managed to break free and scramble to his paws. Blood from his wound spattered in the sand, and his legs felt unsteady.

Sandstorm attacked again, darting rapidly in and out to deal a swift blow before the fox could retaliate, in an effort to lead it away from the kits. The she-cat still crouched in the mouth of the den, protecting her litter. With another vicious snarl the fox lunged for Sandstorm and grabbed her by the hind leg. Sandstorm let out a shriek of pain. Firestar staggered toward them, but pain blurred his vision, and though he clawed at the fox's haunches he couldn't get any strength behind the blow.

StarClan, help us!

A yowl sounded from farther down the gorge. Another cat was racing to join the battle; it was the dark ginger tom who had been hunting among the bushes downstream.

Letting out another furious screech, the rogue sprang up onto the rocks above the mouth of the den. He clung there for a couple of heartbeats, his claws gripping the rough surface, then hurled himself down to land on the fox's head.

The fox let out a squeal of pain and released Sandstorm. She leaped up on three paws and flung herself back into the battle, scoring a deep gash down the fox's side. Firestar's head was clearing now; he bit down on the fox's tail and heard it shriek.

The rogue was balanced on the fox's head, the claws of all four paws sunk deep into its fur. Blood welled from the scratches and began to trickle into the creature's eyes. Suddenly it gave up and began to stumble away. The ginger tom jumped down, and Firestar aimed a final blow at the fox's haunches as it limped into the shadows.

Breathing heavily, the three cats gazed at one another. "Thanks," Firestar panted. "That could have been nasty if you hadn't turned up."

"Don't thank me." The tomcat narrowed his eyes. "I don't like foxes any more than you do. You look a bit battered," he added, his gaze flicking from Firestar to Sandstorm and back again.

Sandstorm flexed her injured leg and put her paw to the ground. "I'll be okay."

Firestar examined his belly wound, drawing his tongue a few times over the blood-soaked fur. To his relief, the scratch wasn't deep, and the bleeding had already stopped. "We'll be fine," he meowed. "We needed a fight to liven us up." To his surprise, he realized that was true; for several days now he and Sandstorm had done little except rest in the warriors' cave and occasionally hunt. Now he felt more alive, more like a true Clan warrior.

"You're all so brave! Thank you so much! You saved my kits."

Firestar turned to see the pale brown she-cat guiding three kits toward them, her tail curled protectively around them: a black tom, a ginger tom, and a tiny white she-cat.

"I'm Clover," the she-cat announced, "and these are Rock, Bounce, and Tiny."

Sandstorm dipped her head. "I'm Sandstorm, and this is Firestar."

Firestar turned to the other rogue, waiting for him to introduce himself. Instead, he met a challenging gaze from green eyes that sparked with intelligence. "Names are easy," the ginger tom meowed, "but who *are* you? What are you doing here, and how long do you mean to stay?"

For a few moments Firestar was taken aback. The questions, and the cat's authoritative tone, reminded him of how he might have spoken if he had come across rogues in ThunderClan territory.

"I saw you farther down the gorge," he began.

"And I saw you." The ginger tom's ears flattened. "You were hunting with those two crazy kittypets. Why do you want to bother with them?"

"Cherry and Boris are okay," Sandstorm mewed defensively.

"What does it matter why they're here?" Clover broke in. "The fox would have eaten my kits if they hadn't come along!"

"*I* was here, wasn't I?" the ginger tom growled. He unsheathed powerful claws and dug them into the sandy earth. "I can see off any fox that's ever been born." His gaze rested on Firestar again. "So, what's your story?"

"You won't go yet, will you?" Clover begged, with a nervous glance into the shadows. "The fox might come back."

"We'll stay for a while," Sandstorm promised.

Clover lay down in the mouth of her den so that her three kits could burrow into her side and feed. The other cats settled down beside her, Firestar and Sandstorm licking their wounds in between telling the ginger tom about SkyClan.

"I've seen that old cat a few times," the rogue meowed when Firestar recounted his meeting with Sky. "I've never spoken to him, though. He looks mad to me."

"He's not mad. He knows more about the lost Clan than any cat alive." Firestar explained what Sky had told them. "The Clan lived here many moons ago, in the caves near the rocks where the river pours out. They're all gone now, but Sky believes that I can find their descendants and rebuild the Clan."

Firestar was suddenly aware of how foolish he sounded. "I know it's a big decision for any cat . . . ," he went on.

"Not for me." Clover looked up, her ears pricked. "I'd come and live in your Clan in a heartbeat. My kits' father went away before they were born, and it's hard bringing them up on my own." She drew her tail more closely around her kits; by now they had finished suckling, and lay sleeping in a tricolored puddle of warm fur. "Suppose that fox comes back when you've gone?"

"*I* could look after you," the rogue tom reminded her. "I turned up in time today, didn't I?"

"But you hardly ever come this far up the gorge," Clover retorted. "How often have we spoken to each other before now?" Ignoring his hiss of annoyance, she turned back to Firestar. "I'll join the new Clan. We'll all come back to the caves with you today."

Firestar felt his paws tingle with excitement. A nursing queen and three kits was a valuable addition to any Clan. "Well, that's great. We can go now. What about you?" he added with a glance at the ginger tom. "Will you join us too?"

"I manage fine by myself, thanks."

Firestar's pelt prickled with disappointment. This proud, strong, intelligent cat would make a good warrior.

"Mind you," the rogue went on, before Firestar could think of a way to persuade him, "I like the idea of training cats to defend themselves. And I liked the fighting moves you used to drive the fox away."

"Come with us and we'll teach you," Firestar offered.

The ginger rogue blinked at him. "You'd really teach me everything you know?" He sounded as if he couldn't believe cats would share battle secrets that would make them easier to fight.

"Of course," mewed Firestar. "Clanmates don't fight one

another, except for training."

"That could be a good way to live," the rogue meowed.

"Then you'll come?" Sandstorm asked eagerly.

The rogue hesitated, then dipped his head. "I'll give it a try. But I'm not promising to stay for good."

"We won't ask you to decide that yet," mewed Firestar. "Just come to the caves for a while, and find out more about what it means to live in a Clan."

"And tell us your name, please," Sandstorm added.

For a few heartbeats the ginger tom was silent, staring into the distance. "Living alone, a cat doesn't need a name, but now . . . A long time ago, I think my mother called me Scratch."

The waning moon floated above the gorge, shedding pale light over the Skyrock. Firestar jumped over the cleft and stood back to wait for Sandstorm.

"Well?" he asked when his mate had landed by his side. "What do you think? Have we got the makings of a new Clan?"

Sandstorm sat down and gave her chest fur a few quick licks. "It's a start," she mewed, "but there's a long way to go yet."

"I know," Firestar replied. "I'm afraid Scratch will decide not to stay. He didn't want to sleep in the warriors' cave with us tonight. He's still thinking like a rogue."

"Give him time. What worries me," Sandstorm went on, drawing one paw over her ear, "is the way Clover wants to be looked after the whole time. I tried to tell her that the proper place for her and her kits is in the nursery—I even offered to collect the moss and bracken for her—but would she listen? She insists on sleeping in the warriors' cave, in case the fox finds her."

"She needs time too," Firestar comforted her, resting his tail tip on her shoulder. "She had a nasty fright today. She'll soon learn fighting skills, and then she'll realize she can look after her kits herself."

"I hope you're right," Sandstorm meowed.

Firestar heard the sound of pawsteps on the trail leading up to the Skyrock. He glanced down, half prepared to see Scratch, but to his surprise the cat who came into sight was Sky.

"What's he doing here?" he murmured to Sandstorm. "The moon isn't full."

Moonlight turned the old cat's gray pelt to silver; he walked with his head raised proudly, like a true warrior of SkyClan. As he approached the Skyrock, he quickened his pace, and leaped across without hesitation to land on the smooth surface.

"Greetings, Sky." Firestar and Sandstorm dipped their heads to him.

The old cat returned their greeting with a brief nod. "I saw more cats arrive today."

"That's right." Firestar expected Sky to sound more pleased, but there was a wary glitter in his eyes. "I think we might be on the way to rebuilding SkyClan."

A low growl rumbled in Sky's throat. "That ginger rogue would tear your throat out as soon as look at you. And as for those kittypets! I don't know why you're wasting your time with them."

"The kittypets will be fine," Sandstorm mewed. "They're young; they've got lots of time to learn. And they're true SkyClan cats! Have you seen how high they can leap?"

Sky just sniffed.

"And Scratch—that's the ginger rogue's name," Firestar went on, "is tough and a fighter, and once he's learned about the warrior code, he'll be just the sort of cat a Clan needs."

To his relief the old cat nodded. "Maybe you're right," he mewed grudgingly. "At least you're keeping your promise."

He raised his head to the glitter of Silverpelt above them. Following his gaze, Firestar wondered if the SkyClan ancestor was watching. *Are you pleased too?* he wondered. *Is this what you wanted from me?*

There was no answer, nothing but the distant blaze of stars.

CHAPTER 23

"Cats who live in a Clan send out hunting patrols several times a day," Firestar explained, pausing at the end of the line of Twoleg fences. "And we patrol the borders twice, once at dawn and once at sunset."

"So are we the dawn patrol?" Boris asked.

"Mouse-brain!" His sister Cherry swiped at him with one paw. "SkyClan doesn't *have* borders yet. We're hunters, aren't we, Firestar?"

"That's right," Firestar meowed. "We'll have borders soon, when I know the territory a bit better, and see how many cats are going to be living here. Meanwhile, this is SkyClan's first proper hunting patrol."

Cherry gave a happy little bounce. "Great! We haven't caught much, though," she added, sounding disappointed. "I can't seem to pick up any scent at all."

"That's because it's wet," Firestar told her. "Even experienced hunters find it hard."

Fog filled the gorge and stretched over the scrubland on the cliff top as far as the Twolegplace. The rising sun shone through it with a milky light. Every grass stem was bent with the weight of water droplets, and dew misted on the cats' fur.

"But that's no excuse for taking risks." Scratch looked up from where he was digging up some fresh-kill they had buried earlier. "I couldn't *believe* you two. You leaped straight into that garden without looking."

"Sorry," Cherry muttered, while Boris scrabbled his forepaws on the ground in front of him.

"'Sorry' is all very well," snapped the rogue. "You nearly landed right on top of that dog. If Firestar hadn't distracted it, you would be dog food by now. *And* you lost the squirrel you were chasing."

Boris sighed. "It was lovely and fat."

Scratch rolled his eyes and went back to scraping away the earth over their prey.

Firestar gave him a quick glance. It was four days since Scratch and Clover had come to live in the caves, and Scratch's hunting skills were already proving useful, but he had no patience with the two kittypets.

"They'll learn," Firestar meowed, and added to Cherry and Boris, "You're coming along really well."

"Can we come and live in the camp all the time?" Cherry begged.

"Not yet." Firestar was relieved the young cat was so keen to join the Clan, but he wondered if she realized what a huge decision she was making. "What about leaving your housefolk?"

Cherry's tail drooped and her eyes grew more thoughtful. "I like sitting on a lap and being stroked, and I like playing with our housefolk and making them laugh . . . but I like hunting too. I wish we could have both."

"Well, we can't," mewed Boris. "I worry about our housefolk missing us, too. If we could just tell them that we'll be okay . . ." He took a deep breath. "But if we are really descendants of the first SkyClan, we belong in the gorge."

Firestar blinked at him. "I think you need to take your time before you make the final decision." Scratch had been right to scold them for dashing into the garden, even though he could have been more tactful. The kittypets' biggest fault was charging blindly into things. But at least it showed they had courage, a valuable quality in a warrior.

"How much longer?" Cherry demanded. "Can we be apprentices soon?"

Before Firestar could reply, Scratch looked up. "Are we just going to stand around here? I want to be back in the gorge before the mist clears. I've never had anything to do with Twolegs, and I don't intend to start now."

"Good thinking," Firestar meowed. Already the Twoleg nests were standing out more clearly against the dawn sky, and he could hear a monster waking up in the distance. "Bring your prey, and let's go."

As he led the way across the scrubland, his jaws full of fresh-kill and his ears pricked for any sound of danger, optimism swept over him. He was leading a patrol, taking prey back to a camp. For the first time since he left the forest, he felt as if he were really part of a Clan.

* * *

By the time they returned to the warriors' cave, the sun had burned off most of the mist. Even though the leaves were beginning to turn yellow, the gorge was still bathed in the heat of greenleaf.

Sandstorm was climbing the trail from the gorge. Her green eyes were sparking with annoyance, and the tip of her tail flicked.

"What's the matter?" Firestar asked, setting down his fresh-kill at the cave entrance.

Sandstorm beckoned with her tail, so he took a few paw-steps down the path to meet her, away from Scratch and the kittypets.

"It's Clover," she murmured when he was close enough to hear. "I've been trying to teach her some fighting skills. She's a strong, healthy cat—she shouldn't have any problem—but can I make her see why she has to learn? 'Oh, you and Firestar are such good fighters I know you'll look after us all.'" Sandstorm let out a sigh. "She's keen enough to join SkyClan, but just for protection. She's not interested in the warrior code, or what *she* might do for other cats."

Firestar narrowed his eyes. "That could be difficult for her to learn right now," he mewed. "It's natural for a queen to put her kits' safety first. And she must be pretty tired, raising those three lively youngsters."

"But at least she could *try*," Sandstorm pointed out. She glanced down into the gorge where Clover was basking on a rock by the side of the pool, with her kits frisking around her. "Bounce and Rock and Tiny were trying to copy what I was showing their mother. Honestly, I think they learned more than she did!"

Firestar pressed his muzzle against hers. "It'll work out. She couldn't have a better teacher."

Sandstorm gave him a sidelong glance, and seemed to relax. "Let's go down to the river," she mewed. "My paws could do with bathing."

Firestar's paws felt sore, too, and as he followed Sandstorm down the stony trail he longed to feel the cool, damp earth of the forest under his pads. A few fox-lengths upstream he could hear the excited squeals of Clover's litter.

"You know, those kits are almost ready to be apprenticed," he remarked as they stood in the shallows.

"They must be nearly six moons old," Sandstorm agreed, blinking against the sunlit dazzle on the water. "But we can't apprentice them until we find a few more mentors."

"I'll ask Scratch and Clover if they know of any more cats," Firestar meowed.

He broke off at the sound of voices calling his name from somewhere up above. Cherry and Boris were charging down the rock face, springing gracefully down sheer stretches of rock where Firestar and Sandstorm had to pick their way more cautiously.

"Firestar!" Cherry panted as she sprang to the ground and pelted along the bank toward him. "We had an idea!"

"You mean *I* had an idea," Boris mewed, bouncing up to stand beside his sister.

Cherry tried to shoulder him into the water, but Boris

ducked away and swiped one paw over her ear. Cherry pounced on him, and the two kittypets wrestled at the very edge of the river.

"When you've quite finished," Sandstorm interrupted, "maybe you'll tell us what your idea is."

The two young cats straightened up, looking embarrassed. "I guess apprentices don't do that," Cherry muttered.

Apprentices do that all the time, Firestar thought. "I'm listening," he meowed.

"I thought you should have a meeting," Boris explained, his fur fluffed up with enthusiasm. "We can tell all the cats who live near here to come, so you can tell them about the new Clan."

"But we don't know any other cats," Firestar pointed out.

"No, hang on," Sandstorm meowed, before Boris could reply. "I think it's a good idea. After all, we're looking for cats who can live together and cooperate with one another, so if they turn up to a meeting they've already passed the first test."

"I hadn't thought of that." Firestar waded out of the river, shook each paw in turn, and sat down on a sun-warmed rock. "Right, go on. Where do we find these cats?"

"*We* find them." Cherry's green eyes sparkled. "We can pass the message on to all the other kittypets. We'll go now if you like."

"They'll all be outside on a day like this," Boris added.

Firestar exchanged a glance with Sandstorm. "Okay," he decided. "We'll give it a try—but if we expect these cats to come to a meeting they deserve to see who'll be talking to them. I'm coming with you."

Firestar peered down through a rustling screen of leaves into the Twoleg garden. He couldn't see much except for a stretch of grass and a few clumps of bright Twoleg flowers, but there was a strong scent of cat.

Cherry and Boris were crouched on the branch below him. "Hey, Oscar!" Cherry called. "Come up here! We want to talk to you."

A moment later Firestar spotted a muscular black tomcat racing across the grass. He launched himself into the tree with a magnificent leap. *SkyClan blood,* Firestar thought as the newcomer balanced on the branch beside Boris and Cherry.

"What's going on?" he asked. His whiskers twitched as he looked up at Firestar. "Who's he?"

Firestar took a deep breath. "My name's Firestar," he meowed, deciding not to confuse the black cat with details about the forest and ThunderClan. That wasn't important now. "Have you ever heard of SkyClan? The cats who used to live in the gorge by the river?"

Oscar swished his tail. "Nope. Never heard of them."

Cherry and Boris exchanged a glance; Cherry opened her jaws to reply, but Firestar silenced her with a flick of his ears.

"But they've heard about you," Firestar went on, "and there are things you need to know about them. We're holding a meeting tomorrow night in the gorge, by the rocks where the river flows out. Will you come?"

Oscar's eyes narrowed to brilliant green slits. He raised one paw and slid the claws out, contemplating them coolly. "Might. Might not."

Firestar bit back his frustration. He guessed Oscar was a bit of a show-off, but at the same time this was a strong cat who would be a useful Clan member. "You see, I'm trying to rebuild SkyClan, and I'm looking for any cats who might be interested in joining."

Oscar stretched his jaws wide in a yawn. "Why would I want to do that?" Not waiting for an answer, he jumped down from the tree and disappeared.

"Come anyway! See what you think!" Firestar called after him.

Cherry's neck fur bristled. "We should have known better than to ask him!" she mewed. "He's a real pain in the tail."

"Never mind," Firestar replied. "We have to ask as many cats as we can."

"Let's get on, then." Boris sprang impatiently to his paws. "I think we should talk to Hutch next."

"Yes, let's." Cherry's eyes gleamed and she swiped her tongue over her whiskers. "His Twolegs give him *cream*!"

The two kittypets led Firestar along the fence of Oscar's garden and down into a narrow alley. Firestar's fur prickled as he remembered being lost in the other Twolegplace while he was looking for Sandstorm, but his two guides trotted ahead confidently.

Before they had gone far, another cat appeared around the corner and halted with its pelt bristling, then relaxed as

Boris and Cherry drew closer.

"Hi, Bella," Cherry greeted her. "Come and meet our new friend."

Firestar padded up to Bella, a pretty tabby-and-white she-cat with warm amber eyes. He was reminded of his sister Princess, who lived in the Twolegplace that bordered the forest. This cat didn't look as if she had SkyClan ancestry; she didn't have the same powerful haunches as Boris and Cherry, and when she raised her paw to dab at a piece of dust on her nose, her pads were soft and pink.

"Hello." Bella dipped her head politely. "You're new around here. Where do your housefolk live?"

"Firestar doesn't have housefolk," Boris informed her. "He's a Clan cat."

Bella's eyes stretched wide with curiosity, changing to wonder as Firestar briefly told his story.

"You'll come to the meeting, won't you?" Cherry prompted when he had finished. "It'll be great, living in a Clan! I'll show you how to catch mice."

Bella shook her head. "I couldn't possibly do that. I would miss my housefolk far too much, and they would miss me."

"But—" Boris began.

"No," Bella repeated more firmly. "The other night I got shut in the neighbor's shed, and when I got back my housefolk's kits were wailing. I can't bear to think of them upset like that again." She pressed her muzzle affectionately against Cherry's. "But I hope you enjoy living in this new Clan, if that's what you want."

"Thanks, Bella." Cherry looked unusually serious. "We'll come and visit you sometimes; I promise." She watched as the she-cat trotted away down the alley. "I'll miss her," she muttered. "She's a good friend."

Boris gave her ear a quick lick. "Come on; let's go and find Hutch."

At the other end of the alley Cherry and Boris paused beside another fence. One of the wooden strips was broken at the bottom, leaving a space just wide enough for a cat to squeeze in.

"We've got to be careful," Boris warned. "Hutch's Twolegs have a dog as well. It should be shut up, but keep your eyes open."

Cherry had already pushed her way through the gap. Firestar followed warily, while Boris brought up the rear.

On the other side of the fence, Firestar found himself in a thicket of strong-smelling bushes. Beyond it a stretch of grass led up to a path made of sharp little stones running around the Twoleg nest.

"Hey, Hutch!" Boris yowled. "Are you in there?"

Firestar stiffened as a flurry of barking came from the nest, but no dog appeared. Instead, a tiny door swung open in the big Twoleg door, and a dark tabby cat poked its head out. Spotting Cherry and Boris, he slid out the rest of the way, bounded across the stony path without flinching, and raced over the grass to meet them in the shadow of the bushes. He was not as powerfully built as Oscar, but he looked strong, and Firestar had noticed when he crossed the path that he had the hard pads that were a mark of SkyClan. He smelled strongly of kittypet food.

"Hi," he meowed with a friendly flick of his ears to Firestar. "My name's Hutch; what's yours?"

Once again Firestar introduced himself and told the story of SkyClan. "The SkyClan cats could live in the gorge because they had strong back legs for jumping, and hard pads for walking over rock. Just like Cherry and Boris." He felt a stirring of relief when Hutch raised one of his own paws to examine his pads. "We're holding a meeting to talk about it."

Hutch looked intrigued. "I've heard about cats living wild in the gorge," he told Firestar. "My mother used to tell me, but I thought they were just stories for kits."

"No, it's all true," Boris mewed, and Cherry added enthusiastically, "We're going to be SkyClan apprentices!"

"So you'll come to the meeting?" Firestar asked. "Tomorrow night, in the gorge where the river flows out."

"Sure," Hutch replied.

Firestar dipped his head. "Then we'll see you there."

Hutch flicked his tail in farewell and turned to go, then glanced back. "Are you hungry?"

Cherry's ears pricked. "Cream?" she mewed hopefully, swiping her tongue around her jaws.

"A whole bowlful."

"Hang on," Firestar meowed, before Cherry or Boris could move. "You can be a SkyClan apprentice, or you can go into Twoleg nests and eat cream. Not both."

"But we're not apprentices yet," Cherry retorted pertly.

Part of Firestar was amused, but he knew that if he gave his permission now the two young kittypets might never really appreciate what it meant to join a Clan. If they weren't ready to give up Twoleg comforts, they weren't ready to live the life of a warrior.

"SkyClan or cream," he meowed. "You choose."

Cherry and Boris exchanged a glance, and Cherry let out a disappointed sigh.

"It's got to be SkyClan," she replied.

"Fresh-kill tastes better anyway," Boris mewed. "Come on; we've got lots more cats to see."

They plunged back into the bushes toward the fence. Firestar waited to say good-bye to Hutch, and saw his own amusement reflected in the dark tabby's eyes. Suddenly he felt encouraged. This was a cat he could work with.

Cherry and Boris led the way back into the alley and around a corner to the edge of a small Thunderpath. Firestar paused by the fence, his neck fur bristling at the reek of monsters. One of them was crouched a few fox-lengths away, but it seemed to be asleep.

"It's okay," Boris meowed, strolling nonchalantly up to the edge of the Thunderpath. "It's pretty quiet at this time of day."

Cherry bounced up to join him; Firestar admitted to himself that he was impressed. These two kittypets had a lot to learn about Clan life and the warrior code, but here they were confident and focused, and they seemed to know every pawstep of the Twolegplace.

Trying not to show his uneasiness, he padded across to join them, glancing both ways along the Thunderpath. No monsters were in sight, and he couldn't hear any approaching.

"Come *on*!" Cherry urged.

Firestar signaled with his tail, though he wasn't sure that the two young cats were waiting for his order. "Okay, let's go."

All three cats darted across; Cherry and Boris swarmed up the nearest fence and balanced on the top, waiting for Firestar.

"We can go along this fence," Boris explained. "We'll pass two or three gardens where cats live. Watch out for this next one, though. The Twolegs here have a dog."

"Noisy little brute." Cherry sniffed. "It'll probably come out, barking its stupid head off."

She was right. As soon as Boris set paw on the next section of fence, a small white dog shot out of the Twoleg nest, yapping furiously. It sprang up at the fence, and Firestar dug his claws hard into the wood as it shook.

"Get lost, flea-pelt," Cherry spat. "Go and drool over your Twolegs. Don't worry," she added kindly to Firestar. "The idiot can't climb."

Firestar felt as if he were the apprentice and the two kittypets were his mentors. "I'm fine with dogs, thanks," he meowed.

The dog went on barking as the three cats continued along the fence top. Firestar hid his relief as the noise died away behind them.

Eventually Boris paused and looked down over a bigger

garden than most of them, with a wide expanse of smooth grass bordered by masses of bright flowers. Firestar picked up a strong scent of cat.

Cherry lifted her tail to point. "Over there."

She was pointing at some wooden Twoleg thing standing at the edge of the grass in front of the flowers. Lying on top of it was a shapeless heap of cream-and-brown fur.

Cherry jumped down from the fence, landing in a clump of flowers; Firestar and Boris followed and skirted the edge of the flower border until they reached the wooden Twoleg thing.

Two identical heads rose from the heap of fur. Firestar's ears pricked with curiosity. He had never seen cats like these before. Their slender bodies were cream-colored, but their legs, tails, ears, and muzzles were brown, and they had the most brilliant blue eyes he had ever seen.

One of them let out a weird high-pitched yowl. "Hi, Cherry. Hi, Boris."

"What do you want?" the other asked, in the same strange voice.

"We've brought Firestar to meet you," Boris meowed. "This is Rose and this is Lily," he added to Firestar, flicking his tail at each cat in turn.

"Greetings," Firestar began. He felt oddly hesitant; these cats couldn't possibly be SkyClan descendants. "I've come to tell you about the cats who used to live in the gorge. . . ."

The two cats listened to him in silence, their vivid eyes fixed disconcertingly on him. When he had finished, they turned the same intense stare on each other.

"What do you think of that?" Rose asked.

"Amazing!" Lily replied.

"You will come to the meeting, won't you?" Cherry urged them. "It's going to be really great!"

"What, us?" Rose's eyes opened wide. "You're joking, of course."

"Us live in a *cave*? With no warm blanket?" Lily added. "No creamed chicken?"

"To chase mice and *kill* them?" Rose's tongue rasped delicately over one brown paw. "How vulgar!"

Moving as one, the two cats rested their heads on their paws again and closed their eyes.

Cherry exchanged a glance with Boris, who gave a tiny shrug. "Sorry," she mewed to Firestar. "It was worth a try."

"Don't worry," Firestar told him. He couldn't imagine these cats ever adjusting to the life of a Clan, but in case they were still listening he kept his thoughts to himself.

Leaping back onto the fence, he was startled to see that the sun was starting to go down. They had spent most of the day in the Twolegplace and now he was ravenous. At the same moment he heard a distant yowling from a Twoleg several gardens away.

"That's one of our housefolk," Boris told him. "We'd better be going." Sadly, he added, "We'll miss them, you know."

"That's not wrong, is it?" Cherry asked anxiously.

"No," Firestar replied, remembering his own pangs of homesickness. "It's not wrong. But you have to choose."

"We've chosen," Boris meowed determinedly, while Cherry whisked her tail and added, "Come on, Firestar! We'll show you the best way out of here."

Padding back across the scrubland on his own, Firestar spotted movement underneath a thornbush. Cautiously he drew nearer, and recognized the brown rogue who had frightened off the sparrow when he first arrived in the gorge. The cat was crouched over a piece of fresh-kill, and looked up suspiciously as Firestar approached.

"Hi." Firestar tried to sound friendly. "Have you heard about the Clan of cats who used to live in the gorge?"

The brown rogue gave a noncommittal grunt and went on eating. Firestar couldn't be sure he was even listening as he told him about SkyClan and the meeting planned for the following night.

"What do you think?" he asked. "Will you come?"

The rogue swallowed the last mouthful of fresh-kill and cleaned his muzzle with one paw. "I'm fine on my own." His eyes narrowed. "And I don't want *you* ordering me around."

"It's not like that—" Firestar protested, but the rogue stalked off without letting him explain. Guilt gnawed at Firestar as he headed back to the gorge. Maybe if he hadn't been so hostile when they first met, he could have persuaded the brown rogue to give SkyClan a chance.

Finding the trail leading down the cliff face, he padded wearily along it to the warriors' cave. Faint squeals of excitement rose from the bottom of the gorge; Firestar peered down to spot Sandstorm and Clover's three kits batting something around at the water's edge. Warmth flooded through him when he saw how happy and relaxed his mate looked as she played with the kits, happier than she had been since they left the forest.

"Hi, Firestar." Scratch's voice interrupted his thoughts. "Sandstorm says you're organizing a meeting to tell more cats about the new Clan. I could take you to some other rogues, if you like. They'll probably come if I ask them."

Firestar was glad Scratch was becoming more committed to SkyClan, but not sure he liked the tabby tom's cool assumption of authority over the other rogues. Still, if they respected him, that would make Firestar's task easier overall.

"Okay, thanks," he meowed.

"Let's go then." Scratch emerged from the warriors' den and set off down the trail.

What, now? Firestar wailed inwardly. *I haven't eaten all day!*

Sighing, he followed Scratch down the cliff face and caught up with him as he was speaking to Sandstorm. "I'm going to introduce Firestar to a few rogues," he was telling her.

"Great." Sandstorm ducked her head as Rock sprang onto her back. "Get *off!*" she mewed, rolling over and padding gently at him with one paw, her claws sheathed. Rock just squeaked happily, and Sandstorm disappeared under a mound of fur as Bounce and Tiny jumped on her too.

"You're obviously busy," Firestar murmured, amused. "I'll see you later."

Scratch and Firestar padded side by side across the rocky spur to the trees and undergrowth downstream. Firestar hadn't visited this part of the territory since his meeting with Cherry and Boris, and his pelt prickled at the memory of being watched. Then he drew to a halt, his heart beginning to thump. This wasn't just memory! The same sensations poured over him, and icy fear trickled through him from ears to tail tip.

"What's the matter?" Scratch, some way ahead, glanced over his shoulder.

"Nothing." Firestar's voice shook, and he forced it to be steady. "I just thought we might stop and hunt. I haven't had so much as the sniff of a mouse since this morning."

"Okay." Scratch retraced his steps and stood tasting the air.

"Do you smell anything . . . odd?" Firestar asked. He had picked up the same prey scent as before, masked by the sharp aroma of crushed leaves.

Scratch paused, drew in more air, then shrugged. "Prey. Grass and leaves. Why?"

"Nothing." Firestar wanted Scratch to respect him, not think he was a coward looking for danger under every bush. "Let's hunt."

Scratch stalked away into the bushes, and Firestar padded off in another direction. While he tried to find prey, his senses stayed alert for whatever hostile creature was watching him.

Is it something to do with why SkyClan left the gorge? he wondered. Sky had been reluctant to answer any questions, but Firestar was certain that the old cat knew more than he was telling. *I'll have to question him again,* he decided. The future of the new Clan might be at risk if Sky insisted on keeping secrets about possible danger.

Firestar stood in the shadows under a thornbush, looking out across a clear space in the midst of the undergrowth. Nothing stirred among the ferns and grasses.

"Who are you?" he whispered. "What do you want?"

There was no reply, only vicious hatred hurled at him with such force that it almost carried him off his paws. In the twilight he thought he could make out dark, glinting eyes. His pelt crawled.

A rustling in a nearby bush made him jump, but it was only a vole, dashing out into the open space. Firestar leaped after it and snapped its neck. As he picked it up the scent masked everything else, and the sense of a hostile presence around him faded a little. Still, he pushed his way to the edge of the thicket and out into the open by the river before he crouched to eat his fresh-kill.

Scratch was sitting a few tail-lengths farther downstream, cleaning his face and whiskers. "Are you ready?" he asked, drawing his paw over one ear. "It'll be dark soon."

Firestar gulped down the rest of the vole. "Okay, lead on."

The tabby rogue bounded alongside the river until he reached the fallen tree that Sky had used to cross a few days before. Leading Firestar over to the far bank, Scratch started to climb another trail that led up the cliff face on the opposite side. Firestar panted after him, wishing he had the rogue's powerful haunches. Scratch was a true SkyClan cat!

Firestar had never climbed the cliff on this side of the river before. At the top there was a wide stretch of grass that gave way to undergrowth and then trees. His spirits lifted as he padded with Scratch underneath the branches. This was more like his territory in the forest.

"When we set the borders, we'll have to make this part of SkyClan territory." Firestar sniffed appreciatively. "There's plenty of prey. Moss, too," he added, flicking his ears toward thick cushions of it growing on the gnarled roots of an oak tree.

Scratch gave him a sidelong glance. "Then you'd better convince the rogues who live here already."

Firestar realized he had a point. He didn't want to start the new Clan by throwing other cats out of dens they had occupied for moons.

Scratch wove his way through the trees until they came to a hollow tree trunk lying amid lush grass in the middle of a clearing. A pale, blurred shape was visible at the mouth of the tree trunk. As Firestar drew nearer he recognized the cream-and-brown tabby she-cat he had surprised in the scrubland near the Twolegplace.

"Scratch?" Her ears twitched warily as the two toms drew nearer. "Who's this with you?"

"Hi," Firestar meowed, slightly embarrassed, when Scratch had introduced him. "We met the other day. . . ."

The she-cat emerged from the end of the trunk; her amber gaze traveled over him steadily. "I remember you," she murmured. "I'm sorry; I didn't mean to snap at you like that. You gave me a fright, practically leaping on top of me."

Firestar dipped his head. "It was my fault."

"My name's Leaf," the she-cat continued, settling down in the long grass and waving her tail to invite Firestar to do the same. "What can I do for you?"

Firestar crouched beside her, tucking his paws underneath him, while Scratch clawed his way to the top of the trunk and gazed out into the trees. Firestar wondered if he was keeping watch, though the hostile sensation had faded as soon as they crossed the river, and now he was aware of nothing more than the ordinary scents and sounds of a forest at dusk.

"You know the place in the gorge where the river flows out?" he began.

Leaf listened in silence to the story of how SkyClan had been forced to flee from the forest. "Why are you telling me?" she asked when he had finished.

"The old SkyClan leader appeared to me in dreams," Firestar explained. "He sent me to rebuild the Clan, and I'm looking for cats who might want to join."

Leaf looked startled, and for several heartbeats she didn't reply, her gaze fixed on the shadows among the trees. "I don't know . . ." she mewed eventually. "I like it here, and I'm fine on my own. Scratch, are you going to join?"

Scratch padded along to the end of the trunk so he could look down at her. "I'm thinking about it. Cats living together could protect one another."

Leaf nodded. "That's true. Living alone is especially hard for old cats and kits. You remember Scree?" she asked Scratch.

"The old rogue who lived by the dead willow tree?"

"That's right." Sadness welled up in Leaf's eyes. "I found him trying to fight off a fox. It turned tail when it saw me, but Scree was badly wounded. I stayed with him that night and tried to help him, but he died before morning." She turned an intense gaze on Firestar. "That wouldn't happen in a Clan, would it?"

"It might," Firestar answered honestly. "But mostly Clan cats don't have to fight alone, and if they're wounded we have a medicine cat to look after them."

Leaf gave her chest fur a couple of thoughtful licks.

"We're having a meeting tomorrow night," Firestar told her. "Why don't you come and find out more?"

"All right," she meowed. "I'll come to the meeting. But I'm not promising anything else."

"I wouldn't expect you to," Firestar assured her.

He glanced back as Scratch led him farther into the wood. He fiercely hoped that Leaf would decide to join SkyClan. She already seemed to be aware of how a Clan could take care of its weaker members. Any Clan would be glad to have her.

Scratch led him along a narrow path that twisted among arching clumps of fern, the thick fronds blocking out the last of the daylight. Firestar picked up a strong cat scent before he saw anything; not long after, a bad-tempered hiss came out of the darkness.

Just ahead of Firestar, Scratch meowed, "Hi, Tangle."

"This is my place," a voice snapped. Peering over Scratch's shoulder, Firestar made out a large tomcat with ragged tabby fur crouched among the roots of a tree. His fur was bristling and his amber eyes glared as if he were about to spring on them. "Go away!"

Stepping around Scratch, Firestar dipped his head in greeting. "My name's Firestar. I'm holding a meeting for all the cats who—"

"I don't like meetings," Tangle rasped. "Don't like other cats much. Now go away, unless you want a clawed pelt."

Scratch touched Firestar on the shoulder. "He means it. We'd better go."

"Tomorrow night in the gorge, if you change your mind," Firestar meowed quickly.

Tangle unsheathed his claws. Scratch butted Firestar in the side with one shoulder and muttered, "Move!" To Tangle he added, "We're going. See you around some time."

"Not if I see you first," Tangle hissed, as Firestar and Scratch retreated into the ferns.

"He's not very friendly, is he?" Firestar commented when they were out of earshot.

Scratch shrugged. "He never has been. I thought we'd better ask him, but I'm not surprised he wouldn't listen."

They came to a narrow stream reflecting the pale evening sky as it wound through clumps of grass and watermint. Scratch leaped across and headed upstream until he came to a place where the bank overhung a narrow strip of pebbles. Once again Firestar picked up a strong scent of cat.

Scratch halted. "Patch, are you there?" he meowed.

A black-and-white head poked out from under the overhang. "Scratch, is that you?"

His voice was cautious, but to Firestar's relief he didn't sound as unfriendly as Tangle.

"I've brought another cat to see you," Scratch replied. "We've come to tell you about the cats who used to live in the gorge."

"Oh, them!" Patch came out of his den and stood on the strip of pebbles, looking up. "I know about them. I hope you haven't brought that mad old rogue who's always going on about them."

"No, he brought me." Firestar stepped forward and looked into Patch's gleaming green eyes. "And Sky isn't mad—far from it. He has kept alive the memory of the Clan for many seasons." Yet again he explained what he was trying to do. "SkyClan could be great again," he finished. "We're looking for strong cats to join, and Scratch thought you might be interested."

"It does get a bit lonely here sometimes," Patch admitted, flicking his tail tip. "I could come to your meeting, I suppose, and have a look at the other cats who might be joining."

"Thank you," Firestar meowed. "You'll be welcome."

When they had said good-bye to Patch they started back toward the river. By now it was almost completely dark; little starlight penetrated the thick canopy of leaves. Scratch checked the opening of a hollow oak tree, but it was empty, and the cat scent that clung around it was stale.

"That's Rainfur's den," he remarked. "It looks like he hasn't been around for a couple of days."

Firestar felt worn-out when they arrived back at the gorge.

But if only a few of the cats they had seen today decided to join, they would have the beginnings of a Clan. *But only the beginning,* he told himself. There was a lot of work to do before SkyClan would truly live again.

They had almost reached the path down the cliff when Sky let out a sharp exclamation and bounded ahead. Firestar caught up to find him talking to a tomcat whose pale gray pelt was marked with darker flecks.

"This is Rainfur," he told Firestar. "We looked for you in your den," he added to the gray tom.

Rainfur flicked his ears. "I've been downstream. Is there a problem?"

"No, just some news. Firestar, tell him what you told the others."

As Firestar launched into his story again he was aware that Rainfur was looking doubtful. He seemed like a strong, proud cat who would need a good reason before he gave up his independence. When Firestar invited him to the meeting, he was quite prepared for him to refuse.

He was surprised when Rainfur nodded. "I'll come," the gray tom meowed, "but I'm not sure I like the idea. What will happen to cats who live here if they *don't* want to join?"

"Nothing." Firestar put as much conviction as he could into his voice. "We don't want to quarrel with any cat."

Rainfur's eyes narrowed. "This is a peaceful place. I wouldn't want anything to spoil it." Abruptly he turned and plunged into the undergrowth.

"See you tomorrow!" Scratch called after him.

Firestar thought over the gray tom's words as he followed Scratch down the path toward the river. He wanted to include at least part of this wood in the new Clan's territory, but he didn't want to cause trouble with the rogues who decided to remain as they were.

When Scratch reached the bottom of the cliff he turned toward the fallen tree trunk, but Firestar raised his tail to stop him and led the way upstream, intending to cross the river by the Rockpile. He still remembered the hostile force he had sensed in the undergrowth, and his belly lurched at the thought of encountering it again.

Moonlight washed over the gorge as Firestar and Scratch crossed the river again. Firestar leaped from the last rock to the ground to see a pale shape rising up from the shadow of the rocks.

"Sandstorm!" Firestar exclaimed. "I thought you'd be asleep. It's late."

His mate padded up and touched noses with him. "I wanted to hear what happened."

"I'll be off, then." Scratch gave them both a wave of his tail, and bounded away to his cave.

Remembering that Clover and her kits would be sleeping in the warriors' den, Firestar settled down on a rock by the side of the river. Sandstorm crouched beside him, pressing her side warmly against his while he told her about meeting the rogues.

"Then it looks as if SkyClan will return after all," she mewed softly.

"Yes, I think it will." But in spite of his optimistic words, Firestar's belly churned when he thought of the meeting to come. He was used to addressing ThunderClan as their leader, but he wasn't the leader of the cats who would gather here on the following night. Would they listen to him?

Am I doing the right thing? Shouldn't there be a sign from StarClan, or from the SkyClan warrior ancestor? Where were all the other warrior ancestors of the shattered Clan?

He sat gazing up at the brilliance of Silverpelt for a long time, until Sandstorm drew her tongue over his ear and urged him back to the cave to sleep.

CHAPTER 24

The half-moon shone coldly as Firestar padded down the stony trail to the Rockpile. No other cats were waiting for him, and he couldn't make out any shadowy shapes approaching down the cliff or along the river. Only Sandstorm was with him, pausing beside him at the foot of the rocks to gaze at him with luminous green eyes.

Firestar shifted from paw to paw, uneasy under the light of the half-moon. This was the time when medicine cats met to share dreams with StarClan. Somehow it felt wrong to be waiting for other cats to gather; the moon should have been full. Could that be a bad omen?

Shaking off the premonition of disaster, Firestar let his gaze follow the twisting line of the river, glittering silver in the starlight. He wanted to leap to the top of the rocks and yowl the words that drew his own Clan to a meeting. But the familiar summons would mean nothing here, and he was not sure there would be any other cats to hear it.

Suppose no cat comes to the meeting? What will I do then?

"You'll be okay." Sandstorm touched his shoulder with the tip of her tail. "It's hard when you're not these cats' leader, but you still have to shape them into a Clan."

"Some of them," Firestar corrected her. Even at his most optimistic, he couldn't believe that all the cats he had spoken to would agree to join the new Clan. The last thing he wanted was to force any cat; it was important that they joined because they wanted to, and were willing to live by the warrior code.

Am I afraid they won't do what I want? No, it was more than that. The cats who joined SkyClan would have to be determined enough to survive after he and Sandstorm had returned to the forest. And they would succeed only if they were committed to the warrior code to the last claw and whisker.

"Go on." Sandstorm nudged him toward the Rockpile. "It's time."

Firestar met her brilliant gaze for a couple of heartbeats, and drank in her sweet scent. New strength seemed to flow into him; he sprang upward and reached the top of the Rockpile in a few vigorous bounds. From this vantage point he could see farther downstream and up the gorge in the other direction, but there was still no sign of any cats, except for Sandstorm sitting patiently at the foot of the rocks. The half-moon floated higher in the sky.

Where are you? Firestar thought desperately.

Then he caught sight of a flicker of movement in the shadows near the cliff face. He heard the scrape of claws on rock, and Sky pulled himself onto the topmost boulder to stand beside him.

"Greetings," he meowed. "I see I'm in time for the meeting."

"You know about that?" Firestar asked, surprised.

Sky dismissed the question with a flick of his ears. His gray pelt was silver in the moonlight, and his pale eyes shone. Firestar wondered if Sky had ways of knowing things that other cats couldn't understand.

"Do you want to speak to them first?" he suggested. "You're a descendant of SkyClan; they'll listen to you."

"Listen to me? The crazy rogue who sits looking at the moon?" A rusty purr of amusement came from the old cat. "No, *you* must speak to them. More than anything, they need a leader to follow, and you can walk that path more easily than I."

"But I am not their leader . . ." Firestar started to protest.

Sky looked deep into his eyes. "You can go back to your own Clan soon," he promised. "But my Clan needs you now."

Firestar bowed his head. "I will try," he whispered.

Straightening up, he saw with a start of surprise that cats had begun to appear in the gorge. He spotted Scratch sitting at the foot of the rocks, half-hidden in shadows. Clover was guiding her kits down the stony trail and thrust them gently toward a niche in the Rockpile itself. All three kits were squeaking with excitement.

"Hush," Clover murmured. "We have to listen to Firestar. He's going to tell us something very important."

An excited yowl drowned out the kits' reply, and Firestar looked up to see Cherry and Boris slip over the edge of the cliff and pad rapidly down the trail until they reached the Rockpile.

"Where are they all?" Boris asked, gazing around indignantly. "I thought they'd be here by now."

"I told you we should have gone to fetch Hutch," Cherry meowed. "He's probably curled up somewhere with his Twolegs. The fat, lazy—"

"Quiet," Sandstorm interrupted. "Look, some cat is coming now."

Firestar had already spotted the slender shape approaching from downstream: it was Lichen, a mottled brown she-cat he and Scratch had met the day before in the woods below the gorge. She halted, clearly nervous at seeing so many other cats waiting, and sat on a stone at the very edge of the river.

Leaf and Rainfur arrived next, padding side by side as if they already knew each other; they spotted Scratch and went to join him at the base of the cliff. At the same time, Firestar glimpsed movement farther up the rock face; Hutch was picking his way cautiously down to join Cherry and Boris, and to Firestar's surprise Oscar was close behind. The black kittypet halted on a ledge a couple of tail-lengths from the ground, and crouched there with his paws tucked under him. Last came Patch, bounding up the path beside the river as if he were afraid of being late; he gave a wary nod to Lichen, and sat near her at the edge of the gathering.

Firestar's pelt prickled as he felt the gaze of every cat trained on him. He exchanged a glance with Sky, who stepped back and slid over the edge of the boulder, leaving Firestar alone at the top of the Rockpile. He straightened up, holding his head high, trying to show in every hair on his pelt the pride he felt in being a warrior.

"Greetings," he began, "and thanks to all of you for coming. Yesterday I told you about SkyClan, who used to live here in the gorge. I told you that I was sent here to rebuild that Clan."

"Get on with it, then." A bored yowl came from the ledge where Oscar sat.

Firestar's ears twitched; had the black cat come just to disrupt the meeting? He ignored the comment and went on.

"Living in a Clan, cats have the support of their Clanmates from birth to death. Mothers look after their kits, while warriors protect the nursing mothers and bring them food. When the kits reach the age of six moons, they become apprentices, with mentors who teach them to fight and hunt."

Excited squeals came from somewhere farther down the Rockpile. "I want to be an apprentice!"

"So do I! Can we?"

"I want to be an apprentice *now*!"

"Hush." Firestar heard Clover's voice. "You'll have to go back to the cave if you can't listen to Firestar quietly."

"When the apprentices are fully trained," Firestar went on, "they become warriors. Warriors are the strength of a Clan. They must be ready to defend it against enemies like foxes or badgers or other cats." A shiver passed through him as he remembered the battle to drive BloodClan out of the forest. "They must hunt for the Clan and make sure every cat is fed."

"And what do the warriors get out of it?" Rainfur called, rising to his paws.

"Honor and respect," Firestar replied. "The loyalty of friends. The satisfaction of knowing that they have served their Clanmates."

Rainfur gave him a brusque nod and sat down again. Firestar didn't think he was very impressed with his answer.

"When warriors grow old," he continued, "they retire and join the Clan's elders. Part of the apprentices' duties is to look after them, to change their bedding and bring them fresh-kill. They are honored because they have given their lives in the service of their Clan.

"Every Clan has a leader and a deputy to oversee training, organize patrols, and decide what to do if danger threatens. Clan leaders are given nine lives by StarClan, so they can be first in every battle, and last to take fresh-kill if the Clan is hungry."

He caught a gleam of interest in Scratch's eyes when he mentioned nine lives, and felt a prickle of unease.

"And if any cat is sick or wounded," he went on, "each Clan has a medicine cat to care for them. Medicine cats have special knowledge of healing herbs, and they guide their Clan through dreams sent from StarClan."

"That's twice you've mentioned StarClan," Leaf mewed. She had listened intently to everything Firestar had said, her shining gaze fixed on him. "What is that?"

Firestar wasn't surprised by the question, but he paused before answering. Was he right to tell these cats that the spirits of their warrior ancestors were watching over them? He wasn't sure that StarClan walked in these skies, and he had seen only one SkyClan warrior ancestor.

"You can see StarClan above you," he explained, raising his tail to point at the glitter of Silverpelt. "Clan cats who die go to hunt with them—I don't know how it is for cats who have no Clan."

An uncertain murmur rose from the cats below. He understood why this was difficult for them; everything else he had told them made practical sense, whether they approved of it or not, but he was asking them to take this on trust.

Clover sprang to her paws. "Well, I'm going to join the new Clan," she meowed. "Firestar, Sandstorm, and Scratch saved my kits from a fox. They'll be safe if we're part of a Clan."

Firestar winced; catching Sandstorm's eye, he saw the same misgivings reflected there. Clover was still thinking of SkyClan as something she could depend on, without considering how she could contribute to the life of the Clan.

Sky jumped up to stand on the boulder beside Firestar. His pale eyes shone as he gazed down at the cats. A ripple of surprise passed through them as he began to speak in a low, husky voice. "I have kept alive the memory of SkyClan all my life," he rasped. "I know that my ancestors have been waiting to see the Clan rebuilt, but sometimes I despaired that it could ever come to be."

Firestar still wasn't sure that the cats below understood the meaning of warrior ancestors, but no cat rose to challenge Sky. Instead, Firestar could see respect dawning in their eyes. This wasn't the cranky elder they had dismissed as mad; this was a cat whose wisdom and experience made him worth listening to.

"Now you have a leader who has come a long way to rebuild SkyClan," the old cat went on. "Listen to him well before you decide. He will show you a way of life that gives honor to every cat."

Yes, I'm a leader, Firestar thought with a sudden stab of panic. *But I'm not* their *leader.* He was a stranger to the gorge, and the cats here were unlikely to listen to him with the same respect they were beginning to show Sky. They were murmuring among themselves again, and so far none of the newcomers had committed themselves to joining SkyClan. Firestar realized that the meeting could be about to break up in failure.

"We're going to join the Clan!" Cherry sprang excitedly to her paws. "Come on; it's going to be great!"

"Count me in too." Scratch turned to Firestar and spoke directly to him. "It makes sense that cats are stronger when they're together."

Instantly Firestar felt more confident. He had hoped Scratch would make this decision; he was a powerful cat, and while he still needed to learn to live by the warrior code, there wasn't much any cat could teach him about hunting and fighting. But had Scratch decided to join because he wanted to become a nine-lived leader?

"Thank you," Firestar meowed, pushing away his concerns. "SkyClan welcomes you."

"Well, I won't join." It was Lichen who spoke, politely but

with no hesitation in her voice. "I'm sorry, but I don't feel comfortable around so many cats. I like my privacy too much."

"That's your decision." Firestar was disappointed; he liked what he had seen of the mottled she-cat. "And if you change your mind, you know where we are."

"Thanks, but I won't. I wish you well, though." With a dip of her head she turned and padded away down the riverbank.

Rainfur watched her go, then rose to his paws. "I haven't heard anything that makes me want to join," he growled. "All I can see is, other cats will be telling me what to do all the time."

"That's not how it works—" Firestar protested. But part of him could understand why the gray tom felt like that. Firestar had no right to tell these cats how to live their lives; why should they listen when so far they had gotten on perfectly well without him?

"I'd sooner hunt for myself," Rainfur went on. "I don't need SkyClan."

"I'm sorry," Firestar mewed. "SkyClan could use you."

Rainfur's pelt bristled. "I don't want to be *used,* thanks," he spat. Whirling around, he bounded downstream after Lichen.

Firestar stared after him, angry that he had spoken so clumsily. Then he noticed that Leaf was gazing up at him with sympathy in her eyes.

"Don't mind Rainfur," she meowed. "He always was a bit touchy. Maybe we can persuade him later, when he sees how the Clan works."

Firestar's ears twitched. "We?"

"Yes, I'll join," Leaf assured him. "If the Clan really works how you say it will, then cats will have a *purpose*. We'll be more than just rogues, just living to stay alive."

Firestar was impressed. Her words might have come from a true Clan cat. He felt a purr rising in his chest.

"Thank you," he mewed. Glancing at the cats who so far had not decided—Patch, Hutch, and Oscar—he added, "All I can tell you is that SkyClan lived here once and could live here again, following the warrior code for the benefit of every cat. Do you want to be part of it?"

Patch rasped his tongue over his chest fur. "Okay, I'll give it a go."

Cherry gave Hutch a nudge with her shoulder. "Come on, Hutch. What about it?"

Hutch looked up at Firestar, embarrassment in his amber eyes. "I'd like to, I really would, but I'm afraid I won't be good enough at all this hunting and fighting. I've always been a kit-typet."

"We're kittypets too," Boris pointed out. "Firestar can teach you all that stuff."

"If you join us, you'll be very welcome," Firestar told him.

The tabby tom nodded. "Okay, then. I'd miss Cherry and Boris if they went off without me."

Firestar flicked his ears toward the one cat who so far had not spoken. "What about you, Oscar?"

The black kittypet rose slowly from the ledge where he had been crouching. "You don't think I came here to *join,* do you? Why would I leave a couple of perfectly good housefolk who give me everything I want? I didn't spend moons training them for nothing."

"Why are you here, then?" Boris demanded.

Oscar's jaws stretched in an insolent yawn. "I just wanted to find out what stupid ideas you'd come up with. And they are stupid. You're all mouse-brained." With a flick of his tail he set off up the trail, back toward the cliff top.

"Mouse-brained yourself!" Cherry yowled after him.

Sky padded forward to the edge of the Rockpile and looked down at the remaining cats. "SkyClan lives again!" he announced. Raising his head to the misty half-moon, he yowled, "SkyClan! SkyClan!"

"SkyClan! SkyClan!" the cats down in the gorge replied.

Firestar shivered from ears to tail tip. What had once seemed so impossible, so far off, was now real. The cats who stood around the Rockpile, yowling to the stars, were the beginnings of a new Clan to replace the one lost so long ago.

Then cold claws seemed to grip his heart. That sense of anger and hatred he had felt in the undergrowth downstream washed over him again. He raised his head to scan the bushes on the cliff top, and was sure he could spot glittering eyes among the branches.

Chapter 25

The following day dawned clear and cool. Firestar stepped out onto the ledge outside the warriors' cave to see Patch and Leaf scrambling over the spur of rock on their way upstream. After the meeting, all the new Clan cats had returned to their own homes; one of the first tasks would be to collect more bedding and sort out the dens so that the caves in the gorge could become a real Clan camp.

Sandstorm joined him, yawning and giving one ear a vigorous scratch with her hind paw. "We'll have to move Clover down to the nursery," she mewed, flicking her ears toward where the mother cat and her kits were sleeping against the far wall of the cave. "There won't be room in here once the warriors arrive."

"We need a den for the apprentices, too," Firestar pointed out. "And the elders, the leader, the medicine cat . . ."

"Well, we'll have one elder, when Sky moves in with us." Sandstorm blinked thoughtfully. "But there's no leader yet, apart from you."

"No! I'm leader of *ThunderClan*. StarClan will show us which cat is meant to be leader of SkyClan."

"And a medicine cat," Sandstorm added. "You can't have a Clan without a medicine cat."

Firestar murmured agreement. He suspected that finding a medicine cat could be even harder than finding a leader, and he hadn't begun to tackle that problem yet. Until the night before, he hadn't been certain that there would be a Clan at all.

He had to push his worries to the back of his mind as Leaf and Patch came into view a little way down the stony trail, calling out a greeting. Patch looked nervous, but Leaf's ears were pricked with anticipation. A heartbeat or two later Firestar heard pawsteps from up above, and Cherry, Boris, and Hutch appeared from the cliff top.

"We're ready for our hunting lesson," Boris meowed, his eyes shining.

"That's good." Sandstorm twitched her tail approvingly. "We'll be able to take out two full patrols."

"Can we lead them?" Cherry bounced forward to stand in front of Firestar. "*Please!* We know all the good places for prey."

"No, you're not warriors yet." Firestar didn't want to dampen the young cats' enthusiasm, but they had to get used to the way things were done in a Clan. "Don't worry," he added when Cherry flattened her ears in disappointment. "You'll be leading patrols before you know it."

"Boris and Leaf, you come with me," Sandstorm mewed. "We'll pick up Scratch on the way, and see what we can find in the bushes downstream. Is that okay with you, Firestar?"

"Fine. The rest of us can hunt on the cliff top."

When Sandstorm had left with her patrol, Firestar led Cherry, Hutch, and Patch up the trail and through the bushes on the edge of the cliff. The sky was bright where the sun would rise, but there was still no sign of movement from the Twolegplace.

"Let's head that way," Firestar suggested, waving his tail toward the huge Twoleg barn. "I haven't tried hunting there yet."

Not much later he was starting to think he had made the wrong decision. The trees and bushes near the fence of the huge nest were oddly lacking in prey. The scent of crow-food and rats from the fence made it almost impossible to taste anything else on the air.

"Sandstorm's patrol will catch much more," Cherry muttered. "And Boris will never let me hear the end of it!"

Almost ready to give up and go somewhere else, Firestar stopped trying to track down prey to give Hutch and Patch their first lesson in the hunter's crouch and the right way to stalk. Hutch concentrated very hard, but found it difficult to get his haunches into the proper position, while Patch had it almost right the first time. Of course, the rogue cats had been hunting for themselves since they were kits; they would need to learn only the skills of hunting in a group before they were as good as any forest warrior.

"Okay," Firestar meowed. "I want you to imagine that there's prey under that gorse bush over there." He waved his tail to show them which bush he meant. "Let me see you stalk up to it."

All three cats set off. Watching them critically, Firestar admired Cherry's graceful, controlled prowl; she had learned a lot since she first tracked him in the undergrowth downstream. Patch was slinking along with his belly fur brushing the ground, and even Hutch seemed to have gotten his paws under control.

"Keep going; you're doing great," Firestar encouraged them.

Suddenly Patch sprang up with a hiss of astonishment. One paw flashed out, and Firestar spotted a small brown shape as it was tossed in the air. Patch grabbed it as it fell to the ground again. He turned back to Firestar with a mouse dangling limply from his jaws.

"Well done!" Firestar meowed. "First catch to you."

"I think it was half-asleep," Patch admitted, dropping the mouse. "It never had a chance."

"Fresh-kill is fresh-kill, however you catch it." Firestar began to scrape at the ground with his hind paws. "We'll bury it now, and take it back with us when we're ready."

Which won't be long, he promised himself. He didn't like this part of the territory; it was too quiet, too bare of prey, and something about the huge Twoleg barn made him uncomfortable.

"Let's see your crouches again," he mewed.

Hutch had drawn a little way ahead of Cherry; the tabby kittypet had nearly reached the gorse bush when a squirrel started up from underneath the branches and raced for the safety of a clump of beech trees. Startled, Hutch waited a heartbeat too long before chasing after it.

"I'll get it!" Cherry yowled, streaking past Hutch with her tail streaming out.

Hutch halted, looking bewildered.

The squirrel reached the tree with Cherry hard on its paws and swarmed up the trunk until it reached the lowest branch.

"Got you!" Cherry hurled herself into the air.

But she had misjudged the leap. A mouse-length short, her paws struck a clump of leaves and she hung there, clawing frantically, kicking her hind legs and scattering scraps of leaf everywhere, until she managed to haul herself up onto the branch. Meanwhile the squirrel had vanished among the leaves farther up the tree.

"Mouse dung!" Cherry spat.

Firestar strolled to the foot of the tree and looked up at her. Privately he thought the young tortoiseshell's failure would do her no harm—she needed to learn not to show off—but he wouldn't say anything to upset her. She looked frustrated enough.

"Are you okay?" he asked.

"No! Stupid squirrel—I *should* have caught it."

"It was my fault." Hutch padded up beside Firestar. "I should have been a bit quicker."

"Don't worry." Firestar touched his shoulder with the tip of his tail. "This is only your first lesson. You're doing fine."

Hutch looked unconvinced. "I feel like I'm letting you all down. No cat will want to hunt for me if I can't hunt for myself."

Firestar let his tail rest on the tabby tom's shoulder for a moment longer. "That's not how a Clan works," he explained. "You'll be allowed your share of the fresh-kill pile like any other warrior. And you *will* hunt for yourself, and the rest of us too, before very long." Looking from Hutch's disappointed face to Cherry's frustrated one, he turned and signaled to Patch with his tail. "Fetch that mouse," he called. "We'll see if there's more prey nearer the cliff top."

Just as Firestar had hoped, there was better hunting in the bushes that edged the cliff. Before very long, the patrol was able to return to the gorge with a good haul of prey. Hutch was bursting with pride at bringing down his first sparrow, with a leap that proved the tabby kittypet bore SkyClan blood.

His jaws full of fresh-kill, Firestar led the way down into the gorge. The sun was up, and warm, honey-colored light pooled on the rocks and dazzled on the smooth curve of water where it poured out of the darkness. Firestar and Sandstorm had kept a small fresh-kill pile near the entrance to the warriors' cave, but that wouldn't do now. They would need to look for a sheltered spot near the waterside, where every cat could come and eat.

As he padded down the trail, Firestar saw that Sandstorm and her patrol had also returned. He paused, stiffening. Close to the Rockpile, Sandstorm and Scratch stood facing each other with their neck fur fluffed out, as if they were quarreling. Leaf and Boris looked on anxiously, while Clover, at the water's edge, gathered her kits to her.

Firestar bounded down the last few tail-lengths of the trail. Sandstorm had deposited her patrol's fresh-kill under an overhang at the bottom of the Rockpile; he added his own before turning to the two cats.

"And I'm telling you that's not the way it's done," Sandstorm growled, her green eyes furious. "In a Clan, the elders and the nursing queens *always* eat first."

Scratch lashed his tail. "That's mouse-brained! It's the warriors who catch the prey!"

"There's no need to argue," Clover interrupted in a soft voice. "I don't mind. You can eat first. There's plenty for every cat."

"That's not the point," Firestar intervened.

Sandstorm's head whipped around; she had obviously been so intent on Scratch that she hadn't heard Firestar approach. When she saw him, the fur on her shoulders began to lie flat. "Thank StarClan you're here! Tell this stupid furball—"

Firestar lifted his tail to silence her. Hurling insults wasn't going to help. To Scratch he mewed, "Sandstorm's right. Just because warriors are strong enough to hunt doesn't mean they have the right to eat first."

"That's not what I meant," Scratch protested, his green eyes wide with indignation. "The Clan depends on its warriors. They should be fed first so that they're always strong enough to deal with unexpected trouble." With a hostile glance at Sandstorm he added, "Some cats won't *listen*."

To Firestar's relief, Sandstorm didn't respond. Brushing

her pelt reassuringly, he padded forward to face the ginger tom. "Yes, it's important for a Clan to have strong warriors. But the warrior code isn't just based on what is practical. Honor matters equally as much. Elders and nursing queens must be shown respect, because without them the Clan wouldn't survive."

"SkyClan *hasn't* survived," Scratch muttered darkly.

"True, but that's no reason to cast the warrior code aside. Whatever happened to the original SkyClan cats"—Firestar wished that he knew what had happened to SkyClan, but there was no time to think of that now—"it wasn't the fault of the elders or the nursing queens. We must continue to honor them."

Scratch hesitated. Then his head whipped around and he glared at Clover. "Okay. Eat."

Looking very embarrassed, Clover darted past him to the fresh-kill pile, snatched a blackbird, and carried it to where her kits were crouched by the side of the water.

Sandstorm let out a sigh, and padded off to say something quietly to Leaf, who rested her tail tip sympathetically on the ginger she-cat's shoulder. Firestar signaled to the other cats to come and take prey from the pile, though he didn't have much appetite himself. He couldn't help wondering how many more arguments there would be before Scratch and the other cats really understood the warrior code.

Sunhigh had come and gone while the cats, full-fed, drowsed in the sunlight or withdrew to the cool shade of the caves. Every cat in the new Clan was there; Firestar had even spotted Sky padding quietly down the gorge and curling up in the shadow of a thorn tree.

Firestar lay beside Sandstorm, his tongue rasping over her shoulder in long, rhythmic strokes. Sandstorm's eyes were green slits, and a purr rumbled deep in her chest.

"I'm sorry I lost my temper with Scratch," she murmured. "You handled him much better."

Firestar gave her another lick before replying. "Scratch is going to make a fine warrior. But he has to see that the warrior code is about more than just strength. He'll learn, given time."

Sandstorm sighed. "Just as Clover has to learn that a Clan is more than protection." She butted Firestar's shoulder affectionately with her head. "We'll have to show them."

"True. And I think I know how to start."

He rose to his paws and arched his back in a long stretch. Then he bounded up to the top of the Rockpile and yowled out the familiar words: "Let all cats old enough to catch their own prey join here beneath the Rockpile for a Clan meeting!"

Sky started and sat up straight, gazing around as if he wasn't sure where the call had come from. Leaf and Patch, who had been drowsing together at the water's edge, raised their heads, then sat up to listen. Scratch popped his head out of his cave. Cherry and Boris came racing down the trail from the cliff top, while Clover's kits bundled excitedly out of the warriors' den and bounced down to the gorge, followed more slowly by their mother. Within a few heartbeats the whole

Clan had gathered and sat around the Rockpile looking up at Firestar.

"Cats of SkyClan," Firestar began. Pride rippled through his fur as he addressed these cats by their Clan name for the first time. "Last night you committed yourselves to this Clan and the warrior code. Today the Clan will honor you with your Clan names. Scratch, Leaf, Hutch, Clover, and Patch, please come to stand at the bottom of the Rockpile."

Exchanging bewildered glances, the five cats rose to their paws and drew closer to the bottom of the rocks. Clover's kits tried to follow her, and Sandstorm gently halted them with a sweep of her tail.

Firestar picked his way down the rocks to stand in front of the group of cats. There had never been a warrior ceremony like this before, and he had to get it right so that it had meaning with their warrior ancestors—if there were any watching.

"I, Firestar, leader of ThunderClan and mentor to SkyClan, call upon their warrior ancestors to look down upon these cats," he began. "They have a true desire to learn the ways of your noble warrior code, and I commend them to you as warriors in their turn." Padding up to Scratch, he went on, "Scratch, do you promise to uphold the warrior code and to protect and defend this Clan, even at the cost of your life?"

Scratch hesitated; Sandstorm slipped up behind him and whispered, "Say, 'I do.'"

"I do," Scratch meowed, his eyes fixed steadily on Firestar.

"Then by the powers of StarClan I give you your warrior name. Scratch, from this moment you will be known as

Sharpclaw. StarClan trusts you will give all your courage and strength to the new Clan."

Sharpclaw blinked, then dipped his head. Firestar bent to rest his muzzle between the new warrior's ears.

"Lick his shoulder," Sandstorm directed.

Sharpclaw obeyed, and stepped back.

"Now we welcome him to the Clan by calling out his name," Sandstorm meowed. "Sharpclaw! Sharpclaw!"

The rest of the Clan echoed her, Cherry yowling, "Sharpclaw!" at the top of her voice and bouncing up and down enthusiastically.

Firestar gave Patch the warrior name of Patchfoot, and Clover became Clovertail. When he turned to Hutch, he saw doubt and fear in the kittypet's eyes, and was half-afraid that when he was asked to take the oath he would back out.

"Hutch, do you promise to uphold the warrior code and to protect and defend this Clan, even at the cost of your life?"

Hutch swallowed; his voice shook as he replied, "I do."

"Then by the powers of StarClan I give you your warrior name. Hutch, from this moment you will be known as Shortwhisker. StarClan trusts you will give all your strength and wisdom to the building of this new Clan."

As he spoke, he saw the doubt fade from Shortwhisker's eyes, to be replaced by determination. Firestar knew he would be a fine warrior when he had learned to trust himself.

Finally he turned to Leaf. She had waited quietly, acknowledging each of her new Clanmates by their warrior names, and he was struck by the intentness in her eyes when he spoke to her. There was no hesitation as she meowed, "I do."

"Then by the powers of StarClan I give you your warrior name. Leaf, from this moment you will be known as Leafdapple. StarClan trusts you will give all your intelligence and loyalty to the building of this new Clan."

Leafdapple's amber eyes glowed as Firestar rested his muzzle on her head.

When the Clan had finished calling Leafdapple by her new name, Firestar raised his tail to beckon Cherry and Boris. Cherry dashed forward at once, eyes sparkling with eagerness, but Boris was hesitant, as if he realized more clearly than his sister what a massive step they were about to take.

"It's time to add two new apprentices to the Clan," Firestar mewed. "From this day forward," he began, touching Cherry on the shoulder with his tail tip, "this apprentice will be known as Cherrypaw. Sharpclaw, you have much to teach an apprentice, so you will be her mentor."

Cherrypaw's head whipped around and she stared at Sharpclaw. "Does that mean I have to do what he says?"

"Yes, it does," Sandstorm replied, an edge to her voice. "Touch noses with him."

Sharpclaw stepped forward; Cherrypaw stretched out her neck, gave him a quick dab on the nose, and moved back again.

"What if she *doesn't* do what I tell her?" Sharpclaw asked, eyeing his new apprentice. "What do I do then?"

Sandstorm's eyes sparkled. "Whatever you like."

"Within reason," Firestar added hastily, twitching his ears

at his mate. "To start with, you'd better ask me or Sandstorm if you need to punish her. We'll tell you what usually happens in our own Clan."

Turning to Boris, who had been listening apprehensively, he touched the young tabby on his shoulder. "From this day forward, this apprentice will be known as Sparrowpaw. Leafdapple, you will be his mentor and share your experience with him."

The newly named Sparrowpaw stepped forward to touch noses with Leafdapple, but for a heartbeat the she-cat held back, her eyes troubled.

"I'm sorry, Firestar, but I don't think I can do this," she meowed. "I'm so new to living in a Clan. How can I train an apprentice properly?"

"Don't worry," he replied. "Sandstorm and I will help you. For a while, every cat will be learning together."

Relief shone in Leafdapple's eyes, and she stepped forward to touch noses with Sparrowpaw. "I'll do my best," she promised him.

The rest of the Clan welcomed the two apprentices by calling their names, while Cherrypaw and Sparrowpaw listened with shining eyes.

"What about us?" Bounce sprang to his paws from where he sat beside his mother Clovertail. "Why can't we be apprentices?"

"We want proper Clan names, too," added his sister Tiny.

"You can't be apprentices until you're six moons old," Firestar explained.

"But that's *ages* away!" Rock complained, lashing his stumpy black tail.

Firestar exchanged a glance with Sandstorm, seeing amusement glimmering in her green eyes.

"All right," he meowed, beckoning with his tail. "Come here. You can't be apprentices yet, but you can have Clan names."

The three kits dashed toward him, falling over their own paws in their eagerness. When they stood in front of him, quivering with excitement, Firestar touched each with his tail on the top of the head. "From now on, these kits will be known as Rockkit, Bouncekit, and Tinykit."

"Rockkit! Bouncekit! Tinykit!" Leafdapple called, and the rest of the Clan echoed her with warm purrs of affection.

The three kits marched back to their mother, their tails high in the air.

"What about a Clan leader?" Sharpclaw asked. "You're not going to stay here forever, are you?"

Firestar wondered if Sharpclaw was nurturing hopes of being SkyClan's new leader. He was strong, he knew the area well, and he wasn't afraid to take authority. But Firestar didn't feel confident about deciding which cat should lead the new Clan—that was a job for their warrior ancestors, surely?

"It doesn't work like that," he told Sharpclaw. "It's not my job to choose a leader. *StarClan* will do that."

Sharpclaw's eyes narrowed and his voice was disbelieving as he asked, "How?"

"They'll send us a sign," Firestar explained.

Sharpclaw let out a snort, but didn't say any more.

"Now I have one more name to give," Firestar announced, relieved that the question of leadership was over for the moment. He turned to where Sky sat in the shade of the cliff. "Sky, come here, please."

The old cat rose to his paws and padded forward. When Sky stood in front of him, Firestar bowed his head in respect for everything the old cat had done to preserve the memory of SkyClan.

"I, Firestar, leader of ThunderClan and mentor to SkyClan, call upon his warrior ancestors to look down upon this cat," he meowed. "He has served the warrior code throughout his life, and it is thanks to him that this Clan stands here today. For that reason, I ask no promise from him, for he is already a true warrior. Sky, from this day forward you will be known as Skywatcher, in memory of your faith and your dedication to SkyClan."

A glow of delight flared in the old cat's pale eyes.

"Skywatcher! Skywatcher!"

Skywatcher gazed deep into Firestar's eyes. "Thank you. I never dreamed this would happen. I . . . I hope my ancestors can see me now."

"I'm sure they can," Firestar told him.

Drawing closer, Skywatcher murmured in his ear, "Come to my den tonight. There's something I must tell you."

Moonlight silvered the rocks as Firestar padded up the gorge. He couldn't shake off a feeling of unease, but this time it had nothing to do with sensations of hostility or a glimpse of bright, cold eyes in the undergrowth. What did the old cat want to tell him that couldn't have been said at the meeting by the Rockpile? Why had he insisted on returning to his den under the tree roots, instead of moving in with the Clan, where he could be treated with all the respect that an elder deserved?

He found the twisting path behind the boulder and began to follow it up the side of the gorge. A chill breeze ruffled his fur, a reminder that the warm days of greenleaf must soon come to an end. As he padded up the steep path, he spotted the blur of a gray pelt beneath the thorn tree, and found Skywatcher crouching at the mouth of his den with his paws tucked under him.

"You asked me to come."

For a few heartbeats Skywatcher held him with eyes like deep pools of water. "I want to thank you," he meowed solemnly. "You have rebuilt the lost Clan."

"There's no need for thanks," Firestar replied. "I did only what I had to."

Skywatcher nodded, blinking thoughtfully. "Do you think you have been a good leader for ThunderClan?"

The question startled Firestar, and at first he wasn't sure how to reply. "I don't know," he mewed at last. "It hasn't been easy, but I've always tried to do what is right for my Clan."

"No cat would doubt your loyalty," Skywatcher agreed. "But how far would it go?"

Puzzled, Firestar stayed silent. Why was Skywatcher asking him about ThunderClan?

"There are difficult times ahead," Skywatcher went on, "and your loyalty will be tested to the utmost. Sometimes the destiny of one cat is not the destiny of the whole Clan."

Firestar tipped his head to one side. Nothing Skywatcher said was making sense. Was ThunderClan in trouble? He had left them in peace, but that was several moons ago. What would happen to a leaderless Clan with rivals like ShadowClan around?

Skywatcher rose to his paws; his eyes blazed with reflected moonlight. For a heartbeat Firestar was sure he could see the glitter of stars tangled in his fur. The old cat's voice was soft, but charged with power, stronger than it had been before.

"Your Clan is safe for now. But there will be three, kin of your kin, who hold the power of the stars in their paws."

Firestar stared at the old warrior. "I don't understand. Why are you telling me this?"

There was no reply, except for a slight twitch of Skywatcher's ears.

"You must tell me more!" Firestar protested. "How can I decide what I should do if you don't explain?"

The old cat took a deep breath, but when he spoke it was only to say, "Farewell, Firestar. In seasons to come, remember me." He waved his tail, a clear indication that Firestar should go.

Firestar gazed at him helplessly for a moment longer before turning and stumbling down the path away from the den. His whole body felt cold. Skywatcher's words had the unmistakable ring of a prophecy from StarClan, but Firestar had no idea what they referred to.

There will be three, kin of your kin, who hold the power of the stars in their paws.

Firestar had no kin in ThunderClan except for Cloudtail, so who could the three be?

As he approached the Rockpile, listening to the unending murmur of the river, he paused and raised his eyes to Silverpelt. In the forest, the light of his warrior ancestors was a comfort to him, but he could not even be sure that they walked these strange skies.

"Can you hear me?" he whispered. "Bluestar, Spottedleaf, Yellowfang, if you are listening, please help me keep ThunderClan safe from what lies ahead."

CHAPTER 26

Firestar slept fitfully and woke at dawn to find that clouds had covered the sky. A stiff breeze was blowing, and a few leaves whirled down from the bushes on the cliff top. Leaf-fall could not be far away. Giving himself a quick grooming, he tried to forget his fears from the night before. The meaning of Skywatcher's prophecy was hidden in the moons to come. He could do nothing about it now.

Clovertail and her kits had finally settled in the nursery, leaving room for the new SkyClan warriors to share the big cave with Firestar and Sandstorm. Restless to be doing something, Firestar padded across the cave and prodded Sharpclaw with one paw.

"Wha . . . ?" Sharpclaw raised his head, blinking.

"Time for a dawn patrol," Firestar announced.

Sharpclaw groaned, then hauled himself out of his nest and shook scraps of moss and fern from his pelt while Firestar roused Leafdapple.

"We'll fetch Cherrypaw and Sparrowpaw and patrol the borders," he explained.

Leafdapple looked puzzled. "We haven't got any borders."

"We're going to set some."

He led the way down the trail to the cave they had chosen for the apprentices' den, wondering how Cherrypaw and Sparrowpaw had coped with their first night away from their Twolegs. He remembered settling them in the night before, helping them to carry moss up from the cave beside the river and arrange it into comfortable nests.

Sparrowpaw's eyes had grown wide with anxiety as the sun set and night crept into the gorge. "I wonder how our housefolk are feeling," he muttered.

Cherrypaw gave him a comforting lick. "They'll be okay, and so will we. We're Clan cats now."

But Firestar had noticed the tip of her tail twitching, and knew she wasn't as confident as she pretended.

When he and the other warriors arrived outside their cave that morning, Cherrypaw shot outside, her fur sticking all over the place.

"Are we going hunting?" she demanded. "I'm *starving*!"

"Elders and nursing queens eat first," Sharpclaw reminded her, with a glance at Firestar.

"That's right, but Sandstorm will lead a hunting patrol later on for the rest of the Clan," Firestar mewed. "We're the dawn patrol, and we can pick up some prey on the way."

"Are we allowed to do that?" Cherrypaw asked.

"Sure," Firestar replied. "It's only hunting patrols who have to bring their fresh-kill back for the Clan."

"Good." Sparrowpaw poked his head out of the den behind his sister. "Let's get going!"

Firestar led the way up the gorge past the path that led to Skywatcher's den, as far as the rocks where they had saved Clovertail and her kits from the fox. He wondered if the first SkyClan warriors had set their boundaries anywhere nearby; he guessed they would have marked out a bigger territory than the new SkyClan needed now, with fewer mouths to feed and fewer warriors to guard the borders.

"We'll set the first scent markers here," he explained. "Then any cat who comes along will know that this is our territory. If you keep renewing the marks, then over a few moons a really strong scent builds up."

A shiver went through him from ears to tail tip. When he first came to the forest, the borders of ThunderClan had been settled for more seasons than any cat could remember. The decisions he made now would affect SkyClan for seasons to come.

"Do other cats respect the boundaries?" Leafdapple asked.

It was a good question, Firestar thought. Cats from other Clans would think twice before crossing border markers, but there were no other Clans in this remote place.

"You might have trouble from rogues—" he began.

"We'll soon teach them to stay out of our territory," Sharpclaw interrupted, flexing his claws.

"Or get them to join us," Leafdapple suggested quietly. "We were rogues ourselves not so long ago."

When the first markers were set, Firestar found a trail that led up to the cliff top on the side opposite the camp. The cats headed downstream again along the top of the gorge.

"Here's a good place for another scent marker," Firestar meowed, pointing with his tail toward a boulder that broke through the thin soil a couple of tail-lengths from the cliff edge. "It's always a good idea to have a marker you can see as well as scent. That way it's easier to remember where they are."

"Can I do it? Please?" Cherrypaw bounced up to the rock.

"Okay. You saw what I did back there. Catch up when you've finished."

While Cherrypaw set the marker, Firestar led the other cats farther along the cliff until they came in sight of the woodland where he had spoken to the rogues. Cherrypaw came bounding up as they paused for Sparrowpaw to set another marker at a spot where the cliff edge crumbled away.

"I want to include some of the woods in the territory," Firestar meowed. "It's the best place for prey. But I don't want to tread on the tails of the rogues who didn't join us. We're not looking for a fight."

Leafdapple nodded. "If we stay on good terms with them, some of them might change their minds."

Firestar let Sharpclaw take the lead as they reached the trees. The two apprentices had never been in thick woodland before; their eyes stretched wide, and Cherrypaw let out an excited squeal before slapping her tail over her mouth with a guilty look at Sharpclaw.

"That's right, frighten all the prey in the forest," Sharpclaw grumbled.

Firestar glanced at the ginger warrior, hoping he wasn't going to be too tough with an apprentice who was less experienced than a Clan cat of her age. But Cherrypaw didn't seem crushed; she had already spotted a blackbird pecking underneath a bush, and had started to creep up on it.

Leafdapple waved her tail at Sparrowpaw. "You can hunt too, if you like."

Sparrowpaw's ears pricked, and he stood tasting the air before stalking through long grass toward some prey Firestar couldn't see.

"I suggest we head for the stream," Sharpclaw meowed, keeping an eye on his apprentice. "If we make that the border, Rainfur's and Lichen's dens will be outside our territory."

"What about Tangle?" Firestar asked, remembering the cranky old tabby.

Leafdapple let out a faint *mrrow* of amusement. "Tangle shifts his den every moon. If he doesn't like being inside our territory, he can move outside it."

Firestar nodded. Sharpclaw's idea was a good one, but he reminded himself to tell the warriors not to attack rogues if they found them on SkyClan territory—at least, not until they had been given plenty of time to get used to the idea of the Clan's presence in the woods.

"The stream it is, then," he meowed.

Just then Cherrypaw gave an enormous leap and snatched the blackbird out of the air as it tried to fly off. Crashing to the ground again she trotted back with her prey in her jaws and laid it at Sharpclaw's paws. "For you," she mewed, dipping her head respectfully. "I can soon catch another."

Sharpclaw stared at her and at the fresh-kill. "Thanks," he

managed to say. "Good catch."

Her eyes gleaming, Cherrypaw padded off again with her tail in the air.

Not to be outdone, Sparrowpaw brought his first catch—a mouse—to Leafdapple, before going off to hunt for his own fresh-kill. Firestar was pleased to see them trying to act like proper Clan cats, and decided not to tell them that apprentices didn't usually catch prey for their mentors. He caught a squirrel for himself, with a leap that was nearly good enough for SkyClan.

When they had finished eating, Sharpclaw led the way to the stream. Before they reached it, Cherrypaw waved her tail excitedly at a dead tree that stood by itself in a clearing. "That's a good place for a marker!"

Firestar halted. "It's okay, but I think this one would be better." He nodded at an ivy-covered oak tree on the nearer edge of the clearing.

"Why?" Sparrowpaw asked. "We'd have more territory if we used the dead tree."

"Yes, but there's no cover in the clearing," Firestar explained. A tingle of excitement went through him. Were these the sort of decisions that ThunderClan warriors had made in the forest so long ago? "No cover for prey, and none for you, if there are foxes or badgers about."

"That makes sense." Sharpclaw padded up to the oak tree and set a marker there.

Following the stream, the cats reached the cliff top and climbed down to where the fallen tree trunk crossed the river.

Firestar took the lead once more, over to the far side of the gorge and up the cliff toward the Twolegplace, setting scent by the tree stump and the deserted fox's den that Skywatcher had told him marked the old border. Then the patrol skirted the edge of the Twolegplace as far as the barn at the end of the row. Firestar felt his fur begin to prick again as they approached it; he didn't like the place and never would, but at least now it was outside the SkyClan borders.

Finally he led his patrol back toward the camp by a route that took in most of the undergrowth on the cliff top. He guessed it was almost sunhigh, though clouds still covered the sky and the wind was scented with rain.

As the patrol approached the bushes, Sandstorm emerged with a mouse between her jaws. "Hi," she mewed, dropping her prey. "I thought you must have gone on patrol."

"We set the borders!" Cherrypaw announced proudly.

"Good." Sandstorm twitched her whiskers with approval. "You'll have to tell the rest of us where they are."

"Over the next few days, every cat can do the patrol," Firestar meowed. "I see you've been hunting," he added, flicking his tail toward the mouse.

"Yes, there's plenty of prey about," Sandstorm replied. "Patchfoot is a good hunter already, and Shortwhisker is coming on really well."

Firestar was glad to hear that. A few successes would give the former kittypet some much-needed confidence.

"There's just one thing that's worrying me," Sandstorm went on in a lower voice meant for Firestar alone. "There's been no sign of Skywatcher this morning."

Apprehension clawed deep in Firestar's belly. Mention of Skywatcher reminded him of the old cat's strange mood the night before, and the ominous words of his prophecy.

"I think you should check on him," Sandstorm prompted. "He should be here in the camp, not stuck out there in that excuse for a den."

"I'll go right away," Firestar meowed.

He picked his way down the stony trail and headed up the gorge. Remembering what Sandstorm had said about the fox, he kept all his senses alert. Skywatcher was a noble old cat, but he would be no match for a strong and determined predator. However, there was no trace of fox scent.

By the time he reached the path behind the boulder a thin drizzle had begun to fall, penetrating his fur with chill claws. As he approached the den, he couldn't see anything of the old warrior. *Maybe he's out hunting. . . .*

Drawing closer, he spotted gray fur half concealed behind the roots of the thorn tree. "Skywatcher!" he called. There was no reply.

When he stood at the mouth of the den, he could see the old cat curled up at the very back, pressed against the earth wall with a tangle of roots over his head.

"Skywatcher?" Firestar repeated.

The gray warrior did not move. Firestar drew in his breath with sudden understanding as he ducked his head to enter the den and took the couple of pawsteps that brought him to Skywatcher's side. The old cat was still, and when Firestar gently laid a paw on his shoulder, he felt cold. Somehow he looked smaller than he had when he was alive.

Grief clawed at Firestar's heart. Perhaps the old cat had clung to life only until he could see SkyClan restored. Firestar hoped he had died happy, knowing that his dreams had been fulfilled.

"Good-bye, my friend." His voice choked in his throat as he stroked his tail over the old warrior's head. "May StarClan light your path."

Firestar jumped to the top of the Rockpile and gazed down at the cats of SkyClan. Clovertail was stretched out by the stream with her kits frisking around her, while Cherrypaw and Sparrowpaw were eating beside the fresh-kill pile. Sharpclaw and Patchfoot were wrestling together at the foot of the cliff in a practice fight. Sandstorm sat watching them nearby, offering some comments on their technique. Firestar's heart was heavy with the news he had to tell them.

"Let all cats old enough to catch their own prey join here beneath the Rockpile for a Clan meeting!" he yowled.

Sharpclaw and Patchfoot broke apart and sat up with ears pricked. The two apprentices swallowed their fresh-kill and looked up, their eyes bright with curiosity. Leafdapple began to pick her way down from the cliff top, joining Shortwhisker as he emerged from the warriors' den.

"I have some bad news to tell you," Firestar meowed when all the Clan had gathered. "Skywatcher is dead."

For a moment there was silence, except for the happy

squealing of Clovertail's kits as they played beside their mother. Clovertail swept them closer to her with her tail. "Hush," she mewed. "Firestar's telling us something very sad."

"It is bad news," Sharpclaw agreed, flexing his claws against the rock. "The Clan will be weaker without his experience to guide us."

Firestar's tail twitched; grief for the old cat swept over him again as he saw that most of the Clan cats were giving one another blank looks. He could see that few of them felt any real sense of loss.

Sandstorm came to meet him as he bounded down the Rockpile again, and pushed her nose into his shoulder fur. "You can't blame them," she murmured. "They hardly knew Skywatcher, and had only just realized he wasn't a mad old nuisance."

"I know." Firestar sighed. "But they need to understand how much he did for this Clan."

He asked Patchfoot to help him and Sandstorm bring the old cat's body back to camp for his burial. The rest of the Clan gathered around as they laid him gently at the foot of the Rockpile.

"Now remember, you have to stay up all night tonight," Clovertail told her kits, keeping the inquisitive little creatures back with her tail. "You mustn't go to sleep, whatever happens."

"No, that's all right," Firestar meowed, surprised that the former loner had heard about the custom of keeping vigil.

"Kits don't need to stay awake."

Clovertail stared at him, her eyes wide with alarm and her neck fur bristling. "Do you want my kits to die?" she screeched.

"What?" Firestar was baffled. "Your kits aren't in any danger."

Shortwhisker shivered. "No, Clovertail's right. You have to stay awake the night a cat dies; otherwise you die too. My mother told me that."

"It's true," Sharpclaw meowed. "Remember Foxy? He went to sleep the night his brother died, and a couple of days later a monster got him."

"Yes, I remember that," Leafdapple put in.

"But it's not true." Firestar spoke firmly, seeing that the former kittypets were giving one another anxious glances. He'd talk to the rogues later about this intriguing superstition that must have sprung from Clan traditions, even though the Clan itself had been forgotten. "We stay awake, yes, but only to honor the fallen cat on its journey to StarClan. It doesn't have anything to do with believing that we'll die if we don't."

"Not every cat sits vigil for the whole of the night," Sandstorm went on. "Just those who were closest to the dead cat. But tonight I think the whole Clan should do it, because there aren't many of us."

"We're his kin, aren't we?" Sparrowpaw asked. "Those of us with SkyClan blood."

Firestar dipped his head. "Yes, you are. We'll all keep

watch, and in the morning we'll bury him. It's usually the elders who do that, but Sandstorm and I will do it for Skywatcher."

"I'd like to help," Cherrypaw mewed; the young tortoiseshell looked unusually subdued. "We never told him we were sorry for calling him names."

"I wish we had," Sparrowpaw added miserably.

Sandstorm touched his ear with her nose. "I think he knew. He saw you become Clan apprentices, and that's what he wanted most of all . . . to see his Clan being made strong again."

As the sun went down and shadows filled the gorge, the Clan gathered for Skywatcher's vigil. Firestar and Sandstorm crouched closest to him, pushing their noses into his cold gray fur. Cherrypaw and Sparrowpaw sat a little way away, with the rest of the Clan. Clovertail hesitated, but settled down at the foot of the cliff with her kits snuggled into her fur as if they were going to sleep as usual. Shortwhisker looked most anxious, and Firestar wondered if he had deliberately sat down on a sharp-edged stone in order to keep him from dozing off.

The last daylight faded from the sky; the clouds had cleared away and the warriors of StarClan began to appear overhead. After a while Firestar realized that the Clan were becoming restless. He could hear shifting and muttering behind him. Cherrypaw let out a huge yawn and her eyes closed; she jerked awake again as Sparrowpaw prodded her in the side.

Then Firestar heard Clovertail's voice whispering in his

ear. "I'm sorry, Firestar, It's getting cold, and if you're sure it's safe to go to sleep, I'd like to take my kits back to the cave."

"That's fine," he murmured.

As she withdrew, he heard another cat rise and follow her up the stony trail; glancing around he saw that it was Sharpclaw. Shortwhisker and Patchfoot were mewing quietly to each other; after a few heartbeats Shortwhisker moved away, but only to sit by himself on a rock a few fox-lengths farther down the stream. Cherrypaw and Sparrowpaw, for all their good intentions, had fallen asleep. Only Leafdapple remained, her gaze fixed on the stars.

Firestar suppressed a sigh. These cats didn't understand properly what it meant to live the life of a warrior and to follow the warrior code. They would need to learn the importance of the vigil—among so many other things—before they would truly be a Clan. But at least they seemed to trust him when he said they wouldn't die if they fell asleep tonight. Perhaps it had been easier to stay awake when they were leading less orderly lives, without dawn patrols and hunting patrols and cave duties to tire them out.

Stretching stiff limbs, he gazed up at Silverpelt's frosty fire and wondered which of those glittering points of light was the spirit of Skywatcher. *Have you found your way to SkyClan's warrior ancestors?* He hoped so; if any cat deserved to walk among the stars, it was Skywatcher.

Moonlight shining through the cave entrance woke Firestar, and glancing around the den he realized that

Shortwhisker wasn't there. Worried, he poked his head outside and spotted the tabby tom sitting on the rock by the river, where he had gone three nights before when the Clan kept vigil for Skywatcher.

Firestar padded down to join him; as he approached Shortwhisker jumped, and a defensive look flickered in his eyes.

"Did you want me?" he began.

"No, not for anything in particular." Firestar sprang up onto the rock beside him. "But I get the feeling you're not happy. If there's anything wrong, you can tell me."

Shortwhisker edged to one side to make room for him. "There's nothing *wrong,*" he meowed. "Everything's fine. I'm learning stuff I never imagined before. It's just . . . well, there are so *many* cats. Especially when we're all sleeping together in the den. I've been used to living on my own with my housefolk."

"I was a kittypet too, you know, and I felt the same when I joined my Clan. But you'll get used to it," Firestar told him. "Soon you'll wonder how you ever managed to sleep without your Clanmates around you."

"Maybe," Shortwhisker meowed, though he didn't sound convinced.

The tabby cat stared into the river, and Firestar got the sense that he wanted to be alone. He jumped down from the rock and returned to the den, wondering what he could do to make Shortwhisker feel more comfortable with Clan life. Perhaps pride in his hunting achievements would do the trick.

A couple of days after his talk with Shortwhisker, Firestar returned from a hunting patrol with Sparrowpaw and Leafdapple to find the camp almost deserted. The warriors' cave was empty, and when the patrol padded down to the riverside, the only cats they found there were Clovertail and her kits.

"Come back, Bouncekit!" Clovertail called, wrapping her tail around the adventurous ginger kit and pulling him back from the edge of the water. Glancing at Firestar, she added, "They're getting so strong and active. And if they get into trouble, you can be sure Bouncekit is at the bottom of it!"

"They're doing really well," Firestar told her. "They'll soon be ready for mentors. And we're so short of warriors," he went on, "that you might have to mentor one of them yourself. It's not ideal for apprentices to have their mother as a mentor, but—"

Clovertail's eyes widened in dismay. "I've no idea how to mentor an apprentice."

"Maybe it's time you started to join the patrols," Firestar suggested. "I'm sure you'll learn quickly."

"Oh, I couldn't possibly!" Clovertail exclaimed. "My kits still need me. Who would keep an eye on them, if I weren't here? Rockkit, come down off there!" she added, raising her voice to the black kit who had started to scramble up the Rockpile. "You'll fall into the water!"

Looking at the three mischievous kits, Firestar supposed she had a point. "Where is every cat?" he asked. "The whole gorge seems deserted."

"They went with Sandstorm," Clovertail replied, pointing up the gorge with her tail. "She said she was taking them for a training session." With a glance at her kits to make sure they weren't misbehaving, she padded over to the newly stocked fresh-kill pile and chose a mouse for herself.

Firestar left her with Sparrowpaw and Leafdapple, and padded up the gorge. A few tail-lengths farther on, the cliff curved inward to leave a wide, flat space with a sandy floor. Firestar reached it in time to see Cherrypaw pounce on Sandstorm; the two she-cats rolled over and over in a fierce tangle of paws and tails. Sharpclaw, Shortwhisker, and Patchfoot were looking on.

At last Sandstorm broke free and stood up, shaking sand from her pelt. "Well done," she meowed. "You've got that leap and claw action just right. If I were a fox, I wouldn't fancy meeting you."

Cherrypaw's eyes glowed.

"Shortwhisker, you have a go," Sandstorm went on. "Pretend I'm a fox that's trying to get into the Clan nursery."

Shortwhisker hesitated, glancing around at the other cats, while Sandstorm crouched, her tail tip flicking impatiently. "Come on," she urged. "I've had time to eat a couple of kits by now."

Shortwhisker hurled himself across the sandy space, his claws extended, but he had misjudged his leap. He fell short, just in front of Sandstorm, who cuffed him over the ears with both her front paws. Shortwhisker let out a growl of frustration, his tail lashing.

"Don't worry," Sandstorm meowed. "Try again."

"No, I've had enough for now." Shortwhisker backed away. "I'll practice on my own for a bit."

For a heartbeat Sandstorm gave him a questioning stare, then nodded. "Okay. We'll have another session tomorrow."

Shortwhisker padded around a curve in the gorge and out of sight. Firestar exchanged a glance with Sandstorm and went after him. Before he caught up with Shortwhisker, the tabby tom realized that some cat was following him, and stopped to wait.

"I'm sorry," he meowed, not giving Firestar a chance to speak first. "I know I messed up." He blinked miserably. "I'm *never* going to get it right. I just feel so awkward, trying to train with all those other cats watching."

Firestar suppressed a sigh. It was the same problem that Shortwhisker had spoken about before, on the rock by the river. He was finding it hard to adjust to living among a large number of cats.

"Well, it's the same for every cat," he began. Shortwhisker tried to interrupt, but Firestar flicked his tail for silence. "I can understand how you feel, but for StarClan's sake, why didn't you tell Sandstorm that? She's not unreasonable. She would give you a one-on-one session if you asked her."

Shortwhisker's forepaws shuffled on the sandy ground. "I don't like to give her any trouble. She works so hard already."

"I know, but it's no trouble, honestly. I'll tell you what," Firestar went on. "Would you like to practice with me, now? No cat is watching us."

Shortwhisker's eyes brightened. "Would you really?"

"Of course. What move was Sandstorm trying to teach you?"

"She showed us how to leap on top of our enemies. That way, she said, it's harder for them to get at you."

"True." Firestar lashed his tail. "Okay—come and get me."

He had hardly finished speaking when Shortwhisker leaped at him, snarling. Firestar sidestepped; Shortwhisker hit the ground beside him, but managed to rake his paws down Firestar's side before he could scramble out of range.

"Good!" Firestar exclaimed.

"I missed you, though," Shortwhisker mewed ruefully.

Firestar gritted his teeth. Was this cat determined to see the bad side of everything? "But you still got a blow in," he pointed out. "Try again, and this time keep fighting until I tell you to stop."

He crouched, waiting for Shortwhisker's leap. For a moment he relaxed as the tabby's gaze drifted to a butterfly fluttering past; the leap when it came took him by surprise. "Sneaky!" He grunted as Shortwhisker landed on top of him, driving the breath from his body. He heard a snarl of satisfaction as Shortwhisker gripped his shoulders with his paws and bit down into his neck fur. Rolling over onto his back, Firestar twisted his haunches, trying to land a blow on Shortwhisker's belly with his hind paws. Shortwhisker lost his grip, all four paws flailing wildly as he tried to claw Firestar again.

"Okay, that'll do," Firestar panted.

Shortwhisker scrambled to his paws. "I didn't hurt you, did I?"

Firestar's flank was stinging, but he shook his head. "That was great. You've got the makings of a really dangerous fighter."

Shortwhisker's eyes glowed with the praise. "Really?"

"Really. There's no need for you to feel ashamed in front of other cats."

The tabby tom shrugged. "I'll get used to it sooner or later, I guess." He dipped his head to Firestar. "I'll just practice the moves on my own for a bit, if that's okay."

"That's fine."

Firestar padded back down the gorge to find that the training session was breaking up, with the other cats heading toward the camp. Sandstorm was sitting in the middle of the training space, grooming sand out of her fur.

"I had a talk with Shortwhisker," Firestar began, telling her what had happened.

"I'll make sure he gets the chance to train on his own," Sandstorm promised. She finished her grooming and stood up. "I'm less worried about him than about Clovertail. She hasn't been to a single training session yet."

"She's still taking care of her kits."

Sandstorm's whiskers twitched. "Her kits are old enough to be left for a short while. They could come and watch, for StarClan's sake!"

"Don't worry." Firestar brushed his tail against her shoulder. "The kits will be apprenticed soon, and then Clovertail will see that she has to join in. Remember, she hasn't been a Clan cat for long."

Sandstorm sniffed. "When she was made a warrior, she promised to protect and defend the Clan. How does she expect to keep her promise if she never learns to fight?"

"Give her time," Firestar urged. "She doesn't understand what the promise means yet. One day she will."

"And the sooner the better," Sandstorm muttered.

Together the two cats strolled back to camp. Without conscious decision, their paws led them to the top of the Rockpile. Sandstorm lay down on one side, closing her eyes to slits as the sun beat down on her. Firestar sat beside her, looking down to where the river poured out. Patchfoot was sitting on a rock by the waterside, stretching down to lap. A couple of tail-lengths away, Cherrypaw and Sparrowpaw were play-fighting, while their mentors looked on and offered advice. Clovertail and her kits had crossed the river, and the kits were exploring the rocks near the water on that side.

"You know, this reminds me of Sunningrocks," Sandstorm murmured. "The warm rock, the sound of the river . . . I wonder what the others are doing back home?"

"Graystripe will keep the Clan safe," Firestar mewed. "I trust him more than any cat."

Homesickness flooded over him. Even though he believed Skywatcher's promise that ThunderClan was safe, he wanted to see his Clan deputy and his best friend more than anything.

Sandstorm stroked his shoulder gently with her tail tip. "I wonder how Sorrelpaw is getting on with Dustpelt." She let out a soft *mrrow* of amusement. "I'd love to watch one of their training sessions!"

Firestar echoed her *mrrow*. "Let's hope Dustpelt survives—"

He broke off at the sound of a terrified shriek from below. Springing up, he saw Clovertail standing at the edge of the river, her fur fluffed out so that she looked twice her size.

For a heartbeat he couldn't locate the kits. Then he spotted Bouncekit, struggling frantically as he was carried along in the surge of water as it flowed out of the cave. He scrabbled with his front paws, letting out a wail of terror that was cut off as his head went under.

By then Firestar was bounding down the rocks with Sandstorm hard on his paws. But Clovertail was faster. Before they reached the path on the other side of the cave she had plunged into the river; she swam strongly to where her kit had vanished and dived down under the water.

Terror stabbed through Firestar. Would he have to save the mother as well as her kit? Then Clovertail reappeared, gripping Bouncekit firmly by the scruff. Dragging him with her, she reached the side of the pool, where Firestar and Sandstorm leaned over to take the kit while Clovertail hauled herself onto dry ground.

"Bouncekit!" she exclaimed. "Bouncekit, are you all right?"

Shivering, Bouncekit let out a feeble cry and vomited up a mouthful of water. His mother nudged him into a patch of sunlight, where he flopped down like a damp leaf. Clovertail crouched beside him and began licking him fiercely, ruffling his fur the wrong way to dry him out and get him warm again.

Firestar looked around for the other two kits and spotted them edging their way nervously along the path that led underneath the rocks to the cave where the moss grew. Emerging from the cave they pattered along the riverbank and halted in front of their mother, their eyes wide with fear.

"Will Bouncekit be okay?" Tinykit asked in a small voice.

Clovertail looked up from her licking. Already Bouncekit's fur was almost dry and he was trying to sit up.

"I don't know what the three of you were thinking of!" she hissed. "You know very well you shouldn't have gone into that cave without me."

"But we knew you wouldn't let us—" Rockkit began.

"Of course I wouldn't let you! And now you can see why." She gave Bouncekit a few more rough licks; Firestar could tell she was angry only because she had been so terrified. "It's dangerous under there, and you're all too small to swim properly. What if I hadn't been here?"

Bouncekit managed to scramble up and stood groggily on all four paws. "It's my fault," he mewed. "It was my idea."

"I don't care whose fault it was." Clovertail rose and shook herself; drops of water spun away from her pelt, spattering Firestar and Sandstorm. "You're all to go straight back to the nursery. No more play for any of you today."

Rockkit let out an indignant wail, then broke off as his mother glared at him. "Go on. *Now,*" she ordered.

Crestfallen, the kits turned away; then Tinykit glanced

back. "There's a cave in there, full of shining moss," she mewed. "And there were voices talking to us."

Startled, Firestar stepped forward. "What did they say?"

"They were so quiet that we couldn't hear," Bouncekit replied.

"Voices, indeed!" Clovertail scolded. "Haven't you been naughty enough without making up stories?"

"But we're *not* making it up!" Tinykit protested, her white tail quivering. "We *did* hear voices—lots of them."

"I don't want to hear any more about it," her mother meowed. "You're never to go into that cave again, and that's the end of it." Snorting in annoyance, she began herding her kits back toward the Rockpile.

Firestar exchanged a glance with Sandstorm. Skywatcher had told them that the SkyClan medicine cats had shared tongues with their ancestors in the cave where the river flowed out. Could the kits possibly have heard the voices of the SkyClan warriors from so long ago?

He and Sandstorm helped the three kits clamber over the Rockpile, but when they had begun to climb the trail to the nursery he held Clovertail back with his tail on her shoulder. "Where did you learn to swim like that?"

Clovertail shrugged. "I haven't always lived in the gorge," she explained. "I was born farther downriver, near an abandoned Twoleg nest. My mother taught me to swim for fish."

Firestar wondered if the Twoleg nest was the one he and Sandstorm had passed on their journey.

"One of the Clans in the forest where I live is called

RiverClan," he told Clovertail. "They swim and catch fish all the time. I've never heard of any other cats who enjoy swimming, until now. I wonder if you have RiverClan ancestry."

Clovertail's eyes widened. "Does that mean I don't belong to SkyClan?"

The dismay in her tone encouraged Firestar. It showed that at least Clovertail *wanted* to be a member of SkyClan, and had the seeds of loyalty to her Clanmates and the warrior code.

"No," Sandstorm meowed, touching her nose to Clovertail's ear. "You're a SkyClan cat through and through, because that's where you've chosen to live."

"Cats can change Clans," Firestar added, remembering how Brambleclaw's sister Tawnypelt had followed their father, Tigerstar, into ShadowClan. "It doesn't happen often, and it doesn't always work. But being a member of a Clan is about more than just blood."

"Even more," Sandstorm went on, "you've proved that you have warrior blood in you. You owe it to your ancestors to learn their skills of hunting and fighting so that the warrior code can live on in you."

Clovertail blinked. "I promised that, didn't I, when I was made a warrior? I'm starting to understand now what the words mean. But I still don't think I'll be much use—not like you and Sharpclaw."

"You were very brave today," Firestar assured her. "*You* saved Bouncekit. You didn't need any other cat."

Clovertail looked thoughtful. At last she nodded. "I never

thought of it like that," she mewed. "Okay, I *will* join in the training from now on."

"Good." Firestar rested his tail tip on her shoulder. "You'll feel you really belong to the Clan when you give something back to it. Think about your kits—they'll become warriors one day, and you could be a great example for them."

"We understand it's not easy," Sandstorm told the she-cat, giving her a friendly lick. "But I promise you, it's worth it."

"And you needn't worry about your kits," Firestar added. "They'll be apprentices soon, and until then we'll make sure some cat keeps an eye on them while you're training. No more expeditions into that cave!"

On the following morning, Firestar took Sharpclaw, Cherrypaw, and Patchfoot on the dawn patrol. When they returned, he saw Sparrowpaw, Shortwhisker, and Leafdapple huddled together at the foot of the Rockpile, mewing urgently to one another. Sandstorm sat a tail-length away, a disgusted expression on her face.

Firestar glanced at Sharpclaw. "What's all that about?"

The ginger tom shrugged. "I've no idea."

Firestar padded forward until he came up to the little group. "Hi, is everything okay?"

The cats all turned worried faces toward him.

"We were talking about the Whispering Cave," Shortwhisker told him.

Firestar stared. "The what?"

"The cave under the rocks." Sandstorm got up, her eyes

narrowed. "That's what they're calling it now. Those silly kits have spread the story about the voices, and—"

"There must be something down there," Sparrowpaw interrupted. "Rockkit said he saw big shiny cats with huge claws. Their eyes glowed like the moon and their teeth were bigger than a fox's."

Patchfoot looked horrified. "Really?"

"Kits will be kits, I know." Leafdapple twitched her tail. "But they looked terrified! Would they really make all that up?"

"Hmm . . ." Firestar could tell that the kits had improved their story since their visit to the cave the day before.

"Suppose these big cats come out?" Shortwhisker mewed.

Sandstorm rolled her eyes. "Suppose hedgehogs fly!"

"If there is something in there, we ought to deal with it." Sharpclaw flexed his claws. "We should go in and attack before they have a chance to attack us."

Firestar lifted one paw to stall him. "We *will* go in there, but not until later on. And I don't believe there's anything to be afraid of. It's time for hunting patrols," he went on. "Sharpclaw, you can lead one, and Leafdapple the other."

The SkyClan cats still gave him doubtful looks as they moved away. Sandstorm lagged behind, drawing closer to him.

"What do you think is down there?" she murmured. "Skywatcher said that the SkyClan medicine cats used to share tongues with their warrior ancestors in that cave."

Firestar nodded. "That's what I'm hoping. Every Clan needs a special place, like the Moonstone, and this cave could be SkyClan's. It worries me that the new Clan doesn't have a medicine cat yet. Maybe if we go into the cave tonight, SkyClan's warrior ancestors will show us which cat to choose."

Sandstorm's eyes gleamed. "Good idea. We can't stay here forever, waiting for a medicine cat to show up."

Firestar pushed away the feeling of homesickness that threatened to cloud his thoughts. This wasn't his Clan, but he couldn't leave until he was sure they could survive without him, and finding a medicine cat was a big part of that. "SkyClan's warrior ancestors must be out there *somewhere*," he meowed, clawing at the sandy ground.

When night had fallen Firestar led his Clan into the cave beneath the rocks. The moon was a thin claw scratch in the sky, and starlight dappled the surface of the river.

Every Clan member followed as he edged along the narrow path beside the water—all except Clovertail. She had stayed to look after her kits; she still refused to believe that there was anything in the cave, and had given Rockkit, Bouncekit, and Tinykit a good scolding for frightening every cat.

"Be careful!" Firestar called, glancing back over his shoulder. "Cherrypaw, no fooling about! You could easily slip on these wet rocks, and we haven't got Clovertail to pull you out!"

"There's something shining up ahead." A quavering voice came from somewhere behind Firestar; it sounded like Shortwhisker.

He was right. Firestar could see a pale light flowing from the cave, reflecting on the surface of the water. "It's okay," he replied. "It's not big scary cats, I promise."

Setting his paws down carefully, he reached the flattened path that led along the side of the underground river and stood back to let the rest of the Clan file inside.

Sandstorm brought up the rear. "See?" she meowed. "It's just moss."

"And it's beautiful," Firestar added. "Look how the light ripples over the roof."

The SkyClan cats gazed around, their eyes reflecting the eerie light.

"Hey!" Sharpclaw meowed. "*We're* scary cats whose eyes glow like the moon."

Leafdapple let out a *mrrow* of amusement; Cherrypaw and Sparrowpaw exchanged glances, looking ashamed for believing the kits' story.

"Skywatcher told us that your SkyClan ancestors called this the Shining Cave," Firestar told them. "It would have been a special place for them."

But the Whispering Cave might be a better name, he thought. He strained to hear any message from SkyClan's warrior ancestors, but all he could hear was the lap of the swift black water and the mews of his Clanmates.

"What was special about it?" Sharpclaw asked.

Firestar gave each of the SkyClan cats a searching glance before he replied. Skywatcher had told them that this cave was a special place for medicine cats, but Firestar didn't want to destroy their confidence by telling the new Clanmates that they still needed a vitally important Clan member before they could be a real Clan. Instead he watched to see if any cat could hear voices; to his disappointment, they were gazing warily around, respectful, but showing no sign of understanding the cave's deeper meaning—not even Leafdapple, who had seemed sensitive enough to be a potential medicine cat.

"We'll find a use for the cave when it's needed," he told Sharpclaw, stifling a sigh. "All in good time."

The ginger tom gave Firestar a look from narrowed eyes, but said nothing more, only turning to lead the way along the ledge and out into the open again.

Firestar waited until every other cat had left before listening one last time for the voices the kits had heard. The hair on his pelt began to rise; perhaps, very faint and far away, there was something, but he couldn't be sure. How could he put the new Clan in touch with the spirits of the former SkyClan when he couldn't hear them either?

"Are you there?" he mewed aloud, hoping that SkyClan's warrior ancestors could hear him. "If you are, show yourselves to us. And for the new Clan's sake, please send us a medicine cat."

CHAPTER 27

Firestar sat at the edge of the sandy training area, watching Sandstorm working with Clovertail. Several days had passed since the pale brown she-cat had agreed to join the sessions. She was still anxious, still unsure about her place within the Clan, but she was trying her best.

She crouched with her tail lashing back and forth, her gaze fixed on Sandstorm. When the ginger she-cat sprang, Clovertail grabbed her and flipped her over to hold her down on the sand. Her three kits, watching beside Firestar, bounced up and down, letting out gleeful meows.

"Yes!" Rockkit yowled. "Go, Clovertail!"

"Bite her throat!" Bouncekit urged.

Sandstorm pushed Clovertail off and glared at the three kits as she spat out a mouthful of sand. "Do you mind?" she meowed. "You just wait until you're apprentices. I'll teach you about throat biting."

All three kits collapsed in *mrrows* of laughter, their tiny tails waving in the air.

"It's no use." Firestar twitched his ears at his mate. "They know you're not as fierce as you sound."

Sandstorm ignored him. "You're coming along very well," she told Clovertail. "You might want to watch out for—"

She broke off at the sound of yowling coming from farther down the gorge. Firestar sprang to his paws. He flicked his tail at Sandstorm. "Come on. Clovertail, keep the kits here."

Not waiting to see if Clovertail obeyed, he raced down the gorge. Sandstorm bounded at his heels. A heartbeat before they reached the Rockpile, the yowling stopped. The silence was almost as frightening as the sound.

Skidding around the lowest rocks of the Rockpile, Firestar came to a slippery halt. A couple of tail-lengths in front of him stood Rainfur, the gray rogue who had refused to join the Clan. His sides heaved as he fought for breath.

Patchfoot was facing him, his pelt bristling and his lips drawn back in a snarl. Leafdapple and Sharpclaw stood close by with their apprentices, looking ready to fight the intruder if they had to.

"Get out," Patchfoot rasped. "You had the chance to stay and you turned it down. Now go, unless you want your fur clawed off."

"Wait," Firestar meowed, padding forward to push himself between Patchfoot and Rainfur. "What's the problem?"

"Rainfur knows he's not supposed to come here now," Patchfoot began.

Firestar touched the black-and-white tom's shoulder with his tail. "Let Rainfur speak for himself."

By this time the gray rogue had gotten his breath back. "I need your help," he meowed. "Please, Firestar. It's not for me;

it's for my mate and her kits."

Until then Firestar hadn't even known that Rainfur had a mate. "What's the matter with them?"

"Petal is a kittypet," Rainfur explained. "She lives down-river"—he waved his tail toward the opposite side of the gorge—"with an old Twoleg who hardly ever feeds her. She used to sneak out to meet me, and I used to catch prey for her. I tried to persuade her to come and live with me, but she was scared, especially when she found out she had kits coming. She thought the Twoleg would care for them."

"When he didn't care for her?" Sandstorm asked, shocked.

Rainfur shook his head helplessly. "I couldn't persuade her. But now that the kits are born the Twoleg is just as bad, if not worse. Petal is getting weaker and weaker, and she hasn't enough milk to keep the kits alive. You've got to help us!"

Leafdapple glanced at Firestar. "I think we should go."

"Just a moment." Without waiting for Firestar to answer, Sharpclaw stepped forward, giving Rainfur a suspicious look. "If your mate could sneak out to see you, why can't she sneak out now, and bring the kits with her?" To Firestar he added, "I think he might be setting a trap for us."

Rainfur's neck fur began to bristle. "Why would I want to do that?" he meowed. "She can't get out because the Twoleg has blocked the gap she used." A shiver ran through him, and he clawed the ground in frustration. "They're all going to die, and I don't know what to do!"

"We'll come," Firestar decided. "How many kits?"

"Two," Rainfur replied, blinking in shocked relief.

"Okay," meowed Firestar. "Sharpclaw, Leafdapple, Patchfoot, you come with me. That'll be enough to distract the Twoleg and carry the kits out. Sandstorm, you're in charge until I get back."

"Fine." Sandstorm's tail curled up. "Good luck," she added.

Rainfur led the SkyClan patrol downstream, and across the river by the tree trunk. They climbed the cliff and crossed the SkyClan border scent marks, still heading downstream. This was new territory to Firestar; he pricked his ears, all his senses alert, but nothing disturbed the quiet of the woods.

Eventually Rainfur halted, raising his tail in warning. "The Twoleg nest is just beyond here," he explained, nodding toward a clump of brambles. "We need to be careful the Twoleg doesn't see us. He's thrown things at me before now."

Firestar took the lead, creeping around the bramble thicket with his belly fur brushing the grass. He paused when the Twoleg nest came in sight, scanning it carefully. A wooden fence surrounded it, but it was partly broken down, with bushes crowding up against it on both sides. Beyond it the nest was dark and silent. Firestar could pick up strong scents of Twoleg and cat, but he couldn't see any movement.

"Okay, come on," he murmured over his shoulder. "But keep quiet."

He crept forward again, following the Twoleg fence until he came to a gap in the bottom, where he slid into the garden. He found himself among thick bushes, so overgrown that hardly any sunlight penetrated their branches. Beyond them was a stretch of long, ragged grass, leading up to the nest itself. Twoleg flowers edged the grass, but they were straggling and overgrown, not neat like in most Twoleg gardens.

Creepers were growing up the walls of the nest, and Firestar spotted a hole in the roof. It looked almost as derelict as the abandoned nest, where he and Sandstorm had stayed on their way upriver.

"Twolegs live *here*?" Leafdapple whispered from beside Firestar's shoulder.

"That's where Petal is." Rainfur pointed with his tail toward a gap in the wall of the nest.

Firestar heard a faint mewing, and made out a pale blur behind the hard transparent stuff that filled the gap.

"There she is!" Rainfur mewed. He shot past Firestar and leaped onto the ledge outside the hole in the wall.

"Idiot," Sharpclaw muttered. "He'll get us all caught."

But almost at once Rainfur leaped down again and slunk back to rejoin the group, barely visible in the long grass. "She wants to come with us," he reported. "But we have to get her out first."

Staying alert for any Twoleg noise, Firestar turned to the rest of his patrol. "Any ideas?"

Sharpclaw surveyed the nest with narrowed eyes. "Maybe we should take a look around the other side. We need a way of getting in."

"But Rainfur said the Twoleg keeps Petal shut up," Leafdapple pointed out. "That suggests there won't be anywhere to get in or out."

"Then we have to make the Twoleg open the door."

Firestar glanced at each of his warriors in turn: Patchfoot looked blank, and Sharpclaw was tearing impatiently at the earth beneath his paws. Rainfur kept casting anxious glances back at the nest, while Leafdapple's eyes were thoughtful.

"Some cat will have to get in there," she mewed. "If Petal's as weak as Rainfur says, she won't be able to carry the kits out."

Firestar could think of a couple of ideas, but he wanted the SkyClan cats to come up with their own solutions. They would never become independent if they relied on him for everything.

"What would fetch the Twoleg outside?" he prompted.

"Fighting cats!" Sharpclaw exclaimed. "Rainfur, you said the Twoleg throws stuff at you if he sees you outside. He'll have to open a door to do that."

"Brilliant!" Rainfur's eyes were gleaming. "Then the rest of us can slip inside to help Petal."

Firestar nodded. "Right. Sharpclaw and Patchfoot, you do the fighting. Make as much noise as you like, but wait for my signal. Leafdapple and Rainfur, come with me."

With the rogue and the tabby she-cat just behind him, Firestar slipped through the long grass until he stood below Petal. She was gazing out with her nose pressed to the shiny window.

Rainfur jumped up beside her again and beckoned Firestar with his tail. "Come on," he meowed. "Tell her what she has to do."

Motioning to Leafdapple to stay where she was, Firestar

leaped up onto the ledge beside the rogue. Every hair on his pelt tingled with pity as he got a good look at Petal for the first time. Her pelt was such a pale gray that it was almost white, and she was so gaunt with hunger that Firestar could see every one of her ribs. Her blue eyes were wide and pleading.

A bit of the transparent stuff had broken away, leaving a gap big enough for a cat to squeeze through, but it was blocked by a piece of wood, trapping Petal and the kits inside.

"Rainfur says you'll help my kits," Petal mewed, putting her mouth close to the edge of the wood.

Firestar quickly told her what he and the other warriors had decided to do. "Once the door is open, the three of us can get inside," he told her. "We'll bring you and the kits out, and join the others. Just be ready to run when I tell you."

Petal nodded. "I'm ready now."

"Okay, let's do it." Firestar jumped down into the grass again beside Leafdapple. As soon as Rainfur joined them, he waved his tail to where he could see Sharpclaw and Patchfoot crouching at the edge of the bushes.

Immediately Sharpclaw let out a fearsome screech. Patchfoot joined in with an eerie caterwauling. The two toms sprang at each other and rolled over together in the grass, their yowling and hissing growing louder and louder.

A moment later Firestar heard a Twoleg voice coming from the nest, bellowing in rage.

"It's working!" Leafdapple whispered.

The door of the nest flew open. A Twoleg emerged, his pelts tattered and his eyes bulging with fury. He had some

Twoleg things clutched in each hand. Still bellowing, he flung one of them at the battling cats; it flew over their heads and crashed into the bushes.

"Now!" Firestar yowled.

He led the other two cats along the wall of the nest until they reached the door and slipped inside. Firestar recognized a Twoleg kitchen, and drew his lips back at the stench of rotting Twoleg food that rolled out to meet them.

Rainfur flicked his tail toward an inside door that stood half-open. "This way."

As Firestar followed him he heard another thump from outside and an even louder screech. *StarClan help us!* he prayed, hoping that the Twoleg hadn't managed to hit one of the warriors.

Beyond the door was a small, dark den. Petal was crouching over a wooden nest beside the wall. A filthy Twoleg pelt covered the bottom; on it lay a gray kit and a pale gray tabby, squirming and mewling helplessly. An empty bowl stood beside the nest, with traces of kittypet food crusted inside and a couple of flies buzzing around it.

"Poor little scraps!" Leafdapple exclaimed, bending over to nose the two kits gently.

"Are you sure it's safe?" Petal asked, her eyes wide with fear. "My Twoleg will see us!"

"Your Twoleg has other things to think about," Rainfur told her. "Come on."

Petal gripped one of the kits in her jaws by the scruff, then stood up and headed for the door, staggering slightly.

"Give me the kit," Firestar directed. "Leafdapple, you take the other one. Rainfur, help Petal."

When he had the kit in a firm grip he signaled with his tail for the others to follow him outside. But as they slipped out of the nest a shadow blocked the light from the outer door. The Twoleg stood there, yowling and waving his forepaws.

Firestar flashed a glance at Leafdapple and the two of them split apart, dodging past the Twoleg on either side. A huge, hairless pink paw swooped down on Firestar, but before it could grab him Rainfur flung himself at the Twoleg, slashing the paw with his claws. The Twoleg let out a screech of pain. Looking back over his shoulder, Firestar caught a glimpse of Petal raking her claws down the Twoleg's hind leg.

Firestar shot through the outer door into the garden. Setting down the kit, he signaled to Leafdapple to join the other warriors in the bushes. Then he whirled to join the fight, but Rainfur and Petal were already fleeing out of the nest behind him. Snatching up the kit again he raced for the fence, where Sharpclaw was waiting beside the gap. He shoved Petal and Rainfur through to Leafdapple. By now, the Twoleg was lumbering across the garden toward them.

"Get a move on!" Sharpclaw hissed.

Firestar slipped through the gap; the ginger warrior followed, and the whole patrol pelted through the woods with the yowls of the Twoleg dying away behind them. They didn't stop until they had crossed the SkyClan scent markers near the top of the cliff.

For a few heartbeats, all the cats could do was catch their

breath. Petal was leaning heavily on Rainfur's shoulder, but she staggered toward her kits as soon as Firestar and Leafdapple set them down.

"What if my Twoleg comes after us?" she mewed anxiously. "What if he tries to steal my kits back?"

"We'll stop him," Rainfur promised, pressing his muzzle into her shoulder.

We? Firestar thought, though he said nothing. Was Rainfur beginning to appreciate the support that he could expect from a Clan?

Petal sank down beside her kits and covered them with comforting licks. The kits burrowed into her pale belly fur, still mewing in distress as they tried to suckle.

"I haven't enough milk for them." Petal's eyes were filled with grief as she gazed up at Firestar. "They're going to die."

"No, they're not," Firestar assured her. "We'll take them back to our camp and look after them there." Clovertail still had milk, and she wouldn't refuse to help these pitiful scraps.

Hope glimmered in the gray she-cat's eyes. "Will you really? Oh, thank you!"

Leafdapple brushed gently against her pelt. "You don't have to worry anymore."

When they reached the camp, Sandstorm and the others were just returning from their training session. Cherrypaw and Sparrowpaw bounded up eagerly to see the kits, with Clovertail's kits hard on their paws.

"You did it!" Cherrypaw exclaimed. "I wish we'd been there to help."

"It wasn't hard." Sharpclaw twitched his whiskers in satisfaction. "You should have seen that stupid Twoleg blundering about."

Sandstorm approached the kits and gave each of them a gentle sniff. Her tail lashed furiously. "Why did the Twoleg want kittypets if he treated them like this?"

"It wasn't so bad before the kits came," Petal mewed. "I could get out of the nest to catch mice. But once they were born the Twoleg blocked the window. . . ."

"You don't have to explain." Clovertail thrust forward and touched noses with Petal. "Bring them up to the nursery and I'll feed them." She turned to her own kits and gave them a hard stare. "You three stay down here, and let these kits sleep in peace for a bit. And *don't* get into mischief."

"What, us?" Rockkit stretched his eyes wide.

"Don't worry," Cherrypaw assured their mother. "Sparrowpaw and I will keep an eye on them. Come on, you lot." She waved her tail to beckon the kits. "We'll teach you the hunter's crouch."

Their eyes sparkling with delight, Clovertail's three kits marched off after the apprentice, back up the gorge toward the training area.

"We're not the littlest anymore!" Tinykit mewed gleefully.

When they had gone, Clovertail led the way up to the nursery and settled down in her mossy nest. The cave was dim and cool, the boulder at the entrance blocking off most of the direct sunlight.

Firestar and Leafdapple laid the two kits next to

Clovertail's belly; within a heartbeat they were both suckling eagerly, pressed against her soft fur.

Petal gazed at them as if she couldn't believe what she was seeing. "I can't thank you enough," she whispered. She staggered as if her legs wouldn't hold her up any longer, and Leafdapple helped her to lie down in the soft moss next to Clovertail and her kits.

"They're beautiful kits," Clovertail murmured. "What are their names?"

"That's Mint," Petal replied, pointing with her ears at the gray kit. "And that one is Sage," she added, indicating the pale gray tabby. "I used to look through the window at the herbs in the Twoleg garden."

Mintkit and Sagekit, Firestar thought, wondering if Petal would want her kits to grow up in the Clan.

"I'll fetch you some fresh-kill," Leafdapple promised, and slipped out past the boulder at the entrance.

Firestar said good-bye to the two she-cats and followed Leafdapple out. Sandstorm was waiting for him a few pawsteps down the stony trail.

"Petal will need something to help her regain her strength," she murmured when Firestar joined her. "She looks so weak and ill."

"Do you know what to do for her?" Firestar asked.

"Juniper berries for strength, Cinderpelt said," the ginger she-cat replied. "But I don't know where to find them." Her tail tip twitched. "They need a medicine cat, don't they?"

Firestar shook his head. "It's not for us to decide," he

meowed. "Medicine cats are chosen by StarClan. And I haven't had any signs at all."

"Well, I wish StarClan would get a move on," Sandstorm responded tartly. "Meanwhile, I'll do what I can for Petal. I'll ask Sharpclaw if he knows where juniper grows." She padded off to join the ginger rogue, who was crouched beside the fresh-kill pile.

Firestar spotted Rainfur a few fox-lengths farther up the cliff, outside the warriors' den. When Firestar climbed up to join him, he sprang to his paws. "Will they be okay?"

"They'll be fine," Firestar meowed, hoping that was true. "Why don't you go and see?"

"I will, if no cat minds." Rainfur gave his chest fur a couple of embarrassed licks.

Firestar guessed he felt awkward about entering the SkyClan dens. "You're welcome to stay here as long as you want," he mewed.

Rainfur met his gaze steadily. "Thanks, Firestar. I—"

"We would have done the same for any cat."

"I wanted to say I'm sorry about what I said at the meeting," Rainfur meowed. "And I'd like to stay with you, for a while at least. Petal's not strong enough to go anywhere yet, and the kits need Clovertail to feed them. But only if that's okay," he added.

"Of course. We'll be glad to have you."

Even while he welcomed Rainfur to the gorge, Firestar felt uneasy. The gray rogue were treating him as if he was SkyClan's leader. He wasn't, and he didn't want to be. The sooner he could find a real leader, the better. Sharpclaw seemed the obvious choice: he was strong and brave, and his fighting skills were better than any other cat's. But he had looked too interested at the meeting when Firestar explained that a Clan leader received nine lives. That was the wrong reason to look for Clan leadership, because it could make a cat foolhardy about leaping into danger—those lives were easily lost if not treated with respect.

This isn't your choice, he reminded himself. *A true Clan leader should be approved by StarClan.* He looked up to where the sky was flooded with scarlet from the setting sun. It was still too early for the stars to show.

Do you walk these skies? he silently asked SkyClan's warrior ancestors. *If you're there, please show me which is the right cat to lead this Clan.*

CHAPTER 28

Cherrypaw crouched at the edge of the training area, her tail lashing from side to side and her eyes gleaming. Her tortoiseshell fur bristled as she sprang forward, her claws lashing at her mentor's shoulders. Sharpclaw dodged to one side, trying to hook the young she-cat's paws from under her; she barreled into him, and both cats wrestled together in the sand.

"Well done!" Firestar meowed. "Cherrypaw, you've learned that move really well."

Both cats sat up, panting and shaking sand out of their pelts. Cherrypaw cast a triumphant glance at her mentor. "I'll beat you one day," she told him.

"I hope you will," Sharpclaw replied calmly. "My job will be done then."

"I think that's enough battle training for today." Firestar rose to his paws. "Sharpclaw, when Sparrowpaw gets back from hunting patrol, I thought you and Leafdapple could give the two apprentices an assessment."

"What's that?" Cherrypaw asked curiously.

"Your mentor gives you a task," Firestar explained. "Usually to go and hunt in a particular place. Then they follow you and see how you get on, but you won't see them. In ThunderClan every apprentice—"

He broke off at the sound of pawsteps dashing along the gorge, and a cat yowling his name. Spinning around, he caught sight of Sparrowpaw, his tabby fur bristling and his amber eyes wide with fear.

"We've been attacked!" He gasped. "Patchfoot's hurt."

"Show me," Firestar snapped.

Sparrowpaw turned and raced back down the gorge; Firestar followed, with Sharpclaw and Cherrypaw hard on his paws.

When he rounded the curve and passed the Rockpile, Firestar saw Shortwhisker and Sandstorm dragging Patchfoot down the lowest part of the trail to lay him in the shade of the cliff. His head hung limply and his tail dragged in the sand; blood dripped from a wound in his shoulder. Firestar's belly lurched.

When he padded up to Patchfoot's side he saw that his chest was heaving with rapid, shallow breaths. His eyes were open, filled with pain and fear.

"What happened?" Firestar asked, turning to Sandstorm.

Sandstorm rested her tail reassuringly on Patchfoot's uninjured shoulder. "Don't worry," she mewed. "We'll fix you up as good as new." Giving her attention to Firestar, she went on, "We were attacked by rats outside the abandoned Twoleg barn."

"More rats than you've ever seen in your life!" Shortwhisker gasped. His fur was still fluffed out with shock.

Icy claws pricked Firestar's spine. "I knew there was something wrong with that place," he meowed.

"We fought them off," Sandstorm continued, "but two of them jumped on Patchfoot."

"You're wounded yourself," Firestar pointed out, noticing a patch of fur matted with blood on her side.

Sandstorm twitched her ears. "That's nothing. I'll see to it when I've done what I can for Patchfoot."

By this time, more of the cats had appeared: Leafdapple came down from the warriors' den, while Petal and Rainfur, who had been playing with their kits a little way downriver, padded up and gazed anxiously at the wounded warrior.

"Will he die?" Petal's voice quavered.

"Not if I can help it," Sandstorm replied. "Cherrypaw, go to the Whispering Cave and get me some moss. Sparrowpaw, you go into some of the unused caves and bring me as many cobwebs as you can find."

Sparrowpaw's whiskers quivered with surprise. "Cobwebs?"

"To stop the bleeding." Sandstorm flicked her tail at him. "Hurry!"

Once the two apprentices had scurried off, Firestar and Leafdapple picked up Patchfoot and carried him to the lowest cave, which Skywatcher had told them once belonged to the Clan's medicine cat. There was a large outer cave with some scrapes in the floor, and a smaller, deeper cave beyond it that would have been the medicine cat's den. In a niche in the rock Sandstorm had discovered a few ancient, crumbled leaves, and the scent of sweet herbs seemed to hang in the air.

Patchfoot let out a groan when his Clanmates moved him, and by the time they laid him down in the medicine cat's cave he had lost consciousness.

"Do you think you can help him?" Firestar asked.

Sandstorm's green eyes were anxious. "I don't know. I can stop the bleeding with cobwebs, but I'm worried the wounds will get infected. Cinderpelt would use marigold or horsetail, but I don't know where they grow around here."

"I do." The voice was Petal's; the pale gray cat had followed them and was looking in through the cave entrance. "There's marigold in my Twoleg's garden."

Sandstorm spun around, hope gleaming in her green eyes. "Can you get some?"

Petal flattened her ears; Firestar could see that she was trembling. "How . . . how important is it?"

"Very," Sandstorm replied.

Petal straightened her shoulders. "Then I'll go fetch some."

"Oh, no, you won't." Rainfur appeared beside Petal. "*I'll* go. I know where the marigold grows." He gave Petal's ear a lick. "You look after the kits, and I'll be back before you know it."

"That would be great," Firestar meowed.

Rainfur darted off, and Firestar padded over to Petal. "Thanks for offering, but you shouldn't have to go back to that Twoleg nest again."

Petal looked up at him, her eyes wide with guilt. "Sometimes I think I should have stayed with my Twoleg," she murmured. "But I can't bear even to think about him."

"You don't have to," Firestar told her. "You're safe here."

Petal dipped her head and went out, calling to her kits.

Sandstorm crouched down beside Patchfoot and began to clean the blood from his shoulder wound with strong rasps of her tongue. Firestar watched her for a couple of heartbeats, then went back outside, passing Cherrypaw as she entered with a huge bundle of moss.

The rest of the Clan was gathered around Shortwhisker, listening to his account of the rat attack. "And then they poured out of the barn as thick as a river!" he meowed. "You couldn't see the ground for rats."

"That's enough." Firestar stepped forward and silenced the tabby warrior with a flick of his tail. The Clan was shocked enough by Patchfoot's injuries without hearing exaggerated stories of how he came by them. "I've dealt with rats before," he went on. "They're nasty creatures, but a strong patrol of cats can beat them. Sharpclaw, you can come with me. And Cherrypaw . . ." He waved the apprentice over as she reappeared from the medicine cat's cave. "We'll go and check this out for ourselves."

"Aren't you glad you practiced those fighting moves?" Sharpclaw muttered to his apprentice.

Cherrypaw's only reply was an enthusiastic wave of her tail; her eyes were gleaming with excitement.

"Leafdapple, you're in charge of the camp while we're away. If I were you, I would get all the kits inside the nursery with Clovertail, and then guard the entrance. Just in case."

The tabby she-cat dipped her head. "Don't worry, Firestar.

We'll be fine." She bounded off to round up the kits.

Firestar took a last look at the camp, then led the way up the stony trails to the top of the cliff. There was no scent of rats here, just the hot reek of Patchfoot's blood, but he ordered the patrol to keep silent, and crept as stealthily as he could through the undergrowth and across the scrubland toward the Twoleg barn.

Long before he reached it he began to pick up a strong rat scent, and as he and his patrol drew closer the sense of a malevolent force, of cold eyes watching him from the shadows, swept over him again. Firestar shivered to the roots of his pelt.

Rats!

That was what he had sensed in the undergrowth downstream. Rats whose hatred of cats spilled out like a dark, poisonous river. He was surprised at the strength of that hatred, and how focused it was. The rats he had met before had been vicious, but not like this, purposeful and cunning.

Everything was quiet as the SkyClan patrol approached the shiny fence that surrounded the barn. The ragged holes in the walls seemed to stare at them, but except for the scent there was no sign of a rat.

"Firestar, over here!" Sharpclaw was sniffing a little farther along the fence, beckoning his leader with his tail.

When he joined the ginger tom, Firestar saw the ground torn up by claws, and patches of soil still darkened by clots of blood.

"This must be where the attack happened," Sharpclaw mewed.

Firestar nodded. Just beyond the clawed-up area was a gap at the bottom of the shiny fence, big enough for a cat to squeeze through. For a heartbeat his paws froze to the ground; then he gave his pelt a shake. This was just a gang of rats, nothing that he couldn't cope with, as long as he had strong warriors to back him up.

"Okay," he murmured. "We're going in. Cherrypaw, follow me. Sharpclaw, keep a lookout behind."

Ears pricked and whiskers twitching, he slid through the gap and padded softly across the white stone surface toward the barn. There was still no sign of movement. Firestar would have liked to think that Sandstorm's patrol had frightened the rats off, if it weren't for that overwhelming sensation of being watched.

"Are we going inside?" Sharpclaw asked.

"Not if we don't have to," Firestar replied. "They can do what they like on their own territory. We'll just take a look around outside and then—"

He broke off, every hair on his pelt rising in horror. With a patter of tiny paws, rats had begun pouring out of one of the holes in the walls of the barn, more rats than he had seen in his life, more than he could have imagined living in one barn. Whipping around, he saw yet more emerging from another hole. The two streams flowed around the three cats, a whispering torrent of brown bodies and long, thin tails. None of them squeaked; there was just the small, terrible sound of their scampering feet as they moved steadily, purposefully, into position. Firestar and his patrol were surrounded; an unbroken mass of rats stood a tail-length away from them, blocking the route to the gap in the fence. Their tiny glittering eyes were filled with malice.

Shortwhisker didn't *exaggerate!* Firestar thought in horror. *You really can't see the ground for rats.*

Sharpclaw had dropped into a crouch, ready to spring, his teeth drawn back in a snarl. Firestar stood beside him, flicking a glance at Cherrypaw. The young tortoiseshell's eyes were glazed with terror, but she was facing her enemies and trying to stand firm, even though her legs were trembling.

"Okay," Firestar murmured. "When I raise my tail, head for the fence."

Sharpclaw acknowledged the order with a lash of his tail. Firestar tensed, ready to give the signal, and wished he could have said good-bye to Sandstorm. But before he could move, the mass of rats parted and a single rat stepped out into the gap between them and the cats. It was bigger than most of the others, with a wiry, muscular body and curving yellow teeth.

"Fine," Sharpclaw growled. "You want to die first, do you?"

The rat's wedge-shaped head swung back and forth as its malignant gaze flicked from cat to cat, and it began to speak. To Firestar's astonishment he could understand what it said, though the words were so twisted it was hard to make them out.

"Rats not die." Its voice grated like a claw dragged over stone. "Cats die."

Sharpclaw slid his claws out. "You're sure of that, are you?"

"Leave," the rat went on. "All cats leave. We killed you before; now we kill you again."

"You killed us before?" Firestar exclaimed.

"This time we let black-and-white cat live." The rat's eyes glittered with hatred. "But only this time. You stay by river, you die."

It kinked its tail over its back, and as if they had been waiting for the signal the other rats separated into two streams again and flowed back into the barn. The rat who had spoken slid in among them and was lost to sight.

Firestar flicked his tail toward the gap. "Go!"

While Cherrypaw and Sharpclaw squeezed out into the scrubland, Firestar turned to face the barn. His heart was thumping hard enough to break out of his chest. "The gorge is our place," he yowled after the river of retreating bodies. "We will not leave."

Then he spun around, slid through the gap, and raced across the open ground with Cherrypaw and Sharpclaw by his side. They didn't stop until they reached the shelter of the bushes at the top of the cliff.

"I've never seen so many rats!" Cherrypaw panted, her eyes wide.

"Nor have I," Firestar admitted. "And I've never come across a rat who could speak to cats before."

Sharpclaw was giving himself a quick grooming, as if he was trying to hide how troubled he was. "I've never met one, but I've heard of rats like that—rats who could think, and plan, and hate. My mother used to tell me stories, and I thought that's all they were—just stories."

"I wish they were." Firestar's alarm was growing. "He said, 'We killed you before.' I've got a horrible feeling I know what he meant."

"What?" Cherrypaw asked.

Firestar wasn't ready to reply; there was something he needed to check. Waving his tail for the others to follow, he pushed through the bushes to the cliff top and down the trail as far as the warriors' den.

"Look at that," he mewed, pointing with his tail to the scratches on the column of rock by the entrance.

"Yes, our ancestors' claw marks." Sharpclaw nodded.

"Look at the smaller claw marks at the bottom, the ones that go across instead of up and down. I always assumed that kits made them, but now I think they're the marks of rats." Peering more closely at the marks, Firestar matched them in his memory with the tiny claws of rats. No kit would have claws so thorn-sharp.

Cherrypaw's eyes stretched wide. "Rats came *here*?"

Firestar nodded. "We've always known that something drove the first SkyClan cats out of here and scattered them so that the Clan was destroyed. Now I think we know what that 'something' was."

"Rats!" Sharpclaw snarled.

"Rats," Firestar agreed.

Gazing down at the thin claw marks, scored across the ones made by cats, Firestar found it was easy to imagine hordes of rats pouring into the gorge and overwhelming the

SkyClan warriors. They had set their marks in this cave to proclaim their victory. Firestar had no doubt that he was looking at a record of SkyClan's defeat.

This was the secret that Skywatcher had refused to tell him, the secret of how the first SkyClan had been driven from the gorge. The rats' hatred had been passed down and now it was being nourished by the leader Firestar and his patrol had met outside the barn—the rat who spoke cat, who must have learned to speak the language of his enemies to let them know exactly what he would do to them. He would stop at nothing to rid his territory of cats, just as his ancestors had done long ago.

Firestar worked his claws in the sandy floor. Were SkyClan doomed to be driven out of their homes again, just as their ancestors had been?

He padded out of the den and gazed across the gorge. Clouds covered the sky, though there was a pale gleam of light where the sun was trying to break through. Slowly the clouds shifted into a pattern of light and dark, until the SkyClan ancestor's face was looking down at him with eyes full of wisdom. Firestar's paws seemed to freeze to the rock, and every hair on his pelt tingled. Why should the SkyClan ancestor appear now, when Firestar had not seen him for so long? Somehow Firestar was convinced it must be because there was a way to defeat the rats and save the Clan.

The clouds shifted again and the face of the ancestor disappeared. But the encouragement he had given Firestar flowed through his body from ears to tail tip. "Come on," he meowed, glancing over his shoulder at Sharpclaw. "I'm going to call a Clan meeting."

"Cats of SkyClan." Firestar stood on top of the Rockpile, his flame-colored pelt gleaming in a shaft of sunshine. "You heard what happened today, first to Sandstorm's patrol and then when I went back with Sharpclaw and Cherrypaw. Now we have to decide what we're going to do."

Pausing, he let his gaze travel over the Clan below. All the cats were sitting close to one another, as if they needed the physical support of their Clanmates. Petal was missing, looking after the kits in the nursery cave, but Rainfur was here, even though he wasn't a Clan warrior. Sandstorm was sitting at the mouth of the medicine cat's den, where she could keep an eye on Patchfoot and still listen to what was being said at the meeting.

"*Can* we do anything?" Leafdapple asked. "If there are as many rats as you say, how can we possibly beat them?" Her eyes met Firestar's as she spoke; she wasn't frightened or despairing, but Firestar could tell she saw no point in facing a battle they couldn't win.

He knew he had to be honest with her. "It's going to be tough. I've never come across rats like these before. But we don't have to kill them all. Just enough to make them stay in their own territory."

"They drove out the first SkyClan," Sparrowpaw mewed nervously. "Why should we be any different?" Shortwhisker murmured agreement, his whiskers twitching.

"At least we know what we have to face," Firestar replied. He scraped his claws along the rock, desperate to turn this huddle of shaken cats into a Clan of loyal, determined warriors. "Your warrior ancestors are watching you now," he told them, hoping it was true. "You should fight for *their* sakes, not just your own. This is your chance to take revenge!"

"Why?" Cherrypaw demanded. "We've never met our warrior ancestors. Okay, we're living in their camp, but that doesn't mean we have to fight their battles."

Clovertail nodded, taking a pawstep that brought her to the young tortoiseshell's side. "Cherrypaw is right. We've got to decide what's right for *us,* not for some dead cats who already lost their battle."

Firestar winced; Clovertail's words were harsh, but she had a point.

"And what about the kits?" Shortwhisker fretted. "*They* can't fight. But the rats will kill them if they come here."

Rainfur bared his teeth. "Over my dead body."

Firestar gazed frustratedly down at them. Shortwhisker obviously didn't understand the warrior code that would protect the weakest members of the Clan above all else. And Rainfur didn't seem to realize that he could rely on the Clan for help.

Before he could speak again, Sharpclaw stepped forward. "What are you, warriors or mice? Are you going to let *prey* beat you? I'll fight to the death if necessary—and as often as I have to," he added, with a dark look at Firestar.

Firestar tensed. Sharpclaw couldn't have given a more

obvious hint that he expected to be chosen as Clan leader. But at least he seemed to have shaken off some of the despondency that had settled over the Clan like a clinging fog.

"There's no point in every warrior fighting to the death," Firestar pointed out quietly. "Then there would be no Clan left to fight for. But think about this," he went on. "If you don't want to fight for your warrior ancestors, then how about fighting for yourselves? You've achieved so much—making a home here, rescuing Petal and her kits. Isn't that worth fighting for?"

His heartbeat quickened when he saw that he was reaching them at last. "This is a good home for you," he meowed, waving his tail to take in the river and the caves of the camp. "You've all worked hard for it, and you deserve to be here. Are you going to let the rats drive you out?"

"No! We're staying," Sharpclaw hissed. "And we'll tear the throats out of any rats who try to stop us."

"Yes!" Cherrypaw screeched, springing forward.

"We'll fight!" Sparrowpaw jumped up to stand beside them, and the rest of the Clan yowled in agreement. "We'll fight!"

Firestar gazed over their heads to where Sandstorm was still sitting outside the medicine cat's den. Their eyes met.

Oh, StarClan, Firestar thought, *I hope I'm not leading them to their deaths.*

CHAPTER 29

"How is Patchfoot?" Firestar asked as he slipped into the medicine cat's cave. Night had fallen, and the half-moon shed silver light into the gorge. Back in the forest the medicine cats would be traveling to Highstones for their twice-moon meeting. Firestar wished he had the benefit of Cinderpelt's wisdom now.

Sandstorm looked up as Firestar entered, her eyes filled with sorrow. "He's getting worse," she mewed. "His wound is infected—just what I was afraid of."

"You've tried marigold?" Firestar asked, padding forward to look down at Patchfoot. The black-and-white warrior shifted restlessly in his sleep and let out a moan of pain.

Sandstorm nodded. "Petal and Rainfur brought me plenty, but it's not doing any good. I wish there was something stronger to use for rat bites, but if there is, Cinderpelt didn't tell me." She lashed her tail in frustration.

"You couldn't learn everything in the time you had before we left," Firestar consoled her. "I know you're doing your best."

"It's a pretty poor best if Patchfoot dies."

Firestar wanted to reassure her, but he knew the words would sound empty. He could feel the heat of fever rising from Patchfoot's body. His legs twitched as Firestar watched; he opened eyes glazed with pain and let out another moan.

Sandstorm rested her tail tip soothingly on his head; the black-and-white tom's eyes closed again and he seemed to sink back into a quieter sleep.

"He can't go on like this," Sandstorm murmured. "No cat has the strength."

Firestar rasped his tongue over her ear, but before he could say anything to comfort her, he heard a soft pawstep behind him. A sweet scent drifted around him and every hair on his pelt started to tingle. *Spottedleaf!*

Spinning around, he saw the pale outline of a tortoiseshell cat with the frosty glimmer of StarClan around her. She set down a mouthful of herbs and padded up to settle close by Patchfoot, between Firestar and Sandstorm.

Am I dreaming? Firestar wondered. *When did I fall asleep?*

Then Sandstorm's ears pricked; she turned and her eyes flew wide with astonishment. "Spottedleaf!"

Firestar opened his jaws to speak, but at first not the faintest mew came out. How could Sandstorm see Spottedleaf if she was inside his dream? "Spottedleaf, how . . . ?"

Spottedleaf silenced him by touching noses with him. "I've come because you both need me." She turned to the herbs she had set down and patted them over to Sandstorm. "Burdock root is best for rat bites."

Sandstorm was staring at the StarClan medicine cat as if

she couldn't believe what she was seeing. As the glossy green leaves rustled around her paws she blinked and looked down, sniffing the roots. "This will help Patchfoot?"

Spottedleaf nodded. "I'll chew the root up. You clean the marigold off his wound."

As if she had made up her mind not to think too closely about what was happening, Sandstorm began licking the chewed-up marigold from Patchfoot's shoulder. Firestar watched numbly as Spottedleaf crouched down beside the burdock, tucked her paws underneath her chest, and began to chew one of the roots. When the pulp was ready she showed Sandstorm how to use it, patting it well down into the wound.

Patchfoot stirred uneasily; Spottedleaf bent over him. "Sleep now," she whispered into his ear. "All will be well; I promise."

As if he could hear her, Patchfoot sighed and seemed to settle more quietly.

Sandstorm blinked anxiously. "Will he really get better now?"

Spottedleaf nodded. "Just keep putting the root on his shoulder. You'll find more in the wood by the stream that marks the boundary. Show the leaves to your warriors; then they'll know what to look for."

"Thank you, Spottedleaf," Firestar meowed. Brushing his pelt against the medicine cat's, he added, "I didn't know you could come so far to help us. I haven't seen you since we left the forest."

Too late, he realized that Sandstorm was bristling beside

him. "You mean you've seen Spottedleaf before?"

Firestar faced her to see anger and hurt in her green eyes. "Spottedleaf visits me in dreams. She helps me—"

"You never told me!"

Firestar's belly churned with guilt. He knew how insecure Sandstorm felt when she thought about Spottedleaf, knowing the connection she had shared with Firestar when she had been ThunderClan's medicine cat. But he had never felt that he was betraying her by meeting Spottedleaf in his dreams.

Before he could reply, Spottedleaf slipped between the two of them and laid her tail tip gently on Sandstorm's shoulder. "Peace, dear one," she murmured. "Firestar loves you."

"He loves you more." Sandstorm's voice was choked.

Spottedleaf hesitated, her amber eyes warm as she gazed at the ginger she-cat. "That's not true. Firestar and I never discovered what we might have meant to each other," she mewed at last. "I was alive in the forest for such a short time after he came to ThunderClan. But I know for sure"—her voice grew more intense—"that he and I could never have been mates. I was and always will be a medicine cat. That comes first, more than any cat who walks the forest, more even than Firestar."

Sandstorm searched the tortoiseshell cat's face. "Is that really true?"

"Of course," Spottedleaf purred. "Even now I'm a medicine cat, not for my Clanmates in StarClan, but for all the cats in the forest below."

"I love *you*, Sandstorm," Firestar put in. "You'll never be second-best for me. My love for you belongs here and now, in the life we share—and it will last for all the moons to come, I promise."

Sandstorm looked from Spottedleaf to Firestar and back again. At last she took a long breath. "Thank you, Spottedleaf. I've never stopped thinking about how you and Firestar seemed to belong together when he first came to the forest. But I understand better now."

"I thought you always knew how I felt about you," Firestar mewed, bewildered.

Sandstorm blinked at him. Even though her eyes were full of love, there was a trace of exasperation there too. "Firestar, you can be so *dense*."

Spottedleaf dipped her head. "I must go, but we will meet again, I promise. Until then, may StarClan light your path."

"Good-bye, and thank you—not just for the burdock root," Firestar meowed.

The tortoiseshell she-cat padded toward the cave entrance and paused for a heartbeat, her pelt brushing against his. Too softly for Sandstorm to hear, she murmured, "Sometimes I would give anything for things to be different."

She did not wait for a reply. The moonlight had faded; for a heartbeat her slender shape was outlined against the first pale light of dawn from the sky above the far side of the gorge; then she was gone.

Sandstorm shook her head. "Have I been dreaming, or did that really happen?"

Firestar stepped to her side and pressed his muzzle against

her shoulder. "It really happened."

"I can't believe she came to help us."

"There'll never be another cat in the forest like her. But she's not you, Sandstorm."

Sandstorm turned to gaze at him. "No more secrets, Firestar. I promise to try to understand how important Spottedleaf is to you, but I need to be able to trust you."

"You can," Firestar vowed.

Patchfoot let out a sigh, distracting Firestar from the depths of Sandstorm's green eyes. The black-and-white warrior was quieter now, his breathing easier. He seemed to be sleeping more deeply.

"He's going to be all right," Firestar mewed. "And I think the rest of the Clan will be, too."

"We'll start extra battle training right away." Firestar stood at the bottom of the Rockpile, with the SkyClan cats clustered around him. The sun had risen over the cliff top, casting long shadows down into the gorge. "We need to be as strong as possible when we go out to fight the rats."

Sandstorm stood beside him. Since Spottedleaf's visit earlier that morning, Patchfoot had improved so much that she had told Firestar she could leave him for a while to come to this meeting. "Don't wait too long," she advised, with a twitch of her ears. "Otherwise the rats will come and we won't be ready for them."

Firestar knew she was right. "I want a permanent watch on the Skyrock."

"We should send extra patrols out to the Twoleg barn, too," Leafdapple suggested.

Firestar nodded. "Right, but not too close. I don't want a fight until we're ready."

"I'll sort out the patrols," Sandstorm meowed. "And the training schedules."

"Watches and extra patrols *and* battle training?" Cherrypaw's eyes were wide with dismay. "It sounds like really hard work."

"You'd rather have your throat torn out by a rat?" Sharpclaw flicked his tail over the young tortoiseshell's ear, and she sprang back with an indignant hiss. "*My* apprentice will do as she's told, and do it without complaining."

Cherrypaw opened her jaws to protest, but Firestar silenced her with a flick of his ears. "We can get started," he meowed, "unless you have any other suggestions?"

Rainfur rose to his paws. "Petal and I want to be trained as well."

"That's right." Petal looked nervous to be speaking in front of the whole Clan. "The kits are too small for us to leave yet, and we want to be ready to defend ourselves."

"Thank you." Firestar dipped his head. "We're glad to have you. Sandstorm will add you to the training schedule."

"Either Clovertail or I must stay with the kits," Petal pointed out.

"Don't worry," Sandstorm replied. "I'll work around that. Are there any more questions? Right," she went on when no cat responded, "Leafdapple and Sharpclaw, you can be the first patrol. Cherrypaw, will you keep watch on the Skyrock? Give me a few moments to check on Patchfoot, and then I'll lead a training session with Sparrowpaw and Rainfur, and Petal, you can join us, as Clovertail's with the kits right now."

"What about me?" Shortwhisker asked.

"You can come with me on a hunting patrol," Firestar replied. "We'll need all the fresh-kill we can get to keep our strength up. One more thing," he added before the cats split up for their duties. "No cat leaves the camp alone from now on. And every cat must stay alert. If the rats come, they'll find us ready and waiting."

He dismissed the meeting with a wave of his tail. Sharpclaw and Leafdapple sprang up the rocks toward the top of the cliff, and Cherrypaw followed, taking the trail that led to the Skyrock. Petal, Rainfur, and Sparrowpaw made their way up the gorge toward the training area.

Asking Shortwhisker to wait for him, Firestar padded beside Sandstorm as she headed for the medicine cat's cave. "You know, Cherrypaw was right," he meowed. "It *will* be hard work. We don't have enough cats to prepare for a rat attack as well as all the regular duties." He sighed. "I'd give my pelt to have a patrol of ThunderClan warriors here now."

"Well, you can't." Sandstorm rasped her tongue over his ear. "But don't worry. You'll find a way. You defeated Scourge, and you'll defeat these rats."

Firestar wished he shared her confidence. "At least Spottedleaf told us what to do for Patchfoot."

"True," Sandstorm replied, "but it just goes to show how

much we need a medicine cat."

"Medicine cats are born, not made. And I've yet to see any SkyClan cat show any connection with their warrior ancestors. None of them heard anything when they went into the Whispering Cave."

"We should have a cat who knows about herbs and can treat injuries, at least," Sandstorm pointed out, with an impatient twitch of her tail. "I could teach one of them what I know. It would be a start."

Firestar paused on the trail just below the entrance to the medicine cat's den. "Sharpclaw wouldn't do," he mused. "He's far too good a warrior. Clovertail has kits. . . . What about Shortwhisker?"

Sandstorm shook her head. "He froze at the sight of blood when Patchfoot was injured."

"Leafdapple, then?"

"Maybe . . ." Sandstorm mused. "She cares about weaker cats."

"I know," Firestar decided. "If Spottedleaf visits me, I can ask her."

Sandstorm glanced away for a moment, then faced him again. "Yes, that's a good idea," she murmured.

Firestar curled up in the warriors' den, his legs aching and his head spinning with tiredness. Three days had passed since he had organized the new schedule of patrols and training, and every cat had been on their paws from dawn to sunset. That morning he had led a patrol to the Twoleg barn, then spent the rest of the day hunting. The moon was already climbing the sky before he had the chance to sleep, and he would have to wake later to take his turn watching on the Skyrock.

How long can we keep this up?

No sooner had Firestar closed his eyes than he found himself standing on the Skyrock. The moon floated high above his head and Silverpelt glittered across the sky. The night was silent except for the rushing of the river far below.

It's not time for my watch yet! Firestar thought confusedly.

"Greetings." A voice spoke behind him, and Firestar spun around to see a cat standing on the very edge of the Skyrock. His thick gray fur was turned to silver by the moonlight, and his eyes shone like pale flames. Frosty starlight glimmered around his paws.

Something about the cat was familiar; Firestar's first thought was that he was the SkyClan ancestor who had been haunting him. Then he caught his breath as he picked up a trace of familiar scent. "Skywatcher!"

The StarClan cat dipped his head. "It's good to see you again, Firestar. Come on," Skywatcher went on, proving that he had lost none of his sharp tongue. "Don't stand there with your mouth open. We haven't got all night."

Firestar made an effort to pull himself together. "Why have you come?"

"SkyClan stands at a fork in the path," Skywatcher replied. "Danger is very near."

"You mean the rats? They're what destroyed the first

SkyClan, aren't they? Why didn't you tell me about them?"

Skywatcher sat down and steadily met Firestar's gaze. "What good would that have done? It would have been wrong to tell you if it made you give up. And how would it have helped you to know about SkyClan's old enemies before they attacked? Now you have a Clan of strong warriors to stand against them."

"But are they strong enough?" Firestar murmured.

"They must be ready to defend themselves," Skywatcher replied. "Perhaps you should see these rats as the first challenge for the Clan to overcome. They will be even stronger afterward."

Firestar nodded; the StarClan cat was right, and yet he wondered how the Clan could be stronger if all its warriors were dead. Thinking about death reminded him that so far the Clan had no way of making contact with their warrior ancestors.

"Can you tell me if SkyClan has a medicine cat yet?" he asked. "No Clan can survive long without one. What about Leafdapple?"

Skywatcher twitched his ears. "No, that is not Leafdapple's destiny."

"But we *must* have a medicine cat!"

"Even now your medicine cat's paws are on the path that will lead her to you," Skywatcher told him. "But you must look farther than the cats of SkyClan. There is a cat who dreams of her warrior ancestors, but she has not heard of the new Clan."

"So I have to go and find her?" Firestar felt a tingle of excitement in his paws. "Where is she?"

But Skywatcher did not reply. Rising to his paws, he swept his tail around in a gesture of farewell and leaped from the edge of the rock into the sky. Firestar bit back a yowl of alarm; any living cat who tried that would have crashed down onto the rocks below. Instead Skywatcher's body dissolved midleap, leaving behind a faint glittering dust that faded as Firestar watched. A heartbeat later he opened his eyes inside the warriors' den, with Shortwhisker prodding him to wake up and go to the Skyrock.

"Sparrowpaw, you can be excused from battle training this morning," Firestar announced. "I want you for a special mission."

The young tabby tom's eyes gleamed with excitement. "What mission?"

"I have to go to the Twolegplace, and I need a cat who knows his way around." Quickly he explained to Sparrowpaw what Skywatcher had told him in his dream.

Though Skywatcher hadn't said that the new medicine cat lived among Twolegs, Firestar thought it was most likely. Sharpclaw and Leafdapple hadn't told him about any other rogues living in the forest, and he couldn't look farther afield because that would mean leaving SkyClan to face the rats without him.

Not long ago they would have raced across the scrubland toward the Twolegplace; now they crept along, slinking from one patch of cover to the next, all their senses alert for any trace of rats. Firestar remembered how he had felt when the dog pack roamed the forest; it went against everything in the warrior code when cats were forced to behave like prey.

Clouds scudded across the sky, driven by a cold wind. Leaves whirled in the air; the warmth of greenleaf would soon be no more than a memory. How would the Clan cope, Firestar wondered, through the harsh days of leaf-bare if they still had to guard against invasion from the rats?

"I hate this," Sparrowpaw hissed as they crouched behind a gorse bush, spying out the next stage of their journey. "This waiting . . . it spooks me. Why don't the rats just attack and get it over with? What are they waiting for?"

"I can't be sure." Firestar flexed his claws. "But I'd guess the rats know exactly how unsettled we are by waiting. They think they're going to win whenever they attack, so they've nothing to lose by making us suffer."

He didn't add that the longer they waited, the more tired the Clan would become. Any cat could see that. The rats probably knew it too; they more were clever than any rats he had ever known. Firestar's respect for them was growing every day, but that only made him hate them all the more. He would have led a patrol to fight the rats on their own territory, to attack them first and win the advantage of surprise, but for one thing: SkyClan didn't have a medicine cat to heal their wounds or read the signs from StarClan.

"Let's keep going," he muttered.

As they paused in the shelter of the fence that surrounded

the first Twoleg gardens, Sparrowpaw peered through a gap with a trace of sadness in his eyes. "That's where Cherrypaw and I used to live," he murmured. Defensively he added, "It's not that I want to go back—"

"I know," Firestar reassured him. "Twolegs aren't our enemies, even if they don't understand the warrior's way of life. Now and then I miss my old Twolegs."

"You do?" Sparrowpaw's eyes widened.

Firestar nodded. "They were good to me. But I was born for the life of a warrior."

Sparrowpaw straightened up; pride replaced the sadness in his eyes. "So was I."

"My Twolegs have a new cat now," Firestar went on. "Her name's Hattie. She seems nice—much better suited to living with housefolk than I was."

For a heartbeat Sparrowpaw looked alarmed at the thought of another cat taking his place. Then he gave his chest fur a couple of quick licks. "I hope my housefolk get another cat, too," he mewed bravely. "Then they wouldn't be sad anymore about losing me and Cherrypaw."

Firestar rested the tip of his tail on the young cat's shoulder. "Come on. We have a cat to find."

He felt his bristling pelt relax a little as he and Sparrowpaw slipped down the first alley that led into the heart of the Twolegplace. Twolegs and dogs he had dealt with before, and here among the Twoleg nests they were less likely to encounter the clever, coldhearted rats.

Sparrowpaw, however, looked much less at ease than he

had when he and Firestar had last visited the Twolegplace. His pelt fluffed up at the distant barking of a dog, and when they emerged from the alley onto the edge of a small Thunderpath, he leaped into the air as a glittering monster snarled past. "I guess I've forgotten what it's like around here," he mewed, giving his shoulder an embarrassed lick.

After carefully checking that no more monsters were around, Firestar led the way down another alley, to be met at once by a powerful scent of cat.

"Well, look who's here," a voice drawled.

Sparrowpaw jumped, his pelt bristling again. Firestar looked up to see the black kittypet, Oscar, stretched out on the top of the wall. His jaws gaped in a yawn, showing sharp teeth.

"If it isn't the mad rogue," he sneered, with a dismissive twitch of his whiskers at Firestar. "And little Boris! Actually, I've been expecting you," he added. "But I thought you'd come a bit sooner than this."

Firestar froze. Surely *Oscar* couldn't be the medicine cat Skywatcher had told him of?

The black tomcat leaped lightly down from the wall and confronted them. "Crawling back to your housefolk, are you, now the weather's turning cold?"

"No, I am not!" Sparrowpaw glared at the black tom. "I'm going to be a warrior. And don't call me Boris. I'm Sparrowpaw now."

Oscar let out a snort of amusement. "*Sparrowpaw!* What sort of name is that?"

"It's *my* name." Sparrowpaw slid his claws out. "Do you want to make something of it?"

Hastily Firestar thrust himself between the two bristling toms. "We're not here to fight," he meowed, though privately he would have liked to see the battle-trained SkyClan apprentice show Oscar just how much he had learned in the past moon. "We're looking for a special cat," he went on to Oscar. "One who has weird dreams. Have you heard about a cat like that?"

Please, Skywatcher, he added silently, *don't let Oscar tell me that* he *dreams about you!*

Oscar's green eyes widened, gleaming with contempt. "No," he replied. "And I haven't heard about any cats who fly, either."

"You think you know everything, you—" Sparrowpaw began hotly.

"I think you are looking for me," another voice interrupted him from behind, clear and young. "My name is Echo. I dream of cats with stars in their fur."

CHAPTER 30

A shiver ran through Firestar from ears to tail tip. A couple of heartbeats passed before he could force his paws to move and let him turn to face the newcomer. He saw a silver-gray tabby she-cat with deep green eyes, small and gracefully built, with tiny dark gray paws. To Firestar she looked almost fragile, and he wondered if she was suited for the tough life of a Clan.

"Greetings," he meowed. "Have you dreamed of . . . of a gray-and-white cat?"

"Yes, many times. And other cats, too. A new one just came to join them—a big cat with frosty gray fur." She blinked at Firestar with growing excitement. "Can you tell me who the starry cats are?"

"Yes," Firestar replied. "They are the spirits of your warrior ancestors."

"Spirits!" Oscar sneered. "I hope you're not listening to this rubbish?" he hissed to Echo.

To Firestar's relief, Echo ignored him. "Do you know why they come to me?" she asked Firestar.

"Have you heard of the Clan of cats who have settled in the gorge?" Echo shook her head. "The gray-and-white cat came to me and asked for my help," Firestar explained. "Many seasons ago, he was leader of SkyClan, but his cats are long gone now. Skywatcher—the new gray cat you saw—challenged me to rebuild the Clan. But they can't be a real Clan until they find a medicine cat," he went on, taking a deep breath. "And you—"

"Last night the gray cat spoke to me in a dream," Echo interrupted, her eyes shining. "He told me to come here today and look for two strange cats. Yes, I will join you."

"What?" Oscar broke in before Firestar could respond. "Go off with these two crazy furballs? You must be as mad as they are."

"Maybe I am," Echo replied calmly. "But no other cat has ever been able to explain my dreams to me. I will come."

"What about your Twolegs?" Sparrowpaw asked.

A hint of sadness appeared in Echo's green eyes. "These last few moons I've felt so restless that I've been roaming farther and farther from my housefolk's nest. I felt that if only I knew how to listen, the stars would give me an answer. Now that I'm leaving for good, my housefolk will just assume that I've found a new nest to stay in. They'll miss me, but they won't be afraid for me."

"Then let's go," meowed Firestar.

"Hang on." Oscar shouldered past him to face Echo. "You're not really going, are you? Just because of a few dreams?"

"This is not for you to understand," Echo murmured gently. She turned back to Firestar, who caught a hint of nervousness in her eyes.

"You're taking a big step," he pointed out, feeling that he had to give her a chance to change her mind.

"I know. But I'm sure this is what I'm meant to do."

Firestar nodded. If she was willing to trust her dreams, then that was enough for him. "Let's go," he mewed.

Oscar stood staring after them, dumbfounded, as they slipped back along the alley and out of the Twolegplace.

"What's it like, living in a Clan?" Echo asked as they made their way back to the gorge.

"You have to be an apprentice first," Sparrowpaw told her. "You learn hunting and fighting and stuff like that. And—"

"Hang on," Firestar interrupted. "Echo might . . . well, she might play a different role, one that involves healing herbs—and more dreams of starry cats."

"How will I learn to do all that?" she asked, her eyes wide.

They were sheltering under the gorse bush where Firestar and Sparrowpaw had paused on the way out. Sparrowpaw padded a tail-length away to check for any signs of marauding rats.

"I don't know," Firestar admitted. "My mate, Sandstorm, can teach you some of the stuff about herbs. As for the rest—if SkyClan's warrior ancestors really mean for you to join us, they'll show you the way."

To his relief, his answer seemed to satisfy Echo. "I will wait for their guidance," she mewed.

When the three cats reached the gorge, Sharpclaw was

keeping watch on the Skyrock. He sprang up to meet them at the top of the cliff.

"Still no sign of rats," he reported, and gave Echo a curious sniff. "Who's this?"

"This is Echo," Firestar replied. "I . . . I think she is going to be your medicine cat."

Sharpclaw's fur began to bristle, and his eyes narrowed. "A stranger? I thought you'd appoint one of us to be medicine cat."

Firestar took a deep breath. "It's not up to me to appoint a medicine cat," he explained. "They have to have a special connection with your warrior ancestors. I think Echo has that. You're all great warriors," he added, "but to defend your Clan fully, you need the support of a cat who can heal and share tongues with your ancestors."

Sharpclaw's fur began to lie flat, but he still looked uneasy. "Where does she come from?" he asked. "Can we trust her to give us the right herbs and remedies?"

"I lived with housefolk." Echo's clear gaze rested calmly on Sharpclaw, though her voice held a trace of uncertainty. "And I promise you can trust me. Once I've learned all about the herbs, I'll do my best for every cat."

Sharpclaw gave her a brusque nod. "We'll see how you get on," he mewed. "Good luck, anyway."

Firestar rested his tail tip on Echo's shoulder. "Come on. Let's introduce you to some more of the cats. Sparrowpaw, you go and tell the others that they have a new Clanmate."

Sparrowpaw took off at once, leaping down the rocks.

Padding more slowly down the stony trail, Firestar glanced into the warriors' den, but at this time of day it was empty. When they reached the nursery, he poked his head around the boulder at the entrance, to find Clovertail keeping watch over the kits. Her own three were play-fighting near the entrance, while Mint and Sage were curled up asleep among the moss.

"Come in, Firestar." Clovertail rose to her paws. "What can I do for you?"

"I want to introduce you to a new member of SkyClan." Firestar slid past the boulder and beckoned Echo with his tail. "This is Echo. Echo, this is Clovertail."

"I'm Rockkit!" The black kit bounced up to Echo and sniffed her; his two littermates joined him and stood gazing up curiously at the newcomer.

Clovertail dipped her head, but Firestar noticed that she looked a little wary.

"I think Echo might become SkyClan's medicine cat," he mewed.

"Are these yours?" Echo asked, twitching her ears at the three kits who surrounded her. "What lovely, strong kits! You must be very proud of them."

"I am," Clovertail purred; Firestar realized that Echo had said exactly the right thing. "But they can be mischievous at times."

Echo gave a soft *mrrow* of amusement. Padding over to the mossy nest where Mint and Sage were asleep, she mewed, "These can't be yours too?"

"No, they're mine." Light from the entrance was blocked off as Petal came in, mumbling around a vole in her jaws. Setting it down in front of Clovertail, she added more clearly, "Sparrowpaw tells me that we might have a new medicine cat." She nodded to Echo. "You're very welcome."

"Thank you." Echo's eyes grew warm as she gazed down at the kits. "They're beautiful—and so tiny!"

"You should have seen them when we came here," Petal replied. "They're much stronger now. Firestar rescued us from my Twoleg. I think my kits would have died if it hadn't been for Clovertail. She fed them and looked after them when I was too ill."

"That's wonderful!" Echo exclaimed.

Clovertail purred, and Firestar could tell that she might decide to be pleased to have Echo join the Clan. When she had spent a little time talking to the two she-cats, Firestar led her out of the nursery again and farther down the cliff. "I'll show you the old medicine cat den," he told her.

Sandstorm was still taking care of Patchfoot in the outer cave, though by now the black-and-white warrior was growing stronger, the infection in his wound almost gone. When Firestar and Echo entered, he was crouched over a piece of fresh-kill, while Sandstorm sat nearby.

She rose to her paws and padded up to Echo to touch noses with her. "Welcome to SkyClan," she meowed.

Echo glanced at Patchfoot, her eyes widening at the ugly wound on his shoulder. "How were you hurt?" she asked.

Patchfoot waved his tail in greeting and gulped down the

last mouthful of blackbird. "Rat bite," he replied when he could speak. "Sandstorm fixed me up, though."

Sandstorm shook her head. "I don't know as much as a real medicine cat—just a few useful remedies."

Echo padded up to Patchfoot, politely asked, "May I?" and then gave his wound a good sniff. "What's that I can smell?"

"Burdock root," Sandstorm replied. "That's best for rat bites, especially if they get infected. For ordinary wounds we usually use marigold. And cobwebs first of all, to stop the bleeding."

Echo blinked admiringly. "You know so much!"

"I had great teachers." Sandstorm caught Firestar's eye as she spoke, and he knew she meant Spottedleaf as well as Cinderpelt. His heart warmed at the glow in her eyes, and he knew that at last she understood his connection to Spottedleaf, without feeling that the tortoiseshell cat was a threat.

One by one the cats leaped the cleft in the rock and landed on the flat surface of the Skyrock. A full moon floated in a sky without any clouds to hide the glitter of Silverpelt. Back in the forest, Firestar thought with a tug of homesickness, the Clans would be gathering at Fourtrees. Here there was only one Clan, but SkyClan would still gather to honor their warrior ancestors.

Rainfur and Petal had stayed behind to look after the kits, but almost all the Clan cats had assembled when Firestar spotted a group of three making their way up the trail:

Sandstorm and Echo—and Patchfoot! Would the black-and-white warrior manage the leap?

He stepped forward, weaving his way between Sharpclaw and Rainfur, but before he could call out Sandstorm had leaped lightly across the gap and turned toward Patchfoot. "Okay," she meowed. "I'm ready."

Patchfoot picked up his pace, though Firestar could see he was limping, and winced with pain when he put his injured leg to the ground. He launched himself into the air and landed with all four paws on the rock, but so close to the edge that he tottered, about to fall backward. Sandstorm sank her teeth into the loose fur on his uninjured shoulder and pulled him to safety. Last of all Echo leaped the gap and gave Patchfoot's shoulder wound a careful sniff.

"Are you mouse-brained?" Firestar hissed, coming up to them. "What if you'd fallen?"

"I'm a member of this Clan." Patchfoot faced him determinedly. "I wanted to be at our first Gathering."

Gazing at the smoldering courage in his eyes, Firestar couldn't go on being angry. "Okay," he mewed, waving his tail. "You're here now. But for StarClan's sake, be careful going back. You're too good a warrior to lose."

He jumped onto one of the tumbled boulders where the Skyrock met the cliff. When the rest of the Clan turned to face him, the pale glow of their eyes set every hair on his pelt pricking. Sharpclaw was scraping at the rock as if he couldn't wait to sink his claws into a rat's pelt. Cherrypaw crouched beside him, as ready for battle as her mentor. Clovertail and

Shortwhisker sat side by side, their ears pricked. Leafdapple beckoned Sparrowpaw over to her with a sweep of her tail, and the two cats settled down to listen at the foot of Firestar's rock.

Firestar knew he was seeing how loyal they were to their Clan, how determined to fight for their right to live in the gorge. In that moment he didn't believe that anything, not even the rats, would overcome them.

"Cats of SkyClan," he began, "when several Clans gather together, they exchange news of what has happened in the previous moon. We can't do that, but we can share our news with one another. Does any cat have something to report?"

Leafdapple raised her tail. "I'd like to say how well Sparrowpaw's hunting skills are coming along. He brought back more prey than any cat yesterday."

"Excellent!" Firestar mewed, while Sparrowpaw licked his chest fur to cover his embarrassment.

"My apprentice is doing well, too." Sharpclaw obviously didn't intend to be outdone. "I promise you, she would have clawed my ear off this morning if Sandstorm hadn't stopped her."

"You just wait!" Cherrypaw muttered, only half joking. "One day when Sandstorm isn't around . . ."

Sharpclaw gave her an affectionate swipe across the haunches with his tail.

"Well done," Firestar told her. "But please leave your mentor in one piece. We need him."

Sandstorm stepped forward. "I'd like to say something

about Petal, even though I know she isn't a member of SkyClan. She volunteered to stay with the kits tonight, so that Clovertail could come here. And she's been so helpful collecting herbs in the forest. I don't know what Echo and I would have done without her."

"I'll mention it to her," Firestar promised.

"There's something else I want to say," Sharpclaw meowed. "We haven't seen so much as the hair of a rat since their leader spoke to us by the Twoleg barn. What are we going to do about them?"

"You know what we're doing," Firestar replied. "The patrols, the battle training—"

Sharpclaw lashed his tail. "But none of that is getting rid of the rats. Why don't we go out there and sort them out once and for all?"

"It's not the right time yet."

"At this rate it will never be the right time." Sharpclaw bared his teeth. "How long do you expect us to live with the threat hanging over us?"

"Not much longer, I hope," Firestar replied. "I hate waiting as much as you do. If you're willing, I think we should attack as soon as Patchfoot is fit."

"It won't be long," Patchfoot put in. "I could fight now if I had to."

"You'll fight when Sandstorm says you can," Firestar told him. "Sharpclaw, does that answer your question?"

Sharpclaw hesitated before giving him a curt nod. Firestar thought he still didn't look happy about the decision, but as important as it was to know when to attack, it was just as important to know when to hold back.

When no other cat spoke, Firestar beckoned to Echo. "Cats of SkyClan," he called, "tonight, under this moon, we welcome a new Clanmate and make her a member of the Clan before the spirits of our ancestors. I, Firestar, leader of ThunderClan and mentor to SkyClan, call upon their warrior ancestors to look down upon this cat," he went on. "She has walked with you in dreams, and I commend her to you as a member of SkyClan." Leaping down from the boulder to stand in front of Echo, he went on. "Echo, do you promise to uphold the warrior code and to protect and serve this Clan, even at the cost of your life?"

Echo raised her head. "I do."

"Then before the spirits of your ancestors I give you your name. From this moment you will be known as Echosong. StarClan honors your wisdom and faith, and we receive you into SkyClan."

He rested his muzzle on Echosong's head, and she licked his shoulder in return.

"Echosong . . . Echosong . . ." The name swept across the Skyrock like a breeze, while the warriors of StarClan blazed down.

Thank you, Skywatcher, Firestar thought.

A few sunrises after the Gathering, Firestar padded down the trail to the river to find Sandstorm sorting out the day's duties. The sun was shining, but there was a crisp tang in the air that promised frost. Leaf-fall was on its way, bringing darker days and less cover for prey to hide in.

"But I'm fed up with rat patrol!" Cherrypaw was protesting. "Why can't I go hunting instead?"

"Because Sandstorm put you on rat patrol." Sharpclaw gave her ear a sharp flick with his tail. "Don't argue."

Cherrypaw gave him a look of smoldering anger. "The stupid rats aren't going to come anyway," she muttered, just loud enough to be heard.

Firestar paused, narrowing his eyes. If the Clan was starting to think like this, they would quickly lose their battle edge. The sooner they could attack, the better.

"Leafdapple, it's your turn to go on watch," Sandstorm continued. "Sparrowpaw is up there now, so you can send him down for battle training."

The tabby she-cat waved her tail in acknowledgment and set off up the trail toward the Skyrock. Sharpclaw followed her on the rat patrol with Cherrypaw and Shortwhisker.

When they had gone, Firestar padded up to Sandstorm. "How's Patchfoot?"

"A lot better." Sandstorm twitched her ears to where the black-and-white warrior was standing a little way downstream with Rainfur and Clovertail. "He's going on hunting patrol this morning, just to see how his shoulder holds up."

"Good. I'll have a word with him when he gets back."

As he was speaking, Echosong appeared from her den, bounded lightly down the rocks, and went up to Patchfoot. She gave his shoulder a careful sniff, then stood back as the hunting patrol waved their tails in farewell and set off downriver. Patchfoot seemed to be walking as well as any cat.

"Echosong has done a marvelous job so far," Sandstorm murmured. "She just seems to know what's right. And she learns so quickly! Soon there won't be anything more I can teach her."

But her words gave Firestar another reason to worry. Without another medicine cat, how could Echosong learn everything she needed to serve her Clan properly? Sandstorm could teach her some things about herbs and treatments, but a true medicine cat's training took many moons, and included mysteries that no other Clan cat knew about.

When the hunting patrol had gone, Echosong padded upstream and joined Firestar and Sandstorm at the base of the Rockpile. "I'm ready," she mewed to Sandstorm.

Firestar flicked his ears inquiringly.

"I'm going to give Echosong some battle training," Sandstorm explained.

Echosong nodded. "Sandstorm says medicine cats don't usually fight, but they need to be able to defend themselves and their Clanmates."

"You might have to, soon," Firestar meowed.

They set off toward the training area, joined by Sparrowpaw, who came bounding down the trail from the Skyrock. At the top of the Rockpile, Firestar heard an excited squeal, and spotted Petal shepherding all five kits from the nursery. He waited for them to catch up, while Sandstorm and the others went on.

"We want to watch the training." Bouncekit scrambled up beside Firestar. "Petal says we can."

"I hope that's okay," Petal added. "It'll give me the chance to do some training myself. You know, in case the rats attack." She lowered her voice and shot a nervous glance at Mint and Sage, stumbling after the older kits.

"Yes, that's fine," Firestar replied. Calling after the kits, he added, "Keep away from the fighting. There'll be claws unsheathed, and I don't want any of you hurt."

"When can we learn to fight?" Tinykit asked as they went on up the gorge.

"Soon," Petal mewed. "When you're apprentices."

"What about us?" Mint asked. "Can we be apprentices too?"

"No," his mother told him. "We don't belong to SkyClan."

"But that's not *fair*!" Sage wailed. "*Why* don't we?"

Petal gave her a gentle tap with her tail. "You're too little to understand."

"Is that why they don't have 'kit' in their names, like us?" Rockkit asked.

Firestar nodded. "If Rainfur and Petal decide to join the Clan, then Mint and Sage will have new names."

Mint's ears pricked up. "You've got to stay," he mewed to his mother. *"Please!"*

Petal shook her head. "It's not as easy as that."

They arrived at the training area, where Sandstorm and Sparrowpaw were already sparring. Firestar was impressed by the tabby tom's speed, flashing past Sandstorm to strike a blow on her shoulder before she had time to dodge.

"Now you, Echosong," Sandstorm meowed. "You've watched Sparrowpaw do that move enough times—see if you can copy him."

The young cat stepped forward, but before she could face Sandstorm they were interrupted by a loud wail of fright from Sage. Firestar's head whipped around. The tiny kit had climbed up onto a rock and was teetering at the very top. Before any cat could reach her she lost her balance and rolled to the bottom in a flurry of legs and tail.

Petal bounded over to her. She sat up, holding out one paw. "It hurts," she whimpered.

Instantly Echosong was beside her, sniffing at the injured paw. "You've snagged a claw," she murmured, giving it a few gentle licks. "I know how painful that can be, but it'll be okay soon."

As she went on licking, Sage's whimpering died away. "You're making it feel better," she mewed.

"You're very brave," Echosong told the tiny kit. "Just like a warrior. Try standing on your paw now."

Sage got up and gingerly put her injured paw to the ground. "It feels fine. Thanks," she added as she scampered off to join her littermate and the other kits. "I'm a warrior," she boasted. "Echosong said so."

Echosong looked after the kit, her eyes glimmering with amusement.

"Well done," Firestar murmured in her ear.

The young cat turned to him. "A snagged claw is easy." But

Firestar could see that her eyes were glowing with new confidence.

As Patchfoot's shoulder improved even more, Sandstorm agreed he could return to limited battle training.

"He's trying hard, but he's still slow," she reported to Firestar. "And he gets tired easily."

"He's not ready to face the rats?" Firestar asked.

"Not yet," Sandstorm replied.

Firestar began to wonder whether they should attack without Patchfoot. He could stay behind with Echosong and one of the nursing queens to defend the camp. Tension among the other cats was building. Sharpclaw and Rainfur, normally the best of friends, almost came to blows over a piece of fresh-kill, while Shortwhisker looked perpetually on edge, glancing over his shoulder as if he expected to see a rat sneaking up on him. Even the kits were affected, boldly playing at rat attacks during the day, but scurrying back to the nursery at any unexpected noise.

But where are they? Firestar wondered. Although he tried to act normally around the cats, fear stalked him day and night. *They threatened to kill us. Why haven't they come?*

He knew the answer already, the same answer he had given Sparrowpaw on the day they traveled to the Twolegplace and found Echosong. The rats hoped to weaken the Clan by keeping them in suspense. They would attack when they were ready.

* * *

Firestar returned from the last hunting patrol of the day to find Echosong waiting for him beside the river where it flowed out from the rocks. The gorge lay in shadow, the last scarlet rays of sunset fading from the sky.

Depositing his fresh-kill on the pile, Firestar padded over to her.

"Firestar, I must talk to you," she mewed. Her eyes were huge and troubled. She looked away to gaze at the smooth curve of water where it left the cave. "When we met in the Twolegplace," she began, "I told you that I dreamed of starry cats."

"Yes, that's how I knew SkyClan's warrior ancestors had sent you to be SkyClan's medicine cat," Firestar reminded her.

Echosong heaved a deep sigh. "But what if you were wrong?" Before Firestar had a chance to reply, she went on, her words forced out as if it hurt to say them aloud. "I haven't dreamed of those cats since I came here. Not once."

Firestar swallowed hard. "You dreamed of them before," he assured her, trying not to let his alarm show in his voice. "You will dream of them again. They know where to find you."

"Then why have my dreams stopped?"

Firestar shook his head. "I don't know. Maybe it would help if you went up to the Skyrock to sleep," he suggested. "That's always been the place where SkyClan were closest to their warrior ancestors."

Echosong's eyes brightened, and her claws flexed in the ground. "I'll sleep there tonight!" she exclaimed.

Firestar pressed his muzzle encouragingly against her shoulder. "I'll come with you."

Night had fallen when the two cats leaped the rift to land on the Skyrock. Silverpelt glittered frostily above, and the moon had waned to the thinnest claw scratch. Firestar fluffed his fur out against the probing wind. "Where's the cat on watch?"

The whole flat expanse of the rock was empty, gleaming faintly in the starlight. Firestar's paws tingled, and he drew in a long breath, tasting the air.

"Can you scent rats?" Echosong asked, her eyes wary.

"No. All I can scent is cat." Firestar padded across to the tumbled boulders near the cliff face, and peered into the deepest shadows. When his eyes adjusted to the dark, he made out a curled-up tabby shape. Shortwhisker.

Firestar felt a growl rising in his throat. He prodded Shortwhisker with one paw. "Wake up."

Shortwhisker stirred, his ears twitching. "Uh . . . wha . . . ?"

Firestar prodded him again, harder. This time Shortwhisker sprang to his paws, his fur bristling. "Are the rats here?"

"No," Firestar replied. "But no thanks to you. What do you think you're doing, sleeping when you should be on watch?"

Shortwhisker gazed around wildly; it was obvious he had no idea where he was or what he was doing there. Then shocked realization flooded into his eyes, and he hung his head.

"I'm sorry, Firestar."

"'Sorry' catches no prey," Firestar snapped. "What if the rats had attacked? We could all have been killed."

"I know. I'm really sorry." Shortwhisker scrabbled on the rock with his forepaws. "I'm just so tired."

"We're all tired," Firestar replied, though his anger was ebbing. Was he expecting too much of the SkyClan warriors, to prepare for the rat attack with every scrap of strength they had? "All right," he went on with a sigh. "I have to be up here now, so you can go and catch up on your sleep in the warriors' den. Who has the next watch?"

"Rainfur."

"Okay, I'll wake him when it's time."

Shortwhisker dipped his head and began pacing across the rock toward the cleft. Then he stopped and glanced back, his eyes filled with shame. "I really am sorry," he repeated. "It won't happen again."

Firestar just nodded, and watched him walk off in silence, his head down and his tail dragging on the rock. He leaped the cleft and disappeared down the trail.

When he had gone, Echosong padded up to join Firestar; she looked thoughtful. "Are there herbs for strength?" she asked. "Or to help cats keep awake?"

"Strength . . . juniper berries, I think," Firestar replied. "Sandstorm might know. But I never heard of herbs to keep cats awake."

"A real medicine cat would know." There was a trace of bitterness in Echosong's voice.

Firestar couldn't help remembering the last time she had

stood on the Skyrock in the light of the full moon, brimming with confidence as she was given her Clan name. Her confidence had waned with the moon, until it was no more than the tiny curved claw that shone above their heads.

"Try to sleep," he suggested. "See if StarClan will speak to you here."

Obediently the silver-gray tabby curled up in the shelter of one of the boulders. Soon her light, regular breathing told Firestar she was asleep. He sat beside her, watching the stars, while his ears were pricked and he kept tasting the air for the first signs of approaching rats.

The moon crept across the sky. There were no sounds except for the distant ripple of the river and the soft hissing of the wind. At last Echosong stirred, blinking and looking up at Firestar. He didn't need to ask what her dreams had been; the desolation in her eyes told him enough.

"I think the starry cats have left me forever," she mewed.

Firestar reached down to give the top of her head a comforting lick. "Did you dream at all?"

"Yes, I thought I was standing on a stretch of moorland. There was mist all around me. I couldn't see anything, but I could sense cats nearby, and I knew they were terribly frightened. And I knew one cat was calling out to me, but I couldn't hear what he wanted to say. He was always out of reach."

Firestar felt his neck fur bristle. "I think you dreamed of the first SkyClan fleeing the forest," he explained. "I've had dreams like that too. The cat who was trying to call to you might have been their leader."

Echosong brightened momentarily, but then the hope faded from her eyes. "It wasn't a proper medicine cat dream, then."

"All dreams can be medicine cat dreams," Firestar told her.

"I'm not sure anymore that I'm meant to be a medicine cat." Echosong shook her head, sighing. "Maybe it's because I was born a kittypet."

"I was born a kittypet too." Echosong looked at him in astonishment, and he went on. "But StarClan still chose me to save my Clan and become its leader. Besides, all cats were wild once, even the ancestors of kittypets."

"Truly?"

"Once there were three Clans of giant cats." Firestar remembered the legends that he had learned when he first became an apprentice in ThunderClan. "LionClan, TigerClan, and LeopardClan. They roamed the forest freely and they were never owned by Twolegs. And a little of their wildness lives on in the heart of every cat."

"Even in kittypets?"

"In every cat," Firestar repeated. "Echosong, don't give up. You dreamed of SkyClan's warrior ancestors before, and you'll dream of them again. Dreams can't be summoned. They're sent, and you'll just have to be patient. SkyClan's ancestors will come to you when they have something to say."

Echosong murmured agreement, but Firestar wasn't sure he had convinced her. Giving her a last reassuring lick, he rose to his paws and went to wake Rainfur for the next watch.

* * *

On the next night, for all his weariness, Firestar found it hard to sleep. After shifting around in his nest for what felt like several moons, he padded out of the warriors' cave to sit on the ledge outside and watch pale dawn light growing over the gorge.

After a little while he smelled Sandstorm's sweet scent and felt her tongue rasping warmly over his ear. "I couldn't sleep either," she murmured.

Firestar turned his head to gaze into her eyes. "If we're going to attack the rats it has to be soon," he mewed. "But is that the right thing to do? Was I right to tell SkyClan that this is their home and they should fight for it?"

Sandstorm's whiskers twitched in surprise. "What else are they going to do? Scatter and live as rogues and kittypets again?"

"There is another alternative." Firestar took a deep breath. "We could take them back to the forest."

"What, after everything we've done to help them make a home here?"

"Why not? The ancestors of the forest Clans drove them out, and we *know* how wrong that was. Maybe now we're supposed to bring them back."

Sandstorm turned her head to smooth a piece of fur sticking up on her shoulder. "I suppose it could work," she meowed. "They would have to split up and join the other four Clans, though. Now that the Twolegplace has been built, there isn't room in the forest for a fifth Clan—that's what caused all the trouble in the first place."

"They won't want to split up now," Firestar warned. "Somehow we would have to find a way of dividing the territory along new boundary lines."

Sandstorm's tail lashed. "There *isn't* a way. You saw that for yourself when Scourge tried to move in with BloodClan. SkyClan's territory was lost when the Twolegs built their Twolegplace. The forest won't support an extra Clan now."

Firestar knew she was right, but guilt filled him up like rain filling an upturned leaf. Was he agreeing just because in his heart he didn't want to give up any of his Clan's territory? Did that make him as bad as the original Clans who had driven SkyClan into exile?

Sandstorm pressed her muzzle against his. "There's no point working yourself up," she mewed. "SkyClan don't *want* to go back to the forest. This is where they feel at home. You know," she added, with a flick of her tail, "you're only saying this because you're afraid of leading them to their deaths. You need to trust their warrior ancestor who told you to come here and rebuild the Clan. He won't let the rats wipe SkyClan out."

"I suppose—" Firestar stopped talking, distracted by movement in the shadowy gorge below. Gazing down, he spotted Echosong climbing to the top of the Rockpile and making her way across to the other side of the river.

"Where is she going?" he wondered out loud.

He set off after her, but by the time he reached the bottom of the gorge, Echosong had disappeared. He tracked her by her scent across the Rockpile as far as the path that led beneath the rocks to the Whispering Cave. Quietly he slipped in after her, along the narrow ledge with the water gliding along just below his paws. Dawn light gleamed on the surface, fading behind him as he went further underground.

He found Echosong sitting by the water's edge in the Whispering Cave, her paws tucked under her and her gaze fixed on the river as it silently slid by, green-black in the eerie half-light. At the sound of his approach she looked up. The pale light of the moss glimmered on her pelt and was reflected in her beautiful eyes.

"Echosong . . . ," Firestar began.

"Tinykit just told me about hearing the voices," she explained. Her eyes sparkled. "And it's true, Firestar! I can hear them, too quiet to make out what they're speaking, but they are all around me, welcoming me. Our warrior ancestors are here, just out of reach. When they are ready, they will come to me."

CHAPTER 31

"Rats! Rats!"

Firestar struggled awake as the terrified yowl split the silence of the night. Darkness filled the warriors' den, and for a few heartbeats he couldn't work out where the entrance was. Guided by the movement of air against his whiskers, he headed outside, only to blunder over another warrior.

"Fox dung!" the other cat spat; Firestar identified Sharpclaw's scent. "Get out of the way."

He scrambled past Firestar and out of the cave. Firestar followed; in the entrance he brushed against another cat's pelt, and Sandstorm's scent wreathed around him. The yowling was drawing closer, and now Firestar could recognize Cherrypaw's voice.

It was the night after he had discovered Echosong in the Whispering Cave. Rain had fallen all night, and clouds still covered the sky, blotting out the stars and the thin sliver of moon. Firestar's paws slipped on the wet rock, and he saw himself plummeting into the gorge below. For a heartbeat his paws froze to the ledge; then as his eyes grew accustomed to the darkness he could just make out the trail leading upward, and a cat pelting toward him.

"It's the rats!" Cherrypaw gasped. "So many rats! They came over the cliff top. . . ."

Firestar looked up. Where the trail met the edge of the gorge, a dark mass was flowing down toward him like water. He couldn't make out individual creatures, but a strong reek rolled ahead of them, and he knew Cherrypaw was right. The rats were attacking at last.

His belly clenched, but his voice was surprisingly steady when he spoke. "Sandstorm, go and make sure that the queens in the nursery know what's happening. Then warn Echosong and Patchfoot. Stay down there and help them."

"I'm on my way." He felt Sandstorm's tail tip brush his ear; then she was gone.

"Cherrypaw." Firestar rested his tail on the panting tortoiseshell's shoulder. "Sparrowpaw will be in your cave. Go and warn him. Then fight where you can do most good."

"Right." The apprentice squeezed past him and vanished down the trail.

"Sharpclaw, are you still there?"

A snarl came out of the darkness just ahead. "I'm over here. What are we waiting for?"

By now the other warriors were emerging from the cave. Firestar picked up Rainfur's scent and Leafdapple's, and a strong reek of fear from Shortwhisker.

"Let's go," he meowed. "Stay in the open if you can. Don't let them trap you in any caves—your advantage lies in being able to run and jump away from them."

He raced up the trail toward the oncoming mass of rats. Sharpclaw bounded beside him, and the others were hard on his paws. Firestar just had time to think, *This is what they were waiting for—a night with no moon!* Then the rats were on him.

Tiny claws gripped his pelt and sank into his shoulders as the sleek brown bodies surged around him. Their hot stink filled his throat, choking his breath. He felt teeth stab into the side of his neck and swatted at the rat with one forepaw. It vanished with a thin shriek. Two more instantly took its place, and Firestar struggled to stay on his paws. If he fell, more rats would be on him and he would have no chance.

Firestar heard a drawn-out caterwaul from the bottom of the gorge, but he couldn't tell which cat it was. *Please, not the nursery!* He could make out the glittering eyes of his enemies now, and their sharp white teeth. Peering among them, he looked for the rat leader, but he couldn't spot him. Either he was hidden by the darkness, or he had stayed behind.

Firestar caught a glimpse of Sharpclaw tossing rats off the boulders to fall into the gorge with shrill wails of fear. Nearby Leafdapple was rolling on the ground with two rats clinging to her pelt. Firestar tried to push his way through the bodies to help her, but just then she bit down hard on the throat of one, and it went limp. The other rat let out a screech of fear and leaped away.

Firestar staggered as another rat jumped onto his back; he scraped himself along a boulder in an effort to throw it off, but it still clung there. Its teeth sank into his shoulder and he felt blood begin to flow. He twisted, vainly trying to grab it with teeth or claws. One hind paw slipped; there was nothing underneath it, and Firestar tottered on the edge of the trail, unbalanced by the weight of the rat on his shoulders.

Then the rat let out a scream, abruptly cut off. Its teeth lost their grip and its weight vanished. Cat claws fastened in Firestar's shoulder fur and hauled him away from the terrifying drop.

"You okay?" Rainfur's voice meowed in his ear.

"Fine, thanks," Firestar panted.

And still the rats came, more and more of them, pouring over the cliff and down the rocks. No matter how many the SkyClan warriors killed, there were still more. Firestar realized that they were being pushed back, past the opening of the warriors' cave, down toward the nursery.

Then another outbreak of screeching and caterwauling broke out far below. Firestar stiffened with his teeth in a rat's throat, and stood peering down for a couple of heartbeats. He couldn't see anything, but terror flowed through his limbs. There must be rats down by the river! A second group must have come along the gorge to attack the SkyClan camp from below.

Tossing his dead enemy aside, Firestar struggled through the writhing swarm of rats. Fear for the apprentices, for Echosong, for the kits, almost overwhelmed him. His claws slashed out and the rats in his path whimpered and fled.

Suddenly the fighting stopped. The rats turned as one, scrambling up the rocks toward the cliff top. Sharpclaw sprang after them with a screech of triumph.

"No!" Firestar yowled. "Wait!"

Sharpclaw turned and looked down at him in furious disbelief. "They're running away! We should go after them."

"No," Firestar repeated. "It could be a trap."

"But we could finish them off once and for all!"

Firestar scrambled up to block Sharpclaw, while the skittering of rats' paws on the rocks faded away. "They could be waiting on the cliff top to ambush us," he insisted. "*Think,* Sharpclaw! Why should they go on fighting to the death? All they need to do is frighten us off. Maybe they think they've already done that."

"Never!" Sharpclaw let out a snarl, but he stayed where he was, glaring into the darkness where the last of the rats had vanished. The noise of fighting in the gorge had died away, too.

Firestar glanced around. As well as Sharpclaw, he could make out the pale blur of Leafdapple's pelt, and the darker bulk of Rainfur. There was no sign of Shortwhisker, and Firestar's belly clenched at the thought of the tabby tom's body broken in the gorge, or lying somewhere among the rocks, bleeding out his life.

"Let's go down," he meowed. "We'll check the nursery first, then Echosong's cave."

The other cats bunched together behind him as he limped down the trail. When he rounded a curve in the rock a furious hiss came out of the darkness. Clovertail was crouched in the narrow entrance between the boulder and the cliff face. Firestar scarcely recognized the cat who had joined the Clan for protection and easy shelter. Her eyes were narrowed with rage and her teeth bared in a snarl.

A heartbeat later she relaxed. "Oh, it's you, Firestar. I thought you were more of those rats."

"The kits?" Firestar asked anxiously.

"The kits are fine." It was Petal who replied, appearing out of the darkness inside the nursery. Rainfur pushed forward to meet her and the two cats touched noses. "Clovertail blocked the entrance and wouldn't let any of them in," Petal added.

Firestar rested his tail on Clovertail's shoulder. "Well done."

The she-cat rose painfully to her paws, revealing the marks of rat bites on her chest and shoulders.

"You should go see Echosong," Petalnose told her. "I can look after the kits."

Clovertail muttered something in agreement; she was obviously exhausted, and staggered as she joined Firestar and the others on their way down the trail. Firestar let her lean on his shoulder until they reached the medicine cat's den.

To his relief, Sandstorm was with Echosong in the outer cave; Echosong was already pulling out her store of herbs. "We'll need a lot of burdock root," she mewed. "It's a good thing Petal and I found a good supply the other day."

"And cobwebs," Sandstorm added. Her gaze traveled over the cats who had just arrived, and locked for a heartbeat with Firestar's eyes before she asked, "Which of you is hurt worst?"

Firestar pushed Clovertail forward. "Where's Patchfoot?"

"He went out to fight," Sandstorm replied. "We realized

there were rats coming up the river only when a couple of them tried to get in here. Patchfoot and I attacked them, but there were swarms of them outside. We got separated in the darkness and I haven't seen him since."

Firestar tried not to let the alarm show in his eyes. Patchfoot would have been in more danger than the other warriors because he didn't have his full strength yet. And what about the two apprentices?

Bracing himself against his bone-numbing weariness, he headed out of the cave to look for them. But when he reached the entrance, he spotted movement among the rocks, and a moment later all three cats appeared, Patchfoot and Sparrowpaw supporting Cherrypaw between them. Blood was flowing from a wound in her neck.

"What happened?" Firestar asked.

"The rats trapped us in our den," Sparrowpaw explained. "We didn't have room to use our fighting moves properly. I think we'd have been in real trouble if Patchfoot hadn't come to help."

"We killed lots of them, though," Cherrypaw rasped, raising her head.

Her Clanmates helped her into Echosong's cave, where she flopped to the ground and closed her eyes. Sandstorm hurried over and started to lick the wound clean. After a moment, glancing up at Firestar, she meowed, "I don't think it's too bad. She'll live."

"Course I'll live," Cherrypaw muttered without opening her eyes. "I'm going to kill more rats."

"That leaves only Shortwhisker unaccounted for," Firestar mewed. "Did any cat see him?"

"Not after the battle started," Sharpclaw replied.

"I'll go and look, if you like," Leafdapple offered. "Though it might be better to wait until dawn. It can't be far off."

"I think you're right," Firestar began, reluctant to let any cat go wandering about in the darkness. They couldn't be sure that the danger from the rats was over. "We'll both go when—"

He was interrupted by a plaintive cry from outside. "Hi! Is any cat there?"

"Shortwhisker!" Sandstorm exclaimed.

Full of relief, Firestar went to the cave entrance again. The first pale trace of dawn had begun to appear in the sky. By its light, he could see Shortwhisker hauling himself up from the river, looking as if he was almost too exhausted to put one paw in front of the other.

"Over here!" Firestar called.

Shortwhisker raised his head and quickened his pace a little. Firestar studied him as he drew closer. He had clumps of fur torn off both shoulders, and the marks of rats' claws stretched along one flank, but apart from that he seemed okay.

"It's good to see you." Firestar touched noses with him as he reached the cave. "That's every cat. And none of us is seriously hurt, thank StarClan."

"I thought I was crow-food for sure." Shortwhisker's eyes were wide with fear. "Three of them drove me into a tiny cave. All I could do was try to keep them off. Then suddenly they turned and vanished."

Firestar nodded. Trapping the cats in confined spaces where they couldn't defend themselves had obviously been part of the rats' strategy. Even if the rats' leader hadn't joined in the attack himself, his clever, controlling mind was behind it.

Gesturing with his tail for Shortwhisker to enter the cave ahead of him, Firestar gazed around at the Clan. Echosong had finished with Clovertail and was examining Patchfoot's old wound, while Sandstorm tended to Cherrypaw. The rest of the cats were lying close together, licking one another's scratches. All of them looked exhausted.

Sparrowpaw raised his head. "We didn't win, did we? The rats *chose* to stop fighting."

"That's true," Firestar replied. "But we didn't lose either. And the battle's not over yet. We're not waiting for them any longer. We must take the fight to them."

Sharpclaw pricked his ears. "Is that wise?"

Firestar realized that the fight had taught Sharpclaw caution. "We don't want the rats to have the advantage of planning the next attack. There won't be so many places to trap cats outside the barn. The time is right."

A murmur of agreement came from the rest of the Clan.

"I'm coming with you," Patchfoot announced. "I fought tonight. No cat can say I'm not fit enough."

"And me." Clovertail lashed her tail. "Petal can look after the kits."

Firestar felt humbled by their courage: Patchfoot, whose

wound would have given him the excuse to stay behind in safety; Clovertail, who was ready to fight not only for her kits but for her Clan; Shortwhisker, who was terrified but determined to overcome his fear. All of them had given up their old lives to make the dream of SkyClan a reality—and they had succeeded. The warrior code lived on in the gorge.

Sharpclaw rose to his paws. "Then we'll go tomorrow night, once the Twolegs are back in their nests," he meowed. "And let's hope there's a moon. I like an enemy I can see."

The Clan yowled in approval of his words. *Sharpclaw would make a good leader*, Firestar thought. He met the ginger tom's gaze; there was a challenge there, almost as if the same thought was going through Sharpclaw's mind too.

But something held Firestar back from offering him the leadership. He still felt it wasn't his choice to make. And while Sharpclaw would be superb at leading his warriors into battle, Firestar wasn't sure he appreciated everything that being Clan leader meant.

It's in the paws of his warrior ancestors, he told himself. *And after tomorrow, who knows whether there will be a Clan left to lead?*

The Clan rested during the morning, but they were awake by sunhigh, gathering in the training area for a last session to hone their battle skills. Firestar felt fresh energy running through his limbs as he practiced fighting moves with Rainfur: this was what he had been trained to do, even if this time he wasn't fighting for his own Clan. Looking at the determined faces around him, watching the expert use of teeth and claws, he knew that SkyClan wouldn't be driven from the gorge a second time. The descendants of the first Clan had returned, and they would fight to their last breath for the right to live here.

Sandstorm was drawing the training session to an end when Echosong and Petal came padding up the gorge, their eyes gleaming with satisfaction.

"We've collected a whole pile of burdock root," Petal announced proudly.

"And poppyseed," Echosong added. "Sandstorm, you said it's good for pain, but I didn't know where to find it before."

"My old Twoleg has poppies in his garden," Petal explained.

"I hope you didn't have any trouble with the Twoleg," Firestar meowed.

Petal flicked her tail dismissively. "He came out of the nest and yowled a bit, but he couldn't catch us."

Firestar couldn't bring himself to warn her about taking risks. There would be wounded warriors after the battle who would be glad of the relief poppyseeds would give them.

Echosong's eyes were brimming with amusement. "Clovertail sent her kits to look for cobwebs," she reported. "You've never seen so many—all over the kits! They worked really hard."

"It's time they were apprenticed," mewed Sandstorm.

"Soon," Firestar agreed. His heart was warmed by the thought of a future for the Clan. SkyClan had so much to lose—but so much to win as well!

Petal padded over to Rainfur and murmured something into his ear. The gray rogue nodded; then both cats approached Firestar.

"We talked things over this morning," Rainfur began, looking unusually hesitant. "We've decided that we want to become members of SkyClan—if you will have us, that is."

"That's great news!" Firestar exclaimed.

Rainfur met his gaze, his eyes wide and serious. "We've seen for ourselves how the warrior code works."

"Yes," Petal agreed. "And there's no other life we want for ourselves and our kits."

Sharpclaw stepped forward to stand beside Firestar. "You're welcome to join us," he meowed, and the rest of the Clan murmured agreement. "You know how much we need strong warriors. We receive you humbly and we give you our thanks."

As the sun went down, Firestar called Rainfur and Petal to the foot of the Rockpile for their warrior ceremony. The rest of the Clan stood in a circle, their eyes bright and their fur already fluffed up in anticipation of the battle.

"I, Firestar, leader of ThunderClan and mentor to SkyClan, call upon their warrior ancestors to look down upon these cats," he began. "They have dedicated themselves to your warrior code, and I commend them to you as warriors in their turn." Padding up to Rainfur, he went on. "Rainfur, do you promise to uphold the warrior code and to protect and defend this Clan, even at the cost of your life?"

Rainfur held his head high; there was no doubt in his voice as he meowed, "I do."

"Then by the powers of StarClan I confirm your warrior name. Rainfur, StarClan trusts you will serve your new Clan with honor and courage."

He rested his muzzle on Rainfur's head, and the gray warrior licked his shoulder.

"Petal," Firestar went on, turning to the pale gray she-cat, "do you promise to uphold the warrior code and to protect and defend this Clan, even at the cost of your life?"

"I do." Petal sounded just as certain as her mate.

"Then by the powers of StarClan I give you your warrior name. Petal, from this moment you will be known as Petalnose. StarClan honors your endurance and your strength, and SkyClan welcomes you."

As he completed the ceremony, the cats of SkyClan called out the names of the new warriors, yowling them like a challenge to the darkening sky. Firestar glowed with pride for all the SkyClan cats; thanks to them, the Clan had gained two strong warriors and two healthy kits. He could see a great future in the Clan for Petalnose and Rainfur.

The yowling died away as the sun sank behind the cliffs and night covered the gorge. The waxing moon gave a fitful light as it appeared from behind the clouds that scudded across the sky. There was a stiff breeze with a hint of frost.

Firestar sent his warriors up to the top of the cliff while he paid a final visit to the nursery. Echosong and Petalnose had returned there with the five kits, who crouched in their nests among the moss and bracken, gazing at Firestar with a mixture of fear and excitement.

"You'll be as safe here as anywhere," Firestar told them. "The entrance is narrow."

Petalnose nodded. "We'll be fine. Don't worry about us, Firestar. And we'll look after the kits, or die trying."

"If the worst happens," Firestar promised, "every warrior who survives will come back here and help you defend them."

"The worst won't happen." Echosong's voice was clear and certain as she padded up to Firestar. "Go now—I'll see you when you come back."

Firestar thought of the brutal battle that lay ahead. Though he still had six lives, they could all be torn from him at once if his wounds were severe enough. He remembered how Tigerstar had died, ripped open by Scourge, and he shivered.

Though he said nothing, he knew that Echosong had guessed where his thoughts were leading. "I *will* see you again," she mewed, and her words had the conviction of a prophecy.

CHAPTER 32

Firestar hauled himself over the edge of the cliff and into the undergrowth. For a heartbeat, until his eyes grew used to the thick darkness under the bushes, he couldn't see any cat, though SkyClan scent was all around him.

Cherrypaw hissed into his ear. "This way."

Following her, he came to the edge of the undergrowth and found the SkyClan warriors crouching under the outermost branches of the thicket, gazing across the scrubland toward the Twoleg barn. He remembered his fears back in the forest, before the battle with BloodClan. He had struggled then with the thought of leading his Clan into a battle from which some of them might not return. His deputy, Whitestorm, had told him that he didn't envy him his position. Bluestar had assured him in a dream that he had the strength he needed. In the end he had understood that making such decisions was part of the burden of being a leader.

Now he looked at the SkyClan warriors, at the eagerness in their eyes as they gazed toward their enemies' nest, and he shrank from the order that he had to give. This battle had been started—and lost—long ago. Firestar was not their leader. What right had he to ask them to fight now? There were so few of them, and they had been given so little time to learn the skills of a warrior.

He was aware of Leafdapple rising to her paws and padding along the line of bushes until she stood in front of him. "You fear for us," she meowed.

Firestar nodded; words stuck in his throat like a tough piece of fresh-kill.

"We fear for ourselves," Leafdapple went on quietly. "But this is our battle, not yours. We owe it to the SkyClan cats who walked here before to try once more to defeat these rats. You do not have to come. Should ThunderClan risk losing their leader for another Clan's sake?"

Firestar gazed at her with a mixture of admiration and disbelief. Where had her courage come from, and her commitment to the warrior code? But what impressed him most was that she realized his first loyalty lay not with this Clan, but with the Clanmates he had left behind in the forest.

He dipped his head to her. "I have brought you this far," he murmured. "I will see you to the end of your journey." Touching noses with Leafdapple, he sprang to his paws. "It's time."

Firestar flattened himself to the ground behind a straggling gorse bush a few tail-lengths from the fence that surrounded the Twoleg barn. Everything was quiet. The barn looked deserted, the moon's pale light reflecting from its shiny surface, the holes in its sides gaping like jaws. The only sign that it was inhabited was the sharp stink of rat and crow-food.

"I wish I knew where the rats had their nest," Firestar muttered.

"Inside, I'd guess," Sharpclaw slid up to him and mewed into his ear. "They're always well hidden during the day. Our patrols have never spotted them."

Firestar dug his claws into the ground. "I'd hoped we wouldn't have to fight inside there."

"It's not like a cave," Sparrowpaw pointed out. "It's *huge*. There's plenty of room to get away."

Firestar knew he was right, but the thought of trying to fight with walls around him and a roof blocking out the sky made him feel trapped and helpless. The former kittypets might see it differently, he supposed. They were used to being inside. But his own kittypet days were so far behind him, it was hard to imagine feeling like that.

"I'll lead half the patrol inside," Sharpclaw offered. "The rest of you can stay out here, and with any luck we'll be able to lure the rats outside and fight in the open."

Firestar nodded. "Good idea. I'll come in with you." He knew he couldn't allow the ginger tom to go somewhere he dared not go himself.

"We want to come too," Cherrypaw whispered.

"Okay. And Shortwhisker," Firestar added. "The rest of you stay outside. Sandstorm, you're in charge."

His mate gave him a brief nod. Keeping low, his belly fur brushing the grass, Firestar led the way up to the fence and crept along it until he found the gap they had used to enter on their previous visit. He slid through with the rest of the patrol close behind.

Firestar's pelt crawled as he surveyed the barn from close up. It loomed over his head, a shiny, unnatural Twoleg thing, with death at its heart. Were the rats aware that their enemies were only pawsteps away? He couldn't feel the malevolent force that had been his first inkling of the rats' presence, but he found it hard to believe that no eyes, glittering and malignant, were watching them now.

"What are we waiting for?" Sharpclaw hissed.

Firestar glanced back to check that Sandstorm and her patrol—Leafdapple, Patchfoot, Clovertail, and Rainfur—were all inside the fence. He gathered his own patrol with a wave of his tail, and crept up to the nearest gap in the barn wall. Leaping through it, he padded forward a pace or two to allow the others to follow, and looked around.

The stench of rat and crow-food was much stronger here. His claws scraped on the hard floor, made of the same white stone that surrounded the barn on the outside, and the sound echoed eerily in the vast space. Firestar remembered Barley and Ravenpaw's barn, made cozy with piles of hay and filled with the rustling and squeaking of mice. The bare, cold emptiness of this barn sent shudders through his fur.

On either side the barn lay in shadow, but moonlight filtering through ragged holes in the roof showed him a huge pile of Twoleg rubbish against the wall at the far end of the barn.

"The rats' nest is probably in there," Firestar whispered to Sharpclaw.

Sharpclaw nodded. "Let's hope the stink of it will hide our scent."

Firestar beckoned the rest of the patrol with his tail. Cherrypaw and Sparrowpaw were glancing around with more curiosity than fear. Shortwhisker looked terrified, his fur fluffed out until he was twice his size, but he padded up determinedly at Firestar's summons.

"We're going to head for the nest," Firestar told them. "When the rats appear, race for the gaps and get outside. With any luck, the rats will follow you."

The patrol spread out into a ragged line across the barn and started to pad up to the pile of rubbish. Firestar felt horribly exposed, his heart pounding so rapidly he could hardly get his breath. Nothing moved among the rotting mounds of Twoleg stuff.

They were less than a fox-length from the pile when Firestar heard a scratching noise behind him, followed by a gasp of terror from Shortwhisker. For a heartbeat he froze, then whipped around to confront rows and rows of rats. More rats than he had ever seen before had crept out of the shadows, covering the floor between the patrol and the gap where they had entered.

Firestar's gaze darted over them, trying to pick out the leader, but all the sleek, dark brown bodies looked the same to him. Then a voice spoke, but the sound echoed around the bare walls of the barn so that he couldn't tell which rat was talking.

"We killed you before. We will kill you again. You are few. We are more."

Sharpclaw let out a snarl of rage and leaped at the first row of rats.

"Stop!" Firestar yowled.

The ginger tom halted, glaring at him. "What now?"

"We must stick together," Firestar explained, drawing the rest of the patrol into a huddle around him with a gesture of his tail. "If they separate us, we're finished. We have to get outside, where we won't be trapped."

He had hardly finished speaking when the first wave of rats crashed over them. Facing outward, lashing out with claws and teeth, the patrol began to force a way through them, back toward the gap where they had entered. There was a second gap, but it was on the far side of the barn, and even more rats blocked their way to it. Firestar reminded himself that he had six lives to lose, while the cats around him had only one; he would have to fight harder to match their courage.

Rats swarmed around them, climbing on top of one another in their eagerness to sink in claws and teeth. But there were too many of them; they hadn't the space to fight effectively. Firestar took a bite on one foreleg and a few nasty scratches around his head, but with the patrol tightly clustered together the rats couldn't attack from behind, couldn't attack at all without coming within reach of the warriors' furious defense.

The gap was only a couple of tail-lengths away; Firestar began to hope that they would make it out into the open.

Then he heard a fearsome screech from outside. Rainfur leaped through the gap, with the rest of the patrol streaming behind him, and fell on the rats from behind.

Firestar let out a yowl of frustration. "No! Get back!"

The outside patrol obviously thought they had to come to the rescue; instead, they were putting every cat in worse danger. Screeching knots of cats and rats writhed on the floor in front of the gap, making it harder to get out. The outside patrol was already separated, each one fighting alone against a swarm of rats.

Before Firestar could yowl an order, his own patrol sprang apart, leaping to help their Clanmates. The whole barn exploded in blood and rage. The warriors' furious screeches mingled with the dying screams of the rats, yet where one fell, two more took its place. Firestar spotted Clovertail batting rats away with both forepaws; Sharpclaw and Cherrypaw fought side by side, forcing their way through wave after wave of attacking rats.

"Out! Every cat get out!" Firestar screeched.

Sandstorm leaped across a cluster of snarling rats and landed at his side. "Sorry!" She gasped. "I couldn't stop them from coming in." She bared her teeth at a rat as it scuttled toward her; it flinched and spun around, right into Firestar's outstretched paws. Fierce satisfaction surged through Firestar as he clawed its life out; whatever the end might be, it was good to fight side by side with Sandstorm again.

Gradually the SkyClan cats won their way back to the gap. Leafdapple shoved Sparrowpaw out and followed him.

Patchfoot slipped out after her, then Shortwhisker. Clovertail shook off one rat with its fangs in her shoulder, struck another across the side of the head with one paw, and sprang out into the open. For the first time, Firestar let himself hope that they would all get out.

He spotted Sharpclaw and Cherrypaw side by side a couple of fox-lengths away, in the midst of a ring of dead or dying rats. "Out!" he yowled, waving his tail at the gap.

Sharpclaw snapped something at Cherrypaw; she opened her jaws to argue, and while she was distracted a rat leaped onto her back. She staggered, her claws skidding on the blood-soaked floor, then collapsed on one side. Sharpclaw leaped for her, tearing the rat off her back and shaking it fiercely before tossing it aside. Hauling his stunned apprentice to her paws, he clawed a way through the horde of rats, driving them back like leaves in the wind. With relief, Firestar saw mentor and apprentice disappear through the gap.

For a heartbeat he thought that only he and Sandstorm were left in the barn. Then he spotted Rainfur still two or three fox-lengths from the gap, in a circle of rats that was gradually closing on him. Rainfur glanced back to see where the gap was, and at that moment a huge rat leaped at him and fastened its fangs in his throat. The SkyClan warrior vanished under a heap of squirming bodies.

"Get out!" Firestar ordered Sandstorm. "I'll help Rainfur."

"I'm not leaving without you," Sandstorm replied.

There was no time to argue. Firestar sprang forward, leaping over one rat and knocking a second out of his path, to fling himself on the creatures that were attacking Rainfur. The gray warrior was barely visible under the mass of rats. They split apart at the sound of Firestar's furious yowl, and Rainfur scrambled to his feet, only to be pulled down again.

Firestar landed among them, clawing and spitting. He bit down on the neck of one rat, and it slumped to the floor. Another fell back, writhing and squealing, its blood spurting as he raked his claws across its eyes and muzzle. He had almost reached Rainfur when more rats surged around him, and a weight landed on his back, carrying him off his paws.

His head struck the hard floor of the barn, stunning him. For a few heartbeats he scrabbled with his paws, trying to get up. Then sharp claws fastened themselves in his throat, and his whole body spasmed with the pain.

Evil rat eyes stared into his, glittering with malice. A voice rasped, "Die, cat!"

Firestar struggled to sink his claws into the body that was pinning him down. This must be the leader of the rats! Kill him, and the battle would be over.

But there was no strength in Firestar's limbs, and the moonlight seemed to be fading, leaving him in a cave of echoing darkness. For a couple of heartbeats longer he was aware of those eyes, twin points of hatred. Then night closed down over him, and he knew nothing more.

CHAPTER 33

Firestar opened his eyes to see a pale light glimmering all around him. At first he thought he was still in the barn. But he couldn't understand the silence, and the lack of any scent of rat.

After a moment's struggle he managed to sit up, and realized that he was in the Whispering Cave, the mosses glowing eerily around him and the underground river sliding past on its way to the opening.

How did I get here? he wondered.

Then he saw that he was not alone. The ancient SkyClan leader was sitting at the other side of the cave. "Greetings," he meowed.

Firestar began to understand. "Have I lost another life?" he rasped.

The SkyClan leader bowed his head. Now Firestar could make out the outline of a flame-colored cat just behind him in the shadows. His pelt and his green eyes glowed; Firestar recognized himself as the shape dipped his head slightly.

Firestar staggered to his paws. "Let me go back," he begged the SkyClan cat. "I've got to help Rainfur. I've got to save

SkyClan—isn't that what you want?"

The SkyClan ancestor rose and padded across the cave to Firestar. His scent was a mingling of frost and wind and the night sky. Breathing it, Firestar felt energy begin to flow back into his aching, exhausted limbs.

"Go now," the SkyClan cat murmured. "And may my strength go with you."

The pale light of the mosses faded, and for a heartbeat Firestar hung in a dark void. Then he felt a paw shaking his shoulder and heard Sandstorm's voice. "Firestar! Firestar!"

He blinked awake to see his mate crouched over him, anguish in her green eyes. "Firestar!" she repeated. "Get up—the rats are coming."

Firestar raised his head to find himself lying on the ground outside the barn. His chest was matted with blood that had flowed from the wound in his throat.

Rats were already swarming through the gap in the barn wall. Sandstorm shoved Firestar to his feet, and with Leafdapple supporting him on the other side, he managed to stagger as far as a stunted tree, several tail-lengths from the fence. The rest of the cats had already scrambled into its branches, all except Cherrypaw and Sparrowpaw, who waited at the bottom.

"Climb!" Cherrypaw urged as Firestar and the other she-cats limped up. "Don't wait for us. We can leap up after."

"No . . ." Firestar tried to hold back. "We'll be trapped. We have to get out through the fence."

Sparrowpaw waved his tail. "Have you seen it?"

Firestar's heart sank. All along the line of the fence, clustering most thickly around the gap the cats had used to get in, were hordes of rats. Their eyes seemed to glitter with triumph. They had the cats trapped now, with all the time in the world to finish them off. The only possible safety, for a short while, was this tree.

Firestar clawed his way up the trunk and found a space to crouch on a broad branch. Looking around, he spotted Shortwhisker, Sharpclaw, Clovertail. . . .

"Rainfur?" He gasped. "Where's Rainfur?"

"I'm sorry." Sandstorm clung to the branch beside him. "Rainfur didn't make it."

Firestar's gaze flew to the barn and he tensed his muscles, half prepared to spring down and battle his way back inside to help the warrior.

"It's no use, Firestar." Sandstorm rested her tail tip gently on his shoulder. "Rainfur is dead." Pain throbbed through her voice as she added, "I could save only one of you, Firestar, and I had to choose you."

Firestar remembered how he and Rainfur had rescued Petalnose, and how Rainfur had saved him from falling into the gorge when the rats attacked the camp the night before. He remembered the great future he had foreseen for the gray warrior. Now he was dead, and the remnants of SkyClan were huddled in this tree while rats swarmed over the ground below, just waiting to finish them off. Firestar had failed: failed the Clan, and Skywatcher, and the SkyClan ancestor who had sent him here. The fifth forest Clan would be destroyed all over again. Sighing, Firestar rested his head against Sandstorm's flank, too weary to move.

"We can't give up!" It was Leafdapple, speaking from a branch just above Firestar's head. "Are we going to let Rainfur die for nothing?" When no cat answered her, she went on. "The rats have no more right to live here than we do. Aren't we going to fight for what's ours?"

Firestar looked up to see the tabby she-cat standing commandingly on her branch. Her eyes glowed with courage. Around her the other cats were stirring, seeming to catch something of the fire that blazed within her.

"I'll fight with you," Sharpclaw snarled. "They'll kill us anyway, but I'll take a few of them with me."

A chorus of voices rose up around Firestar, vowing to fight on, whatever happened. Even Shortwhisker agreed, though his fur was bristling and his eyes were blank with terror.

"We're a Clan now," Clovertail declared, "and this is where we belong. We've *got* to fight for that."

Firestar hauled himself to his feet, digging his claws into the branch. His head was clearing now, and the strength of his next life flowed into his limbs—the strength of the SkyClan ancestor who had brought him here believing that he would not fail.

"I honor your courage," he meowed. "And I'll fight with you. You can have all my lives and all my strength if it will help you beat these rats."

He was aware of Sandstorm's ears pricking in surprise, but he meant every word. This was the right thing to do by the warrior code. For tonight, he was not the leader of ThunderClan, but a member of SkyClan.

"But what are we going to do?" Patchfoot asked in a small voice.

Firestar looked down. The tree was surrounded by sinuous rat bodies, their sharp eyes fixed on the warriors who had taken refuge in the branches. Cherrypaw and Sparrowpaw still stood at its foot, ready to spring up to join their Clanmates if the rats attacked.

But the rats seemed to be in no hurry. Firestar could tell they thought the battle was over, and they could wipe out the remaining cats as slowly as they wished.

"The rats are acting together," he thought out loud. "Like a swarm of bees or a pack of dogs. Last night they stopped attacking us and all turned tail at once. Something is controlling them. They must be taking orders from the leading rat."

"So kill him," Sharpclaw hissed, flexing his claws, "and the rest of them will flee."

"I hope so," Firestar replied grimly.

"That's all very well," Patchfoot meowed. "But how do we tell which one is the leader? They all look the same to me."

Firestar thought back to the last heartbeats of his previous life, when he had faced the rat leader inside the barn. His neck fur bristled at the memory of the malignant eyes and the hoarse voice telling him to die.

"Only the leader can speak the tongue of cats," he meowed. "If we can make him talk to us, we'll know which one he is."

"And then . . ." Sharpclaw slashed one paw, claws extended, through the air.

Firestar glanced around. The SkyClan warriors were ready for action now, their eyes eager, their wounds and weariness forgotten. Even Shortwhisker seemed to have pulled back from the brink of his panic.

"We'll have to climb down," he began. "The rats will sit there forever if we stay up this tree."

Taking the lead, he scrambled down to the cold, hard ground, landing beside the two apprentices. The rest of the Clan followed him in silence and stood gazing out across the mass of rats. Firestar noticed that the SkyClan descendants—Cherrypaw and Sparrowpaw, Shortwhisker and Sharpclaw—moved into position on the outside of the little group, as if they meant to protect their Clanmates who couldn't escape up the tree so easily.

As they descended, a ripple passed through the crowd of rats, and they edged a little nearer. Firestar raised his head and faced them.

"You're brave enough when you're all together," he taunted them. "But I bet you wouldn't be so brave on your own. I don't suppose even your clever leader would come out and face me."

Not a rat moved.

"Cowards!" Sharpclaw sneered. "Crow-food-eating, skulking vermin!"

"Come and fight!" Firestar hurled the challenge against a wall of silence. Panic began to prickle in his fur. The leading rat was obviously clever enough not to show himself.

The cats pressed their backs to the tree as the rats crept a little nearer. Another few heartbeats, Firestar thought, and they would surge forward. The SkyClan cats would fight on for a little while, but sooner or later they would be overwhelmed. Once more SkyClan would become nothing more than a memory. *What can I do?* he asked himself, anguished.

Then a familiar scent drifted around him, and his paws tingled. *Spottedleaf?* He glanced from side to side, but there was no sign of the tortoiseshell she-cat. Only a soft voice that murmured in his ear: *Not many, but one*.

Then the sense of her presence faded. *Wait!* Firestar protested in his head. *I don't understand!* How could Spottedleaf say that there were not many rats here?

He stared out at his enemies, the moonlight washing over them so that their bodies merged together like ripples on a lake. And as he watched the tide ebb and flow, he began to realize what Spottedleaf had meant. He had thought of the rats as a swarm of bees or a dog pack, taking their orders from their leader, but Spottedleaf had shown him it was more than that. These creatures were like a single enemy; the individual rats had no minds of their own. They took their orders from one rat alone, passed from body to body in visible signals, a twitch of fur or flick of tail, the brush of one flank against another. If he watched the ripples, they should lead him to the rat he was looking for.

The rats edged a little closer. Firestar was aware of Sandstorm beside him, her pelt brushing his, her claws digging into the tree root where she stood poised to spring. Hardly daring to breathe, he stared out at the rats, knowing that they could strike at any moment. He forced himself to stop looking at one pair of eyes here, a snakelike tail there, and studied them like the surface of a single lake.

Icy claws pricked his spine. Sure enough, he could make out tiny stirrings of movement circling a central point, the place from where the leader's silent commands rippled outward. And at that central point, a single rat gazed toward the besieged cats.

Firestar narrowed his eyes. There was no time to explain what he was doing to the rest of the patrol. He had just one chance, one chance to ensure that he had not traveled here in vain, and SkyClan would live on. Unsheathing his claws, he leaped, legs outstretched, into the middle of the mass of rats.

Horrified wails rose from the cats behind him. He heard Sandstorm screech, "Firestar!"

Her voice was drowned out by the single shriek that rose from the throats of every rat, and they rushed upon him like a thick brown wave. But Firestar's claws struck their target, tearing at the throat of the rat at the center of the tide. He gazed into the small, hate-filled eyes, and saw their hatred change to terror before the light faded from them. The rat's head dropped back and its body went limp.

For a heartbeat Firestar stood still, his paws sticky with blood. Rats milled around him, squeaking and hissing in confusion. With their leader dead, they did not know what to do next.

"Follow me! Attack!" The yowl came from Sharpclaw, and suddenly Firestar's Clanmates were all around him, claws lashing at their enemies. Gibbering in terror, the rats fled back toward the barn, scrabbling at the shiny walls in their efforts to get in and hide. The SkyClan cats raced past Firestar, dealing a death blow to any rat too slow to get out of their way.

"Stay away from us!" Sharpclaw screeched after them. "The gorge is ours. We'll kill any rats who set paw there!"

Leafdapple halted at the gap, stopping the rest of the SkyClan cats from following the rats inside. "Let them go," she meowed. "They're not dangerous anymore. Not now."

She padded back to Firestar, who still stood over the body of his dead enemy, and bowed her head in deepest gratitude. "The battle is won. Thanks to you, SkyClan is safe."

When the rats had fled, Firestar ventured into the barn with Sharpclaw and Leafdapple. Two or three rats were still visible, sniffing at the bodies of their dead companions, but when they spotted the cats they let out squeals of alarm and scurried into the shelter of the Twoleg rubbish at the far end of the barn.

Rainfur's body lay stretched out on the floor. Dead rats lay all around him, and his claws were still fastened in the throat of one of them. His gray fur was torn with wounds.

"He died like a warrior," Leafdapple murmured.

"We'll carry him back to the gorge and sit vigil for him," Firestar meowed.

In silence they took up his body and maneuvered it through the gap in the barn wall. The rest of the Clan clustered around them to help bear Rainfur through the fence and back across the scrubland to the gorge, under the light of the chill moon. His body drooped, his paws and tail dragging in the dust, and his fur was matted with blood.

As Sharpclaw and Leafdapple carried their dead Clanmate down the stony trail, Echosong appeared at the entrance to the nursery. "You're back!" she exclaimed. She broke off at the sight of Rainfur's broken body, and sorrow welled in her eyes. "I'll tell Petalnose," she whispered.

She slipped around the boulder, and a moment later Firestar heard a wail of anguish.

"Go on," he murmured to Sharpclaw and Leafdapple. "Lay his body beside the Rockpile. I'll join you in a few moments."

Taking a deep breath, he padded into the nursery. Petalnose was crouched over her kits, her eyes wide and staring at nothing. Echosong pressed comfortingly against her side, but Firestar didn't think the gray she-cat was aware of her.

"I'm sorry," he meowed. "He died like a warrior."

Petalnose shivered and focused her eyes on him. "He died protecting what he loved most," she whispered. "Me, and his kits, and his new Clan."

Firestar tried to find words that would comfort her. "He hunts with his ancestors now."

Petalnose's eyes were bleak, and she did not respond. Firestar dared not say any more. This young Clan had no experience of their ancestors yet, so how could Petalnose have faith that Rainfur had found anything after his death?

"He was a brave cat," he mewed instead. "I'm honored to have known him."

As the night went on, the Clan gathered around the body of Rainfur to keep vigil for him. Echosong guided Petalnose and her two kits down from the nursery, and the she-cat crouched beside her mate, pushing her nose into his cold gray fur. Sagekit and Mintkit huddled on each side of her, while Echosong sat at Rainfur's head, her gaze fixed on the distant stars.

Remembering the fidgety, superstitious vigil for Skywatcher, Firestar realized how far the Clan had moved on. Now there was a genuine sense of loss and respect for the fallen warrior. But his heart ached when he reminded himself that rebuilding the Clan had led directly to Rainfur's death. If he had decided to remain a rogue, he would still be alive.

Restlessness pricked at Firestar's paws, and as the sky turned gray with the first light of dawn, he climbed up the trail to the Skyrock and sat alone, looking down into the gorge. *Have I done the right thing?* Since being here he had learned so much about himself and what it meant to be a Clan leader, but that wasn't why he had come. Was it fair to ask these cats to give up their lives for the warrior code, when they had lived happily and peacefully before?

A sweet scent drifted around him, the only scent that could comfort him now. A pelt brushed against his, and a voice murmured in his ear.

"Don't grieve," Sandstorm whispered. "You have saved SkyClan."

"But Rainfur's dead."

"I know. But the SkyClan cats made their own decision to fight for the gorge, and the warrior code—and their *Clan*. The battle has brought them together as nothing else could have."

Firestar shifted uneasily, wanting to believe what his mate said, wanting to believe that what had been won was worth Rainfur's death.

"Life can't go on without death," Sandstorm went on. "Rainfur died like the greatest warrior, fighting for his Clan. Wherever his warrior ancestors are, they will have been watching, and will be waiting for him now."

"I know." Sandstorm's words eased some of the pain in his heart, but Firestar knew that many moons would pass before he could forget the sight of Rainfur's body surrounded by his dead enemies, knowing that he had led the gray cat there to die.

CHAPTER 34

The sun was edging above the cliffs when Firestar and Sandstorm padded down into the gorge again. Rainfur's body still lay at the foot of the Rockpile, but the Clan were relaxing from their vigil; only Petalnose remained close to him, her two kits sleeping beside her. Echosong sat at the entrance to her cave, piles of herbs around her as she examined Patchfoot's fresh wounds.

Firestar knew he should get his own wounds treated, but before he could head for the medicine cat's den, Leafdapple bounded over to him. Firestar saw that her eyes were troubled, and a pang of alarm shot through him. Surely there couldn't be more danger?

"What's the matter?" he asked.

"It's Shortwhisker." Leafdapple glanced back to where the tabby tom was standing beside Sharpclaw, Cherrypaw, and Sparrowpaw. "He says he wants to leave the Clan. He wants to go back to his housefolk."

"What?" Firestar brushed past her and headed for the little knot of cats.

"Are you completely mouse-brained?" Sharpclaw was

arguing as he came up. "You stuck with us through all the danger from the rats, and now that we've shown them this is our home, you want to leave? You've got bees in your brain!"

Shortwhisker flinched and turned to Firestar with a look of relief. "I'm sorry," he began. "But the rat attack just showed me that I'm not cut out for life in a Clan."

"You did your duty like a warrior," Firestar meowed.

"But I was *scared,*" Shortwhisker protested. "Scared to the roots of my pelt."

"And you think the rest of us weren't?" Sharpclaw growled.

Leafdapple padded up and touched Sharpclaw's shoulder with her tail tip. "Don't be angry," she mewed. "We can't force him to understand." Turning to Shortwhisker, she added, "We'll respect your decision. But all the same, we wish you would stay."

"We'll miss you," Cherrypaw told him.

Shortwhisker still faced Firestar, and addressed his words to him. "I was scared," he repeated. "And I knew that I didn't want to give up my life for the sake of my Clan." He hung his head. "I'm a coward, and selfish," he murmured. "But I can't change the way I feel."

"You're not selfish or a coward," Firestar told him. "The warrior code isn't right for every cat." He remembered his friend Ravenpaw, forced to leave ThunderClan for fear of Tigerstar, and now living happily with Barley on the Twoleg farm near Highstones. "You must choose the path that suits you best."

"Then that's the path of a kittypet." Shortwhisker glanced

around the circle of his friends, and though his eyes were regretful, his voice was certain.

"We're still your friends, Shortwhisker—" Sparrowpaw began.

"That's not my name anymore," Shortwhisker interrupted him. "I guess you'd better call me Hutch again."

For the last time he climbed the trail to the top of the cliff; Firestar, Leafdapple, and Sharpclaw followed him. Hutch pushed his way through the belt of undergrowth and paused at the edge of the scrubland.

"Good-bye," he meowed. "I'm proud to have been a SkyClan cat; I really am."

"Good-bye." Cherrypaw nudged him with her shoulder. "Make sure you keep that Oscar in his place."

"And tell the other kittypets about SkyClan," Sparrowpaw added.

Leafdapple dipped her head. "Farewell, Hutch. Don't forget to come and visit us. You helped save SkyClan, and you'll always be welcome here."

Hutch brightened a little. "I won't forget any of you—especially you, Firestar," he added, glancing at the flame-colored tom. "You've taught me so much."

"I've learned from you, too," Firestar replied, meaning it. "May StarClan light your path."

The two toms touched noses; then Hutch turned and began to make his way toward the distant walls of the Twolegplace. His head and tail were held high, and he didn't look back.

"So that's the end," Sharpclaw murmured, looking after him. "The last echo of our battle against the rats."

"No," Leafdapple meowed. "There's one more thing to do."

Firestar and Sharpclaw exchanged a mystified glance, and followed her down the trail to the warriors' cave. Leafdapple stood facing the stone trunk with its ancient claw marks: the marks of many cats and the tiny claw marks of the rats scored across them as a sign of their long-ago victory.

"This," Leafdapple meowed. Extending her claws, she raked them down the stone, then again and a third time, until the rat scratches were obliterated under deep vertical scars. The record of the first defeat was gone.

"Now the gorge belongs to SkyClan again," the tabby she-cat announced.

The days that followed the battle were gray with clouds. Stiff breezes blew with a tang of rain, and one morning Firestar emerged from the warriors' den to find the rocks rimed with frost. He stood sniffing the cold air until Sandstorm appeared, fluffing up her pelt against the claws of the wind.

"We should leave soon," she murmured, with a glance behind to make sure she wasn't rousing the sleeping warriors. "We can't travel in leaf-bare. It'll be too cold to sleep out, and there'll be precious little prey."

"There's a while yet before leaf-bare," Firestar argued.

Sandstorm fixed him with a glinting green gaze. "Don't you trust SkyClan to survive without you?"

"It's not that," Firestar protested.

"The rats aren't a threat anymore," Sandstorm reminded him.

"I know, but the rats aren't the only problem. Will the SkyClan warriors be able to get along with one another without us to help them with patrols and duties? What about the kittypets in the Twolegplace . . . there could be trouble with them. And it'll be harder for them to find prey as the weather gets colder."

Sandstorm scraped her claws along the rock. "Firestar, will you listen to yourself? *Every* Clan has problems like those. Every cat has to work together to follow the warrior code, and if they do that they'll be safe and well fed. The SkyClan cats know that now. You've done your part; you've found them a medicine cat—now it's up to them."

Firestar knew that she was right. If he waited until he could be sure of unbroken peace and an easy life for SkyClan, he would never leave. Yet he knew too that he still had one more task to do.

"We can't leave yet," he meowed. "Not until we can be sure that SkyClan can reach their warrior ancestors. And part of that is finding out which cat StarClan has chosen to be leader."

Sandstorm blew out a long sigh, riffling her whiskers. "I suppose you're right. But I hope it's soon; that's all."

Sandstorm roused Leafdapple; the two cats collected Sparrowpaw and left for the dawn patrol. Firestar padded back into the warriors' den and found Patchfoot stirring. "Hunting patrol?" he suggested.

Patchfoot sat up eagerly. "Sure. I'll be right with you."

"I'll join you." Sharpclaw raised his head from his mossy nest across the cave. "If that's okay."

"I'd rather you led a separate patrol," Firestar told him. "I want to take Cherrypaw and watch her hunting action, without her mentor breathing down her neck. It's time she and Sparrowpaw were made warriors."

"Fine." Sharpclaw's eyes gleamed with approval. "I reckon they're ready, too. I'll take Clovertail and Rain . . ." His voice trailed off. "Just Clovertail, I guess."

Firestar led his patrol downriver, across the spur of rock and into the trees. Leaves whirled in the air; only the last brittle remnants remained on the branches. The cold weather was here, and prey would be much scarcer through the long leaf-bare moons. Yet SkyClan was still small; if they were careful they should be able to feed themselves.

He watched Cherrypaw stalk a squirrel across a stretch of open ground and bring it down with a mighty leap as it tried to escape up a tree. She was easily ready to become a warrior, but Firestar held back from telling her that. He wanted the new leader of SkyClan to give her and Sparrowpaw their warrior names—as soon as there was a sign from SkyClan's warrior ancestors about which cat that would be.

The three cats hunted until they had all the fresh-kill they could carry. There was no sense now of hostile eyes among the undergrowth, no scent or sound to suggest that the rats were still here. SkyClan had made this place their own.

Firestar had returned to camp and was depositing his fresh-kill on the pile when Echosong padded up to him.

"Firestar, I need to talk to you." Her green eyes were puzzled. "Will you come to my den for a moment?"

As she spoke, Firestar was irresistibly reminded of Spottedleaf and Cinderpelt. Echosong fit exactly into the role of a medicine cat now, though he knew her formal acceptance was another ceremony that rested in the paws of SkyClan's warrior ancestors.

She didn't speak again until they were sitting in the outer cave, with the scents of sweet herbs all around them. "I was sorting herbs in here," she began, "and I had a . . . I think you would call it a vision." Looking almost embarrassed, she licked one small gray paw and drew it over her ear.

Firestar's paws tingled, but he made himself remain calm. "What was it?"

"I thought I was gathering herbs in the wood above the gorge. I was alone, and yet I felt so safe and protected! It was as if kind eyes were all around me, watching over me. . . ."

"Go on," Firestar encouraged.

"The sun was shining, as if it was a warm day in green-leaf. And the shadows of leaves were dappling the ground all around me, so perfectly, like pebbles on the riverbed. I noticed them especially, because the leaves are dying now. The pattern of light and shade swirled around me, even though the leaves above my head were still. And then I was back here. It *wasn't* a dream, Firestar," she insisted. "I was awake all the time. Do you think it means anything, or am I making a fuss about nothing?"

"StarClan send their signs for a reason," Firestar replied. "All we have to do is work out what that is." He sat silent for a moment, his eyes narrowed to slits, picturing the small tabby cat in the sunlit forest. "Warm sun. It's leaf-bare now, but there were leaves dappling the ground . . ." he murmured.

"Leafdapple!" Echosong burst out. "My warrior ancestors were telling me something about Leafdapple."

Every hair in Firestar's pelt rose. This must be the sign SkyClan had been waiting for! Echosong's vision showed that the Clan's warrior ancestors really were watching over them. Even more important, they had sent the sign to Echosong and not to him. She was a true medicine cat now, with a connection to the starry spirits that would help her guide her Clan in the moons to come.

The puzzled look gradually cleared from Echosong's eyes. "What this Clan needs more than anything is a leader," she murmured. "Do you think they were showing me which cat it should be?"

Firestar padded over to her and gave the top of her head an affectionate lick. He was purring so hard that he could hardly speak. "Yes, I think they were," he murmured. "Leafdapple will be the leader of SkyClan."

Leafdapple paused with a bite of fresh-kill still between her jaws, her eyes wide with shock. "Me?" She swallowed rapidly. "Leader of SkyClan? Echosong, I think you've got bees in your brain!"

As soon as the dawn patrol had returned to rest and eat, Firestar had taken Sandstorm aside to tell her about the sign. Then he and Echosong had found Leafdapple eating by the fresh-kill pile to give the news to her.

"It's got nothing to do with Echosong," he assured the astonished she-cat. "Your warrior ancestors have chosen you."

"But—but I thought it would be Sharpclaw!"

So did I, Firestar thought. Yet it was Leafdapple who had shown the greater sensitivity to everything that the warrior code meant. She had rallied the Clan in the battle with the rats, and she had understood why Hutch wanted to leave the Clan to be a kittypet again.

Leafdapple took a step back, shaking her head emphatically. "Oh, no, Firestar. I can't do this. Really, I can't."

"I never felt good enough to be Clan leader, either," Firestar confessed. "I was Clan deputy, so of course I'd thought about being leader one day, but when Bluestar died and I had to take her place, I didn't feel that I was ready. But my Clan needed me. And now SkyClan needs you."

Leafdapple seemed to weigh what he was telling her. Then she turned to Echosong. "What do you think?"

Echosong nodded encouragingly. "Our warrior ancestors sent me a vision. I know this is right for you, Leafdapple."

"But I don't understand about our warrior ancestors," Leafdapple protested. "I don't even know that they exist.

And even if they do"—she forestalled Echosong's protest—"why would they choose me? I'm nothing special."

"I don't think you know how special you are," Firestar told her. "Believe me, Leafdapple, you *can* do this."

Leafdapple's amber gaze rested on him for several heartbeats. Then she bowed her head. "What do I have to do?" she asked. "Do I have to call myself Leafstar now? And do I have nine lives?"

"You're not a leader yet," Firestar warned her. "StarClan will give you your nine lives and your name."

"When? How?" Leafdapple looked around as if she expected to see starry warriors stalking up to her in the full light of day.

"Tonight," Firestar meowed. "Your warrior ancestors are watching over you, and we'll meet with them tonight."

Under the frosty light of a half-moon, Firestar led the way up the trail to the Skyrock. Leafdapple padded behind him, and Echosong brought up the rear.

Firestar wasn't sure that he was doing the right thing. He had no doubts about Leafdapple as the destined leader of SkyClan—Echosong's vision seemed too clear for that—but he wondered if he should have taken Leafdapple to the Whispering Cave for her ceremony. That was the nearest the SkyClan cats had to the Moonstone, where the leaders of the forest Clans received their nine lives and their name. Yet tonight the stars seemed particularly bright, and as he looked up they seemed to shift for a moment into the shape of the

SkyClan leader's face, as if he were saying, "Come."

Firestar leaped the cleft and paced into the middle of the Skyrock. Starlight glinted on its surface and the wind buffeted his fur. Leafdapple bent her head into it as she padded across to join him.

"What happens now?" she asked.

"We wait," Firestar replied. "Your warrior ancestors will come to us."

He hoped he was right. He knew of only the SkyClan ancestor who walked these skies, along with Skywatcher. But Leafdapple needed nine cats who would each give her a life. He remembered the pain and terror and wonder of his own leadership ceremony, when the clearing at Fourtrees had been lined with starry spirits. Even if they came to her, would Leafdapple have enough strength to cope? There was only one way to find out.

"Are you sure they'll come? Shouldn't we tell them we're here?" Echosong's voice was eager, her silver tabby fur fluffed up with excitement.

"They'll know," Firestar replied. "Lie down by me," he directed Leafdapple, settling himself on the rock with his paws tucked under his chest.

Hesitantly Leafdapple obeyed him; Firestar could feel a suppressed quivering running all through her body. Echosong crouched on her other side, pressing reassuringly against her fur.

"Don't be afraid," the medicine cat whispered. "I know that our warrior ancestors mean you nothing but good."

Leafdapple still looked unsettled.

"You must trust your warrior ancestors," Firestar told her.

Leafdapple turned her head and gazed at him with eyes that glowed silver in the moonlight. "No," she meowed. "I trust *you*."

CHAPTER 35

The three cats waited silently in the wash of moonlight. Wind swept over the surface of the Skyrock, pressing their fur close to their pelts. "Close your eyes," Firestar whispered.

At first there was only darkness, and he was conscious of Leafdapple shifting restlessly by his side. Gradually she grew still; Firestar's heartbeat quickened as he felt cold creeping over her, until she might have been a cat made of ice. The sound of the wind died away.

Firestar opened his eyes. The Skyrock had vanished; instead, bleak moorland stretched around him, fading into the mist on all sides. No stars could penetrate the cloud, but it shimmered with a pale glow, as if somewhere overhead the moon still shone.

On the other side of Leafdapple, Echosong blinked and raised her head, then rose and arched her back in a stretch. Her gaze, full of wonder, met Firestar's. "Where are we? It's like the place I dreamed of the night I slept on the Skyrock."

"This is the moor where I saw the fleeing SkyClan cats." Firestar stood up, working his claws into the tough grass.

Echosong turned to look down at Leafdapple, laying one

paw gently on her shoulder. The she-cat didn't move.

"She feels so cold," Echosong whispered. Bending down, she breathed softly into Leafdapple's ear; it didn't even twitch. "Firestar, she's not *dead,* is she?"

"No," Firestar reassured her. "Something like this happened to me. I think her old life is being stripped away so that she can receive her nine new ones."

Echosong still looked worried. Firestar guessed that her paws were itching to help Leafdapple, but there was nothing she could do.

It might have been seasons or only heartbeats before Leafdapple sneezed and opened her eyes. Her jaws stretched wide in a huge yawn. Then she seemed to become aware of her strange surroundings; she sprang to her paws, staggering a little.

"Firestar, what's happening?"

"It's okay." Firestar rested his tail tip on her shoulder. "This is where you will meet with StarClan."

As if his words were a signal, the mists swirled in front of him, and the gray-and-white SkyClan ancestor stepped into view. Droplets of water glittered like stars on his fur. "Greetings," he meowed. "I know why you have come."

"Greetings," Echosong replied, her eyes brilliant as she stood face-to-face with a StarClan warrior for the first time.

Firestar padded forward to meet him. "I'm glad to see you again," he meowed. "I've brought Leafdapple. She is the cat you wanted, isn't she?"

"Yes." The former SkyClan leader dipped his head.

"Thank you, Firestar. You have done all you can to rebuild and protect SkyClan once more. Now it's up to the new SkyClan cats."

Firestar took a deep breath. "But how can Leafdapple receive nine lives if you're the only cat here?"

The gray-and-white cat raised his tail commandingly, and Firestar fell silent. He watched the SkyClan ancestor step lightly over the moorland grass to face Leafdapple.

"Do you believe in what is about to happen?" he asked her.

Leafdapple's panic-stricken gaze flew to Firestar and back to the StarClan cat. "I . . . I think so," she stammered. "At least, Firestar says you're going to give me nine lives, and I believe him."

A flicker of sadness passed across the pale warrior's face. "That will have to be enough," he mewed. "Come, and I will give you your first life."

Leafdapple took a step forward so that she stood right in front of the SkyClan ancestor. He bowed his head and touched his nose to hers. Leafdapple stiffened and flinched away, then deliberately moved back so that the SkyClan cat could touch her again.

"I give you a life for endurance," he meowed. "Use it well to strengthen your Clan in times of trouble."

As the SkyClan ancestor finished speaking, Firestar saw all Leafdapple's limbs spasm, and her jaws gaped in a soundless wail of agony. His belly clenched in sympathy; he remembered the terrible pain he had felt when he received his own lives.

"Does it hurt?" Echosong whispered, her eyes wide with shock. "Can't we help her?"

Firestar shook his head. "This is for Leafdapple to bear alone."

Leafdapple trembled as the pain ebbed away, but she stayed on her paws. "Firestar"—she gasped—"do I have to do that eight more times?"

"It's okay," Firestar comforted her. "Not all the lives will feel the same."

The she-cat had a dazed look in her eyes, and a touch of resentment in her voice as she mewed, "You never said it would be like this." She shook her head in mingled astonishment and wonder. Firestar guessed that no cat could go through what she had just endured and still doubt that the experience was real. "I wish we could just get it over with."

"It won't be long," Firestar promised.

"Look!" Echosong exclaimed, whirling around. "Leafdapple, can you see?"

"I-I think so," the tabby she-cat mewed.

A row of cats was appearing faintly through the mist. They encircled the three living cats and the SkyClan ancestor, their outlines indistinct in the drifting clouds. Then one of them strode forward: Skywatcher. Not the scrawny elder who had died in the gorge, but as Firestar had last seen him in his dream, a strong and powerful warrior.

Leafdapple's eyes stretched wide. "Skywatcher," she whispered. "Is that you?"

Skywatcher touched noses with her. "Welcome, Leafdapple.

I give you a life for hope," he meowed. "Use it well to guide your Clan through the darkest days."

Once more Leafdapple tensed as the life surged through her. Firestar could see that the pain was not so great this time, or perhaps she knew what to expect and had braced herself against it. She recovered more quickly, dipping her head to Skywatcher. "Thank you," she murmured. "Thank you for all you have done for my Clan."

Skywatcher stepped back noiselessly to stand with the ranks of misty warriors.

Leafdapple gazed with expectation at the circle of cats whose shapes were gradually becoming more distinct. "I'm ready," she mewed.

The third cat to appear was a tabby she-cat so like Leafdapple that Firestar could hardly tell them apart. She bounded forward and touched noses with Leafdapple: a gesture of pure affection, not the giving of a life.

"My mother!" Leafdapple exclaimed. "But you died . . . I thought I'd never see you again."

"Nothing is lost forever, dear one," her mother replied. Once again she touched noses with her daughter. "With this life I give you love. Use it well for all the cats who look to you for protection."

Leafdapple had stretched forward eagerly to receive this life, and Firestar could see she was unprepared for the piercing agony that came with it. Her limbs went rigid and she dug her claws into the ground, clenching her teeth on a screech of pain. He had experienced the same anguish when Brindleface had given him a life; he had not realized how fierce was a mother's love for her kits, how willing a she-cat was to die to protect her children.

As Leafdapple's pain ebbed, her mother covered her face and ears with loving licks.

"Don't go," Leafdapple whispered.

"Don't be afraid, dear one," her mother reassured her. "I will walk with you many times in dreams, I promise."

As she stepped back, a fourth cat was already walking forward. Firestar caught his breath at a familiar scent, but one he had never expected to smell here. The shape of the cat's head reminded him of the SkyClan ancestor. Then as she emerged fully from the mist he recognized the slender tortoiseshell.

"Spottedleaf!"

She bounded forward and touched noses with him. "Thank you, Firestar," she mewed. "I'm so proud of you! SkyClan owes everything to you. I never told you how much it means to me to see the Clan restored."

Firestar breathed in her sweet scent. "I couldn't have done it without you, Spottedleaf."

The medicine cat dipped her head to him. "I have been given the privilege to walk these skies to give Leafdapple her fourth life." Approaching the tabby she-cat, she went on. "I give you a life for healing wounds caused by words and rivalry. Use it well for all cats troubled in spirit."

This time Firestar could see that there was no pain as the life flowed into Leafdapple. The she-cat let out a blissful purr, her eyes narrowed; for a few heartbeats she looked like a kit in the nursery, safe inside the curve of her mother's paws and belly.

"Thank you, Spottedleaf," she mewed when it was over. "Firestar has told me so much about you. I'm honored to meet you at last."

The medicine cat brushed her tail softly along Leafdapple's pelt, then withdrew once more to the edge of the circle.

Firestar could see that the mist was growing thinner. More of the moorland was opening up, and the moonlight grew stronger, though the moon itself remained hidden. More and more cats were revealed, stretching into the distance. A shiver ran through Firestar, as if his paws splashed into icy water.

As if she felt it too, Echosong pressed against him for a moment. "They're coming home," she whispered. "All the ancestors of SkyClan. I can hear them."

Before Firestar could reply, the cats in the front rank parted to allow four new cats into the center of the circle. He gazed at them, puzzled. They looked vaguely familiar, yet they didn't remind him of SkyClan. They looked nothing like any of the other cats who had given lives. They walked with head and tail high, with all the authority of leaders, yet he had never seen them before, and didn't understand why they should come now to give a life to Leafdapple.

Instead of approaching the she-cat, the newcomers padded over to the SkyClan ancestor, who was staring at them with wide eyes. As the first cat, a muscular bracken-colored tom, drew closer, he gasped. "Redstar!"

To Firestar's astonishment, the bracken-colored cat stood in front of the SkyClan ancestor with his head bowed. "I was wrong all those moons ago," he meowed. "All of Thunder-Clan joins with me to tell you we're sorry for what we did."

Firestar stared: this cat must have been the ThunderClan leader when SkyClan was driven out of the forest.

The next cat, a brown tabby she-cat, crouched beside Redstar. She reminded Firestar of the RiverClan warrior Heavystep, and she had the look of Clovertail too.

"Birchstar?" The SkyClan ancestor's voice was guarded.

"RiverClan says the same. We should never have driven you out. I felt compassion for you, but I did nothing—and that makes my actions worse. I am sorry."

The third cat, an older tom with a gray-black pelt and a long, twitching tail, remained on his paws, but he bowed his head as he meowed, "I am Swiftstar of WindClan, and when I walked the forest I never told any cat I was sorry. But I say it to you now: what we did was wrong."

The fourth cat's creamy brown fur glimmered in the moon-light as she slipped up beside Swiftstar and fixed brilliant green eyes on the SkyClan leader. "ShadowClan is sorry too," she mewed. "We had good reasons for what we did, but I regret that we caused so much suffering to you and your Clanmates."

"Thank you, Dawnstar," the SkyClan cat replied. "Thank you, all of you."

"Nothing can make up for what we did," Redstar went on. "But we have each come here to give a life to the new leader of SkyClan, if we may."

The gray-and-white cat dipped his head, giving his permission.

Redstar stepped forward to touch noses with Leafdapple. "With this life I give you wisdom. Use it well when you have the hardest decisions of all to make."

Leafdapple quivered as the fifth life flowed into her. Firestar remembered how he had felt as the number of his lives mounted up: as though he were a hollowed-out rock, filling up with rainwater that soon would spill over the edges and be lost.

The next cat to approach Leafdapple was Birchstar, the RiverClan leader. "I give you a life for sympathy and understanding," she murmured. "Use it well for the weakest in your Clan, and for all others who need your help and protection."

Swiftstar hardly gave Leafdapple time to receive that life before he strode up and touched noses with her. "I give you a life for selflessness," the former WindClan leader announced. "Use it well in the service of your Clan."

Last of the four came Dawnstar; Firestar gazed at her, astonished that such a graceful she-cat should be leader of ShadowClan, who always seemed to be at the bottom of trouble in the forest. But then, perhaps the ShadowClan of those days had been different—and perhaps they could change again.

"I give you a life for determination," she meowed, stretching her head forward to touch her nose delicately to Leafdapple's. "Use it well to set your paws on the path of what you know to be right."

Leafdapple's legs shook as she received the eighth life. She was breathing hard and fast, as if she had been running. Firestar could see that the effort had drained her strength until she was almost too exhausted to stand on her paws.

When the life had entered into her she gazed at the four rival Clan leaders. "Thank you," she meowed. "The new SkyClan will hold your Clans in honor. The fifth Clan has returned."

The four leaders bowed their heads in reply. Then to Firestar's amazement they turned away from Leafdapple and padded up to him.

"You righted the wrong we did," Redstar meowed. "For that we thank you."

"We thought we had to drive SkyClan away for the sake of our own Clans," Dawnstar added. "But that was a mistake."

Swiftstar twitched his ears. "We've paid for it. None of us could rest easily after SkyClan was gone. Guilt clawed us for the rest of our lives."

"There should always have been five Clans in the forest," Birchstar mewed.

Firestar struggled to find words to reply. When he had first learned of the pain and loss of the SkyClan ancestor, he had blamed the leaders of the other Clans for what they had done. But perhaps they were just leaders like himself, doing their best to make the right decisions for their Clan. "I will never forget you," he murmured.

Redstar remained in front of Firestar as the other leaders turned away. "Your Clanmates are safe and waiting for you," he meowed. "Your work here is over. You can go home now."

The four Clan leaders stepped back to the edge of the circle to stand close to Skywatcher, Spottedleaf, and Leafdapple's mother. The SkyClan ancestor joined them, and all eight starry cats seemed to grow tense and prick their ears, as if they were waiting. No other cat appeared through the mist.

Firestar's belly clenched. Where was the ninth cat to give Leafdapple her last life?

A breeze had risen, tearing the mists into ragged strands. The cats shone out more clearly, with glimmering eyes and pelts dusted with starshine. Beyond them Firestar caught glimpses of a vast expanse of moorland stretching into darkness. Above his head the moon shone fitfully, and stars glittered here and there before the mist drifted over them again. Every hair on his pelt rose.

Beside him, Echosong murmured, "Oh, come—come quickly!"

Then Firestar saw the cats parting to leave a straight path leading far over the moor. At the end of it he could see a single point of light; at first he thought it was a star low on the horizon. It steadily drew closer, and now Firestar could see that it was a cat, racing along with its belly fur brushing the rough moorland grass. Stars streamed from its fur and sparkled at its paws, and its eyes were a blaze of starlight.

The SkyClan ancestor took a single pace forward, his eyes fixed on the approaching cat with a hunger that spoke of moons of starvation.

The shining cat reached the circle, and Firestar saw her clearly for the first time: a beautiful long-furred brown tabby with green eyes fixed intently on the SkyClan ancestor. She padded up to him and lightly touched her nose to his.

"Birdflight!" whispered the SkyClan leader.

"Cloudstar," she purred, twining her tail with his. "I told you I would find you one day."

"And I told you I would wait," Cloudstar replied. He closed his eyes. "I can't believe you're here!"

"I will always be here," Birdflight murmured. "We will walk the skies together forever."

For a heartbeat that seemed to stretch into seasons the two cats stood close together, drinking in each other's scent. Then Birdflight drew back a pace and beckoned with her tail to two other cats who had approached unseen. They padded into the circle and dipped their heads to Cloudstar.

"These are your children," Birdflight explained. "Though they were too small to make the journey with SkyClan, and grew up in ThunderClan instead, Spottedpelt and Gorseclaw have chosen to walk these skies with me in honor of their SkyClan ancestors."

Firestar stared in astonishment. Spottedpelt was a slender tortoiseshell, as like Spottedleaf as if the two cats had been littermates. Gorseclaw was a broad-shouldered tabby tom with glowing amber eyes; Firestar's belly churned at his likeness to his old enemy, Tigerstar. Birdflight had said that the two cats had grown up in Firestar's own Clan. Did that mean that SkyClan's blood ran in ThunderClan? Were Spottedleaf and Tigerstar both descended from Cloudstar?

He caught Spottedleaf's eye and saw her gazing delightedly at the cats in the center of the circle. It must be true! No wonder he had been reminded of the SkyClan leader when she appeared. No wonder she had felt so involved in the destiny of the new Clan.

Cloudstar took a single pace toward his children, his legs stiff with shock. "When I left the forest," he mewed hoarsely, "I vowed my Clan would never look to the stars again. Some of my warriors still followed the old ways, but as time went on and SkyClan was scattered, StarClan was forgotten, and our warrior ancestors were unable to walk these skies. Until now." His brilliant gaze traveled from Birdflight and his children until it rested on Firestar and Leafdapple. "Until now."

Birdflight paced across the circle to where Leafdapple still waited, her eyes filled with wonder, and touched noses with her. "With this life I give you faithfulness," she mewed. "Use it well to hold fast to Clan and kin."

As the ninth life surged into Leafdapple, one more cat appeared from the starry ranks, a small tabby with a white front and paws. She padded across the circle until she stood face-to-face with Echosong.

"My name is Fawnstep," she announced. "I was SkyClan's medicine cat when they fled from the forest. You have my cave in the gorge, and you find herbs in the same places that I once did. Your warrior ancestors have chosen you to be SkyClan's medicine cat from this moment on."

"Thank you," Echosong whispered. "I—"

Fawnstep silenced her by laying the tip of her tail gently over Echosong's mouth. "Peace, dear friend. From now on I will walk in your dreams and watch over you until you have learned how to be a true medicine cat." Her eyes sparkled. "We shall travel far together, you and I."

Echosong raised her head and looked deep into her fellow medicine cat's eyes. "I'll be ready for our next meeting," she promised.

Leafdapple stood in the middle of the circle, a little unsteady on her legs, and looked around. "What happens now?" she asked Firestar in a hoarse whisper.

Firestar had no need to answer. While the new Clan leader was speaking, the last shreds of mist dissolved, revealing a sky where a full moon floated serenely. Stars blazed out as SkyClan's warrior ancestors returned to watch over their descendants who had been lost for so long.

His pelt prickled with recognition as he spotted a strong gray warrior among them, with stars in his fur and the shimmer of starlight in his eyes. Rainfur's gaze met his and he dipped his head.

His belly churning with grief and guilt, Firestar padded over to him. "I'm sorry, Rainfur," he murmured. "If you hadn't joined SkyClan, you would still be alive."

"It was my decision." Rainfur gazed at him with clear eyes. "Now I'll always be part of a Clan, and have a place among the stars. The warrior code is worth dying for." He hesitated briefly and then added, "How are Petalnose and the kits?"

"They grieve for you," Firestar replied. "But they'll always have the support of their Clan."

"I know. I trust SkyClan to look after them." Rainfur dipped his head again, and Firestar felt as though he had been forgiven.

The ranks of cats rose to their paws and sprang up into the sky, setting each star to shine more brightly. Their voices mounted high and tingling to the glittering swathe of Silverpelt. "Leafstar! Leafstar!"

"Leafstar!" Firestar and Echosong joined in to welcome the new leader of SkyClan. "Leafstar!"

The light around him grew so dazzling that Firestar had to squeeze his eyes shut. The voices died away, and when he opened his eyes he was crouching on the surface of the Skyrock, with Leafstar and Echosong beside him. The half-moon still shone in a frosty sky.

Leafstar rose to her paws, staggered to find her balance, and let out a long breath. "Thank you, Firestar," she meowed. "I never imagined . . ." She blinked rapidly, while Echosong brushed her pelt against her flank and pressed her muzzle into the new leader's shoulder.

"You know you mustn't speak of this to any cat?" Firestar warned her.

Leafstar stared at him. "How could I? There are no words. . . ." Shaking her head, she went on. "I understand now. And I promise that I'll be a strong and loyal leader to my Clan, until it's my turn to walk among the stars with my ancestors."

She paused for a moment, then gave her pelt a shake. "Let's go down. My Clan will be waiting for me."

CHAPTER 36

"Let all cats old enough to catch their own prey join here beneath the Rockpile for a Clan meeting!"

Leafstar's voice rang out over the camp as she summoned her Clanmates for the first time. Her body was outlined against a pale blue sky; the day after her leadership ceremony had dawned clear and cold, but now the sun was taking the chill off the rocks and sparkling on the surface of the river. Leafstar waited patiently as her Clan gathered around the foot of the Rockpile.

Firestar had discussed this meeting with her, making sure that she knew what she had to do, but she hadn't told him all the decisions she would make. Whatever they were, he hoped she would have the support of her Clan.

By now they all knew that Leafstar was their new leader; Firestar could see excitement in their pricked ears and shining eyes. Clovertail's kits were bouncing all over the place, getting under every cat's paws, until Bouncekit slipped on a damp stone; Sharpclaw grabbed him by the scruff just in time to save him from a dunking in the river.

"Now stay with your mother," the ginger tom mewed

sternly. "Is that any way for an apprentice to behave?"

Instantly all three kits lined up at Clovertail's side, sitting up straight while their mother gave them a quick grooming. Petalnose and her two kits came to join them; Sagekit and Mintkit eyed the older litter enviously.

"We want to be apprentices," Mintkit mewed to his mother.

"Yes, why can't we?" Sagekit asked.

"You're not old enough," Rockkit retorted in such lofty tones that Firestar exchanged a glance with Sandstorm, sitting beside him, and saw amusement glimmering in her green eyes. "You'll have to wait for *moons* before that happens."

Cherrypaw and Sparrowpaw emerged from their den and padded down the trail to sit together near the fresh-kill pile. Patchfoot joined them, and last of all Echosong appeared from the Whispering Cave, leaped lightly across the Rockpile behind Leafstar, and came to sit with Firestar.

"Cats of SkyClan," Leafstar began when every cat was settled and gazing expectantly up at her, "my first duty as leader is to appoint a deputy." She took a deep breath. "I speak these words before the spirits of my ancestors, that they may hear and approve my choice. Sharpclaw will be the new deputy of SkyClan."

Firestar saw a look of pride spread over the ginger tom's face, along with a touch of uncertainty that was quite unlike him. The warrior rose to his paws, dipping his head to Leafstar. "Thank you," he meowed. "I shall be honored to serve you and our Clan."

Firestar flashed another glance at Sandstorm, feeling very

relieved. Sharpclaw had pushed hard for the post of leader when he hadn't completely understood the full meaning of the warrior code. He could have made Leafstar's life difficult if he had refused to accept her authority. But his fiery courage and fighting skills would balance well with Leafstar's more thoughtful personality. And one day, when he had lived enough moons by the warrior code, he would make a good leader.

"Echosong." Leafstar beckoned with her tail, and the tabby she-cat rose from her place beside Firestar and padded forward to stand at the foot of the Rockpile. "Our warrior ancestors have chosen you to be our medicine cat. Now I give the care of SkyClan into your keeping. We trust you to use your skills for healing and to interpret the signs that the spirits of our ancestors will send us."

A secret look passed between the two she-cats. Firestar guessed they were remembering their extraordinary experiences of the night before.

Echosong bowed her head. "I promise I'll do my best, Leafstar."

"Echosong! Echosong!" The Clan welcomed her by yowling her name; the young medicine cat ducked her head in embarrassment and went back to sit by Firestar.

"My next task is one of the most important that a leader can perform," Leafstar went on. "The making of new warriors." She beckoned Cherrypaw and Sparrowpaw with her tail; the two young cats rose and came to stand side by side at the bottom of the Rockpile, their eyes shining. "Sharpclaw," Leafstar asked, "has your apprentice Cherrypaw learned the skills of a warrior? And does she understand what the warrior code means to every cat?"

"She has and she does," Sharpclaw replied solemnly. "She fought like a seasoned warrior against the rats."

"And I can say the same for my apprentice, Sparrowpaw," Leafstar meowed. She leaped down from the Rockpile and stood in front of the two young cats. "I, Leafstar, leader of SkyClan, call upon my warrior ancestors to look down on these two apprentices. They have trained hard to understand the ways of your noble code, and I commend them to you as warriors in their turn."

A shiver ran through Firestar as he heard the familiar words. Not until today could a SkyClan cat have spoken them with certainty, for no cat knew what had happened to their warrior ancestors. But now he knew—and more important, Leafstar knew—that they walked the skies where they belonged, and would do so for all the seasons to come.

Leafstar went on. "Cherrypaw, Sparrowpaw, do you promise to uphold the warrior code and to protect and defend this Clan, even at the cost of your lives?"

Cherrypaw's fur bristled and she flexed her claws as she replied, "I do."

Sparrowpaw looked calmer, but no cat could doubt the sincerity in his voice as he also promised, "I do."

"Then by the powers of StarClan I give you your warrior names. Cherrypaw, from this moment you will be known as Cherrytail. StarClan honors your bravery and your enthusiasm, and we welcome you as a full member of SkyClan."

Leafstar rested her muzzle on the top of Cherrytail's head; Cherrytail licked her shoulder and moved away to join the other warriors.

Leafstar turned to Sparrowpaw and repeated the same time-honored words. "Sparrowpaw, from this moment you will be known as Sparrowpelt. StarClan honors your courage and your strength, and we welcome you as a full member of SkyClan."

She rested her muzzle on his head, and he too bent respectfully to lick her shoulder.

"Cherrytail! Sparrowpelt! Cherrytail! Sparrowpelt!" the rest of the Clan called to welcome the two new warriors. Cherrytail gave a massive, jubilant leap into the air.

Next, Leafstar beckoned with her tail to Clovertail's three kits. Trying not to wriggle with excitement, they padded up to their Clan leader. Clovertail watched them, looking ready to burst with pride.

"Patchfoot, you have shown courage and endurance," Leafstar meowed. "You will be mentor to Bouncepaw."

Bouncepaw let out a squeal, broke off almost at once, and pattered over to Patchfoot to touch noses with him. Patchfoot looked down at him, eyes glowing with pride at having been chosen as a mentor.

"Cherrytail, you are a new warrior," Leafstar continued, "but the whole of SkyClan has seen your dedication. You will mentor Rockpaw."

The black apprentice bounced up and went to touch noses with his new mentor; Cherrytail looked thrilled.

Leafstar looked down at the last of the three kits, who was hardly able to keep still. "Sparrowpelt, you are young too," Leafstar mewed at last. "But you have excellent fighting and hunting skills. I trust you will pass them on to Tinypaw."

The white apprentice sprang up and, obviously trying to be more dignified than her brothers, padded up to Sparrowpelt and stretched up to touch noses with him.

"For now," Leafstar told them, "all warriors will work together to train the new apprentices. We are a new Clan, and we must learn to depend on one another. I have one more thing to do," she added. "Before Firestar and Sandstorm came to the gorge, we lived separate lives. We were rogues and kittypets. We knew nothing of the life of a Clan, or of the warrior code. Now we belong together and we support one another. Firestar, Sandstorm, we thank you for all you have done for us. Your names will be honored forever by the cats of SkyClan."

"Firestar! Sandstorm!"

Firestar felt himself swelling with pride. He remembered his worries about leaving his Clan, and the dangers of the journey upriver. Every pang of anxiety, every weary pawstep were worth it now that he saw the strong bodies and shining eyes of the new Clan members.

He felt Sandstorm's muzzle brushing his ear as his mate murmured, "It's time for us to leave. We've rebuilt SkyClan, just as we promised. Our own future is waiting for us in the forest."

Firestar knew she was right, but a pang clawed him at the

thought of leaving these cats who had become his friends. They were unlikely to meet again until they walked with StarClan—and even then, would they share the same skies?

He rose to his paws to meet Leafstar as she padded over to him. "Was that all right, Firestar?" she asked anxiously. "I was afraid I wouldn't remember the proper words."

"It was perfect," Firestar told her. "SkyClan is yours now. You don't need us anymore."

A shadow of sadness crossed Leafstar's face, but she didn't try to persuade him to stay. "Your own Clan needs you," she meowed. "But SkyClan will never forget you."

As the rest of SkyClan realized that Firestar and Sandstorm were about to leave, they gathered around, wishing them good-bye and good luck.

"Remember the first time we met?" Cherrytail meowed. "You told us off for making fun of Skywatcher. I thought I'd never seen such a dangerous cat!" Her eyes gleamed with mischief. "Now I'm dangerous, too!"

Sandstorm gave her an affectionate nudge. "I wouldn't be a rat around here for anything."

"Yes, you'll have to keep an eye open for the rats," Firestar reminded Leafstar. "And the kittypets in Twolegplace—Oscar might take it into his head to cause trouble. And—"

Sandstorm interrupted him by prodding him with one paw. "Leafstar *knows* all that," she meowed. "They'll be fine. Let's go."

Calling out more good-byes, Firestar and Sandstorm began to climb up the stony trails to the cliff top. Echosong walked with them as far as her own den. When she reached it, she touched noses with Firestar, her eyes filled with regret. "Maybe we will meet again in the paths of dreaming," she mewed. "But my heart tells me that this is farewell. Thank you, Firestar. You have helped me find my destiny."

Firestar bowed his head. "SkyClan is lucky to have you as their medicine cat, Echosong."

It was hard to look back and see the small tabby figure standing outside her den, watching them leave. Was Echosong *really* ready to take on the role of a medicine cat? Would Sharpclaw understand how a deputy had to support his Clan leader? Would the inexperienced mentors be able to cope with their apprentices?

Then as they paused at the edge of the cliff, Firestar caught sight of a SkyClan patrol among the undergrowth far below. Leafstar was in the lead, with Patchfoot and his apprentice, Bouncepaw, and Clovertail bringing up the rear. As Firestar watched, Clovertail pounced, and stood up with some tiny creature hanging from her jaws.

"See?" Sandstorm purred as she licked Firestar's ear. "There's nothing to worry about. Let's go home."

Firestar let out a long sigh. His quest was over; he had walked with SkyClan to their journey's end—and a new beginning—and now he could go where his heart truly belonged. He pressed his muzzle against Sandstorm's shoulder, and they began to head toward the forest.

Epilogue

Frost glittered on leafless branches as Firestar bounded down the ravine. He felt full of energy, completely recovered from the long journey back from SkyClan three moons before. Brambleclaw and Mousefur followed him: the dawn patrol was returning to the ThunderClan camp, cold and hungry, but with fur unruffled. The borders were peaceful, and leaf-bare would soon give way to the fresh growth of newleaf.

Firestar pushed his way through the gorse tunnel and turned to wait for his Clanmates. "Better get something to eat, and then rest," he meowed. "I want you both to come with me to the Gathering tonight."

"Great!" Brambleclaw's fur bristled with excitement, while Mousefur simply flicked her ears and headed for the fresh-kill pile.

Firestar headed across the clearing toward the nursery, spotting Sorrelpaw, Sootpaw, and Rainpaw wrestling together beside the apprentice's den among the ferns. While he watched, Thornclaw emerged from the warriors' den and called to Sootpaw; mentor and apprentice disappeared through the gorse tunnel.

As he approached the nursery Cinderpelt emerged; Firestar bounded up to her. "Is everything all right?" he demanded.

Cinderpelt's blue eyes glimmered with understanding. "Everything's fine, Firestar. I just took her some borage to help her milk come."

Firestar let out a long breath of relief. "I still can't believe how beautiful they are," he confessed.

Cinderpelt gave his ear a gentle flick with her tail. "In you go, then, and have another look."

Firestar pushed his way through the brambles and into the nursery, the warm, milky scents flowing over him. Sandstorm lay in a deep nest of moss and bracken; huddled close to her belly were two tiny she-kits, their eyes still closed. One was tabby with a white chest and paws, the other a dark ginger like Firestar himself.

Whitekit, Brightheart and Cloudtail's daughter, was looking down at the two kits with as much pride as if they were her own. She was nearly old enough to be apprenticed, and Firestar knew how protective she felt about the new arrivals.

Brightheart roused from her nest and stretched out a paw. "Be careful," she warned her kit. "Don't get too close. They won't be ready to play for a while yet."

As Firestar entered, Sandstorm drowsily raised her head. "I thought of some names," she murmured. "How do you like Squirrelkit and Leafkit?"

"I think they're wonderful names," Firestar replied. The dark ginger Squirrelkit for her fluffy tail, of course, and tabby

Leafkit in memory of Leafstar—and perhaps of Spottedleaf too.

Pride surged through him as he looked at the tiny scraps of fur. He had so many hopes for them: good hunting, happiness, perhaps even leadership of their Clan. Though he had been a kittypet, his daughters were Clanborn through and through. His blood would run through ThunderClan for many seasons to come, even when he no longer walked the forest.

The thought of blood and kinship made Skywatcher's prophecy echo in his ears once more: *There will be three, kin of your kin, who hold the power of the stars in their paws.*

Would these powerful cats be descended from Firestar's two precious daughters? Was the prophecy a warning of great good—or great evil? A chill ran through him, and he shivered as he wondered where the path of his blood would lead.

"*A long, long time ago, long* before bears walked the earth, a frozen sea shattered into pieces, scattering tiny bits of ice across the darkness of the sky. Each of those pieces of ice contains the spirit of a bear, and if you are good, and brave, and strong, one day your spirit will join them."

Kallik leaned against her mother's hind leg, listening to the story she had heard so many times before. Beside her, her brother, Taqqiq, stretched, batting at the snowy walls of the den with his paws. He was always restless when the weather trapped them inside.

"When you look carefully at the sky," Kallik's mother continued, "you can see a pattern of stars in the shape of the Great Bear, Silaluk. She is running around and around the Pathway Star."

"Why is she running?" Kallik chipped in. She knew the answer, but this was the part of the story where she always asked.

"Because it is snow-sky and she is hunting. With her quick

and powerful claws, she hunts seal and beluga whale. She is the greatest of all hunters on the ice."

Kallik loved hearing about Silaluk's strength.

"But then the ice melts," Nisa said in a hushed voice. "And she can't hunt anymore. She gets hungrier and hungrier, but she has to keep running because three hunters pursue her: Robin, Chickadee, and Moose Bird. They chase her for many moons, all through the warm days, until the end of burn-sky. Then, as the warmth begins to leave the earth, they finally catch up to her.

"They gather around her and strike the fatal blow with their spears. The heart's blood of the Great Bear falls to the ground, and everywhere it falls the leaves on the trees turn red and yellow. Some of the blood falls on Robin's chest, and that is why the bird has a red breast."

"Does the Great Bear die?" breathed Taqqiq.

"She does," Nisa replied. Kallik shivered. Every time she heard this story it frightened her all over again. Her mother went on.

"But then snow-sky returns, bringing back the ice. Silaluk is reborn and the ice-hunt begins all over again, season after season."

Kallik snuggled into her mother's soft white fur. The walls of the den curved up and around them, making a sheltering cave of snow that Kallik could barely glimpse in the dark, although it was only a few pawlengths from her nose. Outside a fierce wind howled across the ice, sending tendrils of freezing air through the entrance tunnel into their den. Kallik was glad they didn't have to be out there tonight.

Inside the den, she and her brother were warm and safe. Kallik wondered if Silaluk had ever had a mother and brother, or a den where she could hide from the storms. If the Great Bear had a family to keep her safe, maybe she wouldn't have to run from the hunters. Kallik knew her mother would protect her from anything scary until she was big enough and strong enough and smart enough to protect herself.

Taqqiq batted at Kallik's nose with his large furry paw. "Kallik's scared," he teased. She could make out his eyes gleaming in the darkness.

"Am not!" Kallik protested.

"She thinks robins and chickadees are going to come after her," Taqqiq said with an amused rumble.

"No, I don't!" Kallik growled, digging her claws into the snow. "That's not why I'm scared!"

"Ha! You *are* scared! I knew it!"

Nisa nudged Kallik gently with her muzzle. "Why are you frightened, little one? You've heard the legend of the Great Bear many times before."

"I know," Kallik said. "It's just . . . it reminds me that soon snow-sky will be over, and the snow and ice will all melt away. And then we won't be able to hunt anymore, and we'll be hungry all the time. Right? Isn't that what happens during burn-sky?"

Kallik's mother sighed, her massive shoulders shifting under her snow-white pelt. "Oh, my little star," she murmured. "I didn't mean to worry you." She touched her black nose to Kallik's. "You haven't lived through a burn-sky yet,

Kallik. It's not as terrible as it sounds. We'll find a way to survive, even if it means eating berries and grass for a little while."

"What is berries and grass?" Kallik asked.

Taqqiq wrinkled his muzzle. "Does it taste as good as seals?"

"No," Nisa said, "but berries and grass will keep you alive, which is the important thing. I'll show them to you when we reach land." She fell silent. For a few heartbeats, all Kallik could hear was the thin wail of the wind battering at the snowy walls.

She pressed closer to her mother, feeling the warmth radiating from her skin. "Are you sad?" she whispered.

Nisa touched Kallik with her muzzle again. "Don't be afraid," she said, a note of determination in her voice. "Remember the story of the Great Bear. No matter what happens, the ice will always return. And all the bears gather on the edge of the sea to meet it. Silaluk will always get back on her paws. She's a survivor, and so are we."

"I can survive anything!" Taqqiq boasted, puffing up his fur. "I'll fight a walrus! I'll swim across an ocean! I'll battle all the white bears we meet!"

"I'm sure you will, dear. But why don't you start by going to sleep?" Nisa suggested.

As Taqqiq circled and scuffled in the snow beside her, making himself comfortable, Kallik rested her chin on her mother's back and closed her eyes. Her mother was right; she didn't need to be afraid. As long as she was with her family, she'd always be safe and warm, like she was right now in their den.

Kallik woke to an eerie silence. Faint light filtered through the walls, casting pale blue and pink shadows on her mother and brother as they slept. At first she thought her ears must be full of snow, but when she shook her head, Nisa grunted in her sleep, and Kallik realized that it was quiet because the storm had finally passed.

"Hey," she said, poking her brother with her nose. "Hey, Taqqiq, wake up. The storm has stopped."

Taqqiq lifted his head with a bleary expression. The fur on one side of his muzzle was flattened, making him look lop-sided.

Kallik barked with laughter. "Come on, you big, lazy seal," she said. "Let's go play outside."

"All right!" Taqqiq said, scrambling to his paws.

"Not without me watching you," their mother muttered with her eyes still closed. Kallik jumped. She'd thought Nisa was asleep.

"We won't go far," Kallik promised. "We'll stay right next to the den. Please can we go outside?"

Nisa huffed and the fur on her back quivered like a breeze was passing over it. "Let's all go out," she said. She pushed herself to her massive paws and turned around carefully in the small space, bundling her cubs to one side.

Sniffing cautiously, she nosed her way down the entrance

tunnel, brushing away snow that the storm had piled up.

Kallik could see tension in her mother's hindquarters. "I don't know why she's so careful," she whispered to her brother. "Aren't white bears the biggest, scariest animals on the ice? Nothing would dare attack us!"

"Except maybe a bigger white bear, seal-brain!" Taqqiq retorted. "Maybe you haven't noticed how little you are."

Kallik bristled. "I may not be as big as you," she growled, "but I'm just as fierce!"

"Let's find out!" Taqqiq challenged as their mother finally padded out of the tunnel. He sprinted after her, sliding down the slope of the tunnel and scrambling out into the snow.

Kallik leaped to her paws and chased him. A clump of snow fell on her muzzle on her way out of the tunnel and she shook her head vigorously to get it off. The fresh, cold air tingled in her nostrils, full of the scent of fish and ice and faraway clouds. Kallik felt the last of her sleepiness melt away. The ice was where she belonged, not underground, buried alive. She batted a chunk of snow at Taqqiq, who dodged away with a yelp.

He chased her in a circle until she dove into the fresh snow, digging up clumps with her long claws and breathing in the sparkling whiteness. Nisa sat watching them, chuffing occasionally and sniffing the air with a wary expression.

"I'm coming for you," Taqqiq growled at Kallik, crouching low to the ground. "I'm a ferocious walrus, swimming through the water to get you." He pushed himself through the snow with his paws. Kallik braced herself to jump away, but before she could move, he leaped forward and bowled her over. They rolled through the snow, squalling excitedly, until Kallik managed to wriggle free.

"Ha!" she cried.

"Roar!" Taqqiq bellowed. "The walrus is really angry now!" He dug his paws into the snow, kicking a spray of white ice into their mother's face.

"Hey," Nisa growled. She cuffed Taqqiq lightly with her massive paw, knocking him to the ground. "That's enough snowballing around. It's time to find something to eat."

"Hooray, hooray!" Kallik yipped, jumping around her mother's legs. They hadn't eaten since before the storm, two sunrises ago, and her tummy was rumbling louder than Taqqiq's walrus roar.

The sun was hidden by trails of gray clouds that grew thicker as they walked across the ice, turning into rolls of fog that shrouded the world around them. The only sound Kallik could hear was the snow crunching under their paws. Once she thought she heard a bird calling from up in the sky, but when she looked up she couldn't see anything but drifting fog.

"Why is it so cloudy?" Taqqiq complained, stopping to rub his eyes with his paws.

"The fog is good for us," Nisa said, touching her nose to the ice. "It hides us as we hunt, so our prey won't see us coming."

"I like to see where I'm going," Taqqiq insisted. "I don't like walking in clouds. Everything's all blurry and wet."

"I don't mind the fog," Kallik said, breathing in the heavy, misty air.

"You can ride on my back," Nisa said to her son, nudging him with her muzzle. Taqqiq rumbled happily and scrambled up, clutching at tufts of her snow-white fur to give himself a boost. He stretched out on her back, high above Kallik, and they started walking again.

Kallik liked finding the sharp, cool scent of the ice under the dense, watery smell of the fog. She liked the hint of oceans and fish and salt and faraway sand that drifted through the scents, reminding her of what was below the ice and what it connected to. She glanced up at her mother, who had her nose lifted and was sniffing the air, too. Kallik knew that her mother wasn't just drawing in the crisp, icy smells. Nisa was studying them, searching for a clue that would lead them to food.

"You should both do this, too," Nisa said. "Try to find any smell that stands out from the ice and snow."

Taqqiq just snuggled farther into her fur, but Kallik tried to imitate her mother, swinging her head back and forth as she sniffed. She had to learn everything she could from Nisa so she could take care of herself. At least she still had a long time before that day came—all of burn-sky and the next snow-sky as well.

"Some bears can follow scents for skylengths," Nisa said. "All the way to the edge of the sky and then the next edge and the next."

Kallik wished her nose were that powerful. Maybe it would be one day.

Nisa lifted her head and started trotting faster. Taqqiq dug his claws in to stay on her back. Soon Kallik saw what her mother was heading for—a hole in the ice. She knew what that meant. *Seals!*

Nisa put her nose close to the ice and sniffed all around the edge of the hole. Kallik followed closely, sniffing everywhere her mother sniffed. She was sure she could smell a faint trace of seal. This must be one of the breathing holes where a seal would surface to take a breath before hiding down in the freezing water again.

"Seals are so dumb," Taqqiq observed from his perch on Nisa's back. "If they can't breathe in the water, why do they live in it? Why don't they live on land, like white bears?"

"Perhaps because then it'd be much easier for bears like us to catch them and eat them!" Kallik guessed.

"*Shhhh.* Concentrate," Nisa said. "Can you smell the seal?"

"I think so," Kallik said. It was a furry, blubbery smell, thicker than the smell of fish. It made her mouth water.

"All right," Nisa said, crouching by the hole. "Taqqiq, come down and lie next to your sister." Taqqiq obeyed, sliding off her back and padding over to Kallik. "Be very quiet," Nisa instructed them. "Don't move, and don't make a sound."

Kallik and Taqqiq did as she said. They had done this several times before, so they knew what to do. The first time, Taqqiq had gotten bored and started yawning and fidgeting.

Nisa had cuffed him and scolded him, explaining that his noise would scare away the only food they'd seen in days. By now the cubs were both nearly as good at staying quiet as their mother was.

Kallik watched the breathing hole, her ears pricked and her nose keenly aware of every change in the air. A small wind blew drifts of snow across the ice, and the fog continued to roll around all three bears, making Kallik's fur feel wet and heavy.

After a while she began to get restless. She didn't know how her mother could stand to do nothing for such a long time, watching and watching in case the seal broke through the water. The chill of the ice below her was beginning to seep through Kallik's thick fur. She had to force herself not to shiver and send vibrations through the ice that might warn the seal they were there.

She stared past the tip of her nose at the ice around the breathing hole. The dark water below the surface lapped at the jagged edge. It was strange to think that that same dark water was only a muzzlelength below her, on the other side of the thick ice. The ice seemed so strong and solid, as if it went down forever. . . .

Strange shadows and shapes seemed to dance inside the ice, forming bubbles and whorls. It was odd—ice was white from far away but nearly clear up close and full of patterns. It almost seemed like things were living inside the ice. Right below her front paws, for instance, there was a large, dark bubble slowly moving from one side to the other. Kallik stared at it, wondering if it was the spirit of a white bear trapped in the ice. One that hadn't made it as far as the stars in the sky.